STENDHAL

Lucien Leuwen

BOOK ONE

THE
GREEN
HUNTSMAN

TRANSLATED BY LOUISE VARÈSE

A NEW DIRECTIONS BOOK

INTRODUCTION

HENRI BEYLE

"Begin by affecting deity and you will soon find that you have forgotten your troubles."—STENDHAL

IT IS IMPOSSIBLE to read *Lucien Leuwen,* or any of Stendhal's books, without finding oneself speculating about the author who is so insistently and irresistibly present on every page. His intimate, ironical, effervescent, and impertinent tone tickles readers whom it does not exasperate. Paul Valéry has said of Stendhal: "He is a type of mentality much more than he is a man of letters. He cannot be reduced to a writer. That is why he pleases and displeases—and why he pleases me." Anyone who satisfies this curiosity is richly rewarded, for the story of Henri Beyle (or Stendhal, one of his pen names by which he has come to be better known) is as full of adventure, both physical and psychological—with plenty of "love-interest" —as any novel. As Harry Levin points out in his brilliant study, *Toward Stendhal:* "No historical novelist arranging for his characters to be present at important events could have made more opportune arrangements for Beyle."

The following brief outline of a life in which savor is everything, and which cannot be concentrated into pellet form, can only hope further to whet the reader's curiosity which may now, without a knowledge of French, be more fully satisfied. Both of Stendhal's autobiographies, *The Life of Henri Brulard* and *Memoirs of Egotism,* are available in translation, and there is an excellent and comprehensive biography by Matthew Josephson to which I am much indebted.

Marie Henri Beyle was born in the reign of Louis XVI, lived through the French Revolution, the Directory, the Consulate, the First Empire, the Revolution of July, and twelve years of the Louis-

Philippe regime. He was born in 1783 into a royalist family of Grenoble six years before the storming of the Bastille. It was almost inevitable that a boy with his ardent, generous, romantic nature and inquisitive mind should have espoused the new revolutionary cause and adopted young Bonaparte as his hero. The fact, moreover, that his father whom he loathed, was a royalist and an enemy of the Revolution was reason enough to make the boy abominate the Bourbons. His rejection of religion stemmed from the same source, as he explains in *Henri Brulard,* speaking of his Latin tutor: "I hated Abbé Raillon. I hated my father, the source of the Abbé's power over me. I hated still more the religion in whose name he tyrannized over me." In fact, all the passionate interests of his later life, all his loves and hates, which are woven into the texture of his books, are rooted in his childhood. He remained emotionally a child throughout his life and his pathological need of love is traceable to that mother fixation which, a Freudian before Freud, he himself analyzed. Even his taste for fine clothes and his rationale of feminine conquest were the result of an obsessive memory of his uncle, a dandy and lady-killer of Grenoble. As he grew up among mountains in a country of tall trees, he always despised cities without mountains and with clipped trees. This scorn is reflected in his derisive (as well as inaccurate) description of Nancy in *The Green Huntsman.* His life-long interest in the sciences began in Grenoble when, as a boy, mathematics had seemed to him the glorious antithesis of the lying, hypocritical religion of his father. It will be noticed that in *Lucien Leuwen* he goes out of his way to mention new inventions and to bring in scientific discussions between his characters.

On his way to Paris in 1799 to take his final examinations for the École Polytechnique (which in the end he failed to do, preferring at the moment to dream of writing plays and operas and conquering women) he heard the startling news of the coup d'état of the 18th Brumaire. His hero Napoleon had made himself First Consul. Although this was the death-blow to the Revolution, the sixteen-year-old hero-worshiper did not understand the significance of the event and was, as he says, "delighted that young General Bonaparte should make himself King of France."

Henri Beyle had Napoleon to thank for the fifteen most stirring and mundanely prosperous years of his life. In Paris he had found a powerful protector in his cousin Pierre Daru, whom Napoleon was later to make a count, prime minister, and member of the Academy. After serving two years as a dragoon in the army of reserve in Italy (he promptly fell in love with Italy for life!) and after, on his return, enjoying one of his happiest amorous interludes with an actress in Marseilles, where he was, of all things, a wholesale grocers' clerk, young Beyle was taken under the wing of his cousin, Chief Commissary of the Grand Army, and given a place in the commissary department. As a deputy commissary he followed the Grand Army to Germany, where he witnessed the celebration in Berlin of Napoleon's victory over the Prussians, after the destruction of Prussia's main army at Jena. He soon rose from deputy to full commissary, and then to the post of Intendant of Brunswick. During the next years he traveled constantly as war swept from one end of Europe to the other, each fresh victory giving rise to fresh conflicts. He rushed hither and thither, commandeering quarters and provisions for the army with that tireless and headlong energy he put into everything he undertook throughout his life, whether it was falling in love, playing the wit and the dandy in society, devouring art, or dashing off his teeming ideas in diaries, essays, and novels. In Vienna he was able to satisfy his passion for music, and assisted at the imposing ceremonies in honor of Haydn at which the *Requiem* of his favorite composer, Mozart, was performed. In the interims of war he could also give full rein to his predilection for brilliant society in the *salons* of the First Empire; nor did he ever let his duties interfere with his amorous career which he carried on diligently with varying success. He was finally made an auditor, or secretary, in Napoleon's Council of State and a little later Inspector of Crown Furnishings. At one time he almost fell from grace because of a prolonged leave of absence in his beloved Italy, consummating a passion conceived as a young dragoon eleven years earlier for the voluptuous Gina Pietragrua.

On his return to Paris he writes, rather with a note of satisfaction: "My reputation for being a *wild fellow* has increased . . . I shall have to play five hundred games of whist with old women to get myself forgiven."

In 1812 he returned to active service as a full commissary in the disastrous Russian campaign, and in the nightmare retreat from Moscow displayed extraordinary fortitude as well as his habitual energy and intelligence in emergencies. "I saved myself by force of will," he said afterwards. "I saw many around me give up hope and perish." He lost all his baggage in the retreat—a great loss to literature since it contained notes for a book and his diary of the Russian campaign.

After the Russian adventure Beyle was disappointed in his expectations of preferment, and not a little embittered. Prefectures went to men who had stayed comfortably at home while he was enduring the fatigues and perils of war in Napoleon's service. He was thoroughly disgusted with war, with soldiers, and especially with generals who were "thinking all the time of what every wound was worth in gratuities." And he bitterly added: "The extreme cowardice of these heroes when they became peers of France in 1835 will give posterity an insight into their heroism of 1809." This note is sounded more than once in *Lucien Leuwen*.

"I fell with Napoleon in 1814," Stendhal wrote in *Souvenir d'Égotisme*. War was over for him as was his brilliant life as government official of the Empire. Although he was offered employment under the new government of Louis XVIII, he preferred to exile himself in Italy rather than serve under a Bourbon king. It is probably a lucky thing for letters that with his "fall" he gave up ambition and turned to things his deeper nature craved. In looking back he says: "In reality I have not been ambitious, but in 1811 I thought myself ambitious." He summarized the years from 1814 to 1830 thus: "Travels, great and terrible loves, consolation in writing." He spent seven of those years in Italy, most of the time in Milan, which he came to regard as his true fatherland, devoting himself to painting, literature, music, pursuing his cult of happiness and cultivating "the plant called love." In his biography of Stendhal,

Matthew Josephson points out that in Italy "the impoverished ex-soldier, ex-career official, ex-dandy was turned into the Stendhal we know. Italy helped him 'be himself.' " He spent most of his evenings at La Scala, the great opera house where "all Milan" met to listen to music—but mostly, as Stendhal describes in his *Chartreuse de Parme,* to see and be seen and to gossip. "In Italy I adored opera," he says, "and by virtue of being happy at La Scala, I became a kind of connoisseur."

It was at La Scala that Beyle first met the glamorous Lord Byron, then being lionized by European society. Beyle admired him both as a poet and for his espousal of the cause of Greek freedom. Nor can there be much doubt that Byron's irresistible fascination for women added not a little to the poet's appeal for Stendhal. They met frequently and engaged in stimulating conversations but were fundamentally too incompatible by nature for a real friendship to develop. Despite his profession of republicanism, the aristocratic young English lord was rather a spoiled brat and a real snob. Intellectually, however, they enjoyed each other. They remained on friendly terms and later Byron read Stendhal's books with interest.

Little wonder that Stendhal loved Milan where he felt himself liked and where art was truly appreciated. In Italy, he observed it was free from the venality to be found in his own country where, as he said, literature had become "a vile trade that a M. de V. (Villèle, French prime minister at the time) rewards with places in the Academy and the censorship bureau." In Milan the poets were poor but independent, and their works as they appeared were passionately discussed. Through his connection with this group of intellectuals who were also ardent patriots associated with the political society of the *Carbonari* which was plotting to free Italy from Austrian rule, Stendhal came under the suspicion of the Austrian police. This accounts for his habit of using a code of his own invention in his letters and manuscripts. It was much too simple to worry the police and the only end it served was to complicate a little more the difficulties of his future editors. By one of his revolutionary friends he was taken to the palazzo Viscontini where Countess Métilde Viscontini Dembowska lived separated from her Polish husband. She had fervently adopted the cause of the *Carbonari* and her house was a meeting place for the conspirators of Milan. Stendhal fell violently in love with the beautiful patriotic Métilde who proved to be the most terrible of his "great and terrible loves." As she treated him badly and caused him to experience the whole gamut of sensations known to unrequited love, he was in that state of happy torture which always excited his mind to furious activity and made him turn to his panacea for all ills: writing. It was at this time that he began his *de l'Amour,* an anatomy of love which sets forth his famous theory of the love process for which he invented the term "crystalization."

There now occurred a series of uprisings in many parts of Italy, and after a similar one in Milan had been ruthlessly put down by the Austrian police and many of his friends imprisoned, Stendhal was made to understand that it would be well for him to leave Italy. Like Lucien returning from Nancy, Beyle came back to Paris in despair not knowing whether Métilde returned his love or not. His great preoccupation now was to keep his friends from perceiving his disconsolate state. "The worst misfortune that could befall me, I exclaimed to myself, would be that my friends, those cold-blooded men among whom I am going to live, should discover my passion for a woman I had not even possessed." And he goes on to say that he became a wit in order to hide his feelings. Stendhal had indeed always been an actor, playing a part to correspond to some social ideal he had set himself, and also to hide and to protect his natural self from a society which would certainly have found him ridiculous had it divined his true nature, "a soul," as he once said of himself, "so tender, so timid, and so melancholy." Fortunately he was too exuberant, too intellectually vigorous and fertile not to be forced to find an outlet for his true feelings and thoughts. Casting aside his sophisticated mask when he sat down to write, his nature took its revenge for the indignity of disguise put upon it in public, and reveled quite shamelessly in disclosing itself in words. The consequence is that we today know Henri Beyle much better than did his most intimate cronies. For, with the exception of the women with whom he was hopelessly in love, he was generally considered to be a heartless Lovelace and godless cynic by his contemporaries.

The years between 1821 and 1830 are the ones included in that brief delightful improvisation, *Souvenir d'Égotisme,* written, as Stendhal says, "like a letter," with a living vividness and honesty never found in formal autobiographies. It tells in some detail of his devoted though platonic friendship for the Italian singer Giuditta Pasta, for whom he had an admiration that amounted almost to veneration. It describes his life in different *salons* of Paris, notably that of Destutt de Tracy, the great utilitarian philosopher and a friend of Jefferson, where he used to meet Lafayette. That great general and popular hero, "at the tender age of sixty-five," was usually, according to Stendhal, chiefly concerned with pinching some pretty girl's behind. We are given a glimpse of one of Beyle's ordinary days as, after an "excellent cup of coffee and two brioches" taken late in the morning with one of his friends at the Café de Rouen, he browses at the book-stalls along the Seine on the lookout for one of his favorite engravings and, at the Louvre, gazes miserably at Italian paintings that remind him of Métilde, and, later, as he discusses art, politics, and life in general at cafés or at his habitual *table d'hôte* with such friends as Romain Colomb, his devoted cousin from Grenoble and first publisher of *The Green Huntsman,* and Prosper Mérimée, the author of *Carmen,* whom he admired and of whom he said: "I am not sure of his heart, but I have not the least doubt about his talent." One of his chief evening occupations was going to the Théâtre-Italien, the *Bouffes,* so often mentioned in *Lucien Leuwen,* to hear Italian opera sung by the two greatest prima donnas of those days, Pasta and Malibran. Before settling down to this life in Paris, he made a voyage to London to try to forget Métilde in the pleasure of seeing the famous actor Kean in Shakespeare's plays. "The only writer I found readable," he says of that time, "was Shakespeare." Back in Paris he was obliged to augment his meager income by writing articles for the Paris papers. He was also invited by the English *New Monthly Review* and the *Athenaeum* to send a regular Paris literary *chronique* or letter, which he naturally filled with everything else as well as literature—politics, gossip, and "human interest" stories. Had he lived today he would have been a columnist. Toward the end of this period he wrote *Le Rouge et le Noire,* which was published in Paris several months after the July Revolution. In spite of the excitement over this political upheaval, the novel received far more attention than any of his former books. But the critics were unanimously hostile and treated the author as a kind of moral leper.

Stendhal saw the outbreak of the Revolution in 1830. "I was overjoyed at the July Days," he wrote in *Henri Brulard.* "I watched the firing from the colonnade of the *Théâtre-Français* with very little danger to myself. I shall never forget that fine sunny day and my first sight of the tricolor flag . . ." He now became a functionary of the government of Louis-Philippe, the "crooked" king, as Stendhal was soon to call him when it became apparent that the "Master of the Tuileries" had been liberal in promises only. First appointed consul at Trieste, he was unacceptable to the Austrian government because of his old reputation as a friend of the *Carbonari.* He was then transferred to Civita-Vecchia, near Rome. Desperately bored with his life and duties in that little Mediterranean port, he wrote incessantly—a lucky thing for future Beylists as it is to this period that his two incomplete but precious autobiographies belong, as well as *Lucien Leuwen.* Stendhal could not hope to publish *Lucien Leuwen,* any more than the autobiographies, as long as he was a functionary of the government and "eating off the Budget." His criticism of the Louis-Philippe regime was much too frank and even treasonable.

It was impossible for Beyle to live for any length of time deprived of the stimulating atmosphere of cosmopolitan society, so we find him taking innumerable leaves of absence both in France and Italy. During the longest of them, which lasted three years, from 1836 to 1839, he wrote and published *La Chartreuse de Parme.* Not long afterwards he had his first taste of real literary success when Balzac's glowing encomium of this work brought him what he had missed all his life, the recognition of his peers.

His health had been failing for a long time, and less than three years after his return to Civita-Vecchia, once more on the plea of ill-health, he asked and obtained another leave of absence which proved to be his last. He died of a stroke in Paris on the 23rd of March 1842 after enjoying, in spite of his physical disabilities, almost five months of the old round of social pleasures. He was game to the end and died in his chosen role. He was buried in the Montmartre Cemetery and, in accordance with his request, his head-stone bore the legend he himself had written when, during his self-imposed exile in Italy, he had adopted Milan as his fatherland:

Arrigo Beyle, Milanese
Visse, amo, scrisse.

Henri Beyle, Milanese, lived, loved, wrote.

* * *

Lucien Leuwen, like all Stendhal's heroes, is Henri Beyle himself. He and Lucien share the same tastes, have the same aspirations, the same political convictions. They are both republicans—of a sort. With their hearts full of sympathy for the ideals of freedom and equality, they have a temperamental aversion to the "common man" and delight in aristocratic or at least upper-crust society where people dress well, talk well, and have polished manners. Democracy seems to them "the tyranny of every kind of mediocrity." They were both ill-fated horsemen, as Henri Beyle somewhere exclaims: "I spent my life falling off my horse." As for love, they both held Don Juanesque theories of feminine conquest quite contrary to their warm idealistic natures. When in love they are both perfect fools. There is, however, one touching difference between the young heroes of his novels and Henri Beyle in the flesh: his heroes are all handsome. Much of Stendhal's attitudinizing and play-acting came from the fact that he was rather ugly: short, fat, and red-faced. He was painfully conscious of this handicap, and once failed to take advantage of the advances of a young girl who was in love with him because: "I was not enough in love with her to make me forget that I am not handsome." As for the lovely heroine of *The Green Huntsman,* Bathilde de Chasteller, she is, according to Stendhal himself, Métilde Dembowska. Métilde and Bathilde have the same excessive pride that amounts to prudery, the same piety; they both

make ridiculous scenes for paltry offenses. Stendhal finds it necessary to excuse this childishness in an otherwise exceptionally intelligent woman by saying that, like her religion and her politics, it is a
vice of her convent education. They are both famous for their eloquence in preaching, each her pet cause: Métilde the freedom of
Italy, Bathilde the return of the Bourbons. When Stendhal describes
Lucien's despair at the mere thought of not being allowed to see
Madame de Chasteller every day, he is living over again his own
agony when Countess Dembowska forbade him to come to her
house more than twice a month. There, however, the likeness seems
to end. Métilde with her somewhat sadistic behavior toward her
too ardent lover, her perpetual melancholy and her great tragic eyes,
must have been a very different person from the Bathilde of the
intimate scenes of *The Green Huntsman,* whose greatest charm is
her childlike gaiety and who is capable of melting tenderness. Probably a case of wishful remembering on Stendhal's part. Valéry has
paid high tribute to this love story in his preface to *Lucien Leuwen:*
"I had read nothing before on the subject of love which did not
bore me to excess, did not seem absurd or unnecessary . . . But in
Leuwen, the extraordinary delicacy with which the figure of
Madame de Chasteller is drawn, the kind of noble and profound
feeling in the hero, the progress of an attachment which grows
omnipotent in a sort of silence; and that infinite art with which it
is held back—kept suspended in a state of self-distrust—all this
captivated me and led to a second reading."

* * *

Lucien Leuwen is of course much more than a simple love story.
It is a social and political satire of an entire period, written with
all the irony, subtle humor, and psychological insight that have
come to be associated with Stendhal's name. *The Green Huntsman,*
besides being a picture of fanatical legitimist society in the provinces, made up largely of returned *émigrés* waiting in perpetual fear
for another Reign of Terror and meanwhile despising the middle-
class, middle-way government of Louis-Philippe, is also a frank indictment of the *Juste-milieu* army whose chief function was to en-

gage the troublesome mill-workers in "cabbage wars." In the sequel, concerned with high politics and high finance and their *mariage de convenance,* Lucien tries unsuccessfully to forget his love for Madame de Chasteller while he learns all about the corrupt ways of bankers, ministers, deputies, prefects, and beautiful women of the *haute bourgeoisie.* Stendhal said that his political curiosity kept him from blowing out his brains on his love-sick return from Italy in 1821. This interest in political history appears in all his novels, but in none so constantly as in *Lucien Leuwen.* Stendhal might as truly be called an historical novelist as his famous contemporary Sir Walter Scott, whom he found so boring. But, whereas Scott gives us pictures to look at, we live in Stendhal's novels as we live in our own world, and the social, political atmosphere in his books seems as familiar to us as though we were attached to the events by the umbilical cord of our own newspapers and radios.

But just because Stendhal is so *contemporary,* his references to historical and political events are perhaps a little too casual for some readers who have left their history books far behind. For them the following brief summary of the early years of the reign of Louis-Philippe and the events leading up to the July Revolution, may, perhaps, be acceptable.

A SMALL DOSE OF HISTORY

IN 1814 the allied armies marched into Paris, Napoleon abdicated, and twenty-five years after the execution of Louis XVI, amidst the wild rejoicings of the returned émigrés, the Bourbons were restored to the throne of France. For the royalists the last king had been, not the martyred Louis XVI, but his son the little dauphin who had died in the Temple as Louis XVII. In consequence, the new king was crowned Louis XVIII.

By the First Peace of Paris, France was permitted to retain, in general, the boundaries of 1792, which embraced 3280 square miles more than those of 1790. Considering the havoc wrought on the continent by Napoleon it might be regarded as a mild treaty. In 1815, however, following the "Hundred Days" and the débâcle of Waterloo, the second Peace of Paris severely penalized France for this final Napoleonic conflagration. It brought France back to the boundaries of 1790. She was forced to pay the enormous sum of 7000 million francs for war damages. Her border fortresses were demolished and other forts garrisoned by allied troops at the expense of the French people. The collective shame felt over this treaty was like a wound in the body politic that would not heal, and doomed any regime with the humdrum ideal of peace and prosperity to unpopularity and disorder.

A wave of reaction now swept the country and reached such violence in the anti-Bonaparte south that it was known as the "White Terror." One of the political executions referred to in *The Green Huntsman* which aroused general indignation was that of General Ney. Regarded as a victim of political murder, he became a martyr in the popular imagination.

After the second Restoration, the Chamber, "more royalist than the King," was in constant conflict with Louis' prudent policy. The ultra-royalists or ultras, as they were called, advocated the return of the old monarchy. Other parties gradually gained strength: Guizot's *doctrinaires,* advocating a constitutional monarchy with a strong administration, and the liberal party headed by Casimir Périer and Lafayette. Republicans and Bonapartists continued to work underground allied with a new secret society, the *Charbonniers,* formed for the purpose of overthrowing the Bourbons. It was modeled on the Italian patriotic society of the *Carbonari* and played an important role in all the ensuing uprisings of the Restoration.

Knowing that his monarchy depended on the support of the rich middle class which had emerged from the Empire as a power to be reckoned with, Louis XVIII turned a deaf ear on the royalists' clamor for the return of the estates and property of the émigrés, confiscated by the Revolution and sold as "national property." He gave the "purchasers of national property" formal assurance that they would never be molested. It was not until after his death, at the beginning of the reactionary regime of his brother Charles X, that a decree was finally passed granting the equivalent of 200,000,-000 francs as indemnity to the returned émigrés, *le milliard des émigrés.*

With the Restoration the word Charter took on an almost mystic significance. In 1814 Louis XVIII had "granted" a charter modeled on the English constitution, called the *Charte constitutionelle.* Although anything but liberal in our sense of the word, it was venerated as a guarantee that there would be no attempt to return to the old absolute monarchy. It provided for an hereditary Chamber of Peers nominated by the King, a chamber of elected deputies, freedom of the press, religious liberty, and responsible ministers. This was quite liberal enough to satisfy the wealthiest classes; since the franchise was limited to those who paid a tax of at least 300 francs, they were the only ones who had the right to vote. The King was theoretically free to choose his ministers wherever he pleased, but Louis followed the practice, already established in England, of always choosing members of the chambers. Henceforth the ministers became the real government, and the capture of the ministries the chief stake in the struggle of parties.

Charles X succeeded his brother to the throne in 1824. An ultra of ultras, he had the intelligence of an ostrich and, in spite of the fate of his brother Louis XVI, still suffered from the Bourbon delusion that kings are infallible and know what is best for their people. In the years that followed, the split between the royalist reactionaries and the liberals steadily widened. Charles continued to gaze with blind eyes over the chasm. In January 1830, a surreptitious campaign was begun by Thiers, the rising young leader of the liberals, in their new party organ, the *Nation,* of which Thiers was one of the editors. Under cover of defending the sacred Charter he was preparing the way for a change of dynasty, invoking the English revolution which had established William of Orange in place of the Stuarts. As early as February 1830 he began frankly to advocate the candidacy of the Duc d'Orléans to the throne of France. The ultra-royalist Polignac ministry with its repressive policy of "no more concessions," which had come into power in August 1829, had been growing steadily unpopular. On March 18, 1830, in reply to the King's speech to the Assembly, 221 newly elected deputies signed an address voicing a lack of confidence in the ministry. The King now would either have to yield to the Chamber or resort to a coup d'état. He took the fatal latter course by drawing up ordinances that suppressed the freedom of the press, annulled the late elections by dissolving the chamber, and created a new electoral system still further reducing the franchise. To his ministers, and even to himself, he maintained the fiction that this was not a coup d'état but a perfectly legal proceeding since he was acting within his rights as provided by Article 14 of the Charter: "The King . . . makes the rules and ordinances necessary for the execution of the laws of the State." So utterly unrealistic was the attitude of the King and his ministers that no adequate military preparations were made to quell disorders that the publication of the ordinances was sure to provoke. They appeared in the government newspaper *Le Moniteur* on July 26, 1830.

In reading *Lucien Leuwen* it must be borne in mind that the July Days—the *Glorieuse* so often referred to in *The Green Huntsman* —were not fought and won by those who promptly profited by them. While the politicians were wondering what steps they should take, and the journalists were placarding Paris with their protest, the people took things into their own hands. The deputies and business men who had long been plotting a change of government were scarcely less terrified than the royalists when they saw barricades being thrown up, an armed rabble swarming the streets, and heard the cries of "Long live the Charter!" and "Down with the Ministry!" changed to "Down with the Bourbons!" and "No more kings!" None of the bourgeoisie, high or low, wanted a bloody revolution that might lead to another Reign of Terror. Even Thiers thought it prudent to disappear for two days. Jacques de Bainville recounts a delectable incident about the author of *La Marseillaise,* Rouget de Lisle, then an old man of seventy, who burst into a friend's apartment and announced in a trembling voice: "Things look bad. They are singing *La Marseillaise!*"

Led by republicans, Bonapartists, *Charbonniers* and students from the École Polytechnique, after three days of glorious street-fighting the people of Paris had won another revolution. Then, with victory over the Bourbons assured and the tricolor flag once more floating over the Tuileries, the politicians and bankers took over.

The Orleanist party had the advantage over the Republicans in that the reins of government were already in their hands. After some clever maneuvering, they finally succeeded in getting the deputies to vote in favor of the Duc d'Orléans, thus preventing a political as well as a military victory for the republicans. It also assured eighteen years of disorder and made the Revolution of 1848 inevitable. Even Charles finally admitted that his cause was lost and on August 2nd abdicated in favor of his grandson, Comte de Chambord, posthumous son of the Duc de Berry. The young Prince's claims were set aside and the deputies offered the crown to the Duc d'Orléans who became Louis-Philippe I. Louis-Philippe was descended from the brother of Louis XIV of the younger or Orleans branch of the House of Bourbon. His father, Louis Égalité, a deputy to the Convention in 1791, had given his vote of death for the king. Louis-Philippe himself as a young man had favored the Revolution and had served under Dumouriez at the battles of Valmy and Jemmapes. Later accused of being involved with his General-in-chief in a conspiracy, he was forced to go into exile, and only returned to France with the Bourbons in 1814. Although the republicans were not duped by the democratic role he had chosen to assume, Louis-Philippe was popularly considered a liberal. Lafayette, the people's idol, had dubbed him "the best of republicans."

This time certain additional precautions were taken by the chamber to limit the powers and prestige of the crown. Louis-Philippe was made "King of the French by the grace of God and the will of the nation," not King of France by divine right. He was forced to "accept" a charter drawn up by the deputies instead of "granting" one as Louis XVIII had insisted upon doing in 1814. The new charter was conceived in a somewhat more liberal spirit. Article 14 was suppressed, censorship abolished. The Chamber of Peers was no longer hereditary. The franchise was somewhat lowered to increase the number of voters, but the mass of the people remained disenfranchised.

In Paris the infuriated republicans now began forming secret societies with affiliated committees throughout France. Their political ideas were still somewhat vague but not their determination to get rid of the king who had stolen their revolution. The government knew no respite from the ceaseless barrage of opposition they set up in their newspapers by means of virulent articles and political cartoons such as Philipon's famous "Poire," a caricature of Louis-Philippe in the shape of a pear. Such a paper was *The Aurore,* edited by Lucien's friend the cadastral surveyor of Nancy, Gauthier, who had spent so much time in Louis-Philippe's prisons. The secret societies also kept the country in a constant state of turmoil fomenting riots and insurrections, aided by the growing unrest among the starving workers. Stendhal opens *Lucien Leuwen* with an allusion to one of these uprisings when the republicans tried unsuccessfully to rouse the populace to rebellion on the occasion of the funeral of General Lamarque, a popular leader of the opposition in the chamber. Stendhal's republican-minded hero has been expelled from the École Polytechnique with sixty of his fellow students for participating in that unsuccessful but bloody event which lasted two days —the 5th and 6th of June 1832. As time went on the insurrections took on a more socialistic character. The ideas of Saint-Simon, father of French socialism, of Charles Fourier, and other utopian socialists began to spread through the different political societies. The cause of the miserable journeymen weavers was brought into the political arena. In April 1834 the first of a number of insurrections throughout France known as the "April riots," broke out in Lyons. At the end of February the association of silk-weavers, *Mutualists,* had attempted a general strike in protest against the lowering of their already inadequate wages. On the advice of the republican leaders, who felt that the time was not propitious for a show-down, they returned to work. But hardly had quiet been restored when the news of the law against associations became known, and the city was once more in a tumult of protest. This time the republicans of the *Société des Droits de l'Homme* took the lead.

The government saw its opportunity to crush republicanism in Lyons. A veritable army was brought in, converting the city into an armed camp. All the government's brutal tactics met with the vociferous support of Lyons' manufacturing aristocracy. Now that its interests were threatened the bourgeoisie forgot its liberalism of 1830. The butchery of innocent victims by the soldiers in the Lyons insurrection was repeated a few days later in Paris. The "massacre of the Rue Transnonain" on April 14th was long remembered and always referred to with horror. Soldiers had burst into the house at No. 12 and shot down or bayonetted men, women, and children without the least provocation. Louis Blanc, in his *History of Ten Years,* gives ghastly eye-witness accounts of this insane slaughter, and goes on to show how the government seized upon the April riots, which it had so ruthlessly quelled, to secure dictatorial powers for itself. "On April 15th an ordinance, in utter violation of the charter, transformed the Chamber of Peers into a court of justice, and fourteen million francs of extraordinary supplies were demanded to enable the government to keep up the effective force of the army at 360,000 foot and 6500 horse. . . . With what eagerness they took advantage of an hour of triumph to obtain this authorization to levy, in the height of peace, an army large enough for a vigorous and extensive war!" Louis-Philippe, who had dubbed his form of government the *Juste-milieu,* the exact middle between ultras and republicans, required this enormous army to keep the middle of the road clear for himself and his friends. This was the army Lucien joined with such enthusiasm, but which he soon learned to despise when he discovered that its role was limited to quelling riots and waging war on starving weavers "armed only with cabbages." Yet many young republicans, bursting with idealism, their youthful imaginations fired by the legend of Napoleon and his Grande Armée, like Lucien's anonymous correspondents, were to be found in this unheroic army. It was the only way they had of learning their trade and being prepared for the war that would restore the glory of France and wipe out the shame of the ignominious treaty of 1815.

On July 28, 1835, the anniversary of the July Revolution, occurred one of the many attempts on the life of Louis-Philippe. The King escaped injury, but twenty or more persons were killed by Fieschi's "infernal machine." For the government it served as the excuse it had long been looking for to crack down on the liberties for which the *Glorieuses* had been fought. What are known as "the September laws" were now passed. These created a regime of repression which paralyzed the government's opponents by depriving them of the right to free expression of opinion, the right of association and the right of assembly. It became a crime to publish anything in the nature of criticism of the King, to express the wish to change the established order, to get up subscriptions in favor of newspapers condemned to penalties by the government, or for anyone to declare himself a republican. No drawing or emblematic print could be published or offered for sale without first being submitted to the censor.

During the July Monarchy, after one abortive attempt at insurrection led by the Duchesse de Berry, mother of Henri V, the ultraroyalists, now called legitimists, no longer counted politically. The majority, unwilling to take the oath of allegiance, abstained from voting. They mostly moped and uselessly plotted among themselves. Like Dr. Du Poirier they too were dreaming of war—a war that would restore the great days of the Bourbons and the grandeur of the *ancien régime*. They refused to recognize Louis-Philippe, the "King of the barricades," but were not agreed as to which Bourbon was their sovereign: to some he was still Charles X; others, while accepting the abdication of Charles, looked upon the dauphin as his successor and called him Louis XIX; but the majority swore allegiance to Charles' ten-year-old grandson, Henri V.

Now that absolute monarchy was dead for all time in France, the dictatorship of money took its place. The franchise system, with the privilege of voting reserved to the wealthy, put the power into the hands of a financial oligarchy. The result was constant rivalry among the political leaders of different groups in the chamber, all jockeying for possession of the ministries, and between the king and his ministers. Although romanticism in literature was still in vogue (Victor Hugo's *Hernani* had had its stormy première only a few months before the July Revolution) it no longer represented the spirit of the age. Stendhal and Balzac, "holding a mirror up to nature" were the true chroniclers of the July Monarchy, not the romantic George Sand or de Musset. And, as spiritual brother of the political and financial go-getters, one might cite that old charlatan, Alexandre Dumas, with his factory of ghost writers, his shameless plagiarism and quite unromantic love of money—the oneman Hollywood of his day. As has often been pointed out, Louis-Philippe was the most unromantic king of an unromantic age. Stendhal calls it the "age of charlatanism without talent" and quotes General Lamarque's description as "a halt in the mud." All this perfectly suited the middle classes whose terror of the republicans and a revival of the ideals of liberty, equality, fraternity almost equaled that of the ultras. With Louis-Philippe the one freedom they wanted was assured them, the freedom to make money. The center of the city's social life was now no longer the aristocratic Faubourg Saint-Germain, but the Chaussé d'Antin, the quarter of the new aristocracy of wealth—bankers, merchants and politicians. King and ministers were money-mad, and the Bourse was practically a branch of the government. The "bourgeois king" set the pace. Louis-Philippe's speculations on the Bourse, as well as those of his ministers, occupy a large portion of the sequel to *The Green Huntsman*. The emergent class of big industrialists and big bankers were fully represented in the government, a fact that explains the extreme caution and circumspection of its foreign policy. It was the regime of the Haves, opposed to the Have-nots. It lasted for eighteen years, until the Revolution of 1848 sent Louis-Philippe into exile in his turn, and set up the second Republic.

THE TITLE OF THE BOOK

STENDHAL never succeeded in making up his mind. He toyed with a succession of titles: *Le Chasseur Vert* (The Green Huntsman), *Les*

Bois de Prémol (The Prémol Woods), *Le Rouge et le Blanc* (The Red and the White), *L'Orange de Malte* (The Orange of Malta), *L'Amarinthe et le Noir* (The Magenta and the Black), *Lucien Leuwen* and *Le Telegraphe.* Of these seven titles the first three refer directly to the first volume: The Green Huntsman is the name of a coffee-house in the forest outside Nancy, The Prémol Woods is the forest in which the coffee-house is situated but which Stendhal later called the Burelviller Woods, The Red and the White, according to Stendhal's own note, "is to recall the Red and the Black and furnish a phrase for the critics. Red, the republican Lucien. White, the young royalist Madame de Chasteller." They have no logical excuse as the title of the whole work. Not that logic bothered Stendhal in his choice of titles, as witness *La Chartreuse de Parme* in which the Charter House of Parma is mentioned for the first time on the last page. *The Telegraph* is suitable only for the second volume in which that invention plays an important role, but which is never mentioned in the first part. As for *L'Orange de Malte,* there seems to have been no reason for Stendhal's choosing it except, as he said, "it has such a lovely sound." This leaves two titles that cover subjects relative to both volumes: *The Magenta and the Black* (magenta the color of the lancers' uniforms described in the first volume, black that of Lucien's uniform as *maître des requêtes* at the ministry of the interior in the second), and *Lucien Leuwen.* Since Stendhal could not bring himself to make a choice among all these titles and evidently had moments of fondness for each in turn, for this first English edition of his work, three of them have been chosen with a logic which Stendhal perhaps would have found diverting although unnecessary: For the general title, *Lucien Leuwen,* the one most frequently used in the French editions. *The Green Huntsman* for the first volume, because it is charming, pertinent, and also familiar as the title under which a part of the book was published for the first time in 1885, edited by Beyle's devoted cousin Romain Colomb. For the sequel to *The Green Huntsman,* because of Stendhal's ever-alert curiosity about scientific discoveries and inventions of all kinds, and his particular interest in the Chappe telegraph and the use made of it by the government in its politico-electoral and politico-financial shenanigans, *The Telegraph* has been chosen.

APPENDIX AND NOTES

In an appendix at the back of the book will be found three tentative prefaces which Stendhal wrote for *Lucien Leuwen,* together with some supplementary material left on the backs and margins of his manuscripts. Some or all of this, he may have intended to fit into the story when he reorganized it for publication, but when added without any change in the text as Henri Martineau, the great Stendhal scholar, has done in the Edition du Rocher 1945, it overburdens and weakens the work. The equally eminent Beylist, Henry Debraye reserves this material for an appendix in the Champion Edition of 1927.

Somewhere Stendhal exclaims: "Who will speak of M. de Villèle or M. de Martignac in a hundred years?" Who does? And although Stendhal affirmed many times that he was writing for posterity and not for his contemporaries who were incapable of understanding him, his pages are dotted with ministers and brass hats now forgotten by all but historians. Notes have therefore been provided for those who like information. The pages on which these references occur and the line with the cue words are indicated so that it will be a simple matter to refer to them if desired, but in the text no mark appears to distract the eye of those who dislike being encumbered with unnecessary baggage on a pleasure journey.

I wish to acknowledge my great indebtedness to Robert Allerton Parker in the preparation of this book, and also to thank Aline Caro-Delvaille and Harry Levin for their helpful suggestions.

L. V.

THE
GREEN
HUNTSMAN

THE AUTHOR TO THE READER

To the happy few.
Once upon a time there lived in Paris a family that had been preserved from vulgar ideas by the head of the house who, in addition to being a man of much wit, was capable of making up his mind.—Lord Byron.

Indulgent Reader:

Listen to the title I give you. In truth, if you were not indulgent and ready to take in good part the words and actions of the serious characters I am about to introduce to you, if you were not willing to pardon the author for his total lack of grandiloquence and moral purpose, etc., etc., I should not advise you to go any further. This story was written with a small number of readers in mind, readers whom I have never seen and whom I shall never see, which is a pity: how I should enjoy spending an evening with them!

With the hope of being read by these few, I have made no effort, I confess, to guard the approaches against ill-natured criticism. To be elegant, academic, and eloquent is beyond my powers; or to add a hundred and fifty pages of periphrastic circumlocutions; a hundred and fifty pages that would only please solemn people predestined to detest writers like the one who now in all humility presents himself to you. It is enough that those worthy personages have been a plague to me in real life without letting them spoil my pleasure when I write for the *Bibliotheque bleu.*

Farewell, friendly reader; try not to spend your life hating and being afraid.

Cityold, . . . 1837.

THE GREEN HUNTSMAN

CHAPTER ONE

L UCIEN LEUWEN was expelled from the École Polytechnique for having gone for an untimely walk on
a day when he, with his fellow students, had been
ordered to keep their quarters. It was on one of those famous
days of June, 1832.

Some young men, quite mad but endowed with great courage, had been harboring the design of dethroning the king,
and the École Polytechnique (which enjoys the displeasure of
the Master of the Tuileries) had been officially ordered to stay
off the streets. The day after his promenade, Lucien was expelled as a republican. Very much distressed at first, he had, at
the end of two years, resigned himself to the misfortune of
not having to work twelve hours a day. He spent most of his
time very pleasantly at home, for his father, man-about-town
and rich banker, had a most agreeable house in Paris.

M. Leuwen, one of the associates of the famous banking
house of Van Peters, Leuwen, and Co., feared only two things
in this world: humidity and bores. He never lectured his son,
never adopted a solemn tone, and, when Lucien left Polytechnique, proposed that he should work at the bank one day a
week—Thursdays, the day of the heavy Holland mail. For each
Thursday of work, the cashier counted out for Lucien two
hundred francs; and from time to time also paid a few little
debts, at which M. Leuwen was wont to remark:

"A son is a debtor given us by Nature."

Sometimes he would tease this debtor.

"Do you know," he said to Lucien one day, "what will be
engraved on your marble tombstone at Père-Lachaise, if we

5

should have the misfortune of losing you? *'Siste viator!* Here lies Lucien Leuwen, republican, who for two years waged ruthless war on new boots and cigars.' "

At the time when we take up his story, this enemy of cigars had given up all thought of the Republic which was too slow in coming.* "And besides," he said to himself, "if it amuses Frenchmen to be led monarchically and with a high hand, why disturb them? The majority seem to like this combination of honeyed hypocrisy and lies called *representative government."* †

As his parents did not seek to order his life for him, Lucien spent most of his time in his mother's drawing room. Still young and quite pretty, Madame Leuwen enjoyed the highest consideration; society agreed that she was an infinitely clever woman. But a severe judge might have reproached her for a somewhat excessive delicacy and a too absolute contempt for the arrogance and impudence of our fashionable young gallants.

This proud and exceptional spirit did not even deign to express its contempt, and at the slightest sign of vulgarity or affectation, Madame Leuwen would maintain an impenetrable silence. She was rather inclined to take exception to the most innocent things simply because she had encountered them for the first time in people who make too much noise.

The dinners given by M. Leuwen were famous throughout Paris; they were often perfection. On certain days he would entertain the money-makers and power-seekers; but these gentlemen were not included in his wife's circle. Thus M. Leuwen's business in no way spoiled that society in which money was not the only merit and, unbelievable though it may seem, was not considered the greatest of all advantages! In that drawing room where the furnishings had cost a hundred thou-

* In the opinion of our hero, who is mad and who will change.
† It is a republican speaking.

sand francs, no one hated anyone (strange anomaly!); but everyone liked to laugh and on occasion was not slow to ridicule affectations of every sort, beginning with the king and the archbishop.

As you see, the conversation there was not in the least likely to make for advancement or conquer *fine positions*. In spite of this inconvenience which kept away a great many people who were not missed, the throng was considerable which sought for admission to Madame Leuwen's salon. It would have been the rage had Madame Leuwen been willing to make it more accessible, but one had to combine many different qualifications to be admitted. Madame Leuwen's unique aim was to amuse her husband, who was twenty years older than herself and was said to be on very good terms with the young ladies of the Opera. In spite of this inconvenience and the amenities of her salon, Madame Leuwen was never completely happy unless her husband was present.

In this circle it was agreed that Lucien had an elegant figure, naturalness, and something extremely distinguished in his manners; but here the praise ceased! He was not considered a man of wit. A passion for work, an almost military education, and the free and easy speech of the École Polytechnique had resulted in a total lack of affectation. Each minute he was solely engaged in thinking of what pleased him the most at that very minute, and gave too little thought to *others*.

He regretted the school sword because a very pretty woman, who enjoyed a vogue at the new Court, had said he wore it with an air. . . . He was, moreover, quite tall and rode a horse to perfection. Nice darkish-blond hair prepossessed people in favor of a face that was quite irregular but whose rather large features radiated candor and vivacity. It must be admitted, however, there was nothing overbearing in his manner, he had absolutely nothing of a colonel of a *Gymnase* comedy, still less the tone of importance and calculated arrogance of a young embassy secretary, nothing in his bearing that said: "My father is worth ten million." Thus our hero did not possess that fashionable appearance which, in Paris, is what makes for three quarters of anyone's good looks. Finally, and this was something quite unpardonable in this starched and stuffy century, Lucien appeared to be perfectly carefree and heedless.

"How you are wasting an admirable position!" Ernest Dévelroy, his cousin and a budding young savant, said to him one day. He was already one of the shining lights of the *Revue de* —— and had been promised three votes for the Academy of Moral Sciences.

He was in Lucien's cabriolet when he made this observation, being driven to a soirée at Monsieur N——'s who had been a liberal in 1829, full of sublime and tender thoughts, and who now enjoyed positions worth forty thousand francs, and called republicans the *disgrace of the human race*.

"If you only took things a little more seriously, if you didn't always laugh at the slightest nonsense, you could, in your father's salon or anywhere else as a matter of fact, be one of the foremost among the students of the École Polytechnique expelled for their opinions. Look at your fellow-student Coffe, expelled like you, poor as Job, admitted only out of charity to your mother's drawing room at first; and yet what consideration he now enjoys among all those millionaires and peers of France! His secret is simple enough, anyone can borrow it: he has a solemn manner and never opens his mouth. You really should adopt a rather somber air sometimes. All men of your age try to make people think they're important. You, my poor fellow, through no fault of yours, succeeded in twenty-four hours and you cheerfully fling your advantage away. To see you one would think you were a child and, what's worse, a contented child. I warn you, people are beginning to take you at your word, and in spite of your father's millions, you count for nothing; you have no importance, you are nothing but a

8

nice schoolboy, which at twenty is really a bit ridiculous; and to complete your ruin, you spend hours over your toilet, and everybody knows it."

"To satisfy you," said Lucien, "one should play a part, I suppose? And what a *sad* part! But what would society give me in return for my boredom? With never a moment's relief from this tedium. And wouldn't I be obliged to listen with a straight face to Marquis D——'s long homilies on political economy, and the lamentations of Abbé R—— on the infinite dangers of partition among brothers, provided by the Civil Code? In the first place, perhaps these gentlemen do not even know what they are talking about; and in the second place, which is more probable, they would laugh heartily at the idiot who believed them."

"Well then, refute them, start a discussion, the gallery will be with you. Who said to agree with them? Only be grave. Play a serious role."

"I should be too afraid that in a week the *serious role* would become a habit. What do I care for the world's opinion? I'm not asking it for anything. I wouldn't give three louis to be a member of your Academy; haven't we just seen how M. B—— was elected?"

"But, sooner or later, you will be called to account to the world for the place it accords you on faith, because of your father's millions. If your independence excites the world's displeasure, it will find some way of hurting you. One day it will take it into its head to turn a cold shoulder. Having always been accustomed to being received with open arms, I can imagine your despair, but it will be too late. Then you will feel the necessity of being somebody, of belonging to a group that will stand by you if necessary, and you will frantically take up horse-racing; for my part, I find it less silly to be an Academician."

The sermon came to an end as Ernest got down at the door of the renegade who held twenty offices. "He's fantastic, my

9

cousin," thought Lucien, "just like Madame X who insists that it is important for me to go to Mass: *'It is absolutely indispensable, especially for the heir to a great fortune who is without a great name.'* By gad, I'd be an awful fool to do things that bore me! And who pays any attention to what I do in Paris?"

Six weeks after Ernest Dévelroy's sermon, Lucien was pacing up and down his room. His eye traced with scrupulous attention all the arabesques of a sumptuous Turkish carpet which Madame Leuwen had had taken from her own room one day when her son was confined to his room with a cold. On the present occasion, Lucien wore a magnificent and bizarre dressing-gown in blue and gold, with nice warm pantaloons of magenta cashmere.

He seemed happy in this costume, there was a smile on his face. Each time he turned he would glance a little to one side, but without stopping, and each time his glance would fall on the sofa; on the sofa lay a green coat with magenta pipings; to this coat were attached the epaulets of a second-lieutenant.

And therein lay happiness!

CHAPTER TWO

SINCE M. LEUWEN, that famous banker, gave dinners of rare distinction, really almost perfect, and since he was neither moral, boring, nor ambitious, but only fantastic and original, he had a great many friends. However, through a grave error on his part, he never chose his friends with a view to augmenting the prestige he enjoyed and his importance in the world. They were, first of all, men of wit who liked to enjoy themselves, who perhaps worked seriously every morning at increasing their fortunes but at night laughed at the world in general, went to the Opera, and, above all, tried not to pry too closely into the origins of power; for if they had, it would have been necessary for them to get indignant, denounce and be dull.

His friends had told the reigning minister that Lucien was not a *Hampden,* neither a fanatic on the subject of American freedom nor a man to object to taxes even without the budget, but simply a young man of twenty with the same opinions as everybody else. The result was that for the last thirty-six hours Lucien was a second-lieutenant of the Twenty-seventh Regiment of Lancers, which has uniforms with magenta pipings and is, in addition, famous for its shining valor.

"Perhaps I should have chosen the Ninth which also had a vacancy," Lucien debated with himself as he gaily lighted a cigar he had just rolled in licorice paper sent to him from Barcelona. "The Ninth has canary-yellow pipings . . . that is gayer . . . yes, but less distinguished, less sober, less military. . . . Military! Bah! Regiments paid by a Chamber of Commons will never fight. The important thing in a uniform is that it should look attractive at a ball, and canary-yellow is certainly gayer. . . .

"How I have changed! When I put on my first uniform to enter Polytechnique, how little I cared what color it was; I was thinking of splendid batteries quickly set up under the fire of the thundering Prussian artillery. . . . Who knows, perhaps my Twenty-seventh Regiment of Lancers will one day charge those *hussars of death* whom Napoleon praised in his Jéna bulletin! . . . But to fight with joy, one must feel that one's country is really interested in the combat; if it's only for the sake of this '*halt in the mud*' that has encouraged foreigners in their insolence,* faith, it's not worth it!"

* This young man still speaks the language of his party: this is a republican speaking.

And the idea of facing danger and fighting like a hero lost all its glamor. Because of his beloved uniform he tried to think of all the advantages of the calling: getting promoted, being decorated, money . . . "Come now, why not pillage Spain and Germany at once and have done with it, like N—— or N——!"

His lip curling in profound disgust, he let his cigar fall to the sumptuous carpet his mother had given him. Hastily he picked it up; his mood changed; his contempt for war had vanished.

"After all," he thought, "neither Russia nor the other despotisms will ever forgive the *Three Days*. So it would be a fine thing to fight."

His confidence now restored, after that ignoble momentary contact with the specialists in emoluments, his eyes once more turned in the direction of the sofa where the tailor had spread out his second-lieutenant's uniform. He imagined war from what he had seen of cannon drill in the Park of Vincennes.

He might be wounded! But then he saw himself transported to a thatched cottage in Swabia or Italy and a charming young girl whose language he could not understand nursing him, at first out of simple humanity—but then . . . When his youthful imagination had exhausted all the joys of making love to a fresh innocent peasant girl, it was a young woman of the court exiled on the banks of the Sezia by a churlish husband. First she sent her footman to bring bandages to the young wounded officer, and a few days later she herself appeared leaning on the arm of the village priest.

"But no," went on Lucien, frowning and thinking of all the pleasantries M. Leuwen had heaped on him since yesterday, "I'll never make war on anything but cigars. I'll become the pillar of the military café in some dreary ill-paved little garrison town; my evening diversions will be billiards and beer, and sometimes in the morning we'll wage war with rotten cabbages on dirty workmen who are dying of hunger.

. . . At the most, like Pyrrhus, I'll be killed by a chamber-pot thrown by some toothless hag out of a fifth-story window! What glory! How disconcerted my soul will be when I am presented to Napoleon in the next world, and he says: 'You must have been dying of hunger to engage in this profession?'— 'No, General, I wanted to follow in your footsteps.'" And Lucien burst out laughing. . . . "Our leaders are not firmly enough seated in the saddle to risk a real war. One fine morning a corporal like Hoche will rise from the ranks, and will say to the soldiers: 'Friends, let's march on Paris and make a consul who will not let himself be made a laughingstock by Nicholas.'

"But I want the corporal to succeed," Lucien philosophically continued as he relighted his cigar. "Once the nation is roused to anger and in love with glory, farewell liberty! The journalist who raised any doubts about the bulletin of the last battle would be treated as a traitor, ally of the enemy, and massacred in imitation of the republicans of America. Once more we would turn our backs on liberty for the sake of glory. . . . Vicious circle . . . and so *ad infinitum.*"

It can be seen that our second-lieutenant was not altogether exempt from that disease of *excessive reasoning* which cripples the youth of our time, turning them into old women. "However that may be," he suddenly exclaimed as he tried on his uniform and looked at himself in the glass, "everybody says that one has to be something. Very well, I will be a *lancer;* when I have learned my calling I shall have accomplished my purpose, then come what may."

That evening as Lucien, wearing epaulets for the first time in his life, passed the sentinels at the Tuileries, they presented arms; he was wild with joy. Ernest Dévelroy, who was a *born intriguer* and knew everybody, took him to meet the Lieutenant-Colonel of the Twenty-seventh Lancers, M. Filloteau, who was passing through Paris.

13

In a room on the third floor of a house on the Rue du Bouloi, Lucien, whose heart was pounding and who expected to see a hero, found a man of short stature and wary eye, with great blond side-whiskers, carefully combed, spreading over his cheeks. Lucien was stupefied. "My God!" he thought, "this man is just a pettifogger from Lower Normandy!" He stood gaping in front of M. Filloteau who, in vain, asked him *to have the goodness to be seated*. Between every other word of the conversation, this brave soldier of Austerlitz and of Marengo, always managed to interpolate: *my fidelity to the king,* or *the necessity of suppressing factionists*.

After ten minutes, which seemed like a century, Lucien fled. He walked so rapidly that Dévelroy had difficulty keeping up with him.

"Great God! Do you call that a hero?" Lucien finally burst out, stopping abruptly. "Why, he's nothing but a military policeman, a tyrant's cut-throat paid to kill his fellow citizens, and glorying in it!"

The future Academician saw things in an entirely different light, and on a less exalted plane.

"What do you mean by making such a face? You look as though someone had given you some rotten *pâté de Strasbourg*. Do you or don't you want to amount to something in the world?"

"My God, what riffraff!"

"This lieutenant-colonel is worth a hundred of you. He is a peasant who, by making good use of his sword for anyone who paid him, bagged those epaulets with bullion fringe."

"But he's so coarse, so disgusting! . . ."

"All the more credit to him! It was by disgusting his superiors, if they were worth more than he, that he forced them to favor the advancement he enjoys today. And you, my worthy republican, have you ever earned a penny in your life? You simply took the trouble to get born like the son of a prince.

Your father gives you everything you need. Without that, where would you be? Aren't you ashamed, at your age, not to be able to earn so much as the price of a cigar?"

"But such a vile creature! . . ."

"Vile or not, he's a thousand times superior to you; he has done something, while you have done nothing. The man who, while catering to the passions of the strong, picks up enough pennies to buy himself a cigar, or who, stronger than the weak who are in possession of the money-bags, gets hold of those pennies, may or may not be vile—we'll discuss that later—but he is strong; he's *a man*. You may despise him but first of all you have to reckon with him. You are nothing but a child who counts for nothing, who has discovered some fine phrases in a book and repeats them gracefully like a good actor who knows his part; but as for action—zero! Before despising a coarse Auvergnac peasant who, in spite of his repulsive physiognomy, is no longer a peddler on a street corner, but receives the official visit of M. Lucien Leuwen, a handsome young Parisian and son of a millionaire, just think of the difference in merit between you and him. M. Filloteau probably supports his old peasant father, while your father supports you."

"Oh, you will certainly be a member of the Institute before long!" cried Lucien in despairing tones. "As for me, I'm a fool. You are right, a thousand times right! I see that, I feel it, but I am very much to be pitied. I have a horror of the door through which I shall have to pass. There's too much filth under that door! Good-by."

And Lucien turned on his heels. He was glad that Ernest did not follow him. He rushed upstairs to his room and flung his uniform down furiously in the middle of the floor. "God knows what it will force me to do!"

A few moments later he went down to see his father and embraced him with tears in his eyes.

"Ah, I see how it is," said M. Leuwen in surprise, "you have lost a hundred louis, I'll give you two hundred; but I don't like your way of asking; I'd rather not see tears in the eyes of a second-lieutenant. Shouldn't a valiant soldier think first of all of the effect he is making on his neighbors?"

"Our clever cousin Dévelroy has just been giving me a dressing down. He has convinced me that my only merit is having taken the trouble to get born the son of a man of brains; that by my own wits I have never earned so much as the price of a cigar; that, if it weren't for you, I'd be in the poorhouse."

"And so you don't want a hundred louis?" asked M. Leuwen.

"I already owe much too much to your generosity. What would I be without you?"

"The devil take you," M. Leuwen cried energetically. "Are you becoming a Saint-Simonist, by any chance? What a bore you're going to be!"

Lucien's emotion, which he was unable to hide, began to amuse his father in the end.

"I insist," said M. Leuwen, suddenly interrupting as the clock began striking nine, "that this very moment you go and occupy my box at the Opera. There you will find some young ladies who are worth three or four of you; for, first of all, they didn't take any trouble getting born, and, what's more, on the days they dance they earn fifteen or twenty francs. I insist that you take them to supper in my name, as my deputy, you understand? You will entertain them at the *Rocher de Cancale,* where you will spend at least two hundred francs. Otherwise I disown you, pronounce you a Saint-Simonist, and forbid your seeing me for six months. What a punishment for such a loving son!"

Lucien had a downright fit of tenderness toward his father.

"Do your friends consider me an awful bore?" he asked sensibly enough. "I swear to you that I'll spend your two hundred francs very well."

"God be praised! And remember that nothing could be more

16

ill-mannered than to burst in like this and to begin talking
about serious things to a poor man of sixty-five, who has never
given you the slightest excuse to come loving him furiously in
this way. Devil take you, you'll never be anything but a dreary
republican. I am astonished that you haven't greasy hair and
a dirty beard."

Somewhat nettled, Lucien made himself agreeable to the
young ladies he found in his father's box. At supper he was
very lively and poured them champagne with charming grace.
After seeing them to their door, as he drove home alone in a
cab at one o'clock in the morning, he wondered at his display
of emotion earlier in the evening. "I must be careful of my
first impulses," he said to himself. "I'm not sure of anything
about myself. My affection only succeeded in shocking my
father. . . . I should never have foreseen that. I need action.
I'd better join my regiment."

The next morning at seven o'clock he presented himself in
uniform, and alone, at the door of Lieutenant-Colonel Filloteau's uninviting room. There, for two hours he had the
courage to pay court to the old soldier. He made a serious effort
to accustom himself to military ways. He imagined that all
his fellow officers would have the tone and manners of Filloteau. An unbelievable illusion but one which had its advantages. What he saw shocked him, mortally offended him. "But
I'll go through with it," he said courageously. "I will not make
fun of their manners and I will imitate them."

Lieutenant-Colonel Filloteau talked about himself—talked a
great deal. He told at length how he had obtained his first
epaulets in Egypt in the first battle under the walls of Alex-
andria. The account was magnificent and moved Lucien
deeply. But the old soldier, having been spoiled by fifteen years
of Restoration, was not revolted by the sight of a *Paris dandy*
walking into a lieutenancy without lifting a finger. Calculation having taken the place of heroism in his mind, he began

reckoning the advantages to be derived from this young man. He asked Lucien if his father were a deputy.

M. Filloteau declined Madame Leuwen's invitation to luncheon, conveyed to him by Lucien. But two days later he did not hesitate to accept a superb pipe with meerschaum bowl encased in massive silver. Filloteau had received it from Lucien's hands as a due, and without the least gratitude.

"This," he said to himself, when he had closed the door on Lucien, "means that our dandy, once he's in the regiment, will be asking frequent leaves to go and squander his money in the neighboring town. . . . And," he added, weighing the heavy silver of the pipe in his hand, "you will obtain those leaves, M. Leuwen, and you will obtain them entirely through *me;* you won't catch me passing up a client like that; the popinjay must have five hundred francs a month to spend; his father was certainly in the commissariat during the wars; all that money has been stolen from the poor soldier. . . . Confiscated," he said, smiling to himself. And hiding the pipe under a pile of shirts in the bureau drawer, he removed the key.

CHAPTER THREE

A HUSSAR in 1794, at the age of eighteen, Filloteau had taken part in all the campaigns of the Revolution. For the first six years he had fought with enthusiasm, singing the *Marseillaise*. But Bonaparte made himself consul, and soon all the future lieutenant-colonel's wily common sense told him that it was inept to keep on singing the *Marseillaise*. He was also the first lieutenant in his regiment to obtain the Cross. Under the Bourbons he took his first communion and became an officer of the *Legion d'Honneur*. Now he had come to spend three days in Paris to remind some of his subaltern friends of his existence, while the Twenty-seventh Regiment of Lancers was on its way from Nantes to Lorraine. Had Lucien been wiser in the ways of the world, he would have spoken of the esteem his father enjoyed with the War Office. But such things never occurred to Lucien. Like a restive young horse he saw perils which did not exist, but he also found plenty of courage to brave them.

Having found out that M. Filloteau was leaving the following day by diligence to rejoin his regiment, Lucien asked permission to travel in his company. Madame Leuwen was very much surprised when she saw her son's calash, which she had had stationed under her windows, being unloaded, and all his luggage being sent off to the diligence.

During the very first meal together, the Colonel, seeing Lucien take up a newspaper, reprimanded him sharply.

"In the Twenty-seventh there is a standing order of the day which forbids the officers of this regiment reading the newspapers in public places; there is only one exception—the government's official paper."

"The devil take the paper!" cried Lucien gaily. "Let's try our luck at dominoes and see who is to pay for the punch this evening—that is, if the horses aren't ready yet."

Young though he was, Lucien nevertheless had sense enough to lose six games running, and when they got back into their coach the brave Filloteau had been completely won over. He found that there was something to be said for this young fop after all, and began explaining to him how he should behave so as not to be taken for a greenhorn. Such behavior was just about the contrary of the exquisite politeness to which Lucien was accustomed. For, in the eyes of the Filloteaus of the world (as among monks) exquisite politeness was regarded as a weakness; one must, above all, talk about oneself and all one's advantages, one must exaggerate. As our hero was listening sadly and with great attention, Filloteau fell asleep and left him free to dream at his leisure. On the whole Lucien was delighted to be doing something active and seeing something new.

Two days later, at six in the morning, about three leagues this side of Nancy, our gentlemen caught up with the regiment. They had the diligence stop and deposit them and all their effects on the highroad.

Lucien, who was all eyes, was struck by the air of churlish and vulgar importance that came over the broad countenance of the Lieutenant-Colonel when his orderly opened a portmanteau and took out his uniform with its great epaulets. M. Filloteau had ordered a horse brought for Lucien, and the two of them rejoined the regiment, which had gone on while they were donning their uniforms. Seven or eight officers had taken their place at the extreme rear in honor of their lieutenant-colonel, and to these Lucien was first presented. He found them extremely cold. Nothing could have been less encouraging than the expression of their faces.

"So it's people like these I shall have to live with!" thought Lucien with a lump in his throat like a child. Accustomed as he was to the faces animated by civility and a desire to please in the people he encountered in Paris drawing rooms, Lucien even went so far as to think that the young gentlemen in question were affecting this manner on purpose to discountenance him. He talked too much and nothing he said was allowed to pass without objection or challenge. He stopped talking.

For an hour, without saying a word, Lucien rode on the left of the captain commanding the squadron to which he was to belong. His manner was distant, at least he hoped it was, but his heart was bursting with emotion. The disagreeable dialogue with the officers was hardly at an end before he had completely forgotten their existence. He was absorbed in watching the lancers and found himself transported with joy and astonishment. So these were the companions of Napoleon! So this is the French soldier! He scrutinized the smallest detail, with a ridiculous and passionate interest.

His first transports somewhat moderated, he examined his own situation. "Here I am, provided with a profession, and a profession which is considered the noblest of all and the most amusing. The École Polytechnique would have mounted me with the artillery officers; here I am with the lancers." And he added with a smile, "The only difference is that instead of knowing my trade exceptionally well, I don't know it at all." The captain riding beside him noticed this smile which was more tender than mocking and was annoyed by it. . . . "Bah!" continued Lucien to himself, "Desaix and Saint-Cyr began the same way; those heroes who were not spoiled by dukedoms." *

He could hear the lancers talking among themselves and began to listen to what they were saying. Their conversation was commonplace enough: the quality of their soldier bread, the price of wine, etc., etc. But the frank tone of their voices, the lusty sincerity that shone through every word, fortified his soul like the air of the mountains. There was something simple and unspoiled about them, quite different from the hot-house atmosphere in which he had been living. To feel the difference and to change his whole outlook on life was the matter of a moment. In place of that very agreeable but at bottom very cautious and timorous civility, the tone of these remarks all gaily proclaimed: "I count on myself and to hell with the world!"

"These are really the frankest, the most sincere and perhaps the happiest men in the world!" thought Lucien. "Why shouldn't one of their officers be like them? Like them I'm frank and say what I think; my only thought would be to

---

* A republican is speaking.

contribute to their comfort; after all I really don't give a damn for anything but my own self-respect. As for these pretentious individuals with their cutting and conceited airs who are called my comrades-in-arms, I have nothing in common with them but my epaulets." Out of the corner of his eye he stole a glance at the captain on his right and the lieutenant on the right of the captain. "These gentlemen form a perfect contrast to the lancers. They spend their time acting and, except for death, they are afraid of everything; they are exactly like my cousin Dévelroy."

Lucien once more turned his attention to the lancers, listening to them with delight. Soon his soul was soaring in imaginary space. He keenly relished this sensation of freedom and generosity, and saw nothing but the splendid things to be accomplished, the magnificent dangers. The necessity for intrigue and a life as envisaged by his cousin Dévelroy for him had been forgotten. The idle talk of these soldiers had on him the exhilarating effect of good music; life took on a roseate hue.

Suddenly, between the two rows of lancers who were going along at a walk, slouching in their saddles, the adjutant came riding at a fast trot down the middle of the road. He said something in a low voice to the non-commissioned officers, and Lucien saw the lancers straighten up in their saddles. "How splendid they look now!" he thought.

His young and naïve countenance could not conceal so lively an emotion; gladness and kindliness were written all over it, and perhaps a little curiosity too. This was a great mistake on his part. He should have remained impassive, or better still have assumed an expression contrary to the one that was expected of him. The captain on whose left he was riding immediately thought to himself: "My fine young man is about to ask me a question and I shall put him in his place with a *well seasoned* reply." But not for anything in the world would Lucien have asked his so uncomradely comrades anything. He tried to guess for himself the word that, all at once, had given the lancers such an air of alertness, and, in one second, changed the happy-go-lucky negligence of a long march into all the nobility of military bearing.

The captain kept waiting for a question from Lucien. At last, he could endure the continued silence of the young Parisian no longer.

"It is the Inspector-General we are waiting for, General Count N——, a Peer of France," he finally explained with a cold haughty air and without seeming to be addressing his remarks to Lucien specially.

Lucien looked at the captain coldly and as though merely aroused by the sound of his voice. This heroic soldier's lips were pursed in an outrageous pout; his forehead bore a self-important frown; his eyes, turned ever so slightly to the left, were carefully *not* looking directly at our second-lieutenant.

"What a ludicrous animal," thought Lucien. "Apparently this is that military tone about which Filloteau has had so much to say! Just to please these gentlemen I am certainly not going to adopt such rude and vulgar manners. I shall always be a stranger among them. It may cost me some swordplay, but I am not going to reply to any remark made in such a tone." The captain evidently was expecting some deferential exclamation such as: "You don't mean the famous Count N——, the General so honorably mentioned in the bulletins of the Grand Army?"

But our hero was on his guard. His face continued to have the expression of someone exposed to a bad smell. After a moment of painful silence, and scowling more than ever, the captain was forced to add:

"It was Count N—— who made that magnificent charge at Austerlitz; his carriage will soon come past us. Colonel Malher de Saint-Mégrin, who is not so stupid, at the last relay slipped the postillions a crown; one of them has just now galloped up! The lancers are not to form ranks—that would look pre-arranged. Think what a good impression the inspector will have of the regiment; one should never neglect first impressions. . . . Look at them—those men were born in the saddle!"

Lucien replied only with a nod. He was ashamed of the gait of the old nag they had given him; he let it feel his spurs; it jumped and nearly fell down. "I look like one of our *cabbage-cutter* brothers," he thought to himself.

Ten minutes later they could hear the rumbling of a heavily loaded vehicle and Count N—— came driving along the middle of the highway between the two lines of lancers. Soon his carriage passed Lucien and the captain, but his enormous berlin was so piled high with packages of every size and shape that they did not get even a glimpse of the famous general.

"Case upon case, a caisson," remarked the captain bitterly. "They can't stir without their hams, roasts, turkeys and *pâté de foie gras,* to say nothing of quantities of champagne."

Our hero was forced to reply. And while he is thus engaged with Captain Henriet in the distasteful task of politely returning arrogance for arrogance, we ask permission to turn our attention for an instant to the Lieutenant-General, Count N——, Peer of France, who is this year charged with the inspection of the Third Military Division. . . .

At the moment his carriage rolled over the drawbridge into Nancy, headquarters of the division, seven salvos announced this signal event to the populace.

The sound of the cannon once more sent Lucien's soul soaring into the seventh heaven.

Two sentinels were placed at the inspector's door, and Lieutenant-General Baron Thérance, commander of the division, sent to ask if Count N—— wished to see him at once, or on the following day.

"At once, by God!" said the old general. "Do you think I'm here just to f—— discipline?"

With respect to detail, Count N—— still retained the habits of the army of Sambre-et-Meuse in which he had first made a reputation for himself. These habits were all the more vividly present in his mind since, more than once during the last five or six stages, he had recognized positions which that army of such untarnished fame had formerly occupied.

Although he was certainly not an imaginative man, nor one with many illusions, he caught himself being stirred by memories of 1792. "What a difference between '92 and 183–! Great God, how we used to swear eternal enmity to royalty! And with what conviction! These young non-coms whom Soult has recommended so particularly to my care, why they are ourselves of those days all over again. . . . At that time we used to fight every day; it was an agreeable calling; we liked to fight. Today you have to pay court to a Marshal and Judge in a Court of Peers!"

A rather handsome man of sixty-five or -six, tall and thin, with an erect carriage and finished manners, the General still had a waistline, and a few carefully tended curls between blond and gray gave a certain grace to an otherwise perfectly bald head. His face revealed a steadfast courage and a firm resolve to obey, but was, in every other respect, a total stranger to thought.

It was a face that was much less pleasing at second glance and seemed almost common at the third; there was a vague aura of duplicity about it. One could see that the Empire and its servility had passed that way.

Happy the heroes who died before 1804!

These old figures of the army of Sambre-et-Meuse had been softened in the ante-chambers of the Tuileries and at the ceremonies in Notre-Dame. The Count N—— had seen General Delmas exiled after the famous dialogue:

"What a splendid ceremony, Delmas! Really superb!" said the Emperor on his return from Notre-Dame.

"You are right, General, nothing was missing except the two million men who died to overthrow what you have just restored."

The next day Delmas was ordered never to come within forty leagues of Paris.

When the valet announced Baron Thérance, General N——, who had donned his dress uniform, was pacing the floor still hearing in his imagination the liberating cannon of Valenciennes. Quickly he dismissed all these memories which might so easily lead to indiscretions. And now, for the sake of the reader, as is said by those who hawk the King's speech at the opening of the session, we shall report the dialogue that took place between the two old generals. They knew each other only slightly.

As he entered, Baron Thérance bowed awkwardly. Almost six feet tall he had the look of a Franc-Comtois peasant. Moreover, at the battle of Hanau, where Napoleon had been forced to pierce the ranks of his faithful Bavarian allies to get back to France, Colonel Thérance, who with his battalion covered General Drouot's famous battery, had received a saber blow that had slashed both his cheeks and cut off a bit of his nose. The damage had been more or less repaired, but was still very plain, and this enormous scar across a face furrowed by a perpetual state of dissatisfaction, gave the General a very military air. During the war he had shown extraordinary bravery, but after Napoleon's reign all his boldness had collapsed. On the pavements of Nancy everything terrified him and, above all else, the newspapers. His constant nightmare was the fear of being held up to public ridicule. The dullest pleasantry in a paper with barely a hundred subscribers would put this brave soldier in a panic. He had another vexation: nobody in Nancy paid the slightest attention to his epaulets. He thought himself detested by the youth of the city to whom he had given pretty rough treatment during the riots of 183–.

This once happy man now introduced his aide-de-camp who immediately retired. He then spread out on the table a plan of the disposition of the troops and the hospitals of the division. An hour at least was spent over military details. The General questioned the Baron about the soldiers' frame of mind, about the non-commissioned officers, and from there to the attitude of the inhabitants was but a step. It must be admitted that the replies of the worthy commander of the Third Division would seem pretty long if we set them down with all the flourishes of military rhetoric. We shall therefore content ourselves with the conclusions which Count N——, Peer of France, drew from the remarks, so full of bitterness, of the General of the province.

"Here is a man who is honor itself," thought the Count. "He does not fear death. He even complains, and with all his heart, of the absence of danger. He is, nevertheless, completely demoralized, and if he were called upon to put down an uprising now, his fear of next morning's papers would drive him crazy."

"I am forced to swallow humiliations all day long," repeated the Baron.

"But you must not say it too loud, my dear General; there are twenty general officers, your seniors, soliciting your place. And the Marshal insists on everybody being happy. I am going to repeat to you frankly, as a friend, a remark addressed to me by the Minister—a bit strong, I admit: *'Only an imbecile,'* he said to me a week ago as I was taking leave of him, *'can't make a nest for himself anywhere.'*"

"I should like to see the Marshal here in Nancy," replied the Baron with impatience, "between a rich and thoroughly united aristocracy that openly despises us, and a bourgeoisie led by Jesuits, keen as razors, who control all the women with any money. On the other hand, all the young men of this town who are neither noble nor pious—rabid republicans! If my glance happens to fall on one of them he holds up a *pear,* or some other seditious emblem. Even schoolboys display *pears* for my benefit; and if I happen to be a couple of hundred feet away from my sentinels, the young men hiss outrageously; then later I receive an anonymous letter in which I am offered satisfaction, but should I refuse, the writer covers me with the most fiendish insults. . . . And the anonymous letter always contains a slip of paper with the name and address of the writer. Do you have anything like that in Paris? And if I meet with an affront, the next day everybody is talking and laughing about it. Only the day before yesterday, a very brave ex-officer whose servant had, by chance, been killed during the affair of April 3rd, offered to draw pistols with me outside division limits. Well, yesterday this piece of insolence was the talk of the whole town!"

"In that case a letter to the King's Attorney-General is in order. Does he fail to show the proper energy?"

"He's driven by the devil himself! Being related to the Minister he is sure of promotion with the first political suit that comes up. I made the mistake of going to him a few days after the riots with an atrocious anonymous letter—the first I'd ever received in my life, by gad! 'What do you expect me to do with this rag?' he asked coldly. 'I'm the one who would call on your protection, General, if I had been insulted like this, or else take justice into my own hands.' Sometimes I am tempted to take a slice off the noses of these insolent civilians with my saber!"

"And bid farewell to your post!"

"Ah! If I could only turn the guns on them!" cried the

brave old General with a deep sigh, and raising his eyes to heaven.

"Eh! to be sure," replied the Peer of France. "It has always been my way of thinking. To the cannon of Saint-Roche Napoleon owed the tranquillity of his reign. And has not your prefect, M. Fléron, advised the Minister of the Interior of the temper of the public?"

"Oh, as to that, he scribbles all day long. But he's a child, a hothead of twenty-eight who tries to play the fox with me, is eaten up with vanity and is as timorous as a woman. There's no use my saying to him: 'Come, let's drop these rivalries of prefect and general till happier times. You and I are vilified all day long and by everybody. Has Monsignor, the Bishop, for instance, returned our calls? Does the aristocracy come to your balls or invite you to theirs? And if, according to instructions, we take advantage of certain business relations to bow to a nobleman at the General Council, he returns the bow the first time only, afterwards he is always careful to turn his head the other way. As for the young republicans, they look straight at us and hiss.' All this is perfectly plain. And, believe it or not, the Prefect denies it. 'Speak for yourself,' red in the face with anger, he answers me. 'No one has ever hissed me!' And yet not a week goes by that he isn't hissed two paces away, if he dares appear on the street after dark."

"But are you perfectly sure of this, my dear General? The Minister of the Interior showed me ten letters from M. Fléron in which he represents himself as being on the point of becoming completely reconciled with the Legitimist Party. M. G——, the prefect of N—— with whom I dined day before yesterday, is on fairly good terms with them, and that I saw for myself."

"By God, I believe you! He is a clever man, an excellent prefect, a friend of all the clever thieves, and himself steals thirty thousand francs a year without being caught, which makes him respected in the province. But since what I report of my prefect may be looked upon with a certain suspicion, allow me to send for Captain B——. You know him? He must be in the ante-room."

"He is, if I am not mistaken, the observer sent to the One Hundred and Seventh to report on the temper of the garrison."

"Exactly! He has only been here three months and, in order not to compromise him in his regiment, I make a point of never seeing him by day."

Captain B—— appeared. As soon as he entered, Baron Thérance insisted on retiring to another room. The Captain confirmed, with a thousand instances, each of the poor General's complaints. "In this cursed city the youth is republican, the nobility thoroughly united and devout. M. Gauthier, editor of the liberal paper and leader of the republicans, is determined' and clever. M. Du Poirier, who directs the nobility, is an old fox of the first order with a bewildering fund of energy. Everybody makes game of the Prefect and the General; they are kept out of everything; they don't count at all. The Bishop periodically announces to his whole congregation that we will be out in three months. I am delighted, Monsieur le Comte, to acquit myself of my responsibility. The trouble is that if one writes quite plainly about all this to the Marshal, he replies that one is lacking in zeal. Very convenient for him in case of a change of dynasty . . ."

"Enough, sir!"

"I beg your pardon, General, I forgot myself. Here the Jesuits order the nobility around like charwomen, everybody in fact except the republicans."

"What is the population of Nancy?" the General hastened to ask, finding the Captain's report far too frank.

"Eighteen thousand inhabitants not counting the garrison."

"How many republicans have you?"

"Acknowledged republicans, thirty-six."

"That is two for every thousand. And among them, how many with brains?"

"Only one, Gauthier, the surveyor and editor of the *Aurore*. He is poor and glories in his poverty."

"And you mean to tell me that you can't control thirty-five whipper-snappers and lock up the brains?"

"But let me explain, sir. Just as the aristocrats consider it the proper thing to be religious, all those who are not religious think it smart to imitate the republicans in all their crazy notions. There is that Café Montor, frequented by the youngsters of the opposition. It is just like a club of '93. If four or five soldiers pass by, these gentlemen cry under their breath: *Long live the Line!* If a non-com appears they hail him, talk to him, try to get him to drink with them. But when it's an officer like myself belonging to the government, they heap him with every covert insult imaginable and he has to put up with it. Only last Sunday when I happened to pass the Café Montor, they all, with one movement like soldiers on parade, turned their backs on me; I was terribly tempted to give them a kick in their you-know-what."

"That would have been a sure way of getting put on the unattached list by return post. Aren't you well paid?"

"I receive a thousand-franc note every six months. It was only because I wasn't thinking that I strolled past the Café Montor. Ordinarily I go way out of my way to avoid the cursed café. And to think that an officer, wounded at Dresden and at Waterloo, should be obliged to dodge a pack of civilians!"

"Since the *Glorious Days* there are no more civilians," said the Count bitterly. "But enough of these personal problems," he added, recalling Baron Thérance and ordering the Captain to remain. "Who are the party leaders in Nancy?"

31

The General replied:

"MM. de Pontlevé and de Vassignies are the titular heads of Carlism, commissioned by Charles X. But a confounded intriguer named Dr. Du Poirier is in fact the real head. Officially he is only the secretary of the Carlist Committee. The Jesuit Rey, the Grand Vicar, rules all the women of Nancy from the greatest lady to the smallest shop-keeper; that's as plain as a pikestaff. Just notice if, at the dinner given in your honor by the Prefect, there is a single guest outside government officials. Ask anyone if a single person connected with the government and who is a frequent guest at the prefecture, is ever received by Mesdames de Chasteller, d'Hocquincourt or de Commercy."

"Who are these ladies?"

"They belong to the richest and proudest nobility. Madame d'Hocquincourt is the prettiest woman of the town and lives extravagantly. Madame de Commercy is a sort of Madame de Staël who is always holding forth in favor of Charles X as the Geneva woman used to do against Napoleon. I was in command of Geneva and that madwoman was a terrible nuisance to us."

"And Madame de Chasteller?" asked the Count with interest.

"Well, she's awfully young, although she's the widow of a major-general attached to the court of Charles X. And she preaches the *gospel* in her drawing room. All the young men of the town are mad about her. . . . The other day when a right-thinking young man had lost heavily at cards, Madame de Chasteller had the temerity to go to his house. Isn't it true, Captain?"

"It certainly is, General; I happened to be in the vicinity of the young man's house at the time. Madame de Chasteller gave him three thousand gold francs and a piece of jewelry covered with diamonds which the Duchesse d'Angoulême had given her, and which the young man went to pawn in Strasbourg. I have the pawnbroker's letter on me."

"Enough, enough," said the Count as the Captain produced a fat portfolio.

"There are also," continued General Thérance, "the Puylaurens, the de Serpierres and Madame de Marcilly, where Monsignor the Bishop is received as general-in-chief, and where, devil take me, not one of us ever sets foot. Do you know where the Prefect spends his evenings? In Madame Berchu's parlor—she is the grocer's wife—and the parlor is behind the shop. That is something he doesn't write to the Minister. I have more dignity than that. I go nowhere, so I'm in bed by eight o'clock."

"What do the officers do in the evening?"

"The café and the women of the town, but a bourgeois home—never! We are treated like untouchables. Those devils of bourgeois husbands play the spy for each other with the excuse of *liberalism*. The only happy men here are the artillery and the officers of engineers."

"And what side are they on?"

"They're all infernal republicans—*ideologists* you know! The captain here can tell you that they all subscribe to the *National* and the *Charivari,* all the filthy sheets, and that they openly laugh at my *orders of the day* regarding the press. They have the papers sent to a man in Darney, a little town six leagues from here. And I wouldn't want to swear that they don't have meetings with Gauthier on their hunting parties."

"Who is this man Gauthier?"

"The leader of the republicans, I've already mentioned him, the editor of their incendiary paper called *Aurore*. Last year, he challenged me to a duel, and what makes it really abominable is that he is employed by the government. He is cadastral surveyor, and I can't get him removed. I reported in vain his last contribution to the *National* for the Marshal Ney fund. . . ."

"Let's not talk about that," said the Count, blushing. And he had all the difficulty in the world getting rid of Baron Thérance who found relief in thus unburdening his heart.

CHAPTER FOUR

WHILE BARON THÉRANCE was painting this sad picture of the city of Nancy, the Twenty-seventh Regiment of Lancers was nearing it across the dreariest plain in the world. Nothing could possibly grow in that barren, stony ground, as Lucien noticed at a certain point about a league outside the city from which only three trees in all were to be seen. One growing at the side of the road was sickly and not twenty feet in height. What seemed in the distance a redoubt, he discovered, on nearer approach, to be a row of barren hills. A few meager grapevines were struggling in the gorges formed by these valleys. For a quarter of a league outside the city two pitiful rows of stunted elms marked the course of the highway. The peasants they passed all looked miserable and wore an expression of astonishment. "So this is *la belle France!*" thought Lucien. A little farther along the regiment passed some of those large and useful but dirty establishments which mournfully proclaim an advanced civilization—a slaughter house, an oil refinery, etc., etc. After these lovely sights came vast gardens entirely planted with cabbages—not the tiniest shrub anywhere.

Finally the road made a turn, and the regiment came face to face with the first row of fortifications which, on the side of the town toward Paris, seemed extremely low, as though buried in the earth. The regiment came to a halt and was recognized by the guard. But we forgot to mention that, about a league farther back, the clean-up halt had been made. In a few moments all traces of mud had vanished, uniforms and horses' harness were restored to their former splendor.

At about eight-thirty on a dark cold morning, on the 24th of March, 183–, the Twenty-seventh Regiment of Lancers marched into Nancy. It was preceded by a magnificent band which obtained a signal success with the townsfolk and *grisettes* of Nancy. Thirty-two trumpeters dressed in red and mounted on white horses blew until they almost burst. And the six trumpeters who formed the first row were Negroes into the bargain, while the drum-major was fairly seven feet tall.

All the beauties of the city and particularly the young working girls decked out in lace, were hanging out of the windows, and fully appreciated this ear-splitting music enhanced, it is true, by the trumpeters' scarlet uniforms resplendent with gold braid.

This well-fortified town of Nancy, Vauban's masterpiece, appeared abominable to Lucien. Filth and poverty seemed to have got the better of everything else, and the appearance of the inhabitants reflected perfectly the dreariness of the buildings. Lucien saw nothing all around him but miserly faces— mean, sharp and surly expressions. "These people think of nothing but money and how to make money," he thought with disgust. "Without doubt such is the character and aspect of that America which the liberals so loudly extol."

Accustomed to the courteous faces of his home city, the young Parisian was sincerely distressed. The narrow streets, ill-paved and all twists and turns, had nothing remarkable about them except their disgusting dirt. In the middle ran a gutter filled with muddy water that looked like some slaty concoction.

Suddenly the horse of the lancer marching on Lucien's right, shied and the nag that had been assigned to Lucien was splattered with this foul black mixture. Our hero noticed that this little accident was the cause of the greatest joy to all his new comrades near enough to witness it. The sight of these smiles that tried to appear supercilious cut the wings of Lucien's imagination. They put him in a very bad humor.

"Above all," he said to himself, "I must remember that this is not a camp, that there is no enemy a quarter of a league away, and moreover, that none of these gentlemen who are under forty have ever faced the enemy any more than I have. Hence their habits of meanness, offspring of boredom. These are no longer those young officers full of gallantry, heedlessness, and gaiety, one meets at the *Gymnase*. They are unbearably bored, poor devils, and would like nothing better than to amuse themselves at my expense. They'll bear me a grudge until the day I've fought a few duels, and the sooner the better, so I'll be left in peace. But I wonder if that fat lieutenant-colonel could act as my second? I'm afraid not, on account of his rank; he has to set a good example . . . Where am I to find a second?"

Lucien happened to raise his eyes and noticed a large house that was less shabby than the others the regiment had passed. In the middle of a blank wall he remarked a pair of shutters painted a parrot-green. "What a taste for gaudy colors these provincials have!"

Lucien was feeling pleased with this not very complimentary opinion, when he saw the parrot-green shutters open a little way, and caught sight of a young woman with magnificent blond hair and a haughty air, who had apparently come to the window to watch the regiment march by. All Lucien's gloomy thoughts vanished at the sight of this pretty face; his soul was restored. The dirty scaling walls of the houses of Nancy, the black mud, the envious spirit of his comrades, the inevitable duels, the atrocious paving stones on which his old nag (they had probably given it to him with malice aforethought) kept slipping, all vanished. Because of some stoppage under a covered passage at the end of the street, the regiment had been forced to halt. The young woman closed her window and stood looking out, half hidden by an embroidered muslin curtain. She might have been twenty-four or -five years old. It seemed to Lucien that there was an odd look in her eye; was it irony, was it hate, or simply youth and an inclination to be amused at everything?

The second squadron, to which Lucien belonged, suddenly began to move again. Lucien, his eyes still turned toward the parrot-green shutters, gave his horse a touch of his spurs which startled the old nag; it slipped, fell, and threw Lucien to the ground.

To get up, to give his beast a furious blow with the sheath of his saber was the matter of an instant, but the burst of laughter all around him was general and hilarious. Lucien, back in the saddle, noticed that the lady with the ash-blond hair was still smiling. The officers of the regiment, it was very evident, were laughing *pointedly,* like a member of the *center* in the Chamber of Deputies when one of the ministers has been justly rebuked.

"Never you mind, he's a good little fellow," said an old sergeant with white whiskers.

And one of the lancers added:

"That old screw has never been so well mounted before."

Lucien was very red and affected an air of indifference.

The regiment was hardly settled in barracks and duties assigned, before Lucien rushed to the post stables.

"Sir," he said to the post-master, "I am an officer, as you can see, and I have no horse. This miserable jade which was given me in the regiment, possibly as a joke, has fallen with me—again as you can see." And he blushed as he looked at the vestiges of mud which, having dried, whitened the left side of his uniform. "In a word, sir, is there a passable horse to be bought in this town? I must have one immediately."

"By gad, sir, what a fine chance to swindle you!" Monsieur Bouchard, the post-master, replied. "But that's a thing I wouldn't do."

He was a big man with an air of importance, an ironic expression, and piercing eyes. He watched the elegant young man as he spoke, trying to decide how many louis above the price of the horse he could charge him.

"You are a cavalry officer, sir, and undoubtedly know horses."

As Lucien failed to reply with any humbug, the post-master decided he might safely add:

"Will you permit me to ask, have you ever been to war?"

Thinking the man might be making fun of him, Lucien's frank expression changed instantly at this question.

"It is not a question of my having been to war or not," he replied sharply, "but whether you, the post-master, have a horse for sale."

Monsieur Bouchard seeing himself thus put in his place had some idea of washing his hands of the young man; but to let slip such an occasion for earning ten louis, especially to deprive himself of an hour's gossip was something utterly beyond the worthy post-master. In his youth he had seen active service, and looked upon officers of Lucien's age as children playing a game.

"For many years, sir," Bouchard continued in an ingratiating tone, ignoring the rebuke, "I was cavalry corporal, and then sergeant in the First Cuirassiers; and in that capacity I was wounded at Montmirail in 1814 in the exercise of my functions. That is why I spoke of war. At any rate, as to the question of horses, mine are only hacks at ten or twelve louis, in no way worthy of an officer so well turned out and spruce as yourself, at best only good enough to go on errands—real hacks in short! But if you know how to handle a horse, which I don't doubt"—here Bouchard's eye sought the left sleeve of the elegant uniform, white with dried mud, and, in spite of himself, he resumed his bantering tone—"if you can handle a horse, M. Fléron, our young prefect, has just the thing for you: an English demi-thoroughbred sold to him by an English lord living here, a horse well known to connoisseurs, superb hocks, admirable shoulders, worth three thousand francs, which has only thrown M. Fléron four times for the very good reason that the said prefect only dared ride him four times. His last tumble took place when he was reviewing the National Guard, composed for the most part of old troopers, myself for example, sergeant . . ."

"Let us go then," replied Lucien with ill-humor. "I will buy it on the spot."

The decided tone with which Lucien accepted the price of three thousand francs and the firmness with which he had cut short the former non-com, *carried the day*.

"By all means, let's go, Lieutenant," replied Bouchard with all the respect that Lucien could have asked. And he started off immediately on foot, following Lucien who was still mounted on his old nag. To get to the prefecture they had to go to an out-of-the-way part of the city near the powder-magazine, some five minutes from the residential quarter. It was in a former monastery admirably arranged by the last prefects of the Empire. The pavilion in which the prefect was lodged was surrounded by an English garden. Our gentlemen arrived at the iron entrance door. From the mezzanine, where the offices were located, they were directed to another door ornamented with columns, and leading to a magnificent second-floor where M. Fléron had his private apartments. M. Bouchard rang. No one answered the bell for some time. Finally a most elegant valet came to the door with a bustling air, and ushered them into an untidy drawing room. True, it was only one o'clock. With circumspect gravity, the valet repeated the usual phrases about the extreme difficulty of seeing M. le Préfet, and Lucien was about to lose patience when M. Bouchard intervened with the magic words:

"We have come on a *matter of business* that will interest the Prefect."

This seemed to shock the valet's dignity, but he made no move.

"Eh, by God, it's to sell your Lara for you," said the former sergeant, adding, "the horse that throws M. le Préfet so neatly."

At these words the valet promptly turned on his heel, begging the gentlemen to wait.

After ten minutes, Lucien saw gravely advancing toward him, a young man about four and a half feet tall, who appeared timid and arrogant at the same time. He seemed to bear, with a certain pride, an admirable head of hair so blond as to appear perfectly colorless. Extremely fine and worn too long, it was parted in a meticulously drawn line that separated its owner's head in two equal sections after the German fashion. At the sight of this little figure, which apparently walked on springs, and aimed at grace as well as majesty, Lucien's anger subsided and was followed by a mad desire to laugh. Indeed he had great difficulty to keep from laughing out loud. "His head is a perfect image of a Christ by Lucas Cranach," he thought. "This then is one of those terrible prefects against whom the liberal papers fulminate every morning!"

Lucien was no longer incensed by his long wait. He examined curiously the stuffy little creature coming toward him quite slowly, waddling a little, and assuming the air of someone who is naturally imperturbable, and above the emotions of this mundane sphere. Lucien was so absorbed in his contemplation that a silence ensued.

M. Fléron was flattered by the effect he had produced, and on a military man at that! Finally he asked Lucien how he could be of service to him, but he pronounced the phrase with much gargling of "r"s and in a tone that called for an insolent rejoinder.

Lucien's difficulty was not to laugh in his face. Unfortunately he just then remembered a certain M. Fléron, a deputy. This creature must be the worthy son or nephew of that M. Fléron who fairly wept with emotion whenever he had occasion to mention *our esteemed ministers.*

This recollection was too much for our hero who was still a novice, and he burst out laughing.

"Sir," he said finally, keeping his eyes fixed on the dressing gown, unique of its kind, which was wrapped around the young Prefect. "I am told that you have a horse to sell. I should like to see it, try it out for half an hour, and pay cash for it."

The worthy Prefect looked as though he were dreaming. He had some difficulty accounting for the young officer's laughter. But the main thing in his eyes was to make it perfectly plain that nothing had the slightest interest for him.

"Sir," he said finally and as though reciting a lesson he had learned by heart, "I very much fear that the urgent and grave affairs with which I am overwhelmed, have made me guilty of an incivility. I have reason to suspect that you have been kept waiting. I am very much to blame."

And he lost himself in amenities. The unctuous phrases took some time in coming. As he failed to reach the end of them, our hero, who was less interested than the Prefect in nursing his reputation for perfect manners, took the liberty of bringing the conversation around to the object of his visit.

"I have all due respect for the occupations of M. le Préfet; I should like to see the horse that is for sale and to try it out in the presence of the groom of M. le Préfet."

"It is an English animal," replied M. Fléron in a tone grown almost affable, "a good demi-thoroughbred with all the guarantees. I bought it of Lord Link who has lived here for many years; the horse is well known to connoisseurs. But," he added, lowering his eyes, "I must admit that it is now cared for only by a French servant. I shall place Perrin at your service. You can well imagine that I do not confide such an animal to ordinary hands, and none of the other servants are allowed to go near it."

After giving his orders in a carefully polished style, listening to himself as he spoke, the young magistrate drew his gold-embroidered dressing-gown around him, steadied a sort of bonnet perched over his eyes that looked like the light cavalry's roll and threatened to fall off at any moment. All these little adjustments were made slowly and watched attentively by the post-master whose mocking air changed to a sarcastic smile that was altogether impertinent. But this attitude of Bouchard's was entirely lost on the Prefect who was not in the habit of taking the slightest notice of such people. When he was satisfied that his costume was in order, he bowed to Lucien, gave a curt nod in the direction of Bouchard without looking at him, and returned to his apartments.

"And to think that a nincompoop like that is going to review our troops next Sunday!" cried Bouchard. "Wouldn't it make you puke?"

M. Bouchard, in his animosity against young men higher up in the world than a non-com of Montmirail, soon found ample cause for rejoicing. No sooner did the English horse find itself outside the stable from which it was released much too seldom to suit its taste, than it began galloping around the courtyard and indulging in the most fantastic capers. It leapt into the air, all four feet off the ground, head thrown back as though it were trying to climb into the plane trees surrounding the courtyard of the prefecture.

"It's not a bad beast," said Bouchard, going up to Lucien with a perfidious air. "But probably for the last week neither the Prefect nor his valet Perrin has dared take him out, so perhaps it would be rather imprudent. . . ."

Lucien was struck by the suppressed joy that shone in the post-master's little eyes. "It is written," he thought, "that twice in one day I shall be thrown off a horse; such is to be my debut in Nancy." Bouchard, after getting some oats from a manger, caught and held the animal. But Lucien had all the trouble in the world mounting and mastering the spirited Lara.

He went off at a gallop, but soon succeeded in bringing the horse to a walk. Astonished by Lara's beauty and vigorous gait, Lucien felt no compunction in keeping the jeering post-master waiting. Lara did a league or more, and only reappeared in the courtyard of the prefecture a full half hour later. The valet was beside himself with anxiety at the delay. As for the post-master, he was really hoping to see the horse return riderless. When he saw it appear with its rider still on its back, he scrutinized Lucien's uniform closely. There was nothing to indicate a fall. "Well, well, he's not such a ninny as the others," Bouchard said to himself.

Lucien concluded the affair without getting off his horse. "Nancy must never again see me mounted on that old screw." Bouchard, who did not have the same qualms, mounted the regiment's horse, and M. Perrin accompanied the gentlemen to the collector-general's office where Lucien procured the money.

"You see, Monsieur Bouchard, I never let myself be thrown more than once a day," said Lucien as soon as they were alone. "What really distresses me is that my fall took place in front of that window with the parrot-green shutters—over there—as you come into the town, just before reaching the covered passage—a kind of mansion."

"Ah," said Bouchard, "in the Rue de la Pompe? And there was probably a very pretty lady at the smallest of the windows?"

"Yes, and she laughed at my predicament. It is very disagreeable to be introduced into a garrison in such a fashion, especially such an important garrison. You, who have been a soldier, will understand. What will they think of me in the regiment! But, tell me, who is the lady?"

"She was around twenty-five or -six, wasn't she, with ash-blond hair long enough to touch the ground?"

"And very beautiful eyes, but full of mockery."

"She is Madame de Chasteller, a widow who is courted by all the handsomest men of the nobility because she has millions. Everywhere she goes she preaches the cause of Charles X, and if I were in that little prefect's boots, I'd have her locked up; our province will end up by being a second Vendée. She's a rabid *ultra* who would like to see all of us, who served the fatherland, a hundred feet under ground. She is the daughter of the Marquis de Pontlevé, one of our most zealous *ultras* and," he added, lowering his voice, "he is one of Charles X's commissioners for this province. That's just between you and me. I don't want to be taken for an informer."

"Have no fear."

"They came to sulk here after the *July Days*. They say that what they want is to starve the people of Paris by depriving them of work; but just the same, he's not very smart. Dr. Du Poirier, the best doctor around here, is his right-hand man. Du Poirier is a sly one and bosses both M. de Pontlevé and M. de Puylaurens, Charles's other commissioner; for hereabouts everybody plots quite openly. There's also Abbé Olivier . . . he is a spy."

"But, my dear sir," laughed Lucien, "I have nothing against Abbé Olivier being a spy—there are plenty of others—but do tell me more about the pretty Madame de Chasteller."

"Ah, that pretty little lady who laughed at you when you fell off your horse? She's seen many others fall off their high horses! She is the widow of one of the brigadier generals attached to the person of Charles X, and who was, besides, grand chamberlain and aide-de-camp; in short, a great lord who after the Three Days came here to die of fright. He was always sure the populace *was rising,* as he assured me a dozen times; but a good sort for all that, not insolent at all; on the contrary, very considerate. Whenever couriers arrived from Paris, he always wanted the best pair of horses reserved for them, and he paid well too, by God! he did. For you must know, sir, that it is only nineteen leagues from here to the Rhine by shortcut. He was a tall pale man, and always in a famous funk."

"And his widow?" asked Lucien, much amused.

"She had her own house in the Faubourg Saint Germain, in the street they call Babylone—what a name! You, sir, must know it. She wouldn't mind a bit going back to Paris; but her father is dead-set against it, and tries to separate her from all her old friends, wants to monopolize her in other words! You see, it's like this: during the reign of the Jesuits and Charles X, M. de Chasteller, who was precious pious, made millions on a loan, and now his widow has all that money, and M. de Pontlevé wants to be able to lay his hands on it in case of revolution.

"Every morning M. de Chasteller used to have his carriage hitched up to go to Mass not a stone's throw away; an English carriage that cost at least ten thousand francs and didn't make a sound on the cobblestones. He always said you owed that much to the people. For such things he was a great stickler, always wore his full dress uniform to High Mass on Sunday, with the *cordon rouge* across his coat, and had four lackeys in livery and yellow gloves. But just the same, he never left his servants a thing when he died, because, as he told the vicar who ministered to him at the end, *they were all Jacobins.* But Madame de Chasteller, being still in the land of the living, was afraid, and pretended it was an oversight in the will. She gives them small pensions or else keeps them in her service, and often for practically nothing at all gives them forty francs. She occupies the entire second floor of the Hôtel de Pontlevé; that's where you saw her. But her father insists that she pay rent. It costs her four thousand francs, but you may be sure that the Marquis could never have let that floor for more than a hundred louis. He's a frightful miser. Be that as it may, he speaks to everybody, and very politely too. He says there is going to be another Republic, a new emigration, and that they'll cut off the heads of all the nobles and the priests. And M. de Pontlevé was pretty miserable during the first emigration; they say he worked as a bookbinder in Hamburg, and today he flies into a rage if anyone so much as mentions books in front of him. The truth is, in case of need, he counts on his daughter's fortune; that's why he doesn't want to lose sight of it—he said so to one of his friends . . ."

"But, my dear sir, what do I care for all the absurdities of an old man?" said Lucien. "Tell me about Madame de Chasteller."

"She receives high society in her house every Friday and preaches to them exactly like a preacher, no more no less. Her servants say that she talks like an angel; they all can understand her, and there are days when she makes them cry. Poor fools, I tell them; she's dead-set against the people; if she could put us all in Mont-Saint-Michel she would. But be that as it may, she bewitches them, they love her.

"She blames her father, the valet says, because he refuses to see her younger brother, chief magistrate of the royal court at Metz, for having taken the oath. The Marquis calls that dirtying oneself. No one who is a *Juste-milieu* is received in society here. That fop of a prefect who sold you his horse, swallows insults like water. He doesn't dare present himself at Madame de Chasteller's for she'd tell him just what she thought of him to his face. Whenever he goes to call on Madame d'Hocquincourt, one of our most elegant ladies, she stands in plain sight at one of the windows facing the street and has her porter say that she's not at home. . . . Oh, but excuse me, sir, you are a *Juste-milieu* yourself, I forgot."

This last was said with some glee, and there was a touch of the same in Lucien's rejoinder.

"My friend, you give me information, I listen to it as to a report on the position of the enemy. And now, good-by until we meet again. What is the best apartment-hotel in Nancy?"

"*Hotel of the Three Emperors,* 13 Rue des Vieux-Jesuites. But as it isn't easy to find and I am going that way I'll have the honor of taking you there myself." (I've been badgering him enough, Bouchard said to himself, I'd better let up and talk to the young puppy about the ladies.)

"Madame de Chasteller is the most capricious of all the ladies of the nobility," he went on with the feigned nonchalance of a man of the people trying to hide his confusion. "That is to say, Madame d'Hocquincourt is just as pretty; but Madame de Chasteller has had only one lover, M. Thomas de Busant de Sicile, lieutenant-colonel of hussars—he's the one you're substitute for. She's always sad and peculiar except when she talks about Henri V. Her servants say that she will often order her carriage brought around, and then an hour later order it taken away again without going out. She has the most beautiful eyes in the world, as you saw, and eyes that can say anything they like. Madame d'Hocquincourt is much gayer and wittier, she always has something funny to say, and she twists her husband around her finger. He's a former captain, wounded in the July Days and, my faith, a worthy man. To be sure, they're all worthy men around here! At any rate she does what she pleases with him, and changes lovers every year. At present it's M. d'Antin who is ruining himself for her. I'm always furnishing them with horses for pleasure parties in the Burelviller woods— you can see them over there on the other side of the plain. God knows what they do in those woods! They get my postillions so drunk they can't see or hear anything. And the devil if they have a thing to tell me when they get back."

"But where do you see any woods?" asked Lucien, scanning the dreariest landscape in the world.

"A league away from here, the other side of the plain, magnificent shady woods; a beautiful spot. That's where the *Green Huntsman* is. It's run by Germans so they always have music. It's the *Tivoli* of these part. . . ."

A movement of Lucien's horse alarmed the garrulous postmaster who thought his victim was going to escape him, and what a victim, a handsome Parisian youth just arrived in town and forced to listen to him!

"Every week," he went on hastily, "that pretty woman with blond hair who laughed a little when she saw you fall off your horse, or rather when your horse fell—there's a difference. . . . But to get back to what I was telling you—every week, or just about, she turns down an offer of marriage. M. de Blancet, her cousin, who is always in attendance; M. de Goëllo, the biggest intriguer, a regular Jesuit, you know; Count Ludwig Roller, the most high-and-mighty of the nobles, all have come a cropper. Ah, she's not so dumb as to marry in the provinces! And so, as I told you, to relieve her boredom, she bravely took the lieutenant-colonel of the Twentieth Hussars, M. Thomas de Busant de Sicile in a left-handed marriage. She had him eating out of her hand, but no matter, he didn't budge, and he is one of the greatest nobles of France, they say. Then there are Madame la Marquise de Puylaurens and Madame de Saint-Vincent who never forget themselves; but then the ladies of our city are loath to stoop to anything beneath their rank. They are very strict on this point and I must tell you, my dear sir, with all due respect, and though I've never been anything but a non-com of cuirassiers (as a matter of fact I did ten campaigns in ten years), I have my doubts if the widow of the brigadier-general, M. de Chasteller, who has had a lieutenant-colonel for lover, would ever accept the advances of a simple second-lieutenant, no matter how attractive. For," added the post-master, assuming a pathetic air, "merit doesn't count for much here; rank and nobility are everything."

"In that case, it's all up with me," thought Lucien.

"Good-by, sir," he said to Bouchard, putting his horse to a trot. "I'll send a lancer to your stables for the horse, and a very good evening to you."

He had caught sight of the enormous sign of the *Three Emperors* in the distance.

"Well, anyway, that's one I've baited all right, him and his *Juste-milieu*," said Bouchard to himself, chuckling gleefully. "And a forty-franc tip, besides, *to give to my postillions*—just catch me doing it!"

CHAPTER FIVE

M. BOUCHARD had more reason to be pleased than he knew. When the departure of that individual with the piercing eyes left him to his own thoughts, Lucien found himself in a very bad humor. As an introduction to a provincial city and in a cavalry regiment, the fall from his horse was the worst possible disaster. "It will never be forgotten. Every time I'm seen on the street, even if I ride like the oldest lancer of the regiment, people will say, 'Ah, there goes the young man who fell off his horse the day the regiment arrived.'"

Our hero was suffering the consequences of that Parisian education which develops nothing but vanity, the melancholy portion of the sons of rich men. All this vanity was up in arms, ready for his initiation in the regiment. Lucien had fully expected a duel or two, and had decided that the important thing was to take it all lightly and with firmness; to show oneself bold under arms, etc., etc. But instead, ridicule and humiliation had fallen on him out of the window of the most aristocratic young woman of the place, and a rabid and garrulous *ultra* besides, who would know how to make him the laughing-stock of Nancy. What wouldn't she say about him!

That smile which Lucien had seen straying over her lips when he had sprung up covered with mud and given his horse a furious blow with the scabbard of his saber—he couldn't get it out of his mind. "How stupid of me to have given that blow with my scabbard and with such a show of anger. That was what made me ridiculous! Anyone can fall off his horse, but to hit it angrily, to show how humiliated one is by the fall . . . ! I should have remained impassive; I should have done the opposite of what people expected, as my father says. . . . If ever I meet this Madame de Chasteller, she'll be sure to burst out laughing when she recognizes me! And what are they going to say in the regiment? Ah, as for you, my witty gentlemen, I warn you to lower your voices when you indulge in your bad jokes."

Upset by these unpleasant thoughts, Lucien, who found his man already in the finest apartment of the *Three Emperors,* spent two long hours making his military toilet. "Everything depends on first impressions, and I have much to retrieve."

"My uniform is really excellent," he thought, looking at himself in the two mirrors which he had placed in such a way as to see himself from head to foot. "But those mocking eyes of Madame de Chasteller, those eyes sparkling with mirth and malice, will always see mud on this sleeve," and he looked pathetically at his traveling uniform thrown over the back of a chair. In spite of all the brushing it still kept all too evident traces of his accident.

After an interminable time spent getting dressed, much to the amusement (unsuspected by Lucien) of the hotel personnel and the landlady, who had loaned him her own cheval-glass, Lucien went down to the courtyard where he examined, with no less critical eye, the grooming of his horse. He found Lara presentable except for her back shoes, which he had polished over again in his presence. Finally he vaulted into his saddle, not, however, with military precision and gravity, but with the lightness of an acrobat for he was much too eager to show the hotel domestics gathered in the courtyard that he was perfectly at home on a horse. He asked to be directed to the Rue de la Pompe and started off at a fast trot. "Happily Madame de Chasteller, the widow of a cavalry officer, must be a good judge."

But the parrot-green shutters were hermetically closed, and Lucien rode back and forth in front of the house in vain. Then he went to see Lieutenant-Colonel Filloteau to thank him, and to learn from him all the little social duties that should occupy the first day of a second-lieutenant who has just joined his regiment.

He paid two or three calls of ten minutes each, and displayed that coolness (a *well-chain* is no colder) so especially desirable in a young man of twenty-four, and this proof of a perfect education met with the desired success.

As soon as he was free, he went to visit the scene of his morning disaster again. He arrived in front of the Hôtel de Pontlevé at a fast trot, and there, on the exact spot, he made his horse break into a smooth little gallop that was altogether charming. A few light touches on the bridle, unnoticeable to the profane, gave to the prefect's horse, astonished by the audacity of his rider, those little movements of petulance so delightful to connoisseurs. But, in vain, Lucien held himself straight and motionless in his saddle, even a little stiff—the parrot-green shutters remained closed.

He recognized, in a military sense, the window where he had been laughed at. It had a Gothic frame and was smaller than the others. It was on the second floor of a large house, apparently very ancient, but freshly whitewashed in keeping with the taste of that part of the country. Fine large windows had been cut out on that floor but those of the floor above were the ancient ones with little mullioned panes. This semi-Gothic house had a magnificent modern iron entrance-gate on the Rue du Reposoir which crossed the Rue de la Pompe at right angles. Over the door, in gold letters on a dark marble slab, Lucien read: *Hôtel de Pontlevé*.

It seemed a dreary neighborhood, yet the Rue du Reposoir seemed to be one of the best streets of the city—and one of the loneliest; grass was growing everywhere.

"How I should despise this melancholy house," thought Lucien, "if it were not that it harbored a young woman who laughed at me—and with good reason!

"But the devil take this provincial beauty! Where, I wonder, is the promenade in this idiotic city? Let's find it." In less than three quarters of an hour, thanks to the swiftness of his horse, Lucien had made the tour of Nancy, a wretched hole bristling with fortifications. He looked in vain. All he found in the way of a promenade was a long square crossed at both ends by nauseous ditches that carried off the city's filth, and vegetating all around it, a thousand stunted fan-shaped linden trees pruned with great care.

"Could anyone imagine anything in the world more unpleasant than this town!" our hero kept repeating at each new discovery. And his heart sank.

There was ingratitude in this feeling of profound disgust.

For, during his tours and detours around the ramparts and through the streets, he had been observed by Madame d'Hocquincourt, by Madame de Puylaurens and even by Mademoiselle Berchu, queen of the bourgeois beauties of Nancy. The latter had even remarked: "What a handsome cavalier!"

Ordinarily Lucien could very well have ridden incognito through Nancy. But today all society, high, low and medium, was in a flutter. For in the provinces, the arrival of a regiment is no small event. Paris lives in ignorance of this emotion, and of a great many others too. With the arrival of a regiment the merchant dreams of making the fortune of his establishment, and respectable mothers with marriageable daughters, of marrying off at least one of them. It is entirely a question of pleasing the customers. The nobility ask: "Are there any *names* in this regiment?" The priests, "Have all the soldiers had their first communion?" A first communion of *one hundred subjects* would certainly make a good impression on Monsignor! The world of the grisettes is stirred by emotions, less profound perhaps than those of the ministers of our Lord, but livelier without a doubt.

During Lucien's first peregrination in search of a promenade, the daring (somewhat affected) with which he handled the prefect's notoriously dangerous horse (daring that indicated plainly that he had bought it), had built up his credit with a great many people. "Who," they asked, "is this second-lieutenant who, on his first day in town, treats himself to a horse worth a thousand crowns?"

Among those who were most struck by the probable opulence of the newcomer we should, in all fairness, first mention Mademoiselle Sylviane Berchu.

"Mama, Mama," she shouted on seeing the prefect's horse, famous throughout the city, "look, it's the prefect's Lara! But he has a rider now who certainly isn't scared!"

"He must be a very rich young man," Madame Berchu remarked. And this thought soon absorbed mother and daughter alike.

This same day, it happened that all the nobility of Nancy was dining at M. d'Hocquincourt's, the very rich young man who has already had the honor of being presented to the reader. They were celebrating the birthday of one of the exiled princesses. Besides a dozen noble imbeciles in love with the past and afraid of the future, it is only fair to mention seven or eight former officers, mettlesome young men who, above all else, longed for war and who refused to submit to the fortunes of revolution. Having resigned their commissions after the *July Days,* they did nothing, and thought themselves miserable by right of rank. They chafed under their forced idleness, which by no means amused them; and this boring life did not tend to make them over-indulgent toward the young officers of the present army. Their ill humor marred minds of natural distinction, and betrayed itself in an exaggerated disdain.

In the course of his reconnoitering, Lucien passed three times in front of the Hôtel de Sauve-d'Hocquincourt, the garden of which intercepts the promenade around the ramparts. The company had just risen from table, and Lucien was scrutinized by all that was *purest* in Nancy, both by birth and right-thinking. The best judges of horsemanship—M. de Vassigny, a lieutenant-colonel, the three Roller brothers, M. de Blancet and M. d'Antin, both captains of cavalry, MM. de Goëllo, Murcé, and de Lanfort—all had their word to say. These poor young men had been less bored that day than usual. In the morning the arrival of a regiment had given them an excuse for talking war and horses, the only two things besides watercolor painting that a fine gentleman in the provinces is permitted to know anything about. In the evening they had the rare pleasure of seeing at close range, and of being able to criticize, an officer in the new army.

"That poor horse must be amazed to find itself so boldly handled," said M. d'Antin, Madame d'Hocquincourt's lover.

"The young man is no old hand with a horse, although he rides very well," remarked M. de Vassigny, who was a very handsome man of forty with large features, and who always seemed to be dying of boredom even when he was being witty.

"He is most likely one of those upholsterers or candlemakers called *July heroes*," sneered M. de Goëllo, a tall blond young man, very stiff and supercilious, and already covered with wrinkles of envy.

"How antiquated you are, my poor Goëllo!" cried Madame de Puylaurens, the wittiest woman of Nancy. "Those poor *July Days* have been out of fashion for ages. He is probably the son of one of those corrupt and corpulent deputies."

"One of those eloquent individuals who sit directly behind the minister's back and cry *Sh,* or burst out laughing over an amendment on provisions for convicts at a signal from the minister's *back*." With this fine phrase uttered slowly, the elegant M. de Lanfort developed and illustrated the idea of his witty mistress.

"He must have rented the prefect's horse for a fortnight with the high pay his papa receives from the *Chateau*," said M. de Sanréal.

"Come now, you ought to know people a little better before talking about them like that," M. de Vassigny protested.

> "The ant is not a lender,
> That's the least of all his faults,"

declaimed the somber Ludwig Roller in tragic tones.

"Gentlemen, gentlemen," broke in Madame de Puylaurens, "do make up your minds! Where did this young candle-manufacturer get the money to pay for the horse? For, in spite of all your prejudices, you will hardly go so far as to claim that he is not actually on a horse."

"Money, money," cried M. d'Antin, "nothing could be simpler. Papa, in the assembly, or in the budget committees, supported the *Gisquet musket* contracts, or some such war deal." *

"Live and let live," said M. de Vassigny with an air of political profundity. "That's what our poor Bourbons never understood! They should have *gorged* all the young plebeians, so brazen and garrulous,—today that is called *having talent*. Who can doubt that MM. N——, N——, and N—— would have sold themselves to Charles X, as they sell themselves to the present king? And cheaper besides, for they would have been treated with less contempt. Polite society would have accepted them and received them in their drawing rooms, and that is always the great object of the bourgeois, once his dinner is assured."

"God save us! but here we are head-over-heels in high politics," cried Madame de Puylaurens.

"Well," put in Madame d'Hocquincourt, "July hero, upholsterer, son of a paunchy senator, anything you please, but at any rate he can sit a horse gracefully. And, since his father has sold himself, he, at least, will avoid talking politics and be better company than M. de Vassigny here, who depresses all his friends with his eternal regrets and forebodings. Moaning and groaning should be prohibited—at least after dinner."

"Agreeable company, candle-manufacturer, upholsterer, anything you please," chimed in the tall and puritanical Ludwig Roller whose black hair framed a pale and somber countenance, "but I'll bet you what you like—and I have had my eye on the pretty young gentleman for the last five minutes—that he has not been in the service long."

---

* An *ultra* is speaking; who else would call in question the probity that reigns over the making of contracts?

"In that case he's neither a *July hero* nor a manufacturer of candles," retorted Madame d'Hocquincourt with vivacity, "for it is three years since the *Glorious Days* and he has had plenty of time to acquire poise. He must be the son of a paunchy deputy like M. de Villèle's *Three Hundred,* and it is even possible that he has learned to read and write, and knows how to enter a drawing room like anybody else."

"He does not look common," said Madame de Commercy.

"But his seat on a horse is not as perfect, Madam, as you are pleased to imagine," protested Ludwig Roller, with annoyance. "He is stiff and affected. Just let his horse take a sudden side step and he'll be on the ground."

"Which would be the second time today," cried M. de Sanréal with the triumphant air of a fool who is not accustomed to being listened to and at last has some sensational news to disclose. This M. de Sanréal was the richest and the dullest gentleman of these parts. He now had the satisfaction, a rare one for him, of seeing all eyes turned toward him, and he relished the sensation for some time before he could bring himself to tell the story of Lucien's fall. Trying to be witty, he got so tangled up in the lovely tale that it had to be dragged out of him with questions, and he had the pleasure of beginning his recital all over again. All the time he tried his best to make our hero more ridiculous than he had been in reality.

"You can all say what you like," cried Madame de Sauved'Hocquincourt as Lucien passed by her windows for the third time, "but he is a most charming man. And if my husband weren't such a tyrant, I should be tempted to invite him in for coffee, if only to annoy you."

M. d'Hocquincourt took her seriously, and his gentle and pious face paled with terror.

"Oh, but my dear, a stranger! A man of low extraction, perhaps even a working-man!" he said, looking at his fair better half pleadingly.

"Very well then, I will give him up for you," she rejoined with mock seriousness. Whereupon M. d'Hocquincourt squeezed her hand tenderly.

"And you, wise and *weighty* man," she said, turning to the corpulent Sanréal, "where did you pick up this slander about the poor young man—such a slim, handsome young man!—falling off his horse?"

"From no less a person," replied Sanréal, vexed at her teasing allusion to his own bulk, "than Dr. Du Poirier who was at Madame de Chasteller's at the very moment that this imaginary hero of yours was measuring a fool's length along the ground."

"Whether he's a hero or not, this young officer has already aroused plenty of envy and that's a good beginning. In any case, I should much rather be the one who is envied than the envious. Is it his fault that he isn't the model of Bacchus returning from the Indies, or one of his companions? Wait twenty years and then he will be able to hold his own with anybody. Until then I refuse to listen to you any more," and Madame d'Hocquincourt left them to go and open a window at the other end of the drawing room.

The noise of the opening window made Lucien turn his head, and his horse, becoming a little frolicsome, horse and rider were held for a moment or two before the eyes of that amiable company. As he had just passed the window when it opened, Lucien's horse seemed to be backing-up quickly, as though in spite of his rider.

"That isn't the young woman of this morning," said Lucien to himself, a little disappointed. And he forced his horse, highly excited now, to proceed at the slowest possible pace.

"The puppy!" exclaimed Ludwig Roller, angrily leaving the window. "He is probably one of the riding-masters of Franconi's troup, whom *July* turned into a hero."

"But that can't be the uniform of the Twenty-seventh he's wearing?" said Sanréal with an authoritative air. "Surely the Twenty-seventh has a different colored piping."

At this interesting and learned remark, everyone began talking at once, and the discussion on the subject of the piping lasted a good half hour. Each one of the gentlemen present was anxious to show off his knowledge of this side of military science which extraordinarily resembles the tailor's art, and which was formerly the delight of a great king, our contemporary.

From piping they went on to the monarchical principle, and the women were beginning to get bored when M. de Sanréal, who had left them and had been gone some time, returned breathless.

"I have news!" he cried from the doorway, hardly able to speak. Instantly the monarchical principle found itself miserably abandoned. But Sanréal suddenly became silent. He had seen curiosity in Madame d'Hocquincourt's eyes, and it was only by pulling the words out one by one, as it were, that they learned his story. The prefect's groom had been Sanréal's servant at one time, and zeal for historic truth had taken this noble marquis to the stables of the prefecture. There, from his former servant, he had learned all the circumstances of the sale. But he had also learned unexpectedly from this same source that the price of oats was apparently going to rise. For the deputy head clerk of the prefecture had given the order for the immediate delivery of the prefect's supply; and the clerk, a rich landowner himself, had declared that he would not sell his own oats. Thereupon the noble marquis' preoccupation had suddenly shifted. He congratulated himself on having gone to the prefecture, but was somewhat in the predicament of an actor who, while playing a part on the stage, hears that his house is on fire. Sanréal had oats to sell, and in the provinces even more than anywhere else, the least question of money eclipses instantly any other interest. The spiciest subject of conversation is forgotten; no one any longer has ears for the most scandalous piece of gossip. Returning to the d'Hocquincourts', Sanréal was profoundly occupied with the importance of not letting a single word escape him on the subject of oats. There were several rich proprietors there who could well *take advantage of it* and sell before him.

While Lucien was enjoying the honor of accumulating all the envies of the noble society of Nancy which had learned that he had purchased a horse for a hundred and twenty louis, revolted by the ugliness of the city, he was making his way sadly to the stables of the prefecture to leave his horse, since M. Fléron had graciously put them at his disposal for a few days.

The following day the Twenty-seventh Lancers assembled, and Colonel Malher de Saint-Mégrin formally received Lucien into the regiment as second-lieutenant. After the ceremony Lucien was on inspection duty at the barracks. He had hardly got back to his rooms when the thirty-six trumpeters came under his windows to give him an agreeable aubade. He managed to get through all these more necessary than amusing ceremonies very well.

His manner was cold as a *well-chain,* but not quite cold enough. Several times there was a touch of irony on his lips which did not pass unnoticed. For example, Colonel Malher, when he gave Lucien the accolade in front of the regiment, handled his horse so badly that, at the moment of the embrace, it veered away from Lucien's horse. But Lara, obeying admirably a slight touch of the bridle aided by Lucien's knees, smoothly followed the restive movement of the colonel's mount.

As a corps commander is observed with a more jealous eye than a dandy just arrived from Paris with a second lieutenancy, this maneuver was not lost on the lancers and was a feather in our hero's cap.

"And they say those English horses have no mouth!" said Sergeant La Rose, the same who had come to Lucien's defense after his fall the day before. "They have no mouth for those who can't find it. That whipper-snapper at least knows how to conduct himself. You can see," he added with a swagger, "he's qualified to enter our regiment."

This note of respect for the Twenty-seventh Lancers was generally appreciated by the sergeant's neighbors.

But in maneuvering to follow the colonel's horse, Lucien's expression had unconsciously betrayed his amusement. "Confound the damned republican, he'll pay for that!" the colonel said to himself, and Lucien acquired an enemy in a position to do him a great deal of harm.

When Lucien was at last able to escape from the compliments of the officers on duty at the barracks, from the thirty-six trumpeters, etc., etc., he felt horribly depressed. One thought only was uppermost in his mind: "How empty it all is! They talk of war, the enemy, heroism, honor, when there has been no sign of an enemy for the last twenty years. And my father insists that the miserly Chambers could never be persuaded to vote war credits for more than a single campaign. What use are we soldiers anyway? To make a great show of zeal like a venal deputy!"

As he made this reflection, Lucien, feeling completely disgusted, lay down on an ancient provincial sofa; promptly one of the arms gave way under his weight. He rose in a fury and finished the demolition of this dilapidated relic.

But should he not, on the contrary, have been mad with joy as, in his place, a provincial youth whose education had not cost a hundred thousand francs, certainly would have been? Is there then such a thing as a *false* culture? Is it possible that our civilization has not yet reached perfection? And we spend our days being witty over the endless inconveniences that accompany such perfection!

CHAPTER SIX

NEXT MORNING Lucien took an apartment on the Grande Place, in the house of M. Bonard, the grain merchant, and that evening he learned from M. Bonard, who had it from the butler who supplied the brandy for our second-lieutenant's table, that Colonel Filloteau had declared himself Lucien's patron, and had defended him against certain not very benevolent insinuations of Colonel Malher de Saint-Mégrin.

Lucien's soul was bitter. Everything had contributed to this state: the ugliness of the city, the sight of the dirty cafés filled with officers wearing the same uniform as himself; and among all those faces not one that showed, I will not say the milk of human kindness, but merely that urbanity which is to be found everywhere in Paris. He went to see Filloteau, but the lieutenant-colonel was no longer the same man with whom he had made the trip from Paris. Filloteau had defended him, and to make Lucien appreciate the fact, he took on a self-important and vulgarly protective tone. This put the crowning touch to our hero's ill humor.

"So that's what one has to go through in order to make ninety-nine francs a month," he thought. "What must the men who make millions have to put up with! Confound it!" he went on in a rage, "to think of being patronized, and by such a man, a man I wouldn't have as a lackey!" Misfortune always exaggerates. Hard, bitter and vexed as Lucien was at the moment, if his host had been an *orthodox* Parisian, he and Lucien would not have exchanged ten words in a year. The portly M. Bonard was merely inordinately interested in questions of money, besides being communicative, obliging and *ingratiating,* as long as there was no chance of making four sous on a measure of wheat. He now came to bring his lodger a few little things for his apartment, and at the end of two hours it was evident that they took pleasure in each other's conversation.

M. Bonard advised Lucien to go to Madame Berchu for his supply of liquor. If it had not been for the worthy grain merchant, it would never have occurred to Lucien that a second-lieutenant, who is supposed to be rich, and who is making his debut in the regiment, should be famous for his liqueurs and brandies.

"It's Madame Berchu, you know, who has such a pretty daughter, Mademoiselle Sylviane. Colonel de Busant always dealt with her. It's that fine shop over there by the cafés. And try, while you're striking a bargain, to find some excuse for speaking to Mademoiselle Sylviane. She is our bourgeois beauty," he added in a serious tone that went ill with his rotund countenance. "Except for her virtue, which is still intact, she can vie with my ladies d'Hocquincourt, de Chasteller, and de Puylaurens."

The worthy M. Bonard was the uncle of M. Gauthier, the leader of the republicans of that region, otherwise he would not have indulged in these disparaging remarks. But the young editors of *Aurore,* Lorraine's *American* newspaper, often came to his house to chat over a bowl of punch, and to persuade him that he ought to be offended by certain actions of the noble landowners who sold him their wheat. Although calling themselves, and believing themselves to be, republicans, these young men were really miserable at being inexorably barred from the society of these aristocratic young women whose beauty and charms they could only everlastingly admire from a distance, either on the promenade or at church. They took their revenge by believing all the malicious gossip on the subject of the ladies' virtue. Such calumnies invariably came from the ladies' own lackeys, for in the provinces there is no longer the slightest communication between the hostile classes.

But to return to our hero. Thus prompted by M. Bonard, he picked up his saber and bearskin, and went across the way to see Madame Berchu. He bought a keg of kirschwasser, then a keg of cognac, then a keg of rum that bore the date 1810, and all this with an offhand little air of indifference intended to impress Mademoiselle Sylviane. And these graces, worthy of a colonel of the *Gymnase,* were not without effect he was soon to discover. The virtuous Sylviane Berchu finally made her appearance. She had been spying through a trap-door cut in the floor of the room over the shop, and had seen that this customer who was turning the shop upside down, was none other than the young officer who had appeared the day before mounted on the prefect's famous Lara. This queen of bourgeois beauties condescended to listen to the few courteous remarks Lucien addressed to her. "It is true she is beautiful," he thought, "but not for me. She is a statue of Juno copied from the antique by a modern artist. Subtleties and simplicity are lacking, massive forms and a German freshness, big hands, big feet, extremely regular features, and endless simperings. But all this ill conceals a too visible arrogance. And these people have the temerity to be outraged by the arrogance of good society!" Lucien noticed especially that toss of the head so full of vulgar haughtiness, evidently intended to call to mind her dowry of twenty thousand crowns. However, thinking of the boredom awaiting him at home, Lucien prolonged his visit in the shop. Mademoiselle Sylviane, aware of her triumph, thought fit to bring out for his approbation some quite well-turned platitudes on officers in general, and on the dangers lurking in their civilities. Lucien replied that the dangers were entirely reciprocal, and that he was running a great risk at that very moment. "The young lady must have learned all this by heart," he thought, "for, commonplace as they are, they are certainly not a sample of her ordinary conversation." Such was the admiration that Mademoiselle Sylviane, the belle of Nancy, inspired in Lucien, and, having left her house, the little city seemed to him more forlorn than ever. Thoughtfully he followed his three kegs of *spirits,* as Mademoiselle Sylviane called them. "Now all I have to do is to find some pretext for sending one or two kegs to Lieutenant-Colonel Filloteau."

For this young man, on the threshold of the most brilliant career in the world, as well as the gayest, the evening was deplorable. His servant Aubry, who had been in the family for many years, sought to play the mentor and to give him advice. Lucien promptly sent him packing to Paris with a box of candied fruits for his mother.

This done, he went out. The sky was overcast and there was a cold and piercing little wind blowing from the north. Our second-lieutenant was wearing his dress uniform which, since he was on inspection duty at the barracks, was obligatory; and, moreover, he had learned, among so many other things, that a civilian overcoat was not to be thought of without a special permission from the colonel. He had nothing to do but wander through the dirty streets of this little fortified town, hearing at every two steps the insolent shout, *"Who goes there?"* He smoked countless cigars. After enduring these pleasures for two hours, he looked around for a bookseller's, but found none. He noticed a few books in just one shop, which he hastened to enter. They were *The Christian's Day* on sale at a cheesemonger's near one of the city gates.

He passed in front of several cafés. The windowpanes were foggy with the vapor of many breaths and he could not bring himself to enter any of them; he thought of their unspeakable odor. From these cafés came the sound of laughter, and, for the first time in his life, he experienced the sensation of envy.

That evening he pondered deeply on the different forms of government, and what were the greatest advantages in life. "If there was only a show in this God-forsaken town I'd try courting one of the young ladies of the chorus. I might find her amiability a little less ponderous than that of Mademoiselle Sylviane, and at least she wouldn't want to marry me."

Never had the future looked so black to him. What prevented him from imagining any brighter prospect was the following course of reasoning which seemed to him irrefutable: "I am going to spend at least one or two years like this, and plan as I may, what I am doing at this moment I shall go right on doing forever."

On one of the days that followed, coming from field drill, Lieutenant-Colonel Filloteau passed by our hero's lodgings. At the door he saw Nicolas Flanet, the lancer whom he had assigned to Lucien to look after his horse. (What, an English horse groomed by a soldier! Ah, but Lucien himself went to the stables at least twice a day.)

"Well, Nicolas, and what do you think of the lieutenant?"

"A good sort, Colonel, very generous but not very gay."

Filloteau went upstairs.

"I have come to pass inspection, my dear comrade-in-arms; for I am going to be an uncle to you, as we used to say in Berchiny, when I was corporal of cavalry there, before Egypt, by God! for I was not a sergeant until Aboukir under Murat, and second-lieutenant two weeks later."

But all these heroic details were lost on Lucien who, at the word *uncle,* had given a start. Quickly he recovered himself.

"Well, my dear uncle," he cried gaily, "I'm much too honored by the title, I assure you. I have here three respectable relatives visiting me, whom I should like to have the honor of presenting to you. You see there three kegs: the first is Widow Kirschwasser from the Black Forest . . ."

"I reserve her for myself," cried Filloteau with his coarse laugh. And going over to the keg that had been opened, he took up a small jug.

"It wasn't difficult to find a pretext," Lucien thought to himself.

"Ah, but, Colonel, that respectable relative has vowed never to be separated from her sister who is called Mademoiselle Cognac, 1810."

"Gad, you have wit, my boy! You're a good fellow, really," cried Filloteau, "and I owe a vote of thanks to our friend Dévelroy for having brought us together."

It was not exactly avarice on the part of our worthy colonel; but it simply would never have occurred to him to lay out so much money on two kegs of liquor, and he was delighted to have them fall from the skies. Tasting alternately the kirsch and the brandy, he compared them with great deliberation, and his heart melted.

"But let us get down to business; that is what I came about," he said, adopting an air of mystery, as he sank down heavily on the sofa. "You have been throwing your money around; three horses bought in three days. I don't criticize you for that, it is perfectly all right as far as I am concerned. But what are your comrades going to say who have only one horse, or rather who have only three legs?" And he laughed uproariously. "Well, I'll tell you what they'll say. They will call you a republican." And he added slyly, "That's where the shoe pinches *us*. Now, shall I tell you the answer? A fine portrait of Louis-Philippe on horseback, in a rich gold frame, in the place of honor over your commode; and after that, all pleasure and honor to you!" Then with some difficulty he rose from the sofa. "A word to the wise is sufficient, and you don't look so stupid. Honor!" This was the colonel's form of salutation.

"Nicolas, Nicolas!" he shouted out of the window, "go and get me one of those good-for-nothing civilians hanging around the street to carry these two kegs of liquor, and you be sure to escort them yourself, and damn it all, don't come to me with any story about one of the kegs springing a leak in the street; nothing like that, my boy! But come to think of it," Filloteau said, turning to Lucien, "this is manna from heaven, and a broken jug is always a broken jug; so I'll just follow along a few paces behind without seeming to pay any attention. Farewell, my dear comrade." And pointing with his gloved hand to the place over the chest:

"It's understood, a fine Louis-Philippe up there!"

Lucien thought he had got rid of his visitor but Filloteau reappeared in the doorway.

"And by the way, none of those f—ing books in your trunks, no bad newspapers, no pamphlets. None of the *pernicious press* as Marquin says." With these words Filloteau advanced two steps into the room and lowered his voice: "You know that great pock-marked lieutenant, Marquin, they've sent to us from Paris," and he half covered his mouth with his hand: "He even scares the colonel out of his wits! Enough, enough. Some people I know have ears that aren't just made for ornaments! Right?"

"He's a good sort after all," thought Lucien. "He's like Mademoiselle Sylviane Berchu. I might find them to my taste if they didn't make me sick to my stomach. My keg of kirsch proved successful." And he went out to buy the biggest portrait of Louis-Philippe he could find.

A quarter of an hour later Lucien returned followed by a workman carrying an enormous portrait which he had found all framed and ready, having been prepared for a police commissioner recently appointed through the influence of M. Fléron. Thoughtfully Lucien watched the hammering of the nail and the hanging of the portrait.

"My father has often said to me, and now I understand the wisdom of it: '*No one would ever think you were born a gamin of Paris* among quick-witted people who never fail to see the advantage of a civility. But you imagine men and their affairs more important than they are, and you make heroes of everybody you talk to, good or bad. *You spread your nets too high,* as Thucydides said of the Boeotians.' " And Lucien recited the Greek words, which I do not know.

" 'People in Paris,' my father says, 'if they hear of some profitable meanness or treachery cry: Bravo, that's a stroke worthy of a Talleyrand! and admire it.' I have been racking my brain to think of some delicate and subtle means of ridding myself of my republican varnish and the fatal label: *A student expelled from the École Polytechnique.* Fifty francs for a frame and fifty for a lithograph does the trick; it's just the thing for these people here; Filloteau knows more about it than I do, and that just goes to show the real superiority of a man of genius over an ordinary mortal; instead of a flock of little steps, one decisive action, simple and striking—the answer in a nutshell. I am very much afraid," he added, "that it will be a long time before I am a lieutenant-colonel."

Happily for Lucien, who was beginning to think himself inferior in every way, the trumpet sounded at the corner of the street, and he had to hurry to the barracks where the fear of the sharp reprimands of his superior officers made him very attentive.

That evening M. Bonard's servant handed him two letters. One of them was written on common schoolboy paper and carelessly sealed. Lucien opened it and read:

Nancy, Department of Meurthe
March 8, 183–

Lieutenant Whippersnapper:
Our brave lancers who have fought in dozens of battles, are not the sort to be commanded by a little fop from Paris. You may look

for trouble. You will find Martin-Big-Stick everywhere. Pack your trunks double quick, and get out. We advise you for your own sake. Tremble! [*There followed these signatures written with flourishes:*]

Chaseanass, Hardblade, Outugo.

Lucien was as red as a beet and trembling with rage. He, nevertheless, opened the second letter. "It must be written by a woman," he thought. It was on very good paper and seemed to have been written with care.

Sir:

Pity honest men who blush at the means they are forced to resort to in order to communicate their thoughts. It is not for a generous heart that our names must be kept secret, but the regiment swarms with spies and informers. To think of the noble profession of arms reduced to a school of espionage! How true it is that a great betrayal necessarily carries in its wake a thousand lesser evils! We invite you, sir, to verify, by your own observation, the following facts: Five lieutenants or second-lieutenants, MM. D——, R——, Bl——, V——, and Bi——, very elegant and apparently belonging to the higher classes of society, which makes us fear their attraction for you, are spies trying to track down republican opinion. From the bottom of our hearts we profess those opinions; one day we shall give our life blood for them, and we dare believe that you, at the proper time and place, are ready to make the same sacrifice. When the great day of awakening arrives, sir, count on the undersigned, your friends, who are your equals only through their sentiments of tender pity for our unhappy France.

> Martius, Publius Julius, Marcus,
> Vindex who will kill Marquin.
> In the name of all these gentlemen.

This letter almost wholly wiped out the feeling of *ignominy* and ugliness so painfully awakened by the first. "The letter of insults written on cheap paper," said Lucien to himself, "is the anonymous letter of 1780 when the soldiers were scamps and unemployed lackeys, recruited along the Paris quais. This one is the anonymous letter of 183–.

"Publius! Vindex! my poor friends, you would be right if there were a hundred thousand of you. But you are perhaps not more than two thousand scattered throughout France, and the Filloteaux, the Malhers, even the Dévelroys would, if you declared yourselves, have you legally shot, and they would be approved by the immense majority."

All Lucien's sensations had been so dreary since he came to Nancy, that, for want of anything better to do, he let this republican epistle absorb his attention. "The best thing would be for them all to set sail for America. . . . And would I sail with them?" At this question Lucien began pacing the floor with a troubled air.

"No," he said finally. "Why should I fool myself? I am not quite such an imbecile! I do not possess enough fierce virtues to make me think like *Vindex*. I should be bored in America among men who are, it is true, perfectly just and reasonable, but coarse, and who think of nothing but *dollars*. They would talk to me about their ten cows that in the spring would give them ten calves, while I prefer talking about the eloquence of M. de Lamennais, or the talent of Malibran as compared with that of Madame Pasta. I cannot live with men incapable of clever ideas, no matter how virtuous they may be. I should prefer, a hundred times over, the elegant manners of a corrupt court. Washington would have bored me to death, and I prefer to find myself in the same drawing room with M. de Talleyrand. Therefore, the feeling of esteem is not enough for me. I need the pleasures of a time-honored civilization. . . .

"Well then, donkey, why don't you support the corrupt governments which are the products of civilization? Only a fool or a child is content to harbor two conflicting desires at the same time. I loathe the tedious common sense of an American. The stories of young General Bonaparte, at the time he carried the bridge of Arcole, enrapture me; it is Homer, Tasso, and a hundred times better still! American morality seems to me abominably vulgar, and reading the works of their distinguished men gives me just one desire: never to meet any of them in a salon. That model country seems to me the triumph of stupid and selfish mediocrity, and yet everyone has to court it on pain of death. If I were a peasant with a capital of four hundred louis and five children, I should undoubtedly go to America, buy and cultivate two hundred acres of land in the vicinity of Cincinnati. But what have I in common with that peasant? Have I ever, up until now, been able to earn the price of a cigar?

"Those brave non-commissioned officers would not, in all likelihood, be enraptured by the acting of Madame Pasta; they would not appreciate the conversation of M. de Talleyrand, and what they long for, above all else, is a captain's commission; that is their ideal of happiness. If it were only a question of serving the fatherland, they merit the rank a hundred times more, perhaps, than those who hold it and who, many of them, have got their commissions in the same way I have. They think, and with good reason, that the Republic will make them captains, and feel themselves capable of justifying such a promotion by their deeds of heroism. And what about me? Would I like to be a captain? As a matter of fact, I would not. I really don't know what I want. All I know is that the everyday pleasures of life are to be found only in salons like my mother's.

"Therefore, I am not a republican, but I loathe the meanness of a Malher or a Marquin. What am I then? Not much, I should say. Dévelroy may tell me all he likes: 'You are a very lucky man to have a father who gives you a letter of credit on the Collector-General of the Department of Meurthe. As a matter of fact, I am, from the economic point of view, inferior to my servants. I have suffered horribly ever since I started to earn ninety-nine francs a month.

"But what is it that is most esteemed by the world of which I have caught a glimpse? The man who has amassed a few million or who has bought a newspaper and gets himself praised for eight or ten years at a stretch. (Isn't that the case of M. de Chateaubriand?) For a man with a fortune like myself, isn't the supreme happiness to be considered a man of wit by women of wit?

"Didn't M. de Talleyrand launch his career by holding his own with a clever word against the overweening pride of Madame la Duchesse de Grammont? With the exception of my poor mad republicans, I can see nothing in the world that calls for esteem. As far as I can see there is always some charlatanism in everybody's merit. My republicans are perhaps mad, but, at least, they are not base." Lucien's reasoning could not go beyond this conclusion. A wise man would have said to him: "See a little more of life and you will perceive that things have other aspects. For the moment simply be satisfied not to injure anyone basely. You have really seen too little of life to be able to judge these profound questions. Wait—and keep cool."

Lucien lacked such a counselor, and for want of those words of wisdom lost himself in the clouds.

"So my merit will hang on the opinion of a woman, or a hundred women, of the fashionable world! What could be more ridiculous! What contempt I have always professed for a man in love, like my cousin Edgard, who stakes his happiness, his very self-esteem, on the judgment of a young woman who spends her whole morning at Victorine's discussing the merits of a gown, or ridiculing a man of merit like Monge because he is common-looking!

"But on the other hand, to court the favor of men of the common people, as one has to do in America, is really beyond my powers. I require elegant manners, fruits of the corrupt government of Louis XV; and yet, who were the men of note in such a state of society? A Duc de Richelieu, a Lauzun, whose memoirs are a true picture of life."

These reflections plunged Lucien into a state of extreme agitation. His religion, Virtue and Honor, was at stake, and according to this religion: without virtue, no happiness. "Great God! To whom can I turn for advice? From the point of view of a man's real value, where do I stand? Am I in the middle of the list, or am I at the very end? . . . And Filloteau, in spite of all my scorn for him, has an honorable place; he gave some famous blows in Egypt; he was recompensed by Napoleon who was a good judge of military valor. Henceforth no matter what Filloteau does, that will always remain; nothing can take from him this honorable rank: a brave man, made captain by Napoleon in Egypt!"

This was a profound lesson in modesty, and above all painful. Lucien had vanity, and that vanity had been constantly excited by an *excellent* education.

A few days after the arrival of the anonymous letters, as Lucien was walking through a deserted street, he met two noncommissioned officers. They had slender and well-knit figures and were dressed with remarkable care. They bowed to him in a curious way. Lucien watched them as they passed, and soon saw them retracing their steps in a very pointed manner. "Either I am very much mistaken or these gentlemen may well be Vindex and Julius. They have stationed themselves here from a sense of honor, to sign, as it were, their anonymous letter. It is I who am ashamed now, and I should like to undeceive them. I respect their opinions, their ambition is honorable. But I cannot prefer America to France. Money is not everything to me, and democracy is much too crude to my way of thinking."

CHAPTER SEVEN

THIS DEBATE with himself on the Republic poisoned several weeks of Lucien's inner life. Vanity, that bitter fruit of the education of the upper classes of society, was his tormentor. Young, rich, and to all appearances happy, he could never give himself up whole-heartedly to pleasure. He might have been a young Protestant. He was rarely impulsive; he thought himself obliged to act with a great deal of circumspection. "If you throw yourself at a woman's head, she will despise you," his father once said to him. In a word, society, which in the Nineteenth Century has so little pleasure to offer, frightened him at every turn. For Lucien, as for most of his contemporaries who frequented the *Bouffes,* childish vanity, an extreme and constant fear of not observing the thousand little rules established by our civilization, took the place of all those ardent impulses which, in the reign of Charles X, had stirred the hearts of young Frenchmen. He was the only son of a wealthy man, and it takes many years to overcome such a handicap, the envy of most mortals.

We admit that Lucien's vanity was piqued. For eight or ten hours every day he was thrown among men who knew much more than he did about the only subject on which he would permit himself to talk to them. Lucien's comrades-in-arms, with the polite acrimony of vindictive conceit, tried at all times to make him feel their superiority. These gentlemen were furious because they seemed to realize instinctively that Lucien considered them fools. And you should have seen their superior air when Lucien made a mistake in the time, according to regulations, fatigue cap and stable breeches should be worn.

Lucien remained unmoved and cold in the midst of their affected gestures and politely ironic smiles. He thought his companions were being gratuitously offensive; he was not sufficiently objective to see that it was just their little way of taking revenge for all the display of wealth he indulged in.

"After all, these gentlemen can do me no harm," he said to himself, "so long as I don't talk too much and do as little as possible. Silence is the *watch-word,* to do as little as possible, the *plan of campaign.*" Lucien laughed as he emphasized these words of his new calling. Having no one with whom he could talk freely, he had to laugh with himself.

For eight or ten hours, the time it takes a man to earn ninety-nine francs, he could talk of nothing but maneuvers, regimental accounts, the price of horses, the great question of whether it was better for the cavalry corps to buy directly from breeders, or whether it was more advantageous for the government to take charge of the training from the outset in the remount station. In the latter case the horses came to nine hundred and two francs; but many of them also died, etc., etc.

Lieutenant-Colonel Filloteau had assigned him an old lieutenant, an officer of the Legion of Honor, to teach him the science of war. But this worthy man thought himself obliged to perorate. And what eloquence! Lucien was not able to decline his services and began to read aloud with him the *rhapsody* entitled *Victories and Conquests of the French.* But when Gauthier recommended the Memoirs of Marshal Gouvion-Saint-Cyr, Lucien picked out the accounts of battles in which the brave lieutenant had himself figured, and the latter, moved to tears at hearing these printed accounts of the events of his youth read aloud, would relate in detail all he had seen. The old lieutenant was often sublime, recounting with simplicity those heroic days when no one was a hypocrite! This simple peasant was especially admirable when he described the site of a battle, and recalled a multitude of details which the rest of us would never have remembered, but which, told with that accent of truth, made Lucien's mad love for the armies of the Republic soar with fresh enthusiasm. The lieutenant was extremely entertaining when he described the revolutions that occurred within the regiment after unexpected promotions.

These lessons, from which Lucien came away with sparkling eyes, were very much ridiculed by his comrades. The idea of a man of twenty letting himself be taught like a schoolboy! And worse still, by an old soldier who couldn't open his mouth without murdering the French language! But Lucien's studied reserve and icy gravity disconcerted these would-be wits, and prevented anyone from acquainting him with this general opinion to his face.

Lucien did not see that there was anything wrong with his conduct, and yet, we must admit that it would have been difficult for anyone to commit more blunders than he. There was nothing he did, down to the very choice of an apartment, that was not wrong. What effrontery—a simple second-lieutenant setting himself up in the lodgings of a lieutenant-colonel! (I am simply repeating what everyone was saying.) Before him the apartment of the worthy M. Bonard had been occupied by Monsieur le Marquis, Thomas de Busant de Sicile, lieutenant-colonel of the regiment of hussars which the Twenty-seventh Lancers had just replaced.

Lucien saw nothing of all this. He attributed the more than chilly welcome he was accorded to the aversion of vulgar people to those belonging to a more distinguished class of society. He would have rejected any evidence of friendliness as a snare, and yet this restrained but unanimous hate which he read in every eye, made his heart ache. We beg the reader not to take him for a fool; this heart was still so young! At the École Polytechnique, arduous and constant work, enthusiasm for science, love of liberty, the generosity natural to extreme youth, neutralized vindictive passions and the effects of envy. In the regiment, on the contrary, there reigned a most boring idleness. For, at the end of six months what was there to do, after the duties of the profession no longer constituted the main occupation of life?

Four or five young officers with rather more pleasing manners than the rest, and whose names were not on the list of spies revealed to him by the anonymous letter, might have inspired in our hero ideas of a closer acquaintance had they not evinced perhaps an even more marked aversion to him, or at least their way of showing it was even more stinging. The only friendliness he noticed was in the eyes of a few non-coms who bowed to him eagerly and in a peculiar manner, especially when they passed him in some remote street.

Besides old Lieutenant Joubert, Lieutenant-Colonel Filloteau had engaged a sergeant to teach him the various evolutions of a platoon, a squadron, and a regiment.

"You can't possibly offer this brave old soldier less than forty francs a month," Filloteau told him.

And Lucien, whose bruised heart was about ready to accept Filloteau as a friend (after all, had he not known Desaix, Kleber, Michaud, and the glorious days of Sambre and Meuse), discovered that the brave Filloteau, whom he had cast in the role of hero, appropriated to himself one half of the forty francs intended for the sergeant.

Lucien had had an immense pine table made, and on this table little pieces of wood like two gaming dice joined together, represented the horsemen of a cavalry regiment. Under the direction of the sergeant he practiced maneuvering these soldiers two hours every day; and these were perhaps the best hours of the day.

Little by little, this way of living became a habit. All the sensations of the young second-lieutenant were dulled; nothing any longer gave him either pleasure or pain, and he could see nothing to do about it. He had conceived a profound disgust for all men, even for himself. He had often refused to go to the country Sundays to dine with his host M. Bonard, but one day, having accepted the grain merchant's invitation, he came back to the city with M. Gauthier, whom the reader already knows as the leader of the republicans and the principal editor of the *Aurore.* This M. Gauthier was an enormous young man, built like a Hercules. He had beautiful blond hair which he wore too long, but this was his only affectation. His simple gestures, the extreme energy he put into everything he did, an unmistakable good faith, all saved him from seeming vulgar. On the other hand, the most blatant and cheap vulgarity was the distinguishing mark of his associates. As for him, he was serious; he never lied; he was a sincere fanatic. But through his passion for a France *self-governed,* there shone a beautiful soul. Lucien amused himself on the road home comparing him with M. Fléron, the leader of the opposite party. M. Gauthier, far from profiting by his position, made a bare living at his trade of cadastral surveyor. As for his paper the *Aurore,* it cost him five or six hundred francs a year besides all the many months in prison.

After a few days this man seemed to Lucien the very opposite of everything he had seen in Nancy. Above that enormous body, like his uncle Bonard's, Gauthier had the head of a genius with its beautiful curly blond hair. At times he could be really eloquent when he talked about the future happiness of France and the good times to come when government offices would be held without pay and rewarded only with honor.

Gauthier's eloquence touched Lucien, but did not succeed in destroying his chief objection to a republic: the necessity of paying court to mediocre people.

After six weeks, during which their acquaintance developed almost into intimacy, Lucien discovered by chance that Gauthier was a geometrician of the first order. This discovery moved him deeply; what a difference from Paris! Lucien loved higher mathematics passionately. From now on he spent whole evenings with Gauthier, discussing either Fourier's theories on the heat of the earth, or the soundness of the discoveries of Ampère, or finally that fundamental question: did the habit of analysis make one less able to observe the facts in experimentation.

"Be careful," Gauthier warned him, "I am not only a geometrician, I am a republican and one of the editors of the *Aurore*. If General Thérance or your Colonel Malher de Saint-Mégrin hear of our conversations, they will do nothing to me—they've already done me all the harm they can—but you will be dismissed from the army or sent to Algiers as a bad lot."

"That might be the best thing that could happen to me," Lucien retorted. "Or to speak with the mathematical exactitude we both love, augmentation of punishment in my case would be impossible; I think, without exaggerating, I can say that I have reached the very height of boredom."

Gauthier did not mince words in trying to convert Lucien to American democracy. Lucien listened to him for a long time; he then replied with perfect frankness:

"My dear friend, you really console me. Now I see that if, instead of being a second-lieutenant in Nancy, I were a second-lieutenant in Cincinnati or Pittsburgh, I should be even more bored, and, as you know, the consciousness of a greater evil is always a consolation, perhaps the only one I am capable of appreciating. In order to earn ninety-nine francs a month and my own self-respect, I left my native city where I used to spend my time most agreeably."

"Who forced you to do it?"

"I threw myself into this inferno of my own free will."

"In that case leave it! Fly!"

"Paris is now spoiled for me. If I returned I should no longer be what I was before donning this fatal green uniform: a young man who perhaps one day would amount to something. Now I would be looked upon as a young man incapable of being anything, even a second-lieutenant."

"But what do you care what people think if you are really enjoying yourself?"

"Alas! I possess vanity, a thing which you, my wise friend, cannot understand. My position would be intolerable. I should be unable to answer certain pleasantries. The only thing that could possibly extricate me from the mess I've got myself into without knowing what I was doing, is a war."

Lucien had the courage to write this entire confession and the story of his new friendship to his mother. But he begged her to return his letter. Their correspondence was in the tone of the frankest friendship. He wrote to her: "I won't say my misfortune, but rather my boredom would be intensified if I were to become the subject of my father's jokes and of those amusing men whose absence makes life seem so dull."

Happily for Lucien his intimacy with M. Gauthier, whom he met in the evenings at M. Bonard's, did not come to the knowledge of Colonel Malher. But the commander's ill-will toward Lucien was no secret in the regiment. Perhaps this worthy man would have welcomed a duel to rid him of this young republican who enjoyed protection in too high quarters to permit his persecuting him *on a grand scale*.

One morning the colonel sent for Lucien, and only after waiting for at least three long quarters of an hour in a dirty ante-chamber where three lancers were shining twenty-four pairs of riding boots, was he introduced into the presence of that dignitary. "He has staged all this," Lucien said to himself, "but the only way to defeat his bad faith is not to notice it."

"It has been reported, sir," began the colonel with pinched lips and marked arrogance, "it has been reported that you eat very lavishly in your own lodgings. This I cannot countenance. Rich or poor, you must eat at the forty franc ordinary with

your comrades-in-arms. Good-day, sir. I have nothing more to
say."

Lucien was boiling with rage. No one had ever spoken to
him in such a tone. "So, even at meals, I shall be forced to remain with my amiable comrades whose sole pleasure, it seems,
is to try to crush me with their superiority. I might truthfully
say with Beaumarchais: *My life is a battle*. Oh, very well," he
laughed to himself, "I'll put up with it. Dévelroy shall not have
the satisfaction of repeating that I have taken the trouble to
be born. . . . I shall reply that I have also taken some trouble
to live." And Lucien went off on the spot to pay a month's
board in advance. That evening he dined at the ordinary and
conducted himself with admirable coldness and disdain.

Two days later, at six o'clock in the morning, the non-commissioned adjutant who was supposed to be the colonel's cat's-
paw entered his room. The man said to him smoothly:

"Lieutenants and second-lieutenants, without the colonel's
permission, are not to go farther than a radius of two leagues
beyond the Grande Place."

Lucien made no reply, which nettled the adjutant, who ar-
rogantly offered to leave a written description of all the land-
marks along the different roads to assist him in recognizing
the two-league limit. You must know that the execrable, sterile,
dried-up plain on which the genius of Vauban had seen fit to
place the city of Nancy, has no sign of a passable hill within
three leagues. Lucien at that moment would have given anything in the world to throw the adjutant out of the window.

"May I ask, sir," he said, with an air of innocence, "when
the said lieutenants and second-lieutenants mount their horses
to go riding, are they permitted to trot or only to go at a
walk?"

"Sir, I shall report your question to the colonel," replied the
adjutant, crimson with rage.

A quarter of an hour later, an orderly came galloping back with the following order:

Second-Lieutenant Leuwen will keep quarters twenty-four hours for having held up to ridicule an order of the Colonel.

Malher de Saint-Mégrin.

"O Galilean, thou shalt not prevail against me!" cried Lucien.

This last provocation roused Lucien from his state of listless despondency. Nancy was horrible, the military profession had nothing whatever to recommend it except the far-off echoes of Fleurus and Marengo; but Lucien was determined to prove to his father and Dévelroy that he was able to endure all its vexations.

The very day of Lucien's confinement, the top ranking officers of the regiment had, in their naïveté, attempted to pay their respects on the noble ladies d'Hocquincourt, de Chasteller, de Puylaurens, de Marcilly, de Commercy, knowing, as they did, that some of the officers of the Twentieth Hussars had been received at those houses. We shall not insult our reader's intelligence by pointing out the innumerable reasons that made this proceeding an unbelievable blunder which the most unsophisticated young man from Paris would not have committed.

The visit of these officers belonging to a regiment that was considered *Juste-milieu,* was received with an impertinence which when recounted to our hero did much to enliven his confinement. In his eyes the details were an honor to the wit of the ladies in question.

When Mesdames de Marcilly and de Commercy, who were both indeed very old, saw these gentlemen enter their drawing rooms, they affected an air of terror as though they believed them to be agents of the Reign of Terror of 1793. At Madame de Puylaurens and Madame d'Hocquincourt's, their reception was somewhat different. These ladies had apparently given their servants instructions to make the ranking officers of the Twenty-seventh look ridiculous; for when they left, their passage through the ante-chamber was the signal for a burst of laughter from the lackeys. The rare remarks the two ladies had, in their amazement, been able to think of, had been couched in terms of an impudence that fell just short of the point where it becomes coarseness and is in danger of calling in question the good breeding of those who employ it. At Madame de Chasteller's, where the service was more punctilious, the door was simply closed to these gentlemen.

"And, by gad, the colonel calmly swallowed it all like water," said Filloteau who, under cover of the night when his movements would not be noticed, had come to see Lucien and console him in his imprisonment. "The colonel even wanted to make us believe on leaving Madame d'Hocquin-court, who never stopped laughing at us the whole time, that, after all, we had been received graciously and gaily, one might say, informally, really like old friends! . . . By God! in the old days, when we crossed the whole of France from Mayence to Bayonne on our way to Spain, what wouldn't we have done to the windows of a female like that! A damned old woman, the Comtesse de Marcilly I think it was, who looks ninety at least, had the effrontery to offer us wine when we got up to leave, the way you'd give a drink to a carter!"

Lucien heard many further details as soon as he could go out again.

We forgot to say that M. Bonard had introduced him into several good middle-class homes. He had found the same perpetual affectation that he had encountered at Mademoiselle Sylviane's, and the same pretensions to simplicity. He had noticed, much to his sorrow, that the bourgeois husbands kept reciprocal watch over each others' wives, not through any concerted arrangement but simply through envy and natural meanness. Two or three of *their ladies,* to speak their own language, had very beautiful eyes, and eyes which had deigned to address him. But how could he manage a tête-à-tête? And besides, what affectations surrounded them, to say nothing of their own! What eternal games of Boston he would have to play with the husbands and, above all, what uncertainty of success! Without the least experience and rather dejected by what had happened to him, Lucien preferred to bore himself evenings by himself than to play Boston with these husbands who always took good care to place him with his back turned to the prettiest woman in the room. He was deliberately reduced to the role of observer. The ignorance of these poor women is unimaginable. Fortunes are moderate and the husbands subscribe in common to the newspapers they read and which their better halves never see. Their role is entirely reduced to bearing children and nursing them when they are ill. Only Sundays on the promenade, taking their husbands' arms, they display the dresses and gaudy shawls with which the former have judged fit to reward the faithful accomplishment of their duties as mother and spouse.

If Lucien had shown himself more assiduous in his attentions to Mademoiselle Sylviane, it was only because to see her was such a simple matter. He had only to enter a shop. Our hero was apparently following in the footsteps of M. Fléron the prefect who, every evening, with marked affectation and mawkish air, would knock at the door of the wineshop and, without pausing there, the first magistrate of the department would enter directly into the parlor behind the shop. There he found himself in the home of one of the most influential proprietors of the department, as he took pains to point out in his letters to his minister.

Lucien now only put in an appearance at Mademoiselle Sylviane Berchu's once a week, and each time he came away determined not to go again for a month. He had for a while been a daily visitor. The worthy Filloteau's recital and his resentment against the noble ladies, the discomfiture of Lucien's superior officers whose attitude toward Lucien kept him at such a distance, all awakened in him a spirit of contradiction. "Here is a set of people that refuses to receive anyone who shows himself in the uniform I wear! Well then, let's try to break in. Very possibly they are as boring as the bourgeois, but I must find out. At least, I'd have the satisfaction of triumphing over great odds. I must ask my father for letters of introduction."

But to write to such a father in a serious vein was not easy. It was M. Leuwen's practice, outside his bank, never to read a letter through to the end unless he found it amusing. "The easier the thing is for him to do, the more likely he will be to think up some trick to play on me. He handles all M. Bonpain's business on the Bourse, and M. Bonpain is attorney for the noble Faubourg, the man who manages all the drives for party funds in the provinces, and for everything that is sent to Spain. M. Bonpain, with just a word or two, could assure me a brilliant reception in all the noble houses of Lorraine." With these ideas in mind, Lucien wrote to his father.

Instead of the enormous packet that he awaited with impatience, all that was forthcoming from his father's parental solicitude was the briefest possible letter written on the smallest possible piece of paper.

Most gracious Second-Lieutenant, you are young, you are considered rich, and you no doubt think yourself handsome. At least you have a handsome horse since it cost a hundred and fifty louis. And in your part of the country, the horse is more than half the man. You must be even worse than an ordinary Saint-Simonian not to have been able to force the doors of your petty nobles of Nancy. I wager that Méllinet [one of Lucien's servants] has got farther than you have, and can pick and choose his pleasures any evening. My dear Lucien, *studiate la matematica* and grow profound. Your mother is well, as is also your devoted servant,

François Leuwen.

This letter plunged Lucien into the devil of a mood. But the crowning touch came that evening when, on returning from his ride, within the two-league limit, he caught sight of his servant, Méllinet, sitting outside a shop in the midst of a bevy of women, and every one as merry as possible.

"My father is a sage," he thought, "and I am a simpleton."

Almost at the same moment he noticed a reading room where the lamps were just being lighted. He had his horse taken away, and went in to try to divert his mind and get over his irritation. The next morning at seven o'clock, Colonel Malher sent for him.

"Sir," said his superior with a magisterial air, "republicans, perhaps, exist, but I should prefer not to have them in the regiment which the King has entrusted to me."

And as Lucien looked at him in amazement:

"It is useless to deny it, sir, you spend your time at Schmidt's reading room in the Rue de la Pompe opposite the Hôtel de Pontlevé. It has been called to my attention as a hotbed of anarchy, frequented by the most brazen Jacobins of Nancy. Are you not ashamed, sir, to have associated yourself with the riffraff that forgathers there every night? You have been seen to pass constantly in front of the shop and to exchange signs with these people. One might be readily led to suppose that it was you who were the anonymous subscriber of Nancy mentioned by the Minister to M. le General, Baron Thérance, as having sent a contribution for the *National's* fine . . .

"Silence, sir!" cried the colonel angrily as Lucien seemed to wish to say something in his turn. "If you had the misfortune of admitting such a folly, I should be obliged to send you to General Headquarters at Metz, and I should hate to lose a young man who has already missed his vocation once before."

Lucien was furious. Several times while the colonel was talking, he had been on the point of seizing the pen lying on the large ink-stained and very dirty pine table behind which this uncivil and despotic personage was entrenched, and of writing out his resignation. Only the perspective of his father's teasing restrained him. After a moment or two he began to see that it was more in keeping with manly dignity to force the colonel to recognize that someone had deceived him or tried to deceive him.

"Colonel," he said in a voice that trembled with rage, but on the whole controlling himself rather well, "I was expelled from the École Polytechnique, I was called a republican, that is true. But I was only a rattle-brained schoolboy. Except for mathematics and chemistry, I know nothing. I have never made a study of politics, but I can discern the gravest objections to all the forms of government. It is therefore impossible for me to have an opinion on the one best suited to France. . . ."

"What, sir, you dare to admit that you are not convinced that only the King's government . . ."

Here we suppress three pages of monologue which the worthy colonel recited in one breath, having read them a few days previously in a newspaper subventioned by the government.

"That was way over the head of this cut-throat spy," thought Lucien while the sermon was going on, and he tried to think of a phrase that would say a great deal in few words.

"I entered that reading room yesterday for the first time in my life," he said finally, "and I will give fifty louis to anyone who can prove the contrary."

"Money has nothing to do with the question," replied the colonel sarcastically. "We all know that you have plenty, and it seems that you know it better than anyone else. Yesterday, sir, in Schmidt's reading room, you read the *National* and never even glanced at the *Journal de Paris,* nor the *Débats,* lying in the middle of the table."

"There was evidently a very accurate observer present," thought Lucien. He then began to recount everything he had done while in the place, to the smallest detail, so that the colonel could not deny:

1. That Lucien yesterday, for the first time since he had joined the regiment, had read a paper in a public place;

2. That he had spent only forty minutes in Schmidt's reading room;

3. That he had been occupied all that time solely in reading a long article of six columns on the *Don Giovanni* of Mozart, which he proved by repeating the principal headings.

After a séance of two hours, and the pettiest cross-examination by the colonel, Lucien, pale with suppressed rage, finally left. The colonel's bad faith was evident; but our hero felt a keen pleasure in having reduced him to silence on every one of the charges.

"I'd rather live with my father's lackey," said Lucien to himself, pausing under the *porte-cochère.* "What boors!" he repeated a dozen times during the day. "But all my friends will take me for a fool if at twenty, and with the finest horse in the city, I am a *fiasco* in a *Juste-milieu* regiment, where money is everything. In order to give them something worth talking about in Paris in case I resign, I must fight a duel. That is the custom on joining a regiment, at least so it is thought in our drawing rooms. And, faith, if I lose my life I don't lose very much."

After dinner, at the conclusion of the evening stable call which took place in the courtyard of the barracks, he said to several officers who were leaving at the same time:

"Spies, who are plentiful around here, have accused me to

the colonel of the dullest of sins: I am supposed to be a republican. It seems to me that I have a standing in the world and a fortune to lose. I should like to know who my accuser is, first to clear myself, and after that to give him one or two little caresses with my riding-whip."

There was a dead silence for a moment, then everyone began talking about something else.

That evening, Lucien was returning from his ride, when, in the street, his servant handed him a neat-looking letter carefully folded. He opened it and saw a single word: *Renegade*. At that moment Lucien was perhaps the unhappiest man in all the regiments of lancers in the army.

"That's how they do everything! Like children," he thought. "Who told those poor young men that I thought the way they did? I should be a great fool to dream of governing the State, I haven't even been able to govern my own life." For the first time in his life Lucien thought of killing himself. Excessive boredom had made him bitter, and he no longer saw things as they really were. For example, in his regiment there were eight or ten officers who were very agreeable. He was blind; he could see no merit in them.

Next day when Lucien again spoke of republicanism to two or three of the same officers:

"My dear fellow," one of them rejoined, "you bore us with your eternal refrain. What the devil do we care if you went to the École Polytechnique, or if you were expelled, or if you've been slandered? I've had my own troubles. Six years ago I sprained my ankle, but I don't keep boring my friends with it."

Lucien would not have taken up the accusation of being boring. From the first days of his joining the corps he had said to himself, "I am not here to educate all the unmannerly people in the regiment. I must not protest until one of them

does me the honor to be cruder than usual." At the imputation
that he was boring, Lucien, after a moment's silence, replied:
"I really am boring I am afraid, it happens to me once in
a while, and I am willing to take your word for it, sir. But
I am determined not to allow anyone to accuse me of republicanism. I should like to underline my declaration with a
stroke of my sword, and I should be infinitely obliged if you
would be good enough to measure yours with mine."

This speech seemed to resuscitate all these poor young men.
Soon Lucien was surrounded by twenty officers. This duel was
a stroke of luck for the entire regiment. It took place that
very evening in a perfectly dreary and dirty corner of the
ramparts. They fought with swords, and both the adversaries
were wounded, but without the State's running any risk of
losing either of them. Lucien had a deep cut in his upper arm.

CHAPTER EIGHT

THE CHIEF SURGEON of the regiment, *Chevalier*
Bilars, as he insisted on being called, a kind of charlatan but not a bad sort, who came from the Upper
Alps, made his appearance early the next morning. The adversary's sword had grazed an artery. Chevalier Bilars exaggerated the danger which was naught, and returned two or
three times during the day. The "library," as the Chevalier
called it, of our admirable second-lieutenant, was furnished
with the rarest editions, such as kirschwasser 1810, twelve-
year-old Marie Brizard anisette from Bordeaux, eau-de-vie of
Danzig full of gold flakes, etc., etc. The Chevalier, who was
fond of "reading," spent days on end with his patient, rather
to the latter's annoyance.

From him Lucien learned of a doctor in Nancy who was famous for his exceptional medical skill and who was, moreover, a favorite in royalist circles because of his eloquence and his ferocious support of the legitimate cause. Du Poirier was his name. From everything Chevalier Bilars said, Lucien understood that this doctor might well be the great factotum of Nancy. In any case he must be an amusing rascal quite worth cultivating.

"Tomorrow, my dear doctor, you must bring this gentleman, Du Poirier, to see me, without fail. Tell him that I am in grave danger."

"But you are not in danger at all!"

"Yes, but isn't it logical to begin our acquaintance with so notorious a schemer with a lie? Once he is here you mustn't contradict me. Let me do the talking. We shall certainly hear famous stories about Henri V and Louis XIX, and may possibly have some fun."

"Your wound is entirely surgical, and I don't see what a medical doctor . . ."

In the end Chevalier Bilars consented to fetch the doctor because he knew that if he did not bring him, Lucien could very well write to Du Poirier himself.

The celebrated doctor came the next day. "This man has all the earmarks of a famous fanatic," thought Lucien. The doctor had not been with our hero more than five minutes before he was poking him familiarly in the ribs as he talked. This M. Du Poirier was the worst kind of a vulgarian, and one who seemed proud of his coarse and familiar manners. A hog, in much the same way, wallows in the mire with what seems to the spectator a sort of voluptuous insolence. But Lucien had hardly time to notice his extreme absurdity; it was perfectly evident that it was not through vanity nor for the sake of trying to appear Lucien's equal or superior that Du Poirier took such a familiar tone with him. Lucien was under the impression that he had before him a man of great merit carried away by the urgent need of expressing thoughts which oppressed him by their profusion and compelling force. An older man than Lucien would have noticed that Du Poirier's impetuosity did not prevent him from taking advantage of the familiarity he had assumed, nor from realizing all its advantages. When not carried away by what he was saying, he had just as many little vanities as any other Frenchman. Of all this Chevalier Bilars saw nothing, and thought Du Poirier too uncouth to be allowed in the lowest tavern.

"But no," said Lucien to himself, having for a moment believed in the passionate conviction of a veritable genius, "this man is a hypocrite. He is too clever to let himself be carried away. He never makes a move except after careful calculation. This excess of vulgarity and bad manners, combined with such lofty thinking, must have a purpose." Lucien was all ears. The doctor talked about everything under the sun, but especially about politics. He pretended to have inside information about everything.

"But, my dear sir," cried the doctor, suddenly interrupting his endless dissertation on the happiness of France, "in another moment you will take me for a Paris doctor who tries to be witty, and talks to his patient about everything except his malady."

He then examined Lucien's arm and recommended absolute quiet for a week.

"Away with all these poultices! Forget about medicaments, and if there is no sign of any change you can safely forget all about this little scratch."

While Dr. Du Poirier was examining his wound and taking his pulse, Lucien was satisfied that his own expression had been admirable. Dr. Du Poirier, as soon as he had finished with Lucien's wound, resumed the great topic: the impossibility of the duration of the Louis-Philippe government.*

Our hero had been too quick to decide that he could, without difficulty, amuse himself at the expense of a provincial wit and braggart by profession. He soon discovered that the logic of the provinces is superior to their light verse. Far from making sport of Du Poirier, he had all the trouble in the world not to fall into ridicule himself. One thing was sure, the presence of this strange animal had completely cured his boredom.

Du Poirier might have been fifty years old. His features were large and strongly marked. Two little gray-green eyes, deep-set in his head, kept darting about, moving constantly with extraordinary agility, and seeming to throw out sparks. They made you forget the length of the nose that separated them. At certain angles this unfortunate nose gave to the doctor's countenance the look of an alert fox: a decided disadvantage in an apostle. What completed the likeness, if one had the misfortune of noticing it, was the thick forest of tawny hair bristling over the doctor's head and temples. On the whole, once seen this was a physiognomy that could not be easily forgotten. In Paris it would perhaps have horrified fools; in the provinces where everyone is bored, anything that promises relief is eagerly welcomed, and the doctor was now the rage.

He had a vulgar face and yet his appearance was extraordinary and striking. Whenever the doctor thought his adversary had been convinced—and the moment he met anyone, that person became an adversary to be convinced and an adherent to be gained—his eyebrows would shoot up inordinately and his little gray eyes, wide open like a hyena's, would seem ready to pop out of his head. "Even in Paris," thought Lucien, "this

* This is a legitimist speaking, as above it was a republican.

wild boar's head, this furious fanaticism, these impertinent manners, so fraught with eloquence and energy, would keep him from being ridiculous. A true apostle, a Jesuit." And Lucien watched him with extreme curiosity.

While Lucien was occupied with these reflections, the doctor had plunged into politics and seemed to be quite carried away by his subject. Partition of a patrimony at the death of the head of a family would have to be abolished. Above all the Jesuits must be re-established. As for the elder branch, it was not *legitimate* to drink a single glass of wine in France until it had been restored to its own, that is, reinstated in the Tuileries, etc., etc. And Du Poirier said nothing to soften the blinding glare of these stupendous truths, or to spare the prejudices of his young neophyte.

"How is it possible," cried the doctor all at once, "that you, a man well-born, with elegant manners, a fortune, an enviable position in society, a refined education, should have thrown in your lot with that vile *Juste-milieu!* You have become their soldier, you will fight their wars—not the true war whose very miseries, for generous hearts, are fraught with such nobility and charm, but a constabulary war, a war of rotten cabbages against wretched workingmen half dead with hunger. For you the expedition of the Rue Transnonain is the battle of Marengo . . ."

"My dear Chevalier," said Lucien, turning to the scandalized Doctor Bilars who thought himself obliged to defend the *Juste-milieu.* "My dear Chevalier, I have taken a notion to tell the doctor here certain little peccadillos of my youth which are altogether in the province of medicine, and which I shall confide to you too, but at some other time. There are certain things one only cares to confess to one person at a time."

In spite of this frank declaration, Lucien had some difficulty in getting rid of the Chevalier who was itching to talk politics, and whom Lucien erroneously suspected of being a spy.

The eloquence of Du Poirier was in no way restrained by this episode of the expulsion of the Chevalier. He continued to gesticulate furiously and to talk at the top of his voice.

"Can it be possible," he cried, "that you intend to vegetate in the boredom and pettiness of garrison life? Is this a role for a man like you? You must get out of it at once. The day the cannon will be fired—not the meaningless cannon of Antwerp, but our Nation's cannon, the one that will set French hearts beating, mine, sir, and yours—you will distribute a few louis around the ministry and be a second-lieutenant as before. And for a man of your stamp what does it matter whether he fights as second-lieutenant or captain? Leave the little vanity of epaulets to half-wits. The important thing for a man like you is nobly to pay his debt to his country; the important thing is to lead intelligently twenty-five peasants who have nothing but their courage; the important thing in this dubious age is to give proof of that sort of merit which alone cannot be accused of hypocrisy. The courage of a man who does not flinch under Prussian fire cannot be called hypocrisy. But drawing your sword on workingmen with nothing but fowling pieces with which to defend themselves and who are four hundred against ten thousand, proves absolutely nothing, except the lack of a noble heart and the desire for advancement. And observe the effect on public opinion: in this ignoble duel, homage due to courage will always be, as at Lyons, on the side that has neither cannons nor petards. But reasoning like Barême: even if you kill a great many workingmen, my dear *Second-Lieutenant,* it will take you six years at least to lose that fatal *second.*"

"You'd think the animal had known me for months," thought Lucien. But such things, of so personal a nature and apparently most offensive, cannot be written. One must have heard them spoken with all the vehemence of this fiery fanatic, of a man who knew how to present things with art and even, if necessary, with respect for the susceptibilities of a well-bred young man. The doctor had a gift for saying personal things and giving intimate advice, which in anyone else would have been considered an impertinence, in so spirited a manner, so amusingly, quite inoffensively, with apparently so little intention of assuming a tone of superiority, that everything was forgiven him. Besides he had such a comical way of saying these unwonted things, with such burlesque gestures that Lucien, Parisian though he was, had not the courage to put him in his place, and that was exactly what Du Poirier had counted on. Moreover, I do not think it would have seriously worried him even if he had been severely put in his place. These indiscreet souls are blessed with thick skins.

Finding himself all at once, and in such an unlooked-for fashion, rescued by this provincial doctor from the atrocious boredom which had been slowly killing him for two months, Lucien did not have the courage to deprive himself of such an entertaining spectacle. "I should be ridiculous," he thought, almost bursting with suppressed laughter, "if I let this crusading buffoon see that I found his manners not precisely suitable for a first visit; and besides, what would I gain by frightening him away?"

All that Lucien could do was to frustrate this ardent partisan of the Jesuits and Henri V in his attempt to obtain a confession. So far the most he had obtained was the chance of delivering a profuse and incongruous monologue uninterrupted; but quite like a true apostle Du Poirier appeared to be entirely accustomed to this absence of response, and did not seem to be in the least discountenanced.

For his part, Lucien could not succeed in deceiving this cunning doctor, except in the matter of his health. Anxious to keep the doctor from suspecting that he had been called in only to relieve Lucien's boredom, Lucien pretended to be very much troubled by *flying gout,* a disease his father suffered from and whose symptoms he knew by heart. The doctor questioned him attentively and then gave him serious advice.

After this second consultation, Du Poirier got to his feet but did not leave. He redoubled his brusque incisive flattery. He tried his best to make Lucien talk. Our hero finally decided to master his smothered laughter and to satisfy his visitor. "If on this first call I do not show where I stand, this sycophant will not play out his whole hand, and will be less amusing."

"I do not pretend to deny it, sir; I am aware that I was not born *under a cabbage leaf.* I begin life with certain advantages. Finding two or three great commercial houses here in France which dispute the monopoly of the public's favors, I ask myself: shall I enroll myself in the *House of Henri V & Co.* or in the *National & Co.?* While waiting to make my final choice later on, I have accepted a small interest in the *House of Louis-Philippe,* the only one which is in a position to make any real and positive offers. And I confess that I only believe in something positive. I go so far as always to take for granted that the person talking to me is bent on deceiving me unless he offers me something positive. Under the king of my choice I have the advantage of learning my profession. However respectable and considerable the Republican Party and that of Henri V or Louis XIX may be, neither the one nor the other is able, at the moment, to supply the means of teaching me how to maneuver a squadron in the field. When I have learned my profession I shall no doubt find myself full of respect, as I am today, for the advantages of the mind, as well as for the fine positions to be acquired in society; but with a view to acquiring such a place in society myself, I shall definitely associate myself with that one of the three commercial houses which offers me the most advantageous conditions.

You will admit, sir, that an impetuous choice would be a great mistake, since, for the moment, I lack nothing that I could desire. What I need is a bit of a future, provided anyone does me the honor of considering me."

At this unlooked-for outburst that was uttered with such extraordinary vehemence, for Lucien was afraid of suddenly giving way to his pent-up laughter, the doctor seemed taken aback for a second. Finally he replied in the sanctimonious tone of a village priest:

"My dear sir, it gives me the greatest joy to see that you respect all that is respectable."

The sudden change from the free and satanic vein which until now had characterized his conversation, to this paternal and moral tone, made Lucien flush with pleasure. "I've been crafty enough for the fellow," he thought, "I have forced him to drop political arguments and to try appealing to my feelings." Lucien was in fine fettle.

"I respect everything or nothing, my dear Doctor," he replied lightly, and as the doctor looked astonished: "I respect all that my friends respect. But," he added as though to explain his thought, "who are my friends?"

At this trenchant question, the doctor all at once had recourse to platitudes. He was reduced to discoursing on ideas anterior to any experience in man's consciousness, of secret revelations made to every Christian, of devotion to the cause of God, etc., etc.

"All that may be true, or it may be false, it is immaterial to me," Lucien replied with the most flippant air. "I have not studied theology. In any case we have not got beyond the regions of positive interests. If ever we have the time, we might plunge together into the profundities of German philosophy, so entertaining and so clear, according to privileged persons. A friend of mine who is a scholar says that when

German philosophy is at the end of its arguments, it simply explains by an appeal to *faith* what it is unable to elucidate by means of plain reason. And, as I had the honor of telling you, sir, I don't know yet if, in the future, I shall seek employment in the business firm which considers faith the most necessary part of its capital investment."

"Well, sir, I must be going. I see that it won't be long before you are one of us," replied the doctor with the most satisfied air in the world, adding, as he poked Lucien in the ribs, "We are in perfect agreement. Meanwhile, I shall, I hope, drive away for some time those attacks of *flying gout*."

He wrote out a prescription and disappeared.

"That youngster is much less silly," thought the doctor as he went away, "than the other young Parisians who pass through here every year on their way to the camp of Lunéville or the valley of the Rhine. He recites very intelligently a lesson learned in Paris from one of those atheists of the Institute. All this pretty Machiavellism is happily nothing but idle chatter, and the irony that fills his discourse has not yet penetrated his soul. We shall win. We must get him to fall in love with one of our women. Madame d'Hocquincourt must soon make up her mind to dismiss that fellow d'Antin who amounts to nothing any longer, he is ruining himself."

Lucien now recovered his old Paris energy and gaiety. He had learned to think of all those serious things only since the atrocious void and complete *disinterest* that had assailed him since his arrival in Nancy.

Very late that same evening Gauthier came up to see him.

"You find me altogether enraptured with this doctor," Lucien announced. "There isn't a more amusing charlatan in the world."

"He is more than a charlatan," replied the republican Gauthier. "When he was young and had very few patients, he used to prescribe a medicine and then rush to the apothecary's to make it up himself. Two hours later he would return to his patient to observe the effect. Today, he is to politics what he used to be to his profession. He is the man who should be prefect of the Department. In spite of his fifty years, the foundation of his character is the need of activity, he has the restless energy of a child. In short, he is madly in love with what most men can't abide: work. Talking, persuading, making things happen, and, above all, applying himself to overcoming difficulties, are necessities to him. He will dash up four flights of stairs to advise an umbrella manufacturer on the prevailing conditions in his trade. If the *legitimist* party had two hundred such men in France and knew how to use them, we republicans would be better treated by the government. What you do not realize yet is that Doctor Du Poirier has real eloquence. If he were not so fearful, fearful as a child, fearful to an incredible degree, he would be a dangerous man, even for us. He easily controls all the nobility of the province. He shares the honor with the Jesuit, M. Rey, our bishop's grand vicar. And not a week ago in an incident I shall tell you later, he got the better of Abbé Rey. I watch his moves closely because he is the rabid enemy of the *Aurore*. At the next elections, for which this restless soul is already working, he will permit one, or perhaps two, of the government candidates to win, on condition that the Prefect Fléron will let him suppress our *Aurore* and put me in prison. For he appreciates me as I appreciate him, and we like to argue together on occasion. He has two undeniable advantages over me: he is eloquent and amusing, and is the foremost man in his profession. He is justly considered the cleverest doctor in eastern France and is often called to Strasburg, to Metz, and to Lille. He only returned from Brussels three days ago."

"And so you would consult him if you were dangerously ill?"

"Heaven forbid! An inopportune dose of a good *medicine* would deprive the *Aurore* of the only one of its editors who, as Du Poirier says, is possessed of the devil."

"You tell me that they all have courage."

"Undoubtedly, and some of them are much cleverer than I am, but not all of them have, as their only love, the happiness of France and the Republic."

Lucien had now to endure on the part of the worthy Gauthier what the young men of Paris call a *thick slice* on America, on democracy, on forcing the government to choose prefects from among the members of the general assemblies, etc.

Listening to these arguments which he had already seen printed over and over again, Lucien thought: "What a difference in wit between a Du Poirier and a Gauthier, and yet the latter is probably as honest as the other is unscrupulous. In spite of my profound esteem for Gauthier I am falling asleep. After this, can I possibly say that I am a republican? This proves that I am not made to live in a republic. For me it would be the tyranny of dull people, and I cannot even endure the best of them with patience. What I need is a rascally and amusing prime minister like Walpole or M. de Talleyrand."

Meanwhile Gauthier was terminating his discourse with these words: *But we have no Americans in France.*

"You only have to take any little shop-keeper of Rouen or Lyon, miserly and devoid of imagination, and you have your American."

"Ah, how you grieve me!" cried Gauthier sadly, getting up to leave as one o'clock was striking.

"Grenadier, oh, how you grieve me!" sang Lucien when he was gone. "And yet I respect you with all my heart." After which he thought to himself: "The doctor's visit is a commentary on my father's letter. . . . One must howl with the wolves. M. Du Poirier very evidently wants to convert me.

Well then, I shall give him the pleasure of converting me. . . .
I have just found the way of silencing the rogues: I shall answer
their sublime doctrines, their hypocritical appeals, with this
modest question: 'What do I get out of it?' "

CHAPTER NINE

THE NEXT DAY very early in the morning, that restless soul, Doctor Du Poirier, knocked at Lucien's door.
He too was in favor of avoiding the presence of Bilars.
He counted on making use of arguments which he preferred
to communicate to a single person at a time, it being advisable
to remain in a position to deny them in case of necessity.

"If I cease reasoning like a rogue," thought Lucien as he
saw Du Poirier, "this rogue is going to despise me." The doctor,
bent on seducing this young man deprived of society and
probably dying of boredom, began by flaunting the great aristocratic houses and pretty women of Nancy.

"Ah, you rascal," thought Lucien, "I see what you are driving at."

"What interests me especially, my dear sir," he said aloud with
the dispirited air of a merchant who is the loser, "what interests me the most are your plans for the reform of the Civil
Code and the question of partition. These are questions that
can have a direct effect on my interests. For I am not without
some of *this world's earthly goods*." (It amused Lucien to
borrow the doctor's own provincial expressions.) "At the death
of the head of the house you are opposed, I understand, to
equal partition among the sons."

"Decidedly, sir, or else we shall fall into the horrors of democracy. An intelligent man will be forced, on pain of death,

to pay court to his neighbor, a man who sells matches. Most of our noble and distinguished families who are the hope of France, the only ones who have generous sentiments and lofty ideas, live in the country at this moment. They produce a great many children. Are we to see their fortunes divided, cut up piecemeal among all these children? Why, they would no longer have the leisure to develop distinguished sentiments, to cultivate high-mindedness; they would think of nothing but money, they would be vile proletarians just like the son of the printer next door. But on the other hand, what are we going to do with our younger sons, and how place them in the army as second-lieutenants after the highway robbery we have permitted those cursed non-coms? But that is a question to be taken up later on, a secondary question. First of all we must realize that it is impossible to restore the monarchy without a strong church, without having one priest, at least, to control a hundred peasants, for, with your absurd laws, our peasants have all become anarchists. Consequently, following the excellent example of England, I should place in the church at least one of the sons of every gentleman.

"I insist that even among the lower orders partition should not be equal. If you don't stop this evil pretty soon, all our peasants will know how to read and then, make no mistake about it, you will see an outbreak of incendiary writers. Everything will be called into question and you will soon have no sacred principles left. One must therefore begin with the principle, using as pretext the conservation of the land, that no property can be divided into parcels of less than two acres. . . .

"Let us take as an example what we know best, for that is always the surest way. Let us examine the interests of our noble families of Nancy."

"Ah, you old rascal!" thought Lucien.

Soon the doctor had reached the point where he was telling

Lucien that Madame d'Hocquincourt was the most seductive woman of Nancy; that there wasn't a wittier woman in the world than Madame de Puylaurens who had formerly been one of the shining lights of Madame de Duras' circle in Paris. Then, with a much more serious air, the doctor added that Madame de Chasteller was a very good "catch," and began to detail all her worldly goods.

"My dear Doctor, if I were in a matrimonial frame of mind my father has better than that for me in Paris. There is a certain young woman who is worth more than all these ladies put together."

"But you forget one little detail. What about birth?"

"Certainly it has its price," replied Lucien with a calculating air. "A young person who bears the name of *de Montmorency* or *de la Trémouille* would, in my position, be well worth a hundred, or even two hundred thousand francs. If I myself could boast a noble name, a great name in a wife would be worth a hundred thousand crowns. But, my dear Doctor, your provincial nobility is unknown thirty leagues away from home."

"What do you mean, sir?" exclaimed the doctor indignantly. "Madame de Commercy, cousin to the Emperor of Austria, descendant of the ancient sovereigns of Lorraine, unknown!"

"Absolutely, dear Doctor, like any M. Gontran or M. de Berval, who do not exist. The provincial nobility is known in Paris only through the ridiculous speeches of M. de Villèle's three hundred deputies. I am not considering marriage, however; for the moment I should much prefer prison. If I thought otherwise, my father would unearth some Dutch *bankeress* who would be enchanted to reign in my mother's drawing room, and very eager to buy such a privilege for a million or two, or even three."

Lucien was really comical, looking innocently at the doctor as he said these words.

The sound of that word *million* had a marked effect on the doctor's expression. "He is not impassive enough to make a good politician," thought Lucien. Never before had the doctor met a young man who, though brought up in the midst of great wealth, was absolutely free from hypocrisy. He began to be amazed at Lucien and to admire him.

The doctor was infinitely intelligent but he had never been to Paris, otherwise he would have detected duplicity. Lucien was not a man to be able to fool so arrant a knave as the doctor. Our second-lieutenant was by no means a finished actor. All he could boast was an easy manner and an ardent temperament.

Like all people who make a profession of Jesuitism, the doctor had an exaggerated idea of Paris. He saw it populated by furious atheists like Diderot or ironic ones like Voltaire, and by very powerful Jesuit Fathers who built enormous seminaries, bigger than barracks. He also had an exaggerated idea of Lucien; he was convinced that his patient was absolutely *heartless*. "Such ideas are not acquired," the doctor said to himself. And he began to respect our hero. "If this boy had spent four years in a regiment and taken a couple of trips to Prague or Vienna, he would be way beyond our d'Antins and Rollers. At least when we are alone together he doesn't rant."

After three weeks of an enforced retirement, rendered less tiresome by the almost constant presence of the doctor, Lucien went out for the first time; and for this first outing went to call on the postmistress, the worthy Mademoiselle Prichard, famous for her piety. There, on the pretext of fatigue, he sat down and, with a discreet and modest air, entered into conversation, finally taking out subscriptions to the *Quotidienne,* the *Gazette,* and the *Mode.* The worthy postmistress looked with veneration on this very elegant young man in uniform who took so many subscriptions, and to such papers!

Lucien had realized that in a *Juste-milieu* regiment any role was preferable to that of a republican, that is, the man who fights for a government which has no emoluments to distribute. Many of the *honorable* deputies *literally* could not understand such a degree of absurdity and considered it immoral.*

"It is only too evident that if I go on being a rational man, I shall not find the tiniest drawing room where I can spend an evening. According to the doctor, these people seem to be both too mad and too stupid to understand reason. They never get out of the superlative mood. But it is altogether too dull to be *Juste-milieu* like Colonel Malher, and to wait every morning the arrival of the post to know what platitude one must preach for the next twenty-four hours. As a republican I have just fought a duel to prove that I am not one; there is only one disguise left for me, and that is as the friend of 'privileges' and of the religion which supports them.

"It is the role indicated by my father's fortune. With the exception of a man of great wit, but extraordinary wit like my father, where can you find a rich man who is not a *conservative?* When they take exception to the nudity of my bourgeois name, I shall reply by pointing out the number and quality of my horses. As a matter of fact, isn't whatever distinction I enjoy in Nancy due entirely to my horse? And not in the least because it is a good horse but because it cost a great deal. Colonel Malher de Saint-Mégrin persecutes me, and, by gad, I am going to use high society as a club with which to crush him.

"This doctor should be very useful. He has altogether the air of those people who attach themselves to the privileged class with the function of thinking for them. It was formerly Cicero's role with the patricians of Rome extenuated by a century of happy aristocracy. It would be amusing if at heart this entertaining doctor did not believe in Henri V any more than in God, the Father."

* Historical.

The austere virtue of M. Gauthier might well have taken grave exception to this role assumed so gaily. But M. Gauthier was rather like those virtuous women who speak ill of actresses; he was not even amusing when he talked about people who were considered exceptionally amusing.

The evening of the day on which Lucien had made the acquaintance of Mademoiselle Prichard, the doctor came to see him. He began a sermon on the subject of the workingmen in the tone of an infuriated Juvenal. He spoke of their appalling poverty, exploited by the Jacobin pamphlets, that would be the downfall of Louis-Philippe. All at once, as five o'clock struck, the doctor cut himself short in the middle of a sentence and rose to go.

"Why! what is it, Doctor?" asked Lucien in surprise.

"It is time for Benediction," tranquilly replied the doctor, piously lowering his little eyes, and simultaneously dropping the furious tone of a Juvenal declaiming against the court at the Tuileries.

Lucien burst out laughing. Then sincerely regretting this involuntary outburst, he tried to apologize to the doctor, but an uncontrollable paroxysm got the better of him again and he laughed till tears came to his eyes, and he was soon actually crying with laughter, all the time repeating:

"So sorry, Doctor, forgive me, where is it you are going? I did not quite hear what you said."

"To Benediction at the Chapel of the Penitents." And the doctor gravely and learnedly explained this religious ceremony in a pious, contrite and hardly audible voice, which was a strange contrast to the harsh, impudent, and piercing tones which were habitual with him.

"This is perfect," Lucien said to himself, trying to prolong the explanation and to keep back the laughter that was suffocating him. "This man is my salvation. Without him I was

going into a decline. But I really must find something to say
to him or he will be offended."

"How would it be, Doctor, if I accompanied you?"

"Nothing could do you greater credit," he calmly replied, not
in the least angry at Lucien's unaccountable mirth. "But I must,
for conscience' sake, object to this second outing as I did to
the first. The damp evening air may bring back the inflam-
mation and if we happen to offend the great artery, then we
may have to start thinking of the long journey."

"Have you no other objection?"

"You will expose yourself to the Voltairean witticisms of the
gentlemen who are your comrades-in-arms."

"Bah! I am not afraid of them. They are much too good
courtiers for that. The Colonel told us the first Sunday after
our arrival, and in the most significant manner, that he always
went to Mass."

"In spite of that, nine of these gentlemen, your comrades,
again failed in this duty last Sunday. But, indeed, what difference do their stupid jokes make to you? Your way of silencing
them is already well known in Nancy. And, moreover, your
wise and prudent conduct has already borne fruit. No later
than yesterday, at M. le Marquis de Pontlevé's, when it was
alleged that you were a pillar of the reading room of that
blackguard Schmidt, Madame de Chasteller deigned to come
to your defense. Her maid, who spends her life at the window
overlooking the Rue de la Pompe, had told her that Colonel
Malher de Saint-Mégrin was most unfair to make a scene on
that account; that never once had she seen you go into that
shop although she often sees you ride by on your fine horse
worth a thousand crowns, and that with your elegant and well-
groomed air you didn't look—you must pardon the word, more
accurate than refined, of a servant . . ." and the doctor hesitated.

"Come, Doctor, I won't be offended."

"Well, since you insist: that you didn't look like a *lousy republican."*

"I must admit, sir," replied Lucien gravely, "that I cannot imagine going to read in a *shop!"* This last word was admirably launched. A man born in the Faubourg Saint-Germain could not have done better. "In a few days," continued Lucien, "I shall be able to offer you the few papers an honest man can permit himself to read."

"I know, I know," said the doctor with a little air of provincial smugness. "Mademoiselle Prichard, our postmistress, who *thinks right,* told us this morning that we should soon have a fifth *Quotidienne* in Nancy."

"Oh, this is too much!" thought Lucien. "Is this uncouth individual trying to make fun of me?" Those words *fifth Quotidienne* said with such a contrite air were well calculated to trouble our hero's vanity.

In this as in many other things, Lucien showed that he was young, that is, unjust. Full of good intentions, he believed that he saw everything, whereas he had not seen a quarter of what there was to be seen in life. How was he to know that these little flourishes are as necessary to provincial hypocrisy as they would be ridiculous in Paris. And naturally as the doctor was living in the provinces he had every reason to speak their language.

"I shall soon see if this man is making fun of me or not," thought Lucien, as he summoned his servant to attach the elegant black ribbons that were to tie up the right sleeve of his uniform, and followed the doctor to Benediction. This holy ceremony took place at the Penitents, a charming little church freshly white-washed and without other ornament than a few confessionals of polished black walnut. "A modest place," thought Lucien, "but in excellent taste." He quickly perceived that the congregation was made up only of members of the best society.

Lucien saw the beadle offer a penny to a woman of a lower class, not badly dressed, who, seeing the church open, seemed on the point of entering.

"Go along, my good woman," said the beadle, "this is a private chapel."

The gratuity was evidently an insult. The respectable woman blushed up to her eyes and let the penny fall to the ground; the beadle looked around to see that no one was watching him, picked it up and put it back in his pocket.

"All these women around me and the few men with them certainly have a perfectly well-bred appearance," thought Lucien. "The doctor is not making fun of me any more than of the rest of the world. What more could I ask?" His vanity reassured, Lucien began to enjoy himself immensely. "It is the same here as in Paris, the nobility believes that religion makes people easier to govern. And my father says that it was the people's hatred for the priests that brought about the fall of Charles X! I shall ennoble myself by becoming devout."

He noticed that everyone carried a breviary. "To come here is not enough, one must be exactly like everyone else in the place." He appealed to the doctor. Immediately the latter left his seat and went to borrow one from Countess de Commercy who had brought several with her, carried by her lady companion in a velvet bag. The doctor returned with a superb little *quarto* and explained to Lucien the coat of arms that ornamented the magnificent binding. Across one corner of the escutcheon was the eagle of the House of Hapsburg. Madame de Commercy did indeed belong to the House of Lorraine, but to an elder branch that had been unjustly dispossessed and for some reason, not altogether clear, considered herself nobler than the Emperor of Austria. Lucien listened to all these fine things but feeling himself stared at, and fearing an attack of uncontrollable laughter, he kept his eyes studiously bent on the spread eagle of Lorraine tooled on the cover of the breviary.

Toward the end of the service Lucien, whose chair almost touched the doctor's, felt sure that it would not be considered indiscreet if he let it be seen that he could hear the conversation the doctor was carrying on with five or six ladies, both married and maiden, all well along in years. These ladies addressed themselves to the good doctor, as they called him, but it was evident that their entire dialogue was composed in honor of the brilliant uniform whose presence in the Church of the Penitents was the great event of the evening.

"He is that young millionaire officer who fought a duel a couple of weeks ago," whispered a lady sitting near the doctor. "But it seems he *thinks right.*"

"Why, I thought he had been mortally wounded!" replied her neighbor.

"Our good doctor saved him at the brink of the tomb," added a third.

"Isn't it true that he is a republican, and that his colonel tried to get him killed in a duel?"

"You can see for yourself that he isn't," the first replied with an air of marked superiority. "You can see for yourself he is one of us."

To which the second rejoined tartly:

"You may say what you like, my dear, but I have been assured that he is a near relative of Robespierre who was from Amiens. Leuwen is a North-of-France name."

Finding himself the hero of the conversation, Lucien could not help feeling pleased. Several months had passed since anything of the kind had happened to him. "They are so curious about me, these provincials," thought Lucien, "that sooner or later the doctor will have to present me to all these ladies who do me the honor of thinking that I am a member

of the late **M.** de Robespierre's family. I shall spend my evenings in a drawing room listening to the same sort of stuff I've
just heard, and my father's respect for me will rise: I shall
have got as far as Méllinet. With these respectable people you
can say anything that comes into your head; you need have
no fear of being ridiculous around here; they will never jest
at anybody who caters to their mania." At this moment they
began to talk about a subscription that was being taken up
for the famous Berryer, who twice or three times a year gave
proof of a really first class talent and saved the party from
ridicule. Like all men of genius who are profoundly absorbed
in a single idea, M. Berryer would very probably be obliged to
sell his lands.

"I should gladly contribute a gold piece," said one of the
singular individuals clustered around the doctor [Lucien
learned later that it was Madame la Marquise de Marcilly],
"but this M. Berryer, after all, is not *born* [not noble, in other
words]. I have nothing smaller than gold with me, so I shall
ask our good doctor to send his servant to me tomorrow after
the eight-thirty Mass, and I shall give him some silver."

"Your name, Madame la Marquise," replied the doctor as
though his dearest wish had been fulfilled, "will figure at
the very head of page fourteen of my great register with a
flexible back which I received, or rather, *we* received as a gift
from our friends in Paris."

"I am like M. Jabalot of Versailles in *Je fais mes farces,*"
Lucien was thinking, elated by his success. It is true, all eyes
were bent on his uniform. We should like to say by way of
excuse for our hero, that since he had left Paris he had not
once set foot in a salon. And to live deprived of stimulating
conversation is *no life at all.*

"And I," he said aloud, "shall take the liberty of begging **M.**
Du Poirier to put me down for forty francs. But my ambition

would be to see my name appear immediately after that of Madame la Marquise. That would, I am sure, bring me good luck."

"Very good, young man, very good," cried Du Poirier with the air of a fatherly prophet.

"If my comrades hear of this," thought Lucien, "look out for a second duel. Epithets of *hypocrite* are going to rain down on me. But how will they find out? They see no one belonging to this world. Possibly through the Colonel's spies. And faith, so much the better! I prefer *hypocrite* to republican."

Toward the end of the service Lucien was called upon for a great sacrifice. In spite of his immaculate white trousers he had to kneel down on the dirty stones of the Chapel of the Penitents.

CHAPTER TEN

SOON everyone left the Chapel, and Lucien, seeing that his trousers were hopelessly soiled, decided to go home. "But this little mishap is perhaps a virtue," he told himself. And he endeavored to walk very slowly so as not to pass the groups of devout women who were slowly mincing along the deserted and grass-grown street.

"I am curious to know what the Colonel will find to object to in this," he was thinking as the doctor came up with him. And dissimulation not being one of his accomplishments, it was not difficult for his new friend to guess his thought.

"Your Colonel is nothing but a dull *Juste-milieu*. We know him well," cried Du Poirier with an air of authority. "He is a poor devil always shaking in his boots for fear that any moment he will see his dismissal announced in the *Moniteur*. But I wonder where that one-armed officer is, I don't see him around, that *liberal,* decorated at Brienne, who now serves as the Colonel's spy."

They reached the end of the street and Lucien, walking slowly with his ears open to catch what people were saying about him, was worried for fear he might in some way betray his elation. He allowed himself a slight and very grave bow to three ladies walking almost in a line with him and speaking in loud voices. Then he shook the doctor's hand warmly and was gone. Mounting his horse he gave free rein to the laughter bottled up in him for the last hour. As he passed in front of Schmidt's reading room: "There you have the pleasure of being learned," he thought to himself. He caught sight of the one-armed liberal officer behind the greenish window-pane holding a copy of the *Tribune* and watching Lucien out of the corner of his eye as he passed. The next day among the élite of Nancy there was talk of nothing but the presence of a uniform at the Church of the Penitents and a uniform, moreover, whose right sleeve had been unsewn and tied up with ribbon. This was the young man who had come so near to appearing before his God. It was a day of triumph for Lucien. He did not, however, dare to risk Low Mass at eight-thirty. "This is going to bear fruit," he said to himself. "I must be seen at the Penitents whenever I am not on duty."

Toward ten o'clock he went in grand style to buy a *euchology* or breviary, magnificently bound by Muller. He would not allow the book to be wrapped in tissue paper, finding it amusing to carry it proudly under his left arm. "No one could have done it better in the middle of the *Restoration.* I am imitating Marshal S——, our Minister of War," and he laughed to himself. "With these provincials you can go as far as you please without danger. They don't know the meaning of the word ridicule." Still with his book under his arm, he went in person to take his forty francs to Du Poirier, and so had the opportunity of reading the list of subscribers. The top of each page was reserved for the names preceded by a *de* but, by some lucky chance, the name of Lucien Leuwen was the only exception and began the page immediately following that inscribed with the name of *Madame la Marquise de Marcilly!*

Taking him to the door, M. Du Poirier said with a judicial air:

"You may rest assured, sir, that your Colonel will not leave you standing the next time he has something to say to you. He will at least be polite. As for his good will, that is another question."

Never was prediction destined to be more promptly fulfilled. A few hours later the Colonel, whom Lucien saw some distance away on the promenade, beckoned him to approach, and invited him for dinner the following day. Lucien was disgusted with his oily manner that reeked of bourgeois familiarity. "In spite of his fine uniform and his courage this man is nothing but a churchwarden inviting his neighbor, the district attorney, to dinner." As Lucien was leaving, the Colonel observed:

"Your horse has admirable shoulders. For hocks like those, two leagues is nothing. I authorize you to continue your rides as far as Darney."

Darney was a little town six leagues from Nancy.

"O omnipotent nostrum!" cried Lucien in a burst of laughter as he galloped off toward Darney.

The evening held an even greater triumph for Lucien. Dr. Du Poirier insisted on presenting him at Madame de Commercy's.

The Hôtel de Commercy, situated at the back of a half-paved courtyard ornamented with rows of clipped lindens that formed a high hedge, was at first glance very gloomy, but on the other side of the house, Lucien caught a glimpse of a delightfully green English garden where he would have strolled with pleasure. He was received in a large drawing room hung in red damask with gilded moldings. The damask was a trifle faded but this fault was concealed by family portraits which produced an exceedingly handsome effect. All these heroes wore powdered wigs and were dressed in armor. There were immense armchairs with elaborately carved and gilded frames standing against the walls, and Lucien was terrified when he heard Madame de Commercy, turning to a lackey, utter the sacred words: "An armchair for Monsieur." To his relief, however, a very well-made modern armchair was brought forward instead.

The Countess was a tall thin woman who held herself very erect in spite of her advanced age. Lucien noticed that her laces were white. He detested yellowed laces. As for her expression, the lady had none. "Her features are not noble," thought Lucien, "but she wears them nobly."

Like the drawing room the conversation was noble, monotonous and slow, but without being especially ridiculous. On the whole, Lucien might have imagined himself in a house of elderly people of the Faubourg Saint-Germain. Madame de Commercy did not raise her voice inordinately, her gestures were not exaggerated like those of the young people of good society whom Lucien noticed on the street. "She is a relic of the polite age," he said to himself.

Madame de Commercy noticed with pleasure that Lucien frequently turned an admiring glance toward her garden. She told him that her son, who had lived for twelve years in succession at Hartwell (the house of Louis XVIII in England), had had this exact copy made of the gardens, on a smaller scale of course, as befitted a private individual. Madame de Commercy invited him to come and walk in her garden whenever he liked.

"Several persons come to stroll there without thinking themselves obliged to see the aged proprietress. The concierge has a list of all the strollers."

Lucien was touched by this attention and as he was a well-bred soul, only too well-bred, his reply fully expressed his gratitude. After this invitation, offered with such simplicity, there was no further question of mockery. He felt himself a new man. For several months Lucien had been deprived of polite society.

When he rose to take his leave, Madame de Commercy was able to remark without departing from the general tone of the conversation:

"I must admit, sir, this is the first time that the cockade you wear has been seen in this drawing room, but I hope you will bring it again, and often. It will always be a pleasure to receive a man with such distinguished manners and who, although still in his early youth, is so right-thinking."

"And all this for having gone to the Penitents!" he thought. To relieve his pent-up merriment, he could hardly resist a mad impulse to distribute five-franc pieces to all the lackeys lined up in a row in the ante-chamber as he went out.

And he discovered his own duty in this row of lackeys. "For a man who begins to be as right-thinking as I, it is a grave inconsistency to have only one servant." He asked M. Du Poirier to find him three trustworthy fellows and particularly ones who *thought right*.

Returning home, Lucien was a little like King Midas' barber. He was dying for someone to whom he could relate his good fortune. He wrote eight or ten pages to his mother requesting her to send handsome liveries for five or six domestics. "My father will be convinced, when he pays for them, that I am not yet a very pure Saint-Simonian."

A few days later, Madame de Commercy invited Lucien to dinner. Already assembled in the drawing room, where he had been careful to arrive precisely at half-past three, he found Madame de Serpierre with only one of her six daughters, M. Du Poirier, and two or three ancient ladies with their hus-

bands who were, for the most part, *Chevaliers de Saint Louis.*
They were evidently waiting for someone else. Soon a lackey
announced, *Monsieur and Madame de Sauve-d'Hocquincourt.*
Lucien was impressed: "It would certainly be impossible to
find a prettier woman anywhere. And for once rumor has
not lied." In her eyes was a warmth, a gaiety, a naturalness
that made it a joy just to look at them. On second glance he
found one fault in this charming young woman. Although
hardly twenty-five or -six, she already showed a tendency to
plumpness. A tall blond young man with drooping mustaches,
very pale and with a haughty, taciturn air, walked beside her.
This was her husband. Her lover, M. d'Antin, had come with
them. At table Lucien was placed on her right; she frequently
turned to him, said something in a low voice, and laughed.
"Such a frank gay laugh!" thought Lucien. "What a strange
contrast to the morose and antiquated bearing of the rest of
the company. In Paris we would say that it was a somewhat
daring gaiety. What enemies she must make, this pretty
woman! Even the most indulgent might well blame her for
exposing herself to the terrible disadvantages of calumny
for lack of a little restraint. The provinces offer certain com-
pensations, after all! In the midst of all these faces born for
boredom, the important thing is that the *leading lady* should
be attractive, and, by gad, this one is really charming. For
such a dinner I would be willing to go to the Penitents a
dozen times over."

Being a prudent man, Lucien made every effort to be agreeable to M. de Sauve-d'Hocquincourt, who insisted on always
using his two names, both being illustrious, the first under
Charles IX and the second under Louis XIV.

While listening to the slow, elegant and colorless discourse
of M. d'Hocquincourt, Lucien examined his wife. She might
have been twenty-four or twenty-five years old. She was blond,
with very large blue eyes full of a charming vivacity. They

were never languishing, only a little absent at times when anyone bored her, but a second later, struck by some original or amusing idea, they would again sparkle with the maddest gaiety. Her deliciously fresh mouth, delicately traced and clearly designed, gave an air of nobility to the whole head. A slightly aquiline nose completed the charm of this aristocratic countenance which was as changing as her changing fancies. In Paris Madame d'Hocquincourt would have passed for a beauty of the first rank; in Nancy people barely admitted that she was pretty.

By the end of dinner Lucien had a feeling of positive benevolence toward the Marquis d'Antin and his lovely mistress. When coffee was served, Du Poirier had the opportunity of replying discreetly to Lucien's numerous questions about Madame d'Hocquincourt.

"She sincerely adores her lover and commits the greatest follies for him. Her misfortune, or rather her greatest distinction, is that after two or three years of admiring a lover she begins to find certain things about him ludicrous. Soon he inspires a mortal boredom that nothing can cure. Then it's worth the price of admission to see how her kindness is tortured by her boredom, for she has the kindest heart in the world and cannot bear to be the cause of real suffering. What is really comical, (I'll tell you all the details another time), is that her last lover fell madly, tragically, in love with her at the very moment when he was beginning to bore her. She was terribly unhappy and for six months could not decide how to get rid of him with humanity. I saw the time approaching when she would come to me for a consultation on the subject. At such moments she is infinitely witty."

"And how long has M. d'Antin lasted?" asked Lucien with a candor that repaid the doctor for all his trouble.

"For thirty months. Everybody is astonished. But he has a temperament as mad as hers, and that holds her."

"And the husband? I have observed that bourgeois husbands are devilishly suspicious in this city."

"But have you only just begun to notice," asked Du Poirier with a comically ingenuous air, "that only among the aristocracy is there any gaiety and savoir-vivre left? Madame d'Hocquincourt has made her husband so madly in love with her that he cannot be jealous. It is she who opens all the anonymous letters sent to him. As for him, he is sincerely preparing himself for martyrdom."

"What martyrdom?"

"Another '93, which is a certainty should Louis-Philippe fall."

"And you think he is going to be overthrown! That is too amusing."

The future martyr had been a captain of grenadiers in Charles X's bodyguard, and had shown much valor in Spain and elsewhere. Those pale cheeks took on a little color only when the subject of the antiquity of his house came up, allied, it is true, to the Vaudemont, the Chatellux and the Lillebonne families and all that was noblest in the provinces. Lucien discovered that this brave man entertained a strange illusion. He imagined that his name was known in Paris, and by a sort of instinctive jealousy fell into a terrible rage when he heard of people making names for themselves through their writing. Béranger had just been mentioned, and was cited as a powerful devil who had brought about the fall of Charles X.

"He must be very proud of that," someone said.

"Not as proud, I should imagine," M. d'Hocquincourt energetically retorted, "as if his ancestors had followed Saint-Louis to the crusades."

This dialogue delighted Lucien, who had the double pleasure of learning interesting facts while not being in the least deceived by the speakers; he was brusquely interrupted. Madame de Commercy summoned him to present him to Madame de

Serpierre, a tall, spare woman, extremely devout, who had a rather limited fortune and six marriageable daughters. The one sitting beside her had hair of an incredibly daring red, was very nearly five feet five inches tall, and wore a voluminous white dress with a green sash six inches wide which emphasized her thin flat figure to perfection. This green on white seemed frightfully ugly to Lucien. It was not on account of politics that Lucien was shocked by the bad taste he had found in *foreign parts.*

"Are the other five sisters as seductive as this one?" he asked when he had returned to the doctor.

All at once the doctor assumed an air of profound gravity. His expression changed as if by command, to the great amusement of the second-lieutenant, who chanted to himself with the accentuation of a military command, "Rascal be—*grave!*"

Meanwhile, Du Poirier spoke at length of the high lineage and equally lofty virtue of these young ladies, facts which Lucien never dreamed of disputing. After a lot of pompous phrases, the wily doctor reached the point of his discourse:

"What is the use of speaking ill of women who are not pretty?"

"Ah! I've caught you, Doctor! A most indiscreet speech. *You* are the one who says that Mademoiselle de Serpierre is not pretty, and I shall be able to quote you!" Then, with a profound and serious air, he added:

"If I wished to lie all the time and about everything, I should go to dine with cabinet ministers. They at least have positions or money to distribute. But I have plenty of money and no ambition for any position but the one I hold. Why open one's mouth if it is only to lie. Especially buried here in the provinces, and at a dinner where there is only one pretty woman! That is really too heroic for your humble servant."

After this sally our hero proceeded to follow the doctor's hint. He paid assiduous court to Madame de Serpierre and her daughter, and abandoned in the most marked fashion the brilliant Madame d'Hocquincourt.

In spite of her unfortunate hair, Mademoiselle de Serpierre turned out to be simple, intelligent, and not even malicious, which was a great surprise to Lucien. After a half-hour's conversation with mother and daughter, he left them with regret to follow the advice that Madame de Serpierre had just given him. He went to ask Madame de Commercy to introduce him to the other aged ladies in the drawing room. During the tiresome conversations that followed he glanced over at Mademoiselle de Serpierre on the other side of the room, and found her infinitely less shocking. "So much the better," he thought, "my role will be less painful. It is all right to laugh at the doctor, but I must obey him. Only by courting the old, the ugly, and the ridiculous can I make my way through this inferno. To talk with Madame d'Hocquincourt as much as I should like is, alas, too much for a stranger to expect in this society, a stranger, moreover, who is not noble. The reception accorded me is astonishingly gracious. I wonder what plot is concealed beneath." Madame de Serpierre was so edified by the politeness of this second-lieutenant who soon came over to sit beside her "Boston" table, that instead of finding he had a "Jacobin and July-hero air" (her first comment about him) she declared. that his manners were most distinguished.

"What is his name exactly?" she asked Madame de Commercy, and seemed profoundly grieved when the reply gave her the fatal assurance that it was irremediably bourgeois.

"Why didn't he take the name of the village where he was born, as they all do? It is a civility they really should observe if they want to be tolerated in polite society."

This remark was addressed to Théodelinde de Serpierre who, kindhearted as she was, had suffered all during dinner over Lucien's embarrassment at not being able to use his right arm.

A lady of some importance coming in just then, Madame de Serpierre told Lucien that she intended to introduce him and, without waiting for his reply, began to explain the antiquity of the house of Furonière, to which this lady belonged, loud enough so that the lady could hear everything being said about her.

"This is really farcical," thought Lucien, "addressed to me who am patently not noble, whom she has met for the first time, and to whom she wishes to be obliging! In Paris we would call it tactlessness. In the provinces people are more natural."

Hardly had the presentation to Madame Furonière taken place than Madame de Commercy called Lucien to introduce him to still another lady who had just arrived. "One more call to pay," Lucien thought to himself after each presentation. "I must write down all these names, together with a few historic and heraldic details, otherwise I shall forget them and commit some shocking blunder. The foundation of my conversation when talking with these new acquaintances will be requests for further details on their noble rank."

The very next day, in his tilbury, followed by two lackeys on horseback, Lucien went to leave cards on the ladies to whom he had had the honor of being presented the previous evening. To his great astonishment he was received almost everywhere, everyone being curious to have a closer view of him; and all these ladies who knew about his great fortune were full of solicitude for his wounded arm. His behavior was perfect, but he was worn out when he arrived at Madame de Serpierre's. He consoled himself with the thought that he would find Mademoiselle Théodelinde, the tall girl of the evening before whom he had at first thought so ugly.

A lackey dressed in a light green livery six inches too long, showed him into a perfectly immense drawing room pleasantly enough furnished, but badly lighted. The whole family rose as he entered. "That comes from their gesticulating mania," he thought. And although respectably tall himself, he found himself almost the shortest person in the company. "Now I understand the enormous size of the drawing room. Such a family could never have fitted into an ordinary apartment."

The father, an old gentleman with white hair, startled Lucien. He was the exact replica, in clothes and manners, of a provincial actor in the role of the *noble father*. He wore the cross of Saint-Louis hung on a very long ribbon with a wide white border, indicating, no doubt, the order of the Lily. He spoke very well and with a kind of grace suitable to a gentleman of seventy. Everything was going wonderfully until, speaking of his past, M. de Serpierre told Lucien that he had been King's Lieutenant at Colmar.

At the word Colmar, Lucien was seized with a feeling of horror which his candid and expressive face must have unconsciously betrayed, for the old officer hastened to make it clear in the most honorable way and not in the least offended, that he had been absent from Colmar at the time of the Colonel Caron affair.

This keen emotion made Lucien forget all his plans. He had come disposed to make fun of the sisters with their red hair and grenadier stature, of this mother with such an amiable disposition, always angry, always criticizing, bent on marrying off all her daughters.

The old officer's gallant attitude toward the Colmar affair sanctified the whole household. From that moment there was nothing ridiculous about them in his eyes.

My benevolent reader is asked to remember that our hero is young; very ingenuous, and without the least experience. All this, however, cannot prevent our feeling a painful sensation in being forced to acknowledge that he still had the extraordinary weakness to get indignant over political matters. At that period he was a naïve soul with no knowledge of himself. He was by no means one of those strong-minded individuals of superior intelligence who judge everything in the most categorical fashion. In his mother's drawing room, where people made fun of everything, he had learned to laugh at hypocrisy and to detect it pretty well. But he had no conception of himself or what he would one day become.

When he was fifteen, and had just begun to read the newspapers, the disgraceful trap set for Colonel Caron, which resulted in his death, was the last important act of the government of that day. It had served as a text for all the newspapers of the opposition. This famous piece of knavery was moreover perfectly intelligible to a boy; with all the details in his possession it was like a geometric demonstration.

Having recovered from the emotion caused by the mention of Colmar, Lucien looked at M. de Serpierre with interest. He was a handsome old gentleman about five feet nine inches tall with an erect carriage and beautiful white hair that gave him an altogether patriarchal air. In the bosom of his family he wore an ancient royal-blue costume with a straight collar and a very military cut. "Apparently in order to wear it out," thought Lucien. This seemed to him very touching, accustomed as he was to the vain, coquettish old gentlemen of Paris. The absence of all affectation, and above all the wisdom of his conversation well provided with facts, completed Lucien's conquest. The absence of affectation seemed to Lucien especially incredible in the provinces.

During the greater part of his visit, Lucien paid much more attention to this brave soldier who related at length all the campaigns of the *emigration,* and all the injustices of the Austrian generals who tried to find ways of humiliating the corps of *émigrés,* than to the six great girls who surrounded him. "I must really," he thought finally, "pay some attention to them." All the young ladies were sitting with their needlework around a single lamp, for oil was very high that year.

They spoke in a natural manner. "It is as though they are asking to be forgiven for not being pretty."

They never raised their voices; they never coyly bent their heads at an interesting point in their conversation; they did not seem to be constantly thinking of the effect they were making on the company; they did not give endless details on the rarity or the manufacture of the stuff of which their gowns were made; they did not call a painting a *great page in history,* etc., etc. In short, if it hadn't been for the hard and malicious face of Madame de Serpierre, their mother, Lucien would have been completely happy and uncritical that evening. As a matter of fact, he succeeded in quite forgetting her remarks and found real pleasure in conversing with Mademoiselle Théodelinde.

CHAPTER ELEVEN

DURING THIS CALL, which should have lasted twenty minutes and which lasted two hours, the only disagreeable remarks Lucien heard spoken were a few spiteful words from Madame de Serpierre. This lady had prominent features, imposing but lifeless. Her large eyes, dull and expressionless, followed every move Lucien made and chilled him to the bone. "God, what a creature!" he said to himself.

From time to time, out of politeness, Lucien deserted the circle around the lamp composed of the de Serpierre young ladies, to chat with the former lieutenant to the King. The latter liked to explain that France would never again know peace and tranquillity until the exact conditions of 1786 had been restored.

"That was the beginning of our decadence," the good old gentleman repeated several times. *"Inde mali labes."*

Nothing could have been more absurd in Lucien's eyes, for he believed that it was precisely since 1786 that France had begun to rise from the state of barbarism in which it was still partly submerged.

Four or five young men, aristocrats without a doubt, appeared in the drawing room one after the other. Lucien noticed them taking poses. They would lean one elbow elegantly on the black marble mantelpiece, or on a gilded console between the windows. Whenever they abandoned one of these graceful poses for another equally graceful, they did it with such quick, violent movements one would have thought they were obeying a military command.

Lucien was thinking: "All this is perhaps necessary in order to impress provincial young ladies," when he was roused from his philosophical meditations by a dawning realization that these fine young gentlemen with their affected poses were endeavoring to make him feel the great distance that existed between himself and them, whereupon he tried to make it equally plain that he returned their sentiments a hundredfold.

"Are you, by chance, offended?" asked Mademoiselle Théodelinde, coming up to him.

There was such simplicity and good nature in this question that Lucien replied with the same candor:

"So little offended that I shall ask you to tell me the names of these pretty gentlemen who, if I am not mistaken, are most anxious to make an impression on you. It is, therefore, to your lovely eyes that I owe the marks of aversion with which they honor me at this moment."

"That young man talking to my mother is M. de Lanfort."

"He is very handsome, and that one over there looks civilized. But who is the gentleman leaning on the mantelpiece with such a ferocious air?"

"That is M. Ludwig Roller, former cavalry officer. The two next to him are his brothers, also officers who resigned after the revolution of 1830. They have no fortune of their own and were entirely dependent on their army pay. Now they have only one horse for the three of them and their conversation suffers in consequence. They can no longer talk of what you military men call equipment, the weight of cloth and plate and other amusing things. They have no longer any hope of becoming marshals of France, like Marshal de Larnac who was the great-great-grandfather of their grandmother."

"Your description makes them altogether charming. And that fat fellow, the short stocky one, who looks at me now and then with such disdain, blowing out his cheeks like a wild boar?"

"What! You don't know who that is? He is the Marquis de Sanréal, the richest man in the province."

The conversation between Lucien and Mademoiselle Théodelinde was to all appearances very lively; for that very good reason it was interrupted by M. de Sanréal who, annoyed by Lucien's happy air, came over and spoke to Mademoiselle Théodelinde almost in a whisper, without paying the slightest attention to our second-lieutenant.

In the provinces everything is permitted to a rich and unmarried man.

Suddenly Lucien was reminded of the proprieties by this act of semi-hostility. The antique clock hanging on the wall, almost eight feet from the ground, had a pewter face so ornately decorated that it was impossible to make out either the hours or the hands. It struck, and Lucien was amazed to discover that he had been at the de Serpierre's for two whole hours. He left.

"Now we shall see whether I have those aristocratic prejudices my father is always teasing me about." He went to Madame Berchu's. There he found the Prefect just finishing a game of Boston.

As soon as M. Berchu saw Lucien he said to his wife, an enormous creature of fifty or sixty years of age:

"My little one, aren't you going to offer M. Leuwen a cup of tea?"

And as Madame Berchu did not hear him, M. Berchu repeated "my little one" several times.

"Is it my fault," thought Lucien, "if these people always make me want to laugh?" When he had finished his cup of tea he went over to admire the really very pretty dress Mademoiselle Sylviane was wearing that evening. It was made of some Algerian stuff with very wide stripes of chestnut and pale yellow. In the light, these colors had a most pleasing effect.

The lovely Sylviane responded to Lucien's admiration by recounting in great detail the history of this remarkable dress: it came from Algiers, it had been in Mademoiselle Sylviane's wardrobe a very long time, etc., etc. The lovely Sylviane, oblivious of her rather colossal girth, was careful to bend and to twist and to turn as she pointed out all the most interesting details of this touching history. "Ah, the lovely curves," thought Lucien, trying to be patient. Mademoiselle Berchu could undoubtedly have posed for one of those Goddesses of Reason of 1793, which had just been the subject of M. de Serpierre's long discourse. Mademoiselle Sylviane would have indeed been proud to be carried on a platform by eight or ten stalwart men through the streets of the city.

The history of the dress finished, Lucien no longer felt any desire to talk. He listened to the Prefect reciting an article from the *Débats* with ponderous fatuity. "These people never converse, they lecture," thought Lucien. "If I sit down I shall go to sleep. I must fly while I still have the strength." He looked at his watch in the ante-chamber. He had stayed barely twenty minutes at Madame Berchu's.

So as not to forget his new acquaintances, and, especially, so as not to get them mixed up, which would have been disastrous considering the susceptibility of provincial pride, Lucien took the precaution of drawing up a list of his friends of recent date. He arranged them according to rank like the lists the English papers always publish of the Almack Balls. Here is the list:

"Madame la Comtesse de Commercy, House of Lorraine.

"M. le Marquis and Madame la Marquise de Puylaurens.

"M. de Lanfort, quotes Voltaire and repeats all Du Poirier's arguments on the Civil Code and on partition.

"M. le Marquis and Madame la Marquise de Sauve-d'Hocquincourt; M. d'Antin, Madame's lover. The Marquis a brave man dying of fright.

"The Marquis de Sanréal, short, fat, unbelievably fatuous, and an income of a hundred thousand pounds.

"The Marquis de Pontlevé and his daughter, Madame de Chasteller, the best 'catch' in the province, millions, and the object of the desires of MM. de Blancet, de Goëllo, etc., etc. Warned that Madame de Chasteller would never receive me on account of my cockade; should have to go in civilian clothes.

"The Comtesse de Marcilly, widow of a *cordon rouge;* great grandfather, a marshal of France.

"The three Comtes Roller: Ludwig, Sigismond, and André, brave officers, inveterate horsemen, and very discontented. The three brothers always say exactly the same thing. Ludwig has a ferocious air and looks at me with disapproval and a jaundiced eye.

"The Comte de Vassigny, former lieutenant-colonel, a man of intelligence and wit; try to get better acquainted. Furnishings in good taste, valets well groomed.

"People whom I know but with whom conversation must be avoided, for one conversation leads to a dozen more and they talk like yesterday's newspaper: M. and Madame de Louvalle; Madame de Saint Cyran; M. de Bernheim; MM. de Jaurey, de Vaupoil, de Serdan, de Pouly, de Saint-Vincent, de Pelletier-Luzy, de Vinaert, de Charlemont."

Lucien was such a novice that he was surprised neither by the excellent reception which this noble society of Nancy had accorded him (with the exception of the young men), nor by the doctor's assiduity in cultivating his company and in acting as his patron.

In spite of his passionate eloquence and insolence, Du Poirier was a singularly timid man. He had never been to Paris and life there assumed monstrous proportions in his imagination. He was, however, dying to visit it. His correspondents had long ago told him all sorts of things about M. Leuwen Senior. "In the Leuwen house," the doctor said to himself, "I should find an excellent dinner gratis, influential men with whom I could converse and who, in case of any mishap, would protect me. Thanks to the Leuwens I should not be completely alone in that Babylon. This young fellow writes everything to his parents; they must know already that I am his patron here."

Mesdames de Marcilly and de Commercy, both of them well over sixty, by whom Lucien had the wit to allow himself to be invited frequently to dinner, had introduced him to all Nancy. Lucien followed to the letter the advice that Mademoiselle Théodelinde had given him.

He had not spent a week in this élite society before he observed that it was torn by violent schisms.

At first, terribly ashamed of this disunion, they tried to hide it from a stranger. But animosity and passion were too strong for them. For there is one good thing that can be said for the provinces: *passion still exists there.*

M. de Vassigny, and all reasonable people, believed that they were living under the reign of Henri V, while Sanréal, Ludwig Roller and all the most fanatical, refused to accept the abdications at Rambouillet, and looked forward to the reign of Louis XIX after that of Charles X.

Lucien went often to what was called the Hôtel Puylaurens. It was a big house situated at the extremity of a faubourg occupied by tanners, and in the neighborhood of a very odoriferous river about twelve feet wide.

Above a row of little square windows, that lighted the carriage houses and stables, could be seen a long line of large windows surmounted by little tile roofs. These little roofs were there to serve as protection for the Bohemian glass windowpanes. Thus shielded from the rain for the last twenty years, they had never been washed and suffused the interior with a dim, yellowish light.

In this gloomiest of apartments lighted by these dusty windowpanes, might be seen, seated at an ancient Boule desk, a tall, lean man still wearing, for the sake of his political principles, powder and queue, although he would often frankly admit that short hair without powder was far more comfortable. This martyr to principle was very old and was called the Marquis de Puylaurens. During the emigration he had been the faithful companion of an august personage. Later that personage, when he became all-powerful, had been very much criticized for not having done anything for a man whom his courtiers called a *friend of thirty years' standing*. Finally, after many solicitations, which M. de Puylaurens often found extremely humiliating, he was named Collector-General at ——.

Ever since those days of distasteful soliciting that had finally led to *financial* employment, M. de Puylaurens, bitter against the family to whom he had consecrated his life, saw everything in a somber light. But his principles had remained pure, and he would have sacrificed his life for them. "It is not," he would often repeat, "because he is an amiable man that Charles X is our king. Amiable or not he is the son of the Dauphin who was the son of Louis XV. That suffices." And in intimate gatherings he would add: "Is it the fault of legitimacy that the legitimate heir is an imbecile? Would my farmer be excused from his obligation to pay me the rent of his farm because I am ungrateful and a fool?" M. de Puylaurens loathed Louis XVIII: "That *enormous* egoist has given a sort of legitimacy to the Revolution. Because of him, revolt has a plausible excuse, ridiculous for us, but which can easily mislead the weak."

"Yes, my dear sir," he said to Lucien the day after the latter had been presented, "the crown is a freehold property and possession, nothing that the actual holder may do can bind his successor, not even a vow, for that vow was made at a time when he was a subject and could refuse nothing to his King."

Lucien listened to all this and much more with a very attentive, and even respectful air as became a young man, but he took care that his courteous air should not be mistaken for agreement. "As a plebeian and a liberal, I can only amount to something in the midst of all this vanity through opposition."

Du Poirier, when present, would unceremoniously break into the Marquis' discourse. "The result of so many fine things," he would say, "is that they will succeed in distributing the property of a commune equally among all the inhabitants. While waiting for this final goal of the *liberals,* the Civil Code undertakes to turn *our* children into little bourgeois. What noble fortune could withstand such a constant partition at the death of the head of every house? And that is not all. For our younger sons there was always the army; but as the Civil Code, which should be called the Infernal Code, preaches equality of fortunes, conscription brings with it the principle of equality in the army. Promotion is flatly governed by a law; nothing depends on the King's favor; and so, why please the King? Well, sir, from the moment one can ask that question monarchy no longer exists. Looking at it from another angle, what do I see? The absence of great hereditary fortunes—again, no monarchy! The only thing that is left us is a religious peasantry; for without religion, no more respect for men of wealth and noble birth, nothing but an infernal spirit of criticism; instead of respect, envy, and, at the slightest so-called injustice, revolt." Then the Marquis de Puylaurens would take up the refrain: "We have, therefore, no other resource than the recall of the Jesuits, to whom for the next forty years should be entrusted the dictatorship of education."

The most amusing thing was that in sustaining these opinions, the Marquis proclaimed himself, and believed himself to be, a patriot. In that he was far inferior to the old rascal Du Poirier who, as they were leaving M. de Puylaurens one day, said to Lucien:

"It is not for a man who has been born a duke, a millionaire, a peer of France to inquire whether his position is in accordance with virtue, the general good, and a lot of other fine things. His position is a good one; therefore he should do everything possible to maintain and to improve it; otherwise he is despised as a coward and a fool."

To listen to such discourses with an attentive and courteous air, never to yawn no matter how long and eloquent the development might be, such was Lucien's duty *sine qua non,* such was the price he had to pay for the extreme grace granted him by Nancy's aristocratic society in taking him to its bosom. "It must be admitted," he said to himself one evening as he returned home ready to fall asleep in the street, "it must be admitted that people a hundred times more noble than I am deign to address me in the most flattering and the most noble fashion, but they also overwhelm me with boredom. I cannot stand it any longer. True, when I get home I can go up to my landlord, to M. Bouchard's on the third floor where I am very apt to find his nephew Gauthier. He is a man of unequaled honesty, who will immediately hurl the most incontestable truths at me, but about things that are not in the least amusing, and in a manner whose simplicity approaches crudity when he gets excited. But why should that worry me? Except that they make me yawn.

"Am I doomed then to spend my life between mad, selfish, and polite legitimists in love with the past, and mad, generous, and boring republicans in love with the future? Now I can understand my father's saying: 'Oh, why wasn't I born in 1710 with an income of fifty thousand pounds!'"

The fine arguments which Lucien endured every evening in society and which the reader has only had to endure once, were the profession of faith of all among the nobility of Nancy, and the province rose little above the level of innocently repeating the articles in the *Quotidienne* and the *Gazette de France*. After one month of patience, Lucien began to find really unbearable this society of noble landed proprietors who talked as though they were the only people in the world, and of nothing but politics and the price of oats.

There was only one exception to this general boredom. Lucien was altogether delighted when, arriving at the Hôtel de Puylaurens, he found the Marquise at home. She was a tall woman of thirty-four or -five, or even more, who had superb eyes and a dazzling skin and, in addition, always seemed to be laughing at the whole world. She could tell a story to perfection and tossed off her ironies lavishly, without the least regard to parties. She almost invariably hit the nail on the head and there was laughter in any group where she was to be found. Lucien would willingly have fallen in love with her but the place was already taken, and Madame de Puylaurens' chief occupation was teasing the amiable young man called M. de Lanfort. Her pleasantries were in a tone of the tenderest intimacy, but no one was shocked. "Another advantage the provinces enjoy," thought Lucien. Moreover, he liked M. de Lanfort; he was one of the *natives* who did not shout.

Lucien became very much attached to the Marquise and at the end of two weeks she seemed to him pretty. There was a provoking mixture in her of provincial enthusiasm and Parisian urbanity. She had indeed completed her education at the court of Charles X while her husband was Collector-General in a remote department.

To please her husband and her Party, Madame de Puylaurens went to church two or three times a day; but the moment she set foot in the temple of our Lord it became a salon. Lucien would place his chair as near to Madame de Puylaurens as he could, thus discovering the secret of obeying the mandates of polite society with the least possible boredom.

One day when the Marquise and her friends had been laughing rather too noisily, a priest came over to her and ventured to remonstrate.

"It would seem, Madame la Marquise, that in God's house . . ."

"Is it to me, by chance, that this *Madame* is addressed? But really, my dear Abbé, you are too comical! Your function is to save souls and, considering your eloquence, if we didn't come here for the sake of our principles, you wouldn't have a soul here to save. Talk all you please in your pulpit; but kindly remember that your duty is to answer and not to ask questions. Your father, who was one of my lackeys, should have taught you better."

A burst of laughter, though more or less stifled, greeted this charitable advice. It was all quite amusing and Lucien did not miss the least shade of the little scene. But, to make up for it, he was obliged to listen to the account of it repeated a hundred times at least.

A serious quarrel arose between Madame de Puylaurens and

M. de Lanfort, and Lucien redoubled his assiduities. Nothing could have been more entertaining than the clashes between the two belligerent parties who continued to see each other every day; their behavior toward each other became the topic of the day.

Lucien often left the Hôtel de Puylaurens in the company of M. de Lanfort, and a certain intimacy sprang up between them. M. de Lanfort, who was fortunate enough to be well-born, was also without regrets. At the time of the revolution of 1830 he had been captain of cavalry, and was only too delighted to have an excuse for quitting a profession that bored him.

One morning, leaving the Hôtel de Puylaurens where he had been shockingly and publicly ill-treated, he said to Lucien:

"Nothing could induce me to put myself in the position of having to slaughter weavers and tanners which, as things are today, is your occupation."

"It must be admitted that the service since Napoleon doesn't amount to much," Lucien rejoined. "Under Charles X you were forced to be spies as at Colmar in the Caron affair, or as in Spain to take General Riego by treachery and let him be captured and killed by King Ferdinand. Such heroic deeds, I acknowledge, are neither to your taste nor mine."

"We should have lived under Louis XIV," de Lanfort conceded. "Then one spent one's life at court in the best society in the world, with Madame de Sévigné, M. le Duc de Villeroy, M. le Duc de Saint-Simon, and had nothing to do with soldiers, except to lead them to battle and win all the glory if there was any."

"That is all very well for you, M. le Marquis, but under Louis XIV I should have been nothing but a merchant, or at best a miniature Samuel Bernard."

At this point, much to their regret, Sanréal accosted them,

and the conversation took quite a different turn. They talked about the dry weather that would ruin all the landowners whose fields were not irrigated; they hotly discussed the necessity of an irrigation canal that would have its source in the Baccarat woods.

Lucien entertained himself by making a detailed examination of Sanréal. He was the prototype of the great provincial landed proprietor. He was a short man of thirty-three, with dirty black hair and a thick girth. He had all sorts of affectations and above all that of being good natured and unassuming, but without, for all that, disclaiming pretensions to subtlety and wit. This mixture of opposite pretensions, set off by a fortune which for the provinces was enormous, and a corresponding conceit, made of him a most extraordinary jackass. He was not exactly devoid of ideas, but so vain and conceited that one itched to toss him out of the window, especially when he was bent on being witty.

When he took your hand, one of his amiable pleasantries was to squeeze it until you cried out. He himself always shouted at the top of his lungs when he had nothing to say. He exaggerated all the marks of simplicity and good nature, and you could see that he said to himself a hundred times a day: "I am the greatest landed proprietor in the province and, in consequence, I ought to be different."

If some common carrier happened to have an altercation with one of his servants, he would immediately rush up to settle the quarrel and would have killed the carrier without compunction. His greatest title to glory, placing him at the head of all energetic and right-thinking men of the province, was to have arrested personally, in the midst of a great crowd, a wretched peasant, one of the many who were shot without knowing why by order of the Bourbons after the conspiracies, or rather the riots, which broke out during their reign. Lucien only learned this detail at a later date. Sanréal's own party was ashamed of him, and he himself, amazed at what he had done, began to wonder whether a gentleman, a great landed proprietor, should really have undertaken the office of a policeman, and worse still, have picked a wretched peasant out of a crowd to have him shot, practically without a trial, and after a simple appearance before a military commission.

The Marquis, and in this alone he resembled all the amiable marquises of the Regency, was almost completely drunk every day after one or two o'clock; and it was two o'clock when he accosted M. de Lanfort. At such times he talked without stopping and was the hero of all his stories. "He is not without energy, this man," thought Lucien, "and will never stick out his neck for the axe of another '93 like those devout sheep, the d'Hocquincourts."

The Marquis kept open house morning and evening, and when talking politics never descended from the heights of emphatic pomposity, and for a very good reason: he knew by heart twenty or more of M. de Chateaubriand's sayings, among others the one about needing only a hangman and six other persons to run a department.

To be able to sustain such a degree of eloquence, he always kept on a little mahogany table beside his armchair a bottle of cognac, a few letters from the other side of the Rhine, and a copy of *France,* the paper that contests the abdications of Rambouillet in 1830. No one entered Sanréal's house without drinking the King's health and that of his legitimate heir, Louis XIX.

"Gad, sir," said Sanréal, turning to Lucien, "perhaps one of these days we'll strike a blow together, if ever the great legitimists of Paris have the wit to shake off the yoke of the lawyers."

Lucien's reply had the good fortune of pleasing the Marquis who was already half drunk, and from that morning, which ended with a spiced wine at an *ultra* café of the city, Sanréal became altogether reconciled to Lucien.

But this heroic Marquis had his drawbacks. He could never hear the name of Louis-Philippe pronounced without shouting: *Robber!* in an odd, screeching tone. This was his great witticism which invariably caused all the noble ladies of Nancy to burst into fits of uncontrollable laughter, not once but ten times of an evening. Lucien was shocked by this eternal repetition and eternal mirth.

CHAPTER TWELVE

AFTER OBSERVING for the sixtieth or eightieth time the electrifying effect of this ingenious witticism, Lucien said to himself: "I should be a simpleton to tell these country clowns what I really think; everything about them, even their laughter, is an affectation; even in their lightest moments they are still thinking of '93!"

This observation decided the success of our hero. A few rather too sincere remarks had already tempered the infatuation which he had begun to inspire. The moment he began lying like a singing cicada to all comers, the infatuation began again and stronger than ever. But with spontaneity, all pleasure also vanished. And, by some sad law of compensation, with prudence, boredom returned. At the sight of any of Madame de Commercy's noble friends he knew by heart exactly what he must say to them, and what their replies would be. The most agreeable of these gentlemen had not more than eight or ten jokes at his disposal, and one can judge of their sense of humor by the Marquis de Sanréal's standing witticism, which was considered one of the brightest.

Moreover, boredom is such an irksome thing, even in the provinces, even to the people given to distributing it abundantly, that these vain gentlemen of Nancy, nothing loath to talk to Lucien, would stop him on the street. This bourgeois, who was right-thinking enough despite his father's millions, was a novelty. And in addition, Madame de Puylaurens, the arbiter of wit, had pronounced him witty. That was Lucien's first success. As a matter of fact, he was a little less green than on his departure from Paris.

Among the persons who had adopted Lucien, the one he preferred above any of the others was unquestionably the colonel, Count de Vassigny. Tall and blond and already quite wrinkled although still young, he had an intelligent instead of a haughty air. He had been wounded in July 1830 and yet never took advantage of this immense superiority. When he returned to Nancy he had the misfortune of inspiring a mad passion in little Madame de Ville-Belle. She was full of borrowed wit and had very beautiful eyes in which shone an unpleasant and ill-bred ardor. She dominated M. de Vassigny, annoyed him, prevented him from going to Paris which he was dying to see again, and insisted on his making an intimate friend of Lucien. M. de Vassigny would often come to Lucien's rooms. "This is too much," thought Lucien. "And what is there left me in this hole if I can't even enjoy privacy at home?" Lucien ended by noticing that, having sufficiently and expertly *sweetened* him with compliments and flattery, the count would begin plying him with questions. To get some fun out of the visits, Lucien would try answering in "Norman," since for these provincials, time apparently stood still and a call of two hours was nothing to them.

"What is the depth of the dry moat between the Palace of the Tuileries and the garden?" Count de Vassigny asked Lucien one day.

"I don't know," replied Lucien. "But it would, I judge, be difficult to cross with weapons in hand."

"Approximately, is it twelve or fifteen feet deep? But then the water from the Seine would seep into it."

"Ah, now that I think of it, I seem to remember that the bottom is always wet. However, it may only be three or four feet deep. I really never thought of investigating it, yet I have heard that moat spoken of as a military defense."

And for twenty minutes Lucien amused himself with these ambiguous replies.

One day, Lucien noticed that Madame d'Hocquincourt was getting terribly annoyed with M. d'Antin. This charming young man, so French, so heedless of the future, so ready to please, so inclined to gaiety, was on this particular day quite beside himself with love and dreamy tenderness. He had so far lost his head as to try to make himself more agreeable than usual. Instead of taking Madame d'Hocquincourt's polite hints that he should go for a walk and come back later, he did nothing but pace up and down the drawing room.

"Madam," said Lucien, "I should like very much to offer you a little English engraving in an adorable Gothic frame. I shall ask your permission to hang it in your drawing room, and the day I no longer see it in its place, to show you how bitterly I resent such a dastardly act, I shall never set foot in your house again."

"Now that's what I like, a man with some sense of humor!" cried Madame d'Hocquincourt, laughing. "You, at least, are not stupid enough to fall in love. . . . Great God! Is there anything under heaven more boring than love? . . ."

But such moments were rare for our poor Lucien, and once more his life became very dull and very monotonous. He had succeeded in breaking into the drawing rooms of Nancy, he had servants in attractive liveries, his dashing tilbury and calash could compare favorably by their newness with any of the equipages of M. de Sanréal and the other wealthy landed proprietors of the country, and he had had the satisfaction of being able to tell his father all the gossip of the first families of Nancy. In spite of all this he was quite as bored as when he spent his evenings wandering alone through the streets of Nancy when he didn't know a soul.

Often when he was on the point of entering one of the aristocratic homes, he would stop short in the street hesitating to expose himself to the torture of so many strident voices. "Shall I go in?" he would ask himself. Even from the street he could sometimes hear the shouting. The haranguing provincial is terrible in his distress; when he has nothing more to say he falls back on his lungs; he seems proud of them, and rightly so; for by that means, he very often gets the better of his adversary and reduces him to silence.

"The *ultra* of Paris is tamed," thought Lucien, "but here I find him in his wild state. It is a terrible species—noisy, *insulting,* accustomed never to be contradicted, able to talk for three quarters of an hour with the use of a single phrase. The most unbearable *ultras* of Paris, the ones who quickly empty a salon there, would seem well-bred, moderate, quiet people in the drawing rooms of Nancy."

Their loud voices Lucien found it hardest of all to endure; these he could not get used to. "I really ought to study them the way one studies natural history. M. Cuvier used to tell us in the *Jardin des Plantes* that to study methodically, carefully noting down all the differences and resemblances, was the surest way of curing oneself of the repulsion that worms, insects, and hideous sea-crabs inspire."

When Lucien met one of his new friends on the street, he naturally had to stop to speak to him. They looked at each other; they had nothing to say to each other; they talked about the weather—the heat or the cold. For, your provincial reads nothing but the newspapers, and after the hour for discussing the news is past he is at a loss for something to talk about. "It is really a calamity to be rich here," thought Lucien. "The rich have less to do than others and for that reason appear to be more malicious. They spend their time examining their neighbors' doings under a microscope. They have no other remedy for boredom but to spy on each other, and it is that which, for the first few months, conceals from a newcomer the sterility of their minds. When a father begins to tell some story known to his wife and children, the latter are obviously itching to interrupt, steal it from him, and recount it themselves; and often, with the pretext of adding some omitted detail, they begin the story all over again."

Sometimes, weary of the struggle, after dismounting from his horse, instead of getting himself dressed to go into the noble society of Nancy, Lucien would stay home and drink a glass of beer with his landlord, M. Bonard.

This worthy industrialist, who had little respect for power, said to Lucien one evening: "I could go to the Prefect himself and offer him a hundred louis for permission to import two thousand sacks of wheat from abroad, and yet his father has twenty thousand francs a year in emoluments."

Bonard had no more respect for the nobles of the city than for the magistrates.

"If it weren't for Du Poirier," he said, "these bastards wouldn't be so bad. I know that he comes to see you often. Well, I warn you, be careful! These nobles," he went on, "shake in their boots whenever the post from Paris is four hours late. Then they come running to me to sell their crops of wheat in advance. They are on their knees begging for gold, and next day, reassured by the news which has finally arrived, they barely return my greeting in the street. As for me, I do not think my honesty in the least compromised if I make them pay a louis extra for each rudeness. . . . I have an understanding with the valets they send to deliver their grain. For, would you believe it, sir, miserly as they are, they haven't the guts to come themselves to see their wheat weighed. At the fourth or fifth bushel, fat M. de Sanréal says that the dust hurts his lungs. A funny sort of *individual* to be thinking of re-establishing statute labor, Jesuits, and the ancient regime against us."

One evening after muster, while the officers were riding around the Parade Grounds, Colonel Malher de Saint-Mégrin gave way to an access of animosity against our hero.

"What about those four or five gaudy liveries with all their galloons you display on the streets? It has a very bad effect on the regiment."

"Faith, Colonel, I don't know of any article of the regulations that forbids spending money when one has it."

"Are you mad to talk to the Colonel like that?" his friend Filloteau whispered to him, taking him aside. "He'll do you an ugly turn."

"And what can he do? I think he already hates me as much as anyone can hate a man he sees so rarely. But I certainly am not going to truckle to a man who hates me without my having given him any reason to.

"At this particular moment, Colonel, I have *taken a notion* to these liveries; and, in addition to the liveries, I had twelve pairs of foils sent from Paris at the same time."

"Ah! What a fire-eater!"

"Why! not at all, Colonel! Upon my word, you haven't another officer in the regiment less fatuous or more peaceable than I. I am not looking for trouble and I hope nobody is going to come looking for it. I shall be perfectly polite and perfectly reasonable with everyone. But if anybody tries to plague me, he'll find me ready."

Two days later, Colonel Malher sent for Lucien and, with an embarrassed and hypocritical air, forbade him to keep more than two liveried servants. So Lucien promptly dressed the others in ordinary civilian suits, but which were the last word in elegance and formed a ludicrous contrast to the wearers' naturally coarse and clumsy appearance. He had them made by one of the tailors of Nancy, and this circumstance completed the success of Lucien's jest, doing him much honor in high society. Madame de Commercy complimented him, and, as for Mesdames d'Hocquincourt and de Puylaurens, both these ladies were quite mad about him.

Lucien wrote his mother a detailed description of the incident. The Colonel, on his part, in a letter to the Minister, censured Second-Lieutenant Leuwen severely. This Lucien had expected. About this time it seemed to him that his stock rose in the drawing rooms of Nancy. As it happened, Du Poirier had been showing everybody the answers he had received from friends in Paris to his letters asking for information on the social and business standing of the house of Van Peters, Leuwen and Company. The replies could not have been more favorable. "That house," he was told, "is one of the very few that, on occasion, buys news from the ministers, or exploits it on a fifty-fifty basis."

It was M. Leuwen Senior who indulged particularly in this somewhat risky business which, ruinous in the long run, makes for agreeable and influential connections. He was on the best terms with all the ministries and heard of Colonel Malher's reprimand in time.

This affair over his son's liveries amused him enormously. He at once began pulling strings, and one month later Colonel Malher de Saint-Mégrin received a most unpleasant ministerial letter.

The Colonel was very much tempted to detail Lucien to a detachment being sent to a certain manufacturing city where the workers were beginning to form a *mutual protection society*. But, after all, when one is head of a corps one has to eat humble pie. Meeting Lucien, the Colonel said to him with the perfidious smile of a man of the lower orders who thinks he is being shrewd:

"Young man, I have been informed of your prompt obedience in regard to the liveries. I am pleased with you. Have as many men in livery as you choose. But mind Papa's purse!"

"Colonel, I have the honor of thanking you," replied Lucien deliberately. *"My Papa* has written me on the subject. I should even be willing to wager that he has seen the Minister."

The smile accompanying the last remark was extremely distasteful to the Colonel. "Ah, if only I weren't a colonel with the ambition of becoming a major-general!" thought Malher, "my sword would answer that last remark, the insolent brat!" And he saluted the second-lieutenant with the frank, abrupt air of an old soldier.

And so it was that through a combination of force and prudence, as the serious books say, Lucien fairly doubled the hate against him in the regiment. No unpleasant remark, however, was brought to him officially. Several of his comrades were amiable enough, but Lucien had formed the bad habit of speaking to his comrades only as much as strictest politeness demanded. By means of this amiable way of living he bored himself mortally and contributed in no way to the pleasures of the young officers of his own age; he had the faults of his century.

By this time the effect of novelty, that had at first made Nancy society seem amusing, had completely worn off. Lucien knew all the characters by heart. He was reduced to philosophizing. He decided that there was more naturalness here than in Paris, but, as a natural consequence, that the fools were much more tiresome in Nancy. "What I find completely lacking in all these people," thought Lucien, "is the unexpected." This unexpected Lucien sometimes glimpsed in Doctor Du Poirier and in Madame de Puylaurens.

CHAPTER THIRTEEN

LUCIEN had never yet met in society that Madame de
Chasteller who had seen him thrown off his horse
the day of his arrival in Nancy; he had forgotten her;
but from force of habit he still rode through the Rue de la
Pompe almost every day. He was now much more apt to glance
at the liberal officer, the spy stationed at the bookseller
Schmidt's, than at the window with the parrot-green shutters.

One afternoon these shutters were open. Lucien noticed a
pair of charming embroidered muslin curtains. Almost unconsciously, he began to put his horse through its paces. It was not
the prefect's English horse but a little Hungarian nag that
took it in bad part. Indeed his Hungarian mount was so incensed and gave such extraordinary leaps and bounds that
two or three times Lucien was on the point of being unseated.

"What! on the very same spot!" he thought, flushing with
anger. And to add to his chagrin, at the most critical moment,
he saw the little curtain being discreetly drawn aside. Evidently someone was watching him. It was, as a matter of
fact, Madame de Chasteller who was saying to herself: "Ah!
that's my young officer about to have another fall." She had
often watched him ride past, and thought that he wore his
clothes with an easy elegance quite free from all stiffness. In
the end, Lucien suffered the extreme mortification of being
thrown by his little Hungarian beast not ten paces from the
spot where he had fallen that first day. "It must be fate!" he
said. "I am predestined to appear ridiculous in the eyes of
this young woman."

He could not get over his discomfiture all evening. "I really should try to meet her," he thought, "just to see if she can look at me without laughing."

That evening at Madame de Commercy's he told of his misadventure. It became the topic of the hour, and he had the pleasure of hearing it repeated to each new arrival. He asked Madame de Serpierre why he had never seen Madame de Chasteller in society.

"Her father, the Marquis de Pontlevé," she replied, "has just recovered from an attack of gout. Even though she was brought up in Paris it is his daughter's duty to stay with him; and, moreover, we have not the honor of pleasing her."

One of the ladies sitting next to Madame de Serpierre interjected an acid remark, whereupon Madame de Serpierre capped this with another.

"But here," thought Lucien, "is pure envy; or does Madame de Chasteller's conduct offer them a happy excuse?" And he remembered what M. Bouchard, the post-master, had told him the day of his arrival on the subject of M. de Busant de Sicile, Lieutenant-Colonel of the Twentieth Hussars.

Next morning all through drill Lucien could think of nothing but his misadventure of the previous day. . . . "Yet riding a horse is perhaps the only thing that I can really do creditably. I dance badly. I am not brilliant in a drawing room. It is plain that Providence wishes to humiliate me. . . . By Gad! if I pass her on the street I am certainly going to bow to that young woman; for surely my two falls constitute an introduction; and if she takes my bow for an impertinence, so much the better, it will at least wipe from her memory the recollection of my ridiculous falls."

Four or five days later, going on foot to the barracks for evening stable-call, Lucien saw a rather tall young woman wearing a very simple hat at the corner of the street a few paces ahead of him. He seemed to recognize the lady's hair, remarkable for its abundance and its color, like that hair which had made such an impression on him three months earlier. In fact, the lady was Madame de Chasteller. Her light youthful step reminded him of Paris. It was a pleasant surprise.

"If she recognizes me she can't help laughing in my face."

Lucien looked into her eyes as he passed. But the simplicity and seriousness of their expression suggested a slightly sad reverie without any sign of laughter. "I must say," he thought, "there wasn't the least hint of mockery in the glance she perforce gave me. She was obliged to look at me as one looks at an obstacle or any object that confronts one on the street. . . . I have just played the role of a cart. . . . How flattering! . . . In those beautiful eyes there was even a touch of shyness. . . . But, after all, how do I know that she recognized me as the unlucky horseman?"

Lucien recalled his plan of bowing to Madame de Chasteller only long after she had passed; her modest and even timid glance had seemed to him so noble that, when she passed him again coming from the other direction, he lowered his eyes in spite of himself.

The three long hours of drill that morning did not seem to our hero as long as usual. He kept recalling that glance which had squarely met his, and which had nothing provincial about it. "Since my arrival in Nancy I have really had only one desire in the midst of all my boredom: to wipe out the ridiculous impression which that young woman must have of me. . . . And if I can't even succeed in this innocent project I am worse than bored, I am really idiotic."

That evening Lucien outdid himself in deference and attentions toward Madame de Serpierre and the five or six intimate friends grouped around her. He listened with every appearance of lively interest to an endless and acrimonious diatribe against the court of Louis-Philippe which concluded with a bitter criticism of Madame d'Hocquincourt. This diplomatic maneuver permitted him at the end of an hour to go over to the little table where, with one of her friends, Mademoiselle Théodelinde sat sewing. He gave further details on his latest fall.

"The worst of it is," he added, "that I had an audience, and one for whom such an event was no novelty."

"And who was that?" asked Mademoiselle Théodelinde.

"A young woman who lives on the second floor of the Hôtel de Pontlevé."

"Why, it must be Madame de Chasteller!"

"That consoles me somewhat, for I have heard very bad things about her."

"The fact is she's considered toplofty as the clouds. She is not loved in Nancy, but we only know her through an occasional appearance in society, or rather," added the good Théodelinde, "we really don't know her at all. She takes her time about returning calls. I should venture to say that there is a certain nonchalance in her disposition and that she dislikes living so far from Paris."

"Often," put in Mademoiselle de Serpierre's friend, "she orders her carriage and, after letting it wait for an hour, dismisses it. They say she is odd and unsociable."

"It must be quite annoying for a woman with any delicacy," rejoined Mademoiselle Théodelinde, "not to be able to dance with a man without his planning to marry her."

"Just the opposite for us poor dowerless girls," bewailed her friend. "After all, she is the richest widow in the whole province."

Then they began talking of the excessively arrogant character of M. de Pontlevé. Lucien waited to hear the name of M. de Busant mentioned. "But I am absurd. How could young girls be expected to know about such things?"

At that moment a blond, insipid-looking young man entered the drawing room.

"Look," said Théodelinde, "that is the man who probably

bores Madame de Chasteller the most. He is M. de Blancet, her cousin, who has been in love with her for ten or fifteen years, and is always talking sentimentally about this childhood love of his, a love that has increased notably since Madame de Chasteller became a prodigiously wealthy widow. M. de Blancet's pretensions are looked upon with favor by M. de Pontlevé, whose most humble servitor he professes to be, and M. de Pontlevé insists that M. de Blancet be invited three times a week to dine with his dear cousin."

"And yet my father says that M. de Pontlevé dreads only one thing in the world, the marriage of his daughter, and that he uses M. de Blancet to keep other suitors away, but will never allow him to get control of that handsome fortune. He intends to keep its administration in his own hands. And that's why he won't let her go back to Paris."

"M. de Pontlevé made a terrible scene the other day," continued Mademoiselle Théodelinde, "toward the end of his attack of gout, because she would not dismiss her coachman. 'I won't be going out in the evening for a long time,' he said, 'and my own coachman can very well drive you. Why should you keep a scamp you never use?' He was almost as violent as when he wanted to force her to break off with her best friend, Madame de Constantin."

"Isn't she the very witty woman whose amusing repartee M. de Lanfort was talking about the other day?"

"Exactly! M. de Pontlevé is frightfully avaricious and timorous, and he is afraid of the influence of Madame de Constantin's independent character on his daughter. He has made plans to emigrate in case of the downfall of Louis-Philippe and the proclamation of the Republic. During the first emigration he was reduced to the most desperate extremities. He has a great deal of land but very little ready money, they say, and if he crosses the Rhine again, he counts largely on his daughter's fortune."

The conversation continued thus agreeably between Lucien, Théodelinde and her friend, until Madame de Serpierre thought it her duty as a mother to interrupt this intimate little group, which she, nevertheless, observed with the greatest satisfaction.

"And what are you gabbing about over here?" she said, with a sprightly air. "You look as though you were enjoying yourselves."

"We were talking about Madame de Chasteller," said Théodelinde's friend.

At once Madame de Serpierre's face changed completely and took on an expression of lofty severity. "The adventures of that lady," she said, "have no place in the conversation of young girls. She has brought with her from Paris certain ways that are most dangerous for your future, young ladies, and for the consideration you may expect from the world. Unhappily the immense fortune she enjoys and the glamor it casts over her, may tend to hide the gravity of her faults. And you, sir," she added, turning to Lucien, "will do me the favor, when you talk to my daughters, never to mention the adventures of Madame de Chasteller."

"Horrible female!" thought Lucien. "For once we were enjoying ourselves and she has had to spoil it. And to think that I listened patiently to her deadly stories for a whole hour!"

Lucien took his leave with the haughtiest and coldest air he could manage. He went straight to his house and was delighted to find his landlord, worthy M. Bonard, the grain merchant, at home.

Little by little, through boredom and not in the least thinking of love, Lucien began to act like any lover. This amused him immensely. Sunday morning he stationed one of his servants on sentry duty opposite the door of the Hôtel de Pontlevé. When the man came to report that Madame de Chasteller had just entered the Chapel of the Propagation, one of Nancy's little churches, he hurried after her.

But this church was so tiny and his horses (he had sworn never to go out without them) made such a noise on the paving stones, and his presence in uniform was so conspicuous, that he felt ashamed of his lack of delicacy. He could barely see Madame de Chasteller who was sitting at the back of a dark chapel. It seemed to Lucien that he detected great simplicity in her. "Unless I am very much mistaken this woman gives not a thought to the people around her. Moreover her deportment is perfectly in keeping with the deepest piety."

Next Sunday Lucien arrived at the Chapel of the Propagation on foot; but even so, he felt ill at ease. His appearance was altogether too striking.

It would have been difficult to be more distinguished than Madame de Chasteller. But Lucien, who had taken a seat from which he would have a good view of her when she left, noticed that when she failed to keep her eyes carefully lowered, they were of so singular a beauty that they betrayed all her passing emotions. "Those eyes," thought Lucien, "must often make their mistress very angry with herself; try as she may she cannot make them inconspicuous."

That day they expressed a profound thoughtfulness and melancholy. "Is it still M. de Busant de Sicile who has the honor of affecting those glances?"

This question was enough to spoil all his pleasure.

CHAPTER FOURTEEN

I NEVER SUPPOSED garrison love affairs were subject to such difficulties." This sensible though vulgar thought seemed to sober Lucien, and he fell into a profound reverie.

"Well, *easy* or not," he said to himself after a while, "it would be charming to be able to talk with such a person in simple friendliness." But *charming* was hardly the word suited to the expression of her face. "I cannot," he continued more calmly, "pretend that there is not a painful distance between a lieutenant-colonel and a simple second-lieutenant; and an even more alarming distance between the noble name of M. de Busant de Sicile, companion of Charles d'Anjou, brother of Saint-Louis, and the little bourgeois name of Leuwen. . . . On the other hand, it is possible that my brilliant liveries and my English horses endow me with a semi-nobility in the eyes of this provincial soul. . . . Perhaps," he added, laughing, "even total nobility. . . .

"No," he said, getting up in a sort of fury. "Mean thoughts cannot possibly exist with such a noble countenance. . . . And if she does entertain such ideas, it is only because of her caste. In her they are not ridiculous, because she adopted them, just as she learned her catechism, at the age of six; they are not ideas, they are sentiments. The provincial nobility gives a great deal of importance to liveries and coach varnish.

"But why all these vain scruples? I must admit I am quite ridiculous. What right have I to delve into such intimate questions? I should like to spend a few evenings in one of the drawing rooms where she is in the habit of going. . . . My father has challenged me to get myself admitted to the first drawing rooms of Nancy. I have been admitted. It has been difficult; now it is about time to find something to do in these drawing rooms. I am dying of boredom, and excess of boredom may make me inattentive—a thing that the vanity of these country gentlemen would never forgive me, even the best of them.

"Why shouldn't I make up my mind, if only, as Mademoiselle Sylviane would say, to have an aim in life, to succeed in spending a few evenings with this young woman? It was pretty silly of me to think of love and to reproach myself! This pastime will not prevent my being a man worthy of esteem and serving my country when the occasion arises.

"Besides," Lucien added, smiling sadly, "probably her *amiable* remarks will quickly cure me of the pleasure I anticipate from seeing her. With rather more aristocratic manners and conversation more in keeping with a different station in life, she will be just a second edition of Mademoiselle Berchu. She will be acrimonious and bigoted like Madame de Serpierre, or intoxicated with nobility and talking titles and ancestors, like Madame de Commercy—who told me yesterday, mixing up all the dates and, worst of all, going on forever, how one of her ancestors named Enguerrand had followed François I to the wars against the Albigenses, and was constable of Auvergne. . . . But what of it? She is pretty and what more could I ask to while away two or three hours? After all, while I listen to her nonsense I shall be only a foot or two away from her beauty. It will even be curious philosophically to observe how ridiculous or mean thoughts fail to spoil such features. For nothing could be more absurd than Lavater's theories."

But what finally settled the matter for Lucien was the thought of what a dunce he'd be if he couldn't manage to meet the lady in one of the drawing rooms she frequented, or be received in her own when she stayed at home. "This will require some exertion like the storming of the salons of Nancy." By means of all these philosophical arguments the fatal word of love was avoided, and Lucien felt absolved. He had always made fun of the pitiful state of Edgard, one of his cousins. "To allow one's self-esteem to be dependent on the opinion of a woman whose own self-esteem is dependent on the fact that her great-grandfather killed some Albigenses under François I! What a mixture of absurdities! In such a contest a man is always more ridiculous than a woman."

Despite all Lucien's fine logic, M. de Busant de Sicile occupied our hero's thoughts as much as, if not more than, Madame de Chasteller. He displayed the greatest ingenuity in asking indirect questions on the subject of M. de Busant, and the sort of welcome he had received. M. Gauthier, M. Bonard, and their friends, and all the middle-class society of Nancy with their habitual exaggeration, knew that M. de Busant de Sicile belonged to the highest nobility and had been Madame de Chasteller's lover, and nothing more. In the drawing rooms of Madame de Commercy and Madame de Puylaurens things were not stated quite so frankly. There, when he asked questions about M. de Busant, people seemed to remember that Lucien, after all, belonged to the enemy camp, and he was never able to extract a plain answer. To Mademoiselle Théodelinde he could not very well broach such a subject, and she seemed to be the only person who was not bent on deceiving him. Lucien never succeeded in finding out the truth about M. de Busant. As a matter of fact, M. de Busant was a very worthy and very brave gentleman, but without the least wit in the world. Upon his arrival in Nancy, misunderstanding the welcome he received and quite forgetting his expanding waistline, his insignificant features, and his forty years, he had proceeded to fall in love with Madame de Chasteller. He had annoyed both her father and herself with his incessant calls which she had never succeeded in making less frequent. Her father was particularly anxious to stand in well with the army in Nancy. If his correspondence (entirely innocent) with Charles X were ever discovered, who would be ordered to arrest him? Who would cover his flight? And if suddenly it were learned that the Republic had been established in Paris, who would protect him against the rabble of the province?

But poor Lucien was very far from knowing all this. He noticed that Du Poirier always avoided his questions with admirable skill.

In society he was told repeatedly: "That really superior officer is the descendant of an aide-de-camp of the Duc d'Anjou, brother of Saint-Louis, who helped the Duke conquer Sicily."

He learned a little more from M. d'Antin who said to Lucien one day:

"You were very wise to take his lodgings, for they are by far the most tolerable in town. Poor Busant is the best of fellows, not an idea in his head but excellent manners. He used to give very charming little dinners at the *Green Huntsman* in the Burelviller woods a quarter of a league from here; and every day at midnight he thought he was gay because he was slightly drunk."

By dint of thinking about ways and means of meeting Madame de Chasteller in a drawing room, all desire to cut a figure in Nancy, which Lucien had indeed begun to despise perhaps more than he should, was replaced by the desire to occupy the thoughts, if not the heart, of this pretty toy. "Such a head must contain some curious ideas!" he said to himself. "A young provincial *ultra* going direct from the convent of the Sacred Heart to the court of Charles X, and forced to flee Paris during the *July Days* of 1830." Such indeed had been Madame de Chasteller's history.

In 1814, after the First Restoration, the Marquis de Pontlevé was in despair at finding himself in Nancy instead of being attached to the Court.

"I see," he said, "the same distinction again being made between the nobility of the Court and the rest of us. My cousin, who bears the same name as myself, because he is at Court, will command as colonel at twenty-two the regiment in which, by the grace of God, I shall be a captain at forty." This was M. de Pontlevé's principal grievance, and he made no mystery of it to anybody. He soon acquired another. In the elections of 1816, he presented himself as candidate for the Chamber of Deputies and received six votes—counting his own. He fled Paris, vowing that after such an affront he would never set foot in that city again, and took with him his daughter, then six years old. To give himself a standing in Paris he solicited a peerage. M. de Puylaurens, at that time in favor at court, advised him to place his daughter in the convent of the Sacred Heart. M. de Pontlevé followed his advice and was soon to realize its full value. He himself became assiduous in his devotions, and by these means succeeded in 1828 in marrying his daughter to one of the major-generals attached to the court of Charles X. This was considered a most advantageous marriage. M. de Chasteller was wealthy. He looked older than he really was, not having a hair on his head; but he had astonishing vivacity and a grace of manner that barely escaped being cloying. His enemies at court applied to him Boileau's verse on his wife's favorite novels:

In which even *I hate you* is said with tenderness.

Well schooled by a husband who worshiped all the little punctilios which count for so much at court, Madame de Chasteller was well received by the princesses, and soon enjoyed a very enviable position. She had court boxes at the *Bouffes* and at the Opera, and, during the summer, apartments at Meudon and at Rambouillet. She was lucky enough never to bother her pretty head about politics or reading the newspapers. All she knew of politics was from the sessions of the *French Academy* which her husband, having high hopes of one day being a member, insisted on her attending. He was a great admirer of the verses of Millevoye and the prose of M. de Fontanes.

The musket shots of 1830 came to disturb these innocent ideas. Seeing the *rabble on the streets,* that was his way of putting it, made him think of the murders of MM. Foullon and Berthier in the first days of the Revolution. The proximity of the Rhine seemed to him to offer the greatest assurance of safety, and he had sought refuge on an estate belonging to his wife near Nancy.

Though somewhat affected, M. de Chasteller was most affable and even amusing in the ordinary course of events, but had never been famous for having much character. He could never get over this third flight of the family he adored. "I see God's hand in this," he would say, shedding tears in all the drawing rooms of Nancy. Soon he died, leaving his wife an income of twenty-five thousand pounds in the public funds. He owed this fortune to the King and the loans of 1817; and in the envious gossip of Nancy drawing rooms, it quickly mounted to eighteen hundred thousand or two million.

Lucien had the greatest difficulty in the world gleaning these simple facts. But the hate which Madame de Chasteller inspired in Madame de Serpierre's drawing room and the common sense of Mademoiselle Théodelinde made it easier for Lucien to get at the truth.

Eighteen months after the death of her husband, Madame de Chasteller dared pronounce the words: *a return to Paris.* "What, my daughter!" cried M. de Pontlevé with the voice and gestures of the righteously indignant Alceste in Moliere's play: "Your princes are in Prague and you would dare to show yourself in Paris! What would the shades of M. de Chasteller say? Ah, if we must quit our penates, it is not in that direction we should turn our horses' heads. Stay and take care of your old father in Nancy! Or, if we are still able to put one foot before the other, let us fly to Prague!"

M. de Pontlevé had that ornate and discursive style of speech which had been the fashion in the time of Louis XVI and which then passed for wit.

Madame de Chasteller had to give up all idea of returning to Paris. At the mere mention of Paris her father would become violent and make a scene. But as compensation, Madame de Chasteller had fine horses, a pretty calash, and servants in elegant liveries. This handsome equipage was to be seen more frequently on the neighboring highroads than on the streets of Nancy. Madame de Chasteller went as often as possible to see her old friend of convent days, Madame de Constantin, who lived in a little town a few leagues from Nancy. But M. de Pontlevé was mortally jealous of Madame de Constantin, and had done everything in his power to break up their friendship.

Several times during his long rides, Lucien had seen Madame de Chasteller's calash several leagues from Nancy.

At midnight, the day of one of these chance meetings, Lucien had gone to smoke one of his little cigars rolled in licorice paper in the Rue de la Pompe. There, still relying on Madame de Chasteller's taste for brilliant uniforms, he forced himself to build his hopes on the elegance of his horses and his servants, then dashed those hopes by reminding himself of his bourgeois name. But even as he reasoned thus bravely with himself, his thoughts were very different.

After first hearing her history he had said to himself: "This young woman is vexed with her father; she must be hurt by the interest he displays in her fortune; Nancy bores her; it is quite conceivable that she should seek a little diversion in a harmless flirtation." Then the recollection of that frank, chaste visage gave rise to doubts, even on the subject of a flirtation.

Finally, on the evening of which we are speaking: "What the devil!" said Lucien. "I am really an imbecile! I ought to be overjoyed by her good will toward uniforms."

And the more he insisted on this reason for hope, the more despondent he became.

"Is it possible," he said at length half aloud, "that I am fool enough to be in love?" and he stopped dead in the middle of the street as though a thunderbolt had struck him. Happily, at midnight there was no one on the street to notice the expression of his face, and to laugh at him.

The idea of being in love filled him with shame, he felt himself degraded. "So I am like Edgard after all," he thought. "I must have a very small, feeble soul! Education has been able to strengthen it momentarily, but its true character asserts itself on exceptional occasions and in unusual situations. What! While the entire youth of France takes sides in such great causes, am I going to spend my life gazing into a pair of beautiful eyes like the ridiculous heroes of Corneille? So this is the sad result of this politic and prudent life I have been leading here:

> Who does not have the spirit of his age
> Of his age knows all the sorrows.

I should have done much better to follow my original idea and carry off a little dancer in Metz! Or better still, I should have made love to Madame de Puylaurens or Madame d'Hocquincourt. With these noble ladies I should have been in no danger of a flirtation developing into anything beyond a little society love affair.

"If this goes on much longer I shall become quite mad and altogether tiresome. This is worse than the Saint-Simonism my father accuses me of! Who thinks seriously about women today? A man like my mother's friend, the Duc de ———, who, at the end of an honorable career, having paid his debt on the battlefield, and also in the House of Peers by refusing his vote, amuses himself feathering the nest of some little dancer as one would play with a canary.

"But for me, at my age . . . ! What young man today would dare even mention a serious passion for a woman? If this is just a simple pastime, all very well; but if it is a serious attachment there is no excuse for me; and the proof that I am getting serious, that this folly is not a simple pastime, is that Madame de Chasteller's weakness for brilliant uniforms, instead of delighting me, makes me sad. I believe in my duty to my country. So far my self-respect has been due principally to the fact that I am not just a selfish egotist thinking of nothing but enjoying the prize I owe to chance; I respect myself, above all, because I have recognized my duties to the fatherland, and felt the need of winning the respect of men with high ideals. I am at the age of action; at any moment the voice of the fatherland may make itself heard; I may be called; my whole mind should be bent on trying to discover the true interests of France which scoundrels are trying to obscure. A single head, a single soul, are not enough to see them plainly in the midst of such intricate duties. And yet this is the moment I choose to become the slave of a little provincial *ultra!* The devil take her and her street!" And Lucien suddenly left the Rue de la Pompe and went home. But a lively sense of shame kept him awake. Daylight found him pacing up and down in front of the barracks waiting impatiently for the sound of the bugle. After roll-call, he walked a little way with two of his comrades; for the first time he found their company agreeable.

When he was alone once more: "Do what I will," he said, "I cannot see in those eyes of hers, so penetrating yet so chaste, the counterpart of a ballet dancer of the Opera." During the whole day he was unable to make up his mind about Madame de Chasteller. No matter how hard he tried he could not picture her in the role of the mistress whom every lieutenant of a garrison thinks himself in honor bound to have. "And yet," whispered reason, "she must be so terribly bored! Her father holds her here while she pines for Paris; he tries to separate her from her best friend; a little flirtation is really the only consolation for the poor soul."

This very logical excuse only served to redouble our hero's depression. In reality he saw very well the absurdity of his position: he was in love, and obviously with the desire of being successful, yet he was unhappy and ready to despise his mistress precisely because of this possibility of success.

It was a painful day for Lucien. Everyone seemed to have conspired to talk to him about M. Thomas de Busant and the agreeable life he had led in Nancy. They compared it with the café and tavern existence of Lieutenant-Colonel Filloteau and the three squadron commanders.

Enlightenment seemed to come to him from every side, for the name of Madame de Chasteller was linked on every lip with M. de Busant; and yet his heart persisted in holding her up to him as an angel of purity.

He no longer took the least pleasure in showing off for the admiration of the whole town his elegant liveries, his fine horses, his calash that rattled all the wooden houses of Nancy as it rolled by. He almost despised himself for having found amusement in such petty things, and forgot the excess of boredom they had been called upon to dispel.

During the days that followed, Lucien was very much perturbed. No longer was he that thoughtless soul amused by the least trifle. There were moments when he despised himself with all his heart. But in spite of his remorse he could not keep himself from riding through the Rue de la Pompe several times a day.

On entering Madame de Commercy's drawing room a week after he had made this humiliating discovery about himself, Lucien found Madame de Chasteller there paying a call. He was unable to say a word; he turned every color of the rainbow; and, although he was the only gentleman present, when Madame de Chasteller rose to go, he did not have wit enough to offer her his arm to escort her to her carriage. He left Madame de Commercy's despising himself just a little more.

This republican, this man of action, who loved horse drill as preparation for battle, had never thought of love except as a dangerous and despised precipice into which he felt sure of never falling. Moreover, he believed this passion to be extremely rare everywhere except at the theater. He was astonished at everything that was happening to him, like a wild bird caught in a snare and caged; and like this terrified captive, he could do nothing but beat his head against the bars of his cage. "Think of it!" he cried, "being unable to say a word, and forgetting the simple rules of good breeding! Thus my weak will succumbs to the attraction of a transgression I have not even the courage to commit!"

Next day Lucien was not on duty. He took advantage of the permission he had received from his Colonel, and plunged deep into the Burelviller woods. . . . Toward evening he learned from a peasant that he was seven leagues from Nancy.

"I must admit I'm a greater fool than I thought! Is it by dashing through the woods that I am going to win the good will of the drawing rooms of Nancy, and have another chance of meeting Madame de Chasteller and of making up for my idiotic behavior?" He hastened back to town and went to Madame de Serpierre's. Mademoiselle Théodelinde was his friend, and this soul that thought itself so indomitable had need of a friendly face that day. Lucien by no means dared to speak of his weakness; but sitting beside her, his heart felt more at peace. He had the highest esteem for M. Gauthier but the latter was a priest of the Republic, and anything which did not directly contribute to the happiness of France, a *self-governing* France, seemed unworthy of his attention, and childish. Du Poirier would have been the ideal counselor, for, besides his general knowledge of the people and affairs of Nancy, he dined once a week with the person whom Lucien had such an overwhelming desire to know. But Lucien was determined, above all things, not to give the doctor a chance of betraying him.

While Lucien was engaged in recounting to Mademoiselle Théodelinde all the things he had observed during his long ride, Madame de Chasteller was announced. Instantly all Lucien's powers forsook him; he tried in vain to talk; what little he said was very nearly unintelligible.

He could not have been more surprised at himself if, galloping into battle with his regiment, he had suddenly turned tail and fled. This thought plunged him into the most violent distress. So then, he could not depend upon his conduct under any circumstances. What a lesson in humility! What a need for action, so that at last he could be sure of himself, trusting no longer to vain probabilities but to deeds.

Lucien was torn out of his profound reverie by a very startling event: Madame de Serpierre was introducing him to Madame de Chasteller, and accompanying this ceremony with the most excessive flattery. Lucien turned crimson and tried in vain to find something courteous to say, while he was being extolled above all for his ready wit, so remarkable for its aptness and Parisian elegance. Even Madame de Serpierre at last became aware of the state he was in.

Madame de Chasteller had recourse to some pretext to cut short her visit. When she rose, Lucien this time thought of offering her his arm to her carriage, but his legs were trembling so, that he decided it would not be prudent to leave his chair;

he was afraid of making a spectacle of himself in public. Madame de Chasteller would have had reason to say: "I think, sir, it is I who should offer you my arm!"

CHAPTER FIFTEEN

I NEVER THOUGHT you were so susceptible to ridicule," said Mademoiselle Théodelinde when Madame de Chasteller had left the drawing room. "Is it because Madame de Chasteller saw you in the not very heroic position of Saint Paul when he beheld the vision of the third heaven, that her presence so petrified you?"

Lucien accepted this interpretation; he was afraid of betraying himself should he offer the slightest explanation, and as soon as he felt that his departure would not seem odd, he made his escape. The moment he was alone he found some consolation in the very excess of the absurdity of what had befallen him. "Have I by chance the pest?" he said to himself. "Since the physical effect was so overwhelming I am not morally responsible! If I broke a leg, I should not be able to march with my regiment."

There was to be a dinner-party at the de Serpierres'—a modest affair, for they were anything but affluent. But, thanks to those prejudices of the nobility which are so tenacious in the provinces and which alone could nourish the hope of finding husbands for the six daughters of the former King's Lieutenant, it was no small honor to be invited to dinner at their house. Madame de Serpierre had indeed hesitated for a long time before inviting Lucien, his name being really too bourgeois. However, as usual in the Nineteenth Century, expediency finally won.

The kindly and simple Théodelinde did not approve this strategy, but she was obliged to obey. The little card placed on the napkin next to hers bore Lucien's name. The former King's Lieutenant had written: "M. le *Chevalier* Leuwen." Théodelinde knew that Lucien would be shocked by this gratuitous ennoblement.

Madame de Chasteller, having been unable to come to another dinner given two months before because of M. de Pontlevé's gout, was invited this evening. Utterly ashamed of her mother's high diplomacy, just before the arrival of the guests Théodelinde got permission, not without considerable difficulty, to place Madame de Chasteller's card on M. le *Chevalier* Leuwen's right, her own on his left.

When Lucien arrived, Madame de Serpierre, with all the duplicity of a mother with six marriageable daughters, drew him aside and said:

"I have put you next to the beautiful Madame de Chasteller; she is the best match in the province and has the reputation of not being indifferent to uniforms; so you see you can thank me for giving you an opportunity of cultivating this acquaintance."

During dinner, Théodelinde found Lucien pretty dull; he said little and what he said was not worth saying.

Madame de Chasteller talked to our hero on the subject that was monopolizing all the conversations of Nancy at the moment. Madame Grandet, the wife of the Collector-General, was about to arrive from Paris and would undoubtedly give the most brilliant affairs. Her husband was very rich, and she had the reputation of being one of the prettiest women in Paris. This subject of conversation was only languidly pursued by our second-lieutenant; he tried to show some animation but his mind was a blank, and all he could manage were the briefest questions addressed to Madame de Chasteller, which were almost curt.

After dinner an excursion was proposed, and Lucien had the honor of escorting Théodelinde and Madame de Chasteller on the pond that was dignified by the name of the Lac de la Commanderie. Several times before, Lucien had taken the de Serpierre young ladies out rowing in perfect safety, but he now barely escaped capsizing the boat and shipwrecking Théodelinde and Madame de Chasteller in a lake that boasted a depth of four feet.

Two days later occurred the birthday of a certain august personage who no longer resided in France. Madame de Marcilly, the widow of a *cordon rouge,* thought it incumbent upon her to give a ball; but the reason for giving the ball did not appear on the card of invitation; and this omission seemed a reprehensible timidity to seven or eight excessively right-thinking ladies, who therefore failed to honor the ball with their presence.

Of the entire Twenty-seventh Lancers, only the Colonel, Lucien and young Riquebourg were invited. But once they had entered the Marquise de Marcilly's drawing rooms, partisan spirit made the noble society, habitually so polite—so boringly polite—forget the simplest rules of good breeding. Colonel Malher de Saint-Mégrin was treated as an intruder and almost as a police spy; Lucien, on the other hand, as the spoiled child of the house. A real infatuation for this pretty lieutenant was quite evident.

When the company had assembled, everyone proceeded to the ballroom. In the middle of a garden planted by King Stanislas, the father-in-law of Louis XV, and laid out in a labyrinth of hedges after the fashion of the day, rose a very elegant pavilion, but badly neglected since the death of Charles XII's friend. To conceal the ravages of time it had been transformed into a magnificent tent. The Commander of the town, very much annoyed at not being able to attend the ball and to celebrate the birthday of the august personage, had taken from the army stores and loaned for the occasion, two enormous tents known as *marquises*. They had been set up alongside of the pavilion with which they communicated through two great doors ornamented with Indian trophies, the color white being everywhere predominant. Paris could not have done it better. And all these decorations were the devoted work of the three Roller brothers.

Thanks to these charming tents, to the lively atmosphere of the ball, and also, undoubtedly, to the flattering reception accorded him, Lucien completely forgot his mortification and dejection. He was as pleased as a child by the beauty of the garden and the ballroom; these first sensations made another man of him.

This grave republican took a schoolboy delight in passing back and forth in front of Colonel Malher without speaking to him, without even deigning to look his way. In this he followed the general example: not one word was addressed to this colonel so proud of his reputation; he was left to himself *like a mangy dog,* the expression everyone had adopted to describe his unhappy position. And he did not even have the wit to leave the ball and to escape from this unanimous rudeness. "Here," thought Lucien, "it is he who does not *think right,* and I am even with him for his insolence over the reading room in the Rue de la Pompe. With these coarse souls one must lose no opportunity of making one's contempt felt; when simple people fail to notice them they merely put it down to the fear they inspire."

Upon his arrival, Lucien noticed that all the ladies were wearing green and white ribbons, which did not offend him in the least. "This insult is addressed to the head of the State, and a perfidious one. The exalted position of the State itself makes it impossible for any family, even a family of heroes, to insult it."

Behind one of the adjacent tents Lucien noticed a little retreat that was ablaze with light; there were perhaps forty
burning candles that attracted Lucien by their dazzling effect.
"It is like one of those street altars of the Corpus Christi procession," he thought. In the place of honor among the candles,
like a sort of monstrance, hung the portrait of a young Scotsman. In this boy the painter (more right-thinking than right-
painting) had tried to combine the amiable smiles of youth
and a forehead charged with the thoughts of genius! He had
thus succeeded in making an astonishing caricature with something monstrous about it.

All the ladies who entered quickly crossed the ballroom and
went directly up to the portrait of the young Scotsman. There
they would remain in silence for an instant affecting a very
solemn air, then, turning, would resume their festive expression
and go to shake hands with their hostess. Two or three ladies
who went to greet Madame de Marcilly before honoring the
portrait, were received very coldly and appeared in such a
ridiculous light that one of them decided it would be the
part of wisdom to swoon. Not one detail of all these rites was
lost on Lucien. "We aristocrats," he laughed to himself, "if
we stick together need fear no one; but, also, what nonsense
one has to swallow with a straight face! It is amusing," he
thought, "that the two rivals, Charles X and Louis-Philippe,
both on the nation's pay-roll, while paying the nation's servants
with the nation's money, think we are in debt to them personally."

After a cursory survey of the ball, which was really very
beautiful, Lucien went dutifully over to the Boston table of
Madame de Commercy, the "cousin of the Emperor," a title
which Lucien heard her give herself five or six times during
the course of a deadly half-hour.

"The vanity of these provincials inspires them with the

most incredible notions," he thought. "I feel like a traveler in a strange land."

"You are delightful, my dear sir," said the cousin of the Emperor, "and I certainly hate to part with such a *charming cavalier,* but I see that some of the young ladies over there are pining to dance; they will be looking daggers at me if I keep you any longer."

And Madame de Commercy pointed out several young ladies of the very *highest rank.*

Bravely our hero resigned himself to his fate; not only did he dance, but he talked; he found a few little ideas on a level with the intelligence, left uncultivated with intent, of these maidens of the provincial nobility. His courage was rewarded by the unanimous approval of Mesdames de Commercy, de Marcilly, de Serpierre, etc. He was the rage. Uniforms are popular in the East of France, a profoundly military region; and it was thanks largely to a uniform, so gracefully worn and almost unique in this society, that Lucien could be accounted the most brilliant guest at the ball.

At last he was able to dance a quadrille with Madame d'Hocquincourt. He proved himself brilliant, witty, quick in repartee. Madame d'Hocquincourt complimented him highly.

"You have always been most agreeable, but tonight you are another person," she said.

This remark was overheard by M. de Sanréal, and Lucien began to be very unpopular with the young men of society.

"Your success is putting these young gentlemen in a very bad humor," said Madame d'Hocquincourt. And as MM. Roller and d'Antin came up to her, she called out to Lucien who had moved away:

"Monsieur Leuwen, will you dance the next quadrille with me?"

"This is charming," reflected Lucien, "and something no

one would dream of doing in Paris! Really, there is something
to be said for these foreign countries. People here are less
timid than we are."

While he was dancing with Madame d'Hocquincourt, M.
d'Antin approached them. Pretending that she had forgotten
that she was engaged to him for this dance, Madame d'Hocquincourt began making excuses that were so droll and yet
so stinging that Lucien, still dancing with her, could hardly
keep from laughing aloud. Madame d'Hocquincourt was evidently trying to make M. d'Antin angry, and he kept pro-
testing in vain that he had never counted on this quadrille
with her.

"How can a man allow himself to be treated like that?"
Lucien asked himself. "What won't a man stoop to for love!"

Madame d'Hocquincourt addressed the most amiable remarks to Lucien and spoke almost exclusively to him; but Lucien resented seeing poor M. d'Antin placed in such a humiliating position and, leaving Madame d'Hocquincourt, went to
the other end of the ballroom and danced several waltzes with
Madame de Puylaurens who was also extremely charming to
him. He, who was such a bad dancer, was clearly the idol of
the ball; he knew it very well and for the first time in his
life he found some pleasure in that exercise. He was dancing
a galop with Mademoiselle Théodelinde when, in a corner of
the room, he caught sight of Madame de Chasteller.

All Lucien's dashing ease deserted him, all his wit vanished
in the twinkling of an eye. Madame de Chasteller wore a
simple white gown, and the simplicity of her attire would
have seemed really ridiculous to the young men if she had
been without fortune. In these cities of puerile vanity, balls are
battlefields, and to neglect any advantage seemed a very
marked affectation. It was felt that Madame de Chasteller
should have worn her diamonds. The choice of such a modest
and inexpensive gown was an act of eccentricity, deprecated

with an exaggerated show of profound pain by M. de Pontlevé, and secretly disapproved of by the timid M. de Blancet, who gave her his arm with ludicrous dignity.

These gentlemen were not altogether wrong. Nonchalance was probably the most profound trait of Madame de Chasteller's character. Behind that air of perfect gravity which her beauty rendered so imposing, she hid a happy, even a very gay disposition. Day-dreaming was her supreme pleasure. She seemed to pay little or no attention to all the little happenings around her, but not one of them escaped her. She saw them all, and it was indeed these little happenings that served to feed her pensiveness which everybody took for haughtiness. Although no detail of life escaped her, there were very few things that succeeded in touching her, and never the ones other people considered important.

For example: the very morning of the ball, Monsieur de Pontlevé had had a serious quarrel with her because of the indifference with which she had read a letter announcing a bankruptcy. And a few minutes later on the street, passing a tiny little old woman, hardly able to walk, almost in rags, whose shriveled skin was visible through a torn shirt, she had been moved to tears. No one in Nancy had divined her character; her intimate friend, Madame de Constantin, alone at times was the recipient of her confidences and would often make fun of her.

Madame de Chasteller, like the rest of the world, talked enough to keep up her end of a conversation, but to begin talking was always a trial for her.

There was only one thing in Paris she really missed and that was Italian music, which had the power of increasing to an amazing degree the intensity of her spells of dreaming. She thought very little about herself and even the ball we are describing had not been able to make her conscious of the role she should play, or to awaken in her an honest dash of coquetry which most people believe to be innate in the character of all women.

As Lucien escorted Mademoiselle Théodelinde back to her mother, Madame de Serpierre could be heard loudly exclaiming:

"What is the meaning of that little white muslin frock? Is that the way to present oneself on such a day as this? She is the widow of a general officer attached to the very person of the King; she enjoys a fortune tripled and quadrupled by the generosity of the Bourbons. Madame de Chasteller should understand that to come to Madame de Marcilly's on the birthday of our adorable Princess is equivalent to presenting oneself at the Tuileries. What will the republicans say—seeing us treat the most sacred things so lightly? And isn't it the moment, when the entire mass of the common people is attacking these sacred things, for each one of us, according to our individual position, to show all the more courage and to do our duty? And she of all people," added Madame de Serpierre, "the only daughter of M. de Pontlevé who, rightly or wrongly, is the head of the nobility of this province, or at least gives us instructions as the commissioner of the King. That little head of hers understands nothing of all this!"

Madame de Serpierre was right; of course Madame de Chasteller was to be blamed, but not as much as she was blamed. "What will the republicans say?" cried all the noble ladies; and they thought of the next number of the *Aurore* which was to appear in two days.

CHAPTER SIXTEEN

MADAME DE CHASTELLER came up to Madame de Serpierre's group as the latter, in a very loud voice, was continuing her critical and monarchical reflections. Brusquely these acrimonious criticisms gave place to those trite and extravagant compliments which, in the provinces, pass current for urbanity. Lucien was delighted to find Madame de Serpierre ridiculous. A quarter of an hour before he would have been highly amused; now this malicious woman had the same effect on him as another rock on a rough mountain trail. These endless civilities to which Madame de Chasteller was necessarily forced to respond, gave Lucien plenty of time to examine her at leisure. Madame de Chasteller's complexion had that inimitable freshness which seems to give evidence of a soul aloof from the petty vanities and little animosities of a provincial ball. Lucien was grateful to her for this, although the idea was pure invention on his part. He was absorbed in his admiration when the eyes of this pale beauty turned toward him; he could not endure their splendor; they were so altogether beautiful and simple in all their changing expressions! Without thinking, Lucien stood stock-still three paces from Madame de Chasteller, on the spot where her eyes had struck him.

All the sprightliness and brilliant effrontery of the man of fashion left him; he no longer thought of charming society, and if he remembered the existence of that monster at all, it was only to dread its tongue. Was it not this very society that was constantly talking to him about M. Thomas de Busant?

Instead of bolstering up his courage with action, he now succumbed to the weakness of meditating—philosophizing. To excuse the weakness and the misfortune of falling in love, he told himself that never before had he met with such celestial loveliness; he gave himself up to the pleasure of examining all this beauty, and his awkwardness increased accordingly.

Under his very nose, Madame de Chasteller promised M. d'Antin a quadrille, for which Lucien had been trying for the last half-hour to make up his mind to ask her. "Up till now," he reflected as he watched Madame de Chasteller being carried off, "the ridiculous affectations of all the pretty women I have met have served me as a shield against their charms. The coldness of Madame de Chasteller, the moment she speaks or makes a gesture, is transformed into a charm I should never have dreamed possible."

We must admit that while Lucien was indulging in these eulogistic reflections, standing motionless and stiff as a post, he looked like an idiot.

Madame de Chasteller had remarkably lovely hands. Since her eyes terrified him, our hero kept his own fastened on her hands, following them as she danced. His shyness had not been lost on Madame de Chasteller who had heard Lucien talked about daily by everyone who came to her house. Our second-lieutenant was at last roused from his happy state by the painful notion that everybody not engaged in dancing was looking at him with hostile eyes, bent on ridiculing him. His uniform and his cockade alone were enough to alienate, and violently, all persons at the ball who did not belong to the highest society. Lucien had long ago observed that in *ultraism* the less intelligent people were, the more rabid they became.

But all these prudent reflections were quickly forgotten; he found much too much pleasure puzzling over the character of Madame de Chasteller.

"How shameful!" suddenly objected the anti-love party, "how shameful in a man who has loved duty and the father-land with a devotion that he can truthfully call sincere! He has eyes for nothing but the charms of a little provincial legit-imist with a soul so base that it prefers the particular interests of her class to those of France."

"Soon," he said to himself, "I shall be putting the happiness of two hundred thousand nobles before that of thirty million Frenchmen. And the only excuse I could offer would be that these two hundred thousand privileged persons have elegant salons providing refined pleasures I should look for in vain elsewhere; in other words, salons that are necessary to my own private happiness. The vilest of Louis-Philippe's courtiers do not reason otherwise."

It was a cruel moment for Lucien, and his expression was far from gay as he tried his best to drive away these terrible thoughts. He was standing at the moment motionless near the quadrille in which Madame de Chasteller was dancing. Immediately the pro-love party, quick to confound reason, led him to invite Madame de Chasteller to dance. She looked at him, but this time Lucien was incapable of analyzing that look; it seemed to burn through him, to set him on fire. And yet, that look meant nothing more than a pleasurable curiosity at finding close at hand a young man everyone was talking about, who had such extreme passions, who fought a duel every day 'and who rode past her windows with remarkable frequency. And the splendid horse of this young officer always seemed to become skittish at the very moment when she happened to be at her window! It was plain that the horse's rider wished to appear very much taken with her, at least when he rode through the Rue de la Pompe, and she was not at all scandalized. She did not consider it an imperti-nence. It is true that when he had sat next to her at Madame de Serpierre's dinner, he had seemed completely devoid of wit, his manner had even appeared to her crude. But he had, after all, rowed the boat on the *Lac de la Commanderie* with gallantry, but with the cold gallantry of a man of fifty.

The result of all these various ideas was that, while dancing with Lucien and without looking at him, without departing from the most decorous gravity, Madame de Chasteller was very much preoccupied with him. She had soon noticed that he was shy to the point of awkwardness.

"I suppose," she thought, "that it rankles his pride to re-member that I saw him thrown off his horse the day his regiment arrived." Thus Madame de Chasteller found no objection to admitting that Lucien's timidity was due to her. This doubt of oneself had a certain charm in such a young man, especially in the midst of all these provincials so sure of their own importance and whose stature was not diminished in the least now as they danced. This young officer was at least not timid on horseback; every day she trembled at his temerity, a temerity that was frequently unfortunate, and she almost laughed aloud at the recollection.

Lucien was tortured by his own persistent silence. At last, making a prodigious effort, he found enough courage to ad-dress a few words to Madame de Chasteller, and succeeded only with the greatest difficulty in expressing very badly very commonplace ideas which is the just punishment for anyone who fails to exert his memory.

Madame de Chasteller avoided the invitations of several of the fashionable young men whose prettiest speeches she knew by heart, and after having succeeded in dancing in the same quadrille as Lucien, by one of those adroit feminine maneuvers that we understand only after we have no longer any interest in understanding them, she quickly came to the conclu-sion that his intelligence was really not distinguished, and almost stopped thinking of him altogether. "He is nothing but a horseman like the others; only he rides more gracefully and makes a more interesting appearance." No longer was he that smart, high-spirited young man with an air of being indifferent and superior to everything, who so often rode past her window. Vexed by this discovery which seemed to increase for her the boredom of Nancy, Madame de Chasteller turned to Lucien and almost coquettishly began chatting with him. She had been watching him ride by for such a long time now that, although he had been presented only a week ago, he seemed to her almost like an old acquaintance.

Lucien only at intervals summoned up enough courage to look at the severely cold countenance of this lovely person talking to him, and was far from realizing all the friendly attention being lavished upon him. He danced, and in dancing made too many movements, and his movements were totally lacking in grace.

"Decidedly this fine young gentleman from Paris is at his best only on a horse; the moment his foot touches earth he loses half his merit, and when he starts dancing he loses the rest. He isn't intelligent; too bad, for his face seemed to promise such keenness and naturalness! It must be the *naturalness* that comes from a lack of ideas." And she began to breathe more freely. Yet by nature she was not ungenerous, but she loved her freedom, and she had been frightened.

Now altogether reassured as to Lucien's fatal fascination, and not inordinately affected by his single gift of horsemanship: "Like all the others," she said to herself, "this handsome young Parisian wants to play the lover overcome by my charms." And she thought of all those young men who flocked around her trying so hard to find amiable things to say. M. d'Antin occasionally succeeded. While granting M. d'Antin his due, Madame de Chasteller was annoyed that

Lucien, instead of saying a word, confined himself simply
to smiling at M. d'Antin's gracious remarks. And to crown
her displeasure, Lucien kept gazing at her in so marked a
manner that it might very well have attracted attention.

Our poor hero was much too profoundly preoccupied, both
with his remorse at being in love and an absolute inability to
find one passable word to say, for him even to give a thought
to controlling his eyes. Since he had left Paris he had seen
nothing, from the moral point of view, that was not, so it
seemed to him, distorted, dull and disagreeable. Duly weighing
my words, I can assert that the base ambitions, the puerile
pretentiousness, and above all the crude hypocrisy of the provinces, had succeeded in shocking a young man thoroughly in-
ured to all the vices of Paris.

Quite forgetting his ironic and pessimistic pose for the
past hour, Lucien had not had eyes enough for gazing, soul
enough for admiring. His remorse at falling in love had been
battered in breach and destroyed with delicious celerity. His
youthful vanity reminded him from time to time that the
continued silence in which he was happily basking, would
do nothing to enhance his reputation for affability; but he
was so amazed, so transported, that he had not the power
to give any serious consideration to the effect he was producing.

In charming contrast to everything that had been offending
his eyes for so long, there standing before him, not six paces
away, was a woman whose heavenly beauty made her worthy
of adoration; but that beauty was almost the least of her
charms. In place of the assiduous, importunate, tiresome civilities of the lady of the house of de Serpierre, in place of that
mania for being witty on all and every occasion, like Madame de Puylaurens, Madame de Chasteller was simple and
cold, but with the kind of simplicity which is charming
because it does not try to hide a soul made for the noblest

emotions, with that coldness which is so close to fire, and which seems ready to burst into tenderness and even into transports, had one the gift to inspire them.

CHAPTER SEVENTEEN

MADAME DE CHASTELLER went to take a turn around the ballroom. Having resumed his post, M. de Blancet offered her his arm with an air of authority; one could see that he was anticipating the happiness of giving her his arm as her husband. As luck would have it, they came upon Lucien again in another part of the hall. Finding him there before her eyes once more, Madame de Chasteller felt a flash of impatience with herself. How could she have wasted a second glance on so commonplace a person, a man whose sublime virtue, like that of those heroes of Ariosto, consisted in being a good horseman! She engaged him in conversation, trying her best to make him talk.

Suddenly, listening to Madame de Chasteller, Lucien was transformed into another man. He believed that her noble glance which had deigned to fall on him absolved him from repeating all those commonplaces which bored him to say, which he said so badly, and which, in Nancy, still formed the staple of conversation between persons who had met for the eighth or tenth time. Suddenly he dared to talk, and to talk a great deal. He talked about everything that might interest or amuse this pretty woman who, still leaning on her tall cousin's arm, deigned to listen to him with a look of amazement in her eyes. Without losing in the least its tone of quiet and respectful courtesy, Lucien's voice grew clearer, took on a new resonance. At no loss for apt and amusing ideas, he found lively and picturesque words in which to express them. Into this noble simplicity of tone which he spontaneously assumed, he was able to instill, without of course permitting himself anything that might shock the most scrupulous delicacy, that shade of delicate familiarity permissible between kindred souls when they meet and recognize each other in the midst of the masks of that ignoble masquerade known as society. Thus might two angels address each other if, having descended from heaven on some mission, they should meet here below. Indeed such noble simplicity is not without a certain kinship to the informality of speech permitted by long acquaintance. But in delicate reassurance each word seemed to say: "Bear with me for a moment; as soon as you wish to put on your mask again, we shall once more become complete strangers to one another—as is proper. Never fear that tomorrow I shall presume on this moment, but deign to enjoy yourself for an instant in all security."

In general women are terrified by conversations of this sort, but in practice never know how to stop them. For the man, apparently so overjoyed to talk to them, seems always to be saying: "Souls like ours should ignore considerations that were made for common mortals, and you surely feel as I do that . . ."

But for this unlooked-for eloquence, one should not fail to give due credit to Lucien's inexperience. It was through no effort of will that he had suddenly assumed a tone so favorable to his aspirations; he sincerely thought what this tone seemed to say, and thus, for reasons by no means flattering to his powers of diplomacy, his manner of expressing it was perfect. It was the illusion of a child-like heart. Lucien had always had a certain instinctive horror of all the base things that rose like a forbidding wall between himself and experience. He turned his eyes away from everything that seemed to him too ugly, and at twenty-three was as naïve as any sixteen-year-old Parisian youth of good family would be ashamed of being in his last year of school. It was by pure chance that Lucien adopted the tone of a clever man of the world. He was certainly no expert in the art of winning a woman's heart and arousing her senses.

This tone, so singular, so attractive, so dangerous, was shocking, and practically unintelligible, only to M. de Blancet who, nonetheless, insisted on putting in a word now and then. Lucien had taken possession of all Madame de Chasteller's attention as though it were his due. Terrified though she was, she could not help thoroughly approving Lucien's ideas and sometimes replying to them in almost the same tone; but finally, without precisely ceasing to listen with pleasure, she fell into a brown study.

To justify her involuntary smiles of approbation in her own mind, she said to herself: "He talks about everything happening here at the ball and not a word about himself." But the very fact of his daring to talk to her in this manner, even about unimportant things, was in itself a way of speaking of himself and of putting himself on a footing that was by no means negligible in the eyes of a woman of her age, and one accustomed, as she was, to so much reserve: such a footing would have been nothing less than unique.

At first Madame de Chasteller was amazed and amused by the transformation she was witnessing, but not for long. Soon she ceased to smile. Now it was her turn to be afraid. "In what a way he dares to talk to me, and I am not in the least shocked! I do not feel in the least offended! Heavens! he is not by any means just another nice, simple young man . . . what an idiot I was to think so! On the contrary I am confronted with one of those clever, attractive, and profoundly insidious men, such as one meets in novels. They know how to make themselves attractive precisely because they are incapable of loving. There he stands before me, happy and gay, occupied in assuming a role—certainly a most pleasing one—but he is happy only because he feels that he is talking so well. . . . Apparently he decided to start his conquest by appearing completely dazzled for an hour, even to the point of being stupid. But I shall certainly find a way of breaking off all relations with such a dangerous, such an accomplished actor."

But even as she was making this sage reflection, formulating this magnificent resolution, her heart was already involved. From this moment may be reckoned the birth of a particular sentiment for Lucien, setting him apart. All at once Madame de Chasteller was struck with remorse at having remained there so long talking to Lucien, away from all the other women, and having as chaperon only the worthy M. de Blancet who, in all probability, did not understand a word of all he was hearing. To extricate herself from this embarrassing situation, she accepted Lucien's request that she should dance with him in the quadrille.

After the quadrille and during the waltz that followed, Madame d'Hocquincourt called out to Madame de Chasteller to come and sit beside her in a corner where there was a little more air and some relief from the increasing heat of the ballroom.

Lucien, who was on the friendliest terms with Madame d'Hocquincourt, remained with the two ladies. There Madame de Chasteller could see for herself that he was the rage that evening. "And it really isn't surprising," she thought, "for in addition to the handsome uniform, which he wears so well, he is always the center of mirth and gaiety wherever he happens to be."

The guests were now beginning to drift toward a tent

nearby where supper was being served. Lucien managed it
so that he could offer Madame de Chasteller his arm. It seemed
to her that whole days must have intervened between her
present feelings and her state of mind at the beginning of
the evening. She had almost entirely forgotten the boredom
that had fairly extinguished her voice after the first hour spent
at the ball.

It was midnight; the supper had been laid out in a charming
open-air hall formed by the walls of hedges twelve to fifteen
feet high. Over these verdant walls a tent roof with broad red
and white stripes sheltered the guests from a possible heavy
fall of dew. These were the colors of the exiled personage
whose birthday was being celebrated. Here and there, through
the leaves of this living wall, could be seen a lovely moon
lighting up a wide and peaceful landscape. This ravishing
scene of nature was in tune with the new emotions struggling
for the possession of Madame de Chasteller's heart, and was, in
part, responsible for putting off and weakening the protests
of her reason. Lucien did not take his place next to Madame
de Chasteller (one had to have a certain regard for the old
friends of his new acquaintance, as a look, more friendly than
he would ever have dared hope for, had warned him), but
where he could both see and hear her perfectly.

He had the happy idea of expressing his real feelings by
means of remarks apparently intended for the ladies sitting
near him. This necessitated his talking a great deal, yet, without
saying too many preposterous things, he was successful. He
soon dominated the conversation; and while greatly entertaining the ladies around Madame de Chasteller, he began au-
daciously expressing things that could have an infinitely
tender implication, something he would otherwise never have
dreamed of attempting so soon. He knew that Madame de
Chasteller could very well pretend, if she chose, not to understand these words addressed to her indirectly. Lucien even

succeeded in entertaining the men who stood behind the ladies, for they did not yet view his success with out and out envy.

Everyone was talking, and there was a great deal of laughter at Madame de Chasteller's end of the table. People at the other end fell silent hoping to have some part in all the merriment centered around her. Madame de Chasteller was doubly occupied, both with what she heard, which often made her laugh, and with those very serious reflections forming such a strange contrast to the gay and festive tone of the evening.

"So this is that timid fellow whom I thought devoid of ideas? What a terrifying creature!" It was perhaps the first time in his life that Lucien had been witty, brilliantly witty. Toward the end of the supper he noticed that his success went beyond anything he could have dreamed of. He was happy, extremely animated, and yet, by some miracle, he said nothing that was offensive, in spite of the fact that here among the proud families of Lorraine, he was hemmed in by three or four fierce prejudices of which Paris had but the palest copies: fanatical belief in Henri V and the Nobility, and a duplicity and stupidity toward the lower orders which amounted to a veritable crime against humanity. None of these great verities, the foundation head of the credo of the Faubourg Saint-Germain, received the slightest wound from Lucien's gaiety.

It was because his generous heart had, in fact, infinite sympathy for the situation of these poor young gentlemen around him. Four years ago, out of loyalty to their political beliefs and ideas of a lifetime, they had deprived themselves of a small portion of the budget, useful if not absolutely necessary to their subsistence. They had lost even more: the only occupation in the world that could save them from boredom, the only one, they were convinced, that did not dishonor them.

The ladies decided that Lucien was *eminently correct*. Madame de Commercy it was who pronounced the sanctifying word in that corner of the ballroom reserved for the highest nobility. For there was a little group of seven or eight ladies who despised the rest of this society, which, in turn, despised the rest of the city, very much as Napoleon's Imperial Guard would, in case of a revolt, have terrified that army of 1812 which itself was the terror of Europe.

At this conclusive word of Madame de Commercy, the gilded youth of Nancy almost revolted. These young gentlemen, so adept in how to be elegant and how to appear to advantage at the entrance of a café, were usually silent at balls, content to reveal their prowess simply as lusty and indefatigable dancers. When they saw Lucien talking volubly, contrary to his habit, and noticed, moreover, that he was listened to, they began saying that he was very noisy and quite insufferable; that such loud amiability might be the fashion in *bourgeois* circles in Paris and in the back parlors of the shops of the Rue Saint-Honoré, but would certainly never succeed with good society in Nancy.

While these gentlemen thus declared themselves, Lucien's witty remarks were succeeding admirably and giving them the lie. They were reduced to repeating to one another with a lugubriously self-satisfied air: "After all, he is only a bourgeois, born nobody knows where, and the only nobility he can hope to enjoy is that conferred by his epaulets."

This remark of the resigned officers of Lorraine sums up the great quarrel that afflicts the Nineteenth Century: the resentment of rank against merit.

But none of the ladies gave a thought to such melancholy ideas; they had completely escaped, for the moment, from the sad civilization that so weighs on the male mind in the provinces. The supper finished brilliantly with champagne; and without ill effect this wine brought greater gaiety and freedom to everyone's manners. As for our hero, he was elevated by the tenderest sentiments which, disguised by the mask of gaiety, he had the temerity to address to the lady of his thoughts. It was the first time in his life that success had thrown him into such a state of intoxication.

Returning to the ballroom, M. de Blancet danced a waltz with Madame de Chasteller, and was succeeded after a few turns by Lucien, in accordance with the German custom. During the dance, with a skill that was not skill but the offspring of chance and passion, Lucien was able to resume their conversation in a tone which, although altogether respectful, was, nevertheless, in more ways than one, that of an old acquaintance.

Taking advantage of a grand cotillion, which neither Madame de Chasteller nor Lucien cared to dance, he was able to say to her, laughing and without its being too out of keeping with the general tone of their colloquy: "All for the sake of getting nearer to your beautiful eyes I bought a missal, I fought a duel, and I cultivated the acquaintance of Dr. Du Poirier." Madame de Chasteller's face grew very pale at that moment, and her startled eyes expressed profound surprise, and almost fright. At the name of Du Poirier she replied in a low voice and as though loath to pronounce the words: "He is a dangerous man!"

Lucien was mad with joy, for Madame de Chasteller had showed no anger at the motives he gave for his conduct in Nancy. But he hardly dared believe what seemed evident.

A silence of two or three seconds followed, pregnant with meaning; Lucien fixed his eyes on those of Madame de Chasteller, until at last he dared to say:

"He is admirable from my point of view; if it had not been for him, I should not be here tonight. . . . But," he added, with all his imprudent artlessness, "I have a terrible suspicion."

"What? What is it?" asked Madame de Chasteller.

She felt right away that so direct, so impulsive a response on her part was a hopeless indiscretion; but she had spoken without thinking. She blushed deeply. Lucien was very much moved to see the crimson flush spreading even over her shoulders.

But, as it happened, Lucien could not reply to Madame de Chasteller's simple question. "What will she think of me?" he said to himself. Instantly his expression changed; he paled as though struck by some sudden malady; his features betrayed the terrible pain caused by the thought of M. de Busant de Sicile which, having left him for several hours, now suddenly returned.

That was it! What he had obtained was only a favor conferred on a uniform no matter who wore it! His thirst for the truth, coupled with the impossibility of finding admissible words to express such an odious idea, threw him into a profound embarrassment. "One word and I am lost forever!"

The unlooked-for emotion that seemed to have chilled Lucien, was in an instant communicated to Madame de Chasteller. She turned pale seeing the cruel suffering, no doubt related in some way to her, that had so suddenly appeared on Lucien's open and youthful countenance: his features seemed to have shrunk; his eyes, so brilliant before, now appeared dull and sightless.

There was an exchange of one or two insignificant words. "But what is the matter?" said Madame de Chasteller.

"I don't know," Lucien replied mechanically.

"But, how can you say, you don't know?"

"No, Madam . . . My respect for you . . ."

Can the reader ever believe that Madame de Chasteller, more and more perturbed, was imprudent enough to add: "Has this suspicion anything to do with me?"

"Would I have hesitated the fraction of a second?" cried Lucien with all the ardor of a first sorrow keenly felt. "Would

I have hesitated had it had nothing to do with you, with nobody but you in the whole world? Whom else could I think of but you? And hasn't this suspicion stabbed me through the heart a hundred times a day ever since I came to Nancy?"

Nothing more was needed to stimulate Madame de Chasteller's growing interest than to have her honor called in question. It did not occur to her to hide her astonishment at the tone of Lucien's reply. The fervor with which he had just spoken to her, the evidence of the extreme sincerity in this young man's words, all at once changed her pallor to an imprudent blush. Even her eyes blushed! But dare I admit in such a prudish age which seems to have contracted a marriage with hypocrisy, that it was with happiness that Madame de Chasteller first blushed and not because of what the dancers might be thinking about her as they passed back and forth in front of them through the figures of the cotillion.

She might decide to respond, or not to respond, to his love; but how sincere it was! with what devotion she was loved! "Perhaps, even most probably, this infatuation will not last," she said to herself. "But how real it is! No ranting, no flowery phrases! Surely this is true passion; surely this is the way it would be sweet to be loved. But that his suspicion should be such as to arrest his love . . . why, the implication is infamous!"

Madame de Chasteller remained pensive, her head resting on her fan. From time to time, her eyes turned toward Lucien who was standing as still and pale as a ghost, intent upon her alone. Lucien's eyes were indiscreet to a degree that would have made her tremble had she still had her wits about her.

CHAPTER EIGHTEEN

ANOTHER much more perturbing thought now came to agitate her heart. "At the beginning of the evening it was not any lack of ideas that kept him from talking, as, in my innocence, I had imagined. Could it have been because of that suspicion, that horrible suspicion which made him falter in his esteem for me? . . . Suspicion of what? What calumny black enough to produce such an effect in anyone so young and so good?"

Despite her seeming calm, Madame de Chasteller was so overwrought that without thinking of the temerity of what she was saying, and still under the influence of the gay tone of the conversation at supper, she let this strange question escape her:

"But why is it . . . at the beginning of the evening you found only the most insignificant things to say to me? Was it your exaggerated sense of politeness? Was it . . . the reserve so natural between two people who hardly know each other?" (Here she lowered her voice in spite of herself.) "Or was it," she finally added, "the effect of that suspicion?" And her voice at these last two words suddenly resumed a tone of restraint without losing any of its intensity.

"It was because of my extreme shyness: I have no experience of life, I had never been in love before; your eyes, when I saw them so close, terrified me."

This was said with such an accent of sincerity, with such tender intimacy, with such real love that, before she could think, Madame de Chasteller's eyes—those eyes whose expression was so profound, so sincere—had replied for her: "I, too, am in love."

After half a second, as though coming out of a trance, she turned her eyes away, but not before Lucien's had garnered the full force of that telltale look.

He flushed almost absurdly red. He hardly dared believe the extent of his good fortune. Madame de Chasteller, for her part, felt that her cheeks were on fire. "My God! I am compromising myself in the most frightful way. All eyes are turned on this stranger with whom I have been talking so long, and with such a show of interest!"

She beckoned to M. de Blancet who was dancing in the cotillion.

"Take me to the terrace in the garden. I have been feeling ill from the heat for the last five minutes, I am suffocating. I drank half a glass of champagne at supper, and I really believe I am intoxicated."

But what was frightful for Madame de Chasteller was that instead of adopting a sympathetic tone, M. de Blancet only sneered derisively as he listened to these lies. He was mad with jealousy at the air of intimacy, of pleasure, with which she had been listening to Lucien for so long and, moreover, he had been warned in his regiment never to credit the indispositions of lovely ladies.

He offered her his arm and was escorting her out of the ballroom when another equally luminous idea occurred to him. Madame de Chasteller seemed to be leaning heavily on his arm with a really singular abandon.

"Does my lovely cousin wish me to understand that she reciprocates at last, or that she has, at least, a certain feeling of tenderness for me?" M. de Blancet asked himself. But trying to recall all the little incidents of the evening, he could find nothing that seemed to presage such a happy change. Was it a sudden impulse, or was it willful dissimulation on her part? He led her to the other side of some flower-beds where he discovered a marble table placed in front of a garden chair with back and foot rest. He had some difficulty in getting Madame de Chasteller comfortably seated, for she seemed almost incapable of movement.

While M. de Blancet, instead of seeing what was happening under his own nose, was engaged with these chimerical fancies, Madame de Chasteller was reduced to utter despair. "My conduct is shocking!" she said to herself. "I have compromised myself in the eyes of all those women, and at this moment I am the subject of the most unflattering and humiliating re-marks. I have behaved, for I don't know how long, as though no one were looking at me, or at M. Leuwen. Nancy society will never overlook anything as far as I am concerned. . . . And M. Leuwen?" This name, as she said it to herself, made her tremble. "And I have compromised myself in the eyes of M. Leuwen!"

That was the real cause of her wretchedness. And it found no relief in any of the thoughts that came crowding in upon her as she reviewed all that had happened that evening.

Soon another suspicion came to add to her unhappiness. "If M. Leuwen acts with such assurance it must be because he knows that I spend whole hours hidden behind the shutters at my window, waiting for him to ride past."

We hope our reader will not think Madame de Chasteller too absurd. Inexperienced as she was, she had no idea of all the pitfalls into which a loving heart may lead one; never had she felt anything to resemble what had been happening to her during this painful evening. She could not find an idea in her head to come to her rescue, and had no real experience to help her. The strongest emotions that had, up till now, troubled her equanimity had been the slight timidity she felt when being presented to a great princess, or profound indigna-tion against the Jacobins who were trying to undermine the throne of the Bourbons. Over and above these theories which were largely sentimental and only succeeded in touching her heart for an instant, Madame de Chasteller had an earnest and tender nature, which at this moment could only be expected to add to her unhappiness. Unfortunately the little daily interests of life did not touch her. Thus she had always lived in false security. For natures that have the misfortune of being above the trifles which form the chief occupation of the majority of human beings are all the more disposed to think exclusively of the things that have once succeeded in really touching them.

CHAPTER NINETEEN

TO CROWN her misery, and as a result of that savoir-vivre which makes a sojourn in the provinces so agreeable, several women, who were certainly not very intimate friends of Madame de Chasteller, promptly left the ballroom and together invaded the terrace, crowding around the marble table. Several had brought candles. Each one of them chirped something about her friendship and her eagerness to do something for her *dear* Madame de Chasteller. M. de Blancet had not had enough backbone to safeguard the entrance of her garden retreat and to prevent this intrusion.

The accumulation of worry and unhappiness, aided by this abominable uproar, was about to drive Madame de Chasteller into a fit of hysterics in good earnest.

"Let's see now," these kind friends were thinking, "just how this woman, so proud of her wealth and with all her haughty airs, behaves when she is in such a state."

Hearing them approach, Madame de Chasteller had said to herself:

"Whatever I do, I am sure to be guilty of some horrible new blunder." She decided to keep her eyes closed and not to reply.

Madame de Chasteller could find no excuse for her self-styled obliquities. She was as miserable as anyone could possibly be in life's most trying moments. If the unhappiness of tender souls does not at such times reach the maximum of their endurance, it is perhaps because the necessity of action prevents the soul from being wholly absorbed by the contemplation of its misfortune.

Lucien was dying to follow the indiscreet ladies out to the terrace; but he had hardly taken a step in that direction before he was horrified by this grossly selfish impulse and to avoid all temptation he left the ball, but with lingering steps. He regretted missing the end of the evening. He was amazed, and, at the bottom of his heart, worried. He had no idea of the extent of his victory. He felt an instinctive urge to review, and to weigh, with all the calm of reason, the events that had happened with such rapidity. He was in need of reflection, of deciding what he *ought* to think.

His heart, still so young, was dazed by these concerns of great moment, which he had treated as if they had been mere trifles. He could see nothing clearly. While the skirmish lasted, he had probably never allowed himself to stop for an instant to think, fearing to let the least opportunity for action escape him. Now in retrospect he saw that things of the utmost importance had been happening. He did not dare give himself up to the visions of happiness he vaguely glimpsed, and he trembled suddenly as he reviewed the events, recalling some word, some act that might separate him forever from Madame de Chasteller. As for his remorse at being in love with her, there was now no longer any question of it.

Dr. Du Poirier, who, shrewd man that he was, never neglected small opportunities while giving serious attention to large ones, now fearing that some young doctor, a good dancer as well, might make the most of Madame de Chasteller's indisposition, soon appeared in front of the marble table which still afforded Madame de Chasteller some slight protection against the zeal of her loving friends. With her eyes closed and head resting on her hands, motionless and silent, surrounded by twenty candles that curiosity had assembled, Madame de Chasteller was now the center of attack from a group of twelve or fifteen women all talking at once of their friendship for her and of the best remedies for fainting fits.

Since Du Poirier had no interest in saying the contrary, he told them the simple truth, that what Madame de Chasteller needed, above all, was calm and silence.

"Ladies, please be good enough to return to the ballroom. Leave Madame de Chasteller alone with her doctor and with M. de Blancet. We shall take her home just as quickly as possible."

Hearing the doctor give this order, the poor afflicted soul was profoundly grateful.

"I'll see to everything!" cried M. de Blancet who always came off with flying colors on those all too rare occasions when physical energy takes precedence over everything else. He was gone like a flash, in less than five minutes had reached the Hôtel de Pontlevé at the other end of the town, had the horses in harness, had indeed harnessed them with his own hands, and soon Madame de Chasteller's carriage, driven by M. de Blancet himself, could be heard clattering up at a gallop.

Safe in her own apartment at last, Madame de Chasteller had presence of mind enough to dismiss her maid who hoped for nothing so much as a full account of her mistress's mishap. Madame de Chasteller thought bitterly of her dear friend Madame de Constantin whom M. de Pontlevé's calculated

politeness had succeeded in keeping away. Madame de Chasteller dared write in the letters entrusted to the post only the
vaguest assurances of affection, having reason to believe that
her father had all her letters shown to him. The postmistress
of Nancy *thought right,* and M. de Pontlevé was the head of
a sort of commission established in the name of Charles X
for Lorraine, Alsace, and Franche-Comté.

"And so I am alone, utterly alone in the world with my
shame," Madame de Chasteller said to herself.

She wept without restraint in the silence and secrecy of a
great open window from which, two leagues away toward
the east, could be seen the somber mass of the Burelviller
woods, and overhead a dark, cloudless sky strewn with twinkling stars. At last she grew calmer, and summoned the courage
to call her maid and to dismiss her for the night. Until then
the presence of any human being would have painfully intensified her shame and distress. As soon as she heard the
maid climbing the stairs to her own room, bravely she forced
herself to turn her mind to an examination of all her hideous
errors of that fatal evening.

At first her distress and confusion were extreme. It seemed
to her that no matter where she turned she discovered some
new reason for despising herself, and a boundless humiliation.
What shocked her most of all was that suspicion which Lucien had dared to mention. To think that a man, a young
man, should permit himself such a liberty! Lucien seemed to
be well-bred. Then it must be that she had given him extraordinary encouragement. What had she done? She could
remember nothing except that sort of pity and disappointment
she had felt at the beginning of the evening because of the
singular lack of ideas displayed by a young man she found
attractive. "And to think I took him merely for a very *accomplished* horseman like my cousin, Blancet!"

But what could have been that suspicion he spoke of?

This was her worst torment. She wept for a long time. Her tears were the honorable amends she made herself.

"Well, let him have all the suspicions he likes," cried Madame de Chasteller. "It must be some calumny he has heard. If he believes it, so much the worse for him; it only proves that he has very little intelligence or discernment! I am innocent!"

This display of pride was sincere. Little by little she ceased to wonder what that suspicion might be. Her real faults seemed to her at that moment even more unbearable and innumerable. And she wept again. At last, after all the anguish of extremest bitterness, weak and half-dead from grief, it seemed to her that she could clearly distinguish two things for which she must blame herself in particular: first she had let that contemptible and stupidly malicious audience which she despised, catch a glimpse of what was happening in her heart. She felt her unhappiness redoubled as she thought of all the many reasons she had to dread its cruelty and to despise it. All those gentlemen on their knees before wealth, or at the least show of favor from the King or from a minister, how pitiless they are toward any fault not derived from the love of money! Thinking of all her scorn for this high society of Nancy in whose eyes she had compromised herself, she felt a pain, a *detailed* pain, if I may be permitted the expression, that burned like a red-hot iron. She imagined all the glances cast her way by the women who had danced past her in the cotillion, imagined all their scorn.

After having wantonly exposed herself to the stings of this pain, Madame de Chasteller reverted to a much deeper grief, the thought of which seemed, in a flash, to divest her of all her courage. It was her own condemnation for having violated, in the eyes of Lucien, that feminine reserve without which a woman cannot hope to enjoy the esteem of a man who is himself worthy of esteem. Faced by the chief article of her indictment, she felt something like a respite from her suffering. She even brought herself to say, and aloud, in a voice half-strangled by sobs:

"And if he didn't despise me, it is I who would despise him! Can it be possible," she cried after a moment of silence, and as though yielding to her rage against herself, "a man entertains doubts about my conduct, and far from turning away, I seem to want to justify myself. And as though this indignity were not enough, I make a spectacle of myself, I lay my heart bare to those vile creatures who, whenever I stop to think of them seriously, make me sick for days at a time; and then, in the end, my imprudent eyes give M. Leuwen the right to place me among those women who throw themselves at the head of the first man who pleases them. For why shouldn't he have the insolence of his age? Hasn't he every justification?"

And she soon denied herself the delight of thinking of Lucien, to revert to those terrible words: *who throw themselves at the head of the first man who comes along.*

"But M. Leuwen is right," she continued with savage courage. "I see clearly enough myself that I am a dissolute woman. I did not love him before this fatal night; I thought of him only in a perfectly rational way, and as a young man who seemed to be a little above the usual run of gentlemen whom chance sends our way. He speaks to me for an instant, I think him frightfully shy, and a stupid arrogance makes me trifle with him as someone of no consequence; it amuses me to try to force him to talk; and then, all at once, I find myself thinking of nothing but him. It was evidently simply because I found him handsome. Could the most depraved woman have acted any worse?"

This new access of despair was more violent than all the others. At last, as the white light of dawn paled the sky above the black woods of Burelviller, exhaustion and sleep came to suspend for a little while Madame de Chasteller's remorse and sorrow.

During this same night, Lucien thought of her ceaselessly, and with a feeling of adoration that was indeed very flattering. What a consolation could she only have witnessed all the timidity of this young man who seemed to her like the most terrible and accomplished Don Juan! Lucien could not make up his mind what to think of the events of this decisive evening. He could not help trembling as he pronounced the word "decisive." He believed that he had read in her eyes the promise that one day she would love him.

"But, Great God! have I no other merit in the eyes of this angelic creature than to be an exception to the rule which makes her prefer lieutenant-colonels! Great God! How can such behavior, apparently so vulgar, be reconciled with all the appearances of a noble soul? I can see that heaven has not given me the gift of understanding the heart of woman. Dévelroy was right: I shall be a simpleton all my life, always more amazed at my own heart than at all that is happening to me. This heart of mine, which should be wild with happiness, is, quite the contrary, in deep distress. Ah! If only I could see her! I should ask her advice; the soul that spoke from those eyes would understand my suffering; to vulgar souls it would seem too ridiculous. What! I win a hundred francs in a lottery and I am in despair because I did not win a million! I devote all my attention to the prettiest woman of the city in which I happen to find myself. First weakness: I try to resist her. I am beaten. And now here I am trying to do everything to please her, just like any of those poor ineffectual little nobodies who clutter up the salons of Paris. Finally, the woman, with whom I have the signal weakness of being in love, seems to receive my advances with pleasure and a coquetry which is, at least in its manner, adorable. She plays her role as though she guessed that the passion

I am weak enough to entertain for her is serious. Instead of enjoying my good fortune, not so bad after all, I spoil it by indulging in false delicacy. I torture myself because the heart of a lady of the Court has been stirred by others before me! But, great God, have I the art to win the heart of a truly virtuous woman? Every time I have aspired to a woman a little better than the common run of grisettes, haven't I always failed in the most ridiculous fashion? Hasn't Ernest, who, after all, possesses intelligence despite all his pedantry, explained to me how totally lacking I am in sang-froid? With my choir-boy face everybody knows exactly what I am thinking. . . . Instead of taking advantage of my little conquests and forging ahead, I stand stock-still like a donkey, rolling them around on my tongue with relish. For me the pressure of a hand is a city of Capua; instead of advancing I stand in ecstasy over the rare delights of so decided a favor. In short, I have no talent for this sort of warfare, and I have the temerity to be exacting! Poor idiot, if you please her it is quite by chance, pure chance. . . ."

After pacing up and down his room a hundred times:

"I love her," he said aloud, "or at least I want her to love me. I have even an idea that she *is* in love with me. And yet I am miserable. I could certainly pose for the portrait of the perfect fool. Apparently, in my plans for winning her, I should first of all require her not to love me! Wonderful! I want her to love me and I am miserable because she seems to have taken a fancy to me! When one is an idiot, one should at least try not to be a coward as well."

At daybreak he fell asleep with this lovely thought, and with half a mind to ask Colonel Malher to have him transferred to N——, twenty leagues from Nancy where a detachment of his regiment was engaged in keeping an eye on the Mutualist workers.

How it would have added to the torture of poor Madame

de Chasteller, who, almost at the same hour, had succumbed to fatigue at last, had she been aware of the seeming contempt which, twisted and turned in every sense, looked at from every angle, was keeping awake the man who, in spite of herself, was uppermost in her own thoughts!

CHAPTER TWENTY

WHATEVER LUCIEN'S THOUGHTS may have been, he was not master of his actions. Early next morning, having donned his uniform and started out to present himself to Colonel Malher, he passed within sight of Madame de Chasteller's street. He could not resist the desire to have another glimpse of those windows with the parrot-green shutters which, if the Colonel granted his request, he might never see again. He had hardly turned into the street than his heart began pounding so that he could scarcely breathe: the mere idea that he might catch sight of Madame de Chasteller almost drove him out of his mind. It was even a relief not to find her at her window.

"And what would become of me," he asked himself, "if after obtaining permission to leave Nancy, I should long just as madly to return? Since last night I am no longer master of myself, I follow every idea that suddenly strikes me and that a second before I'd never thought of."

After this bit of reasoning worthy of a student of the École Polytechnique, Lucien mounted his horse and did five or six leagues in two hours. He was running away from himself. Morally he suffered all the anguish of physical thirst in the urgent need he felt of submitting his own to another man's judgment, of asking advice. He had just enough reason left to believe and to feel that he was going mad; yet his entire happiness depended on the opinion he should finally form of Madame de Chasteller.

He had had the good sense not to go beyond the bounds of the most circumspect reserve with the officers of his regiment. So he had no one near him to encourage him, he had not even the expedient of the vaguest, most remote opinion. M. Gauthier was away, and, besides, Lucien felt sure, would not have understood his folly except to upbraid him and advise him to go away.

Returning from his ride, and passing once more through the Rue de la Pompe, he had an access of madness that astonished him. It seemed to him that if he were to encounter Madame de Chasteller's eyes at that moment, he would fall off his horse for the third time. He felt that he lacked the courage to leave Nancy, and he did not go to see Colonel Malher.

M. Gauthier returned from the country that same evening. Lucien attempted to speak to him of his situation in veiled terms, trying him out, as they say. And, after a few conventional phrases, this is what Gauthier said:

"I too have my worries. Those workers of N—— have me bothered. What will the army have to say? . . ."

The very day after the ball Doctor Du Poirier came to pay his young friend a long call, and without preamble began talking about Madame de Chasteller. Lucien felt himself blushing to the whites of his eyes. He opened the window and stood in the shadow of the blinds so that the doctor could not see his face clearly.

"That old duffer has come here to cross-examine me. We'll see about that!"

Lucien launched forth in praise of the beauty of the pavilion where the dancing had taken place the night before. From the courtyard he proceeded to the magnificent stairway and the vases of exotic plants with which they had been decorated; then, in mathematical and logical order, from the stairway he passed on to the antechamber, thence to the first two drawing rooms. . . .

The doctor soon broke in, turning the conversation to the subject of Madame de Chasteller's indisposition, and speculating on what might have been the cause. Lucien was careful not to interrupt him. Each word was a treasure, for the doctor had just come from the Hôtel de Pontlevé. However, Lucien succeeded in keeping himself well in hand; at the slightest pause he gravely resumed his dissertation on the probable cost of those elegant tents with crimson and white stripes. The sound of these words, that fell so strangely from his lips, seemed to increase his coolness and perfect self-possession. Never had he had more need of them: the doctor, who wanted at any cost to make him talk, told him priceless things about Madame de Chasteller, things about which Lucien would have paid any price to hear more. And the situation was tempting: he felt that with a little adroit flattery the doctor could be led to betray any secret in the world. But Lucien was cautious to the point of diffidence. He never pronounced the name of Madame de Chasteller except in replying to the doctor; to do so at any other moment would have been a serious blunder.

Lucien overplayed his part, but, not being accustomed to people who replied to exactly what was said, Du Poirier failed to notice. Lucien made up his mind to be ill the next day; he hoped to find out from the doctor many more details about M. de Pontlevé and the daily life of Madame de Chasteller.

The following day the doctor had changed his tactics. Madame de Chasteller, according to him, was a prude, imbued with an insufferable pride, much less rich than people said. She had, at most, an income of ten thousand francs. But, in spite of all the doctor's barely disguised spite toward Madame de Chasteller, he did not even mention M. Thomas de Busant de Sicile, lieutenant-colonel of Hussars. This was a precious moment for Lucien. Almost as precious as that moment the night before when Madame de Chasteller had looked at him after asking if his suspicion had anything to do with her! And so there had been no scandal connected with her affair with M. Thomas de Busant!

Lucien paid many calls that evening, but said not a word beyond making the most conventional inquiries on the state of everyone's health after such an extraordinarily exhausting ball.

"What a boon to these bored provincials the spectacle of my real preoccupation would be—if they only knew!"

Everybody criticized Madame de Chasteller with the exception of the good Théodelinde; but then Théodelinde was quite ugly and Madame de Chasteller extremely pretty. Lucien felt for Théodelinde an affection that almost amounted to love.

"Madame de Chasteller fails to share these people's taste in the matter of amusement," she observed. "That is something that is forgiven nowhere. Such differences are unknown in Paris."

During his last calls Lucien, certain now of not meeting Madame de Chasteller who, it was said, was still indisposed, thought how pleasant it would be to see those little embroidered muslin curtains lighted by her candles.

"I am a coward," he finally decided. "Very well! I shall give in to my cowardice and enjoy it."

> And if you must be damned, at least
> Be damned for pleasant sins!

These were perhaps his last sighs of remorse at being in love, and over his lost love for his poor betrayed fatherland. One cannot have two loves at the same time.

"I am a coward," he said to himself as he left Madame d'Hocquincourt's drawing room. Since in Nancy the streetlights were extinguished at ten-thirty by order of the Mayor, and since, with the exception of the nobility, everybody then went to bed, he could, without being too ridiculous in his *own* eyes, pace back and forth under the parrot-green shutters, although almost immediately after his arrival the lights had gone out in the little room. Embarrassed by the sound of his own footsteps, Lucien took advantage of the profound darkness and settled himself for a long time on a large stone directly across the street from the window, from which he never once took his eyes.

His was not the only heart to be disturbed by the sound of his footsteps. Until ten o'clock Madame de Chasteller had spent an evening haunted by somber thoughts and filled with remorse. She would have been less melancholy in company, but she was afraid to risk meeting Lucien or hearing his name mentioned. At ten-thirty, seeing him appear, her deep and lonely sadness was all at once interrupted by the pounding of her heart. She hastened to blow out her candles, but, in spite of all her remonstrances with herself, did not leave the window. Her eyes were guided in the darkness by the tip of Lucien's little cigar. Lucien had finally triumphed over the last vestige of remorse.

"All right—I shall love her and despise her," he said to himself. "And after she loves me I shall say to her: 'Ah, if only your soul had been pure, I should have cherished you for the rest of my life!' "

The next day, wakened at five o'clock for drill, Lucien felt a passionate desire to see Madame de Chasteller. He now felt sure of her heart.

"One look told me everything!" he repeated when common sense tried to raise some objection. "But I would to God she were more difficult to please! I should not complain."

Finally, five days after the ball, which seemed like five weeks to Lucien, he met Madame de Chasteller at the Comtesse de Commercy's. Madame de Chasteller was ravishing. Her natural pallor had vanished as she heard the lackey announcing: *M. Leuwen.* As for Lucien, he could hardly breathe. But Madame de Chasteller's costume seemed to him far too elegant, too gay, too sophisticated. Madame de Chasteller was indeed exquisitely dressed in a style that Paris would have approved.

"Why should she go to so much trouble simply to pay a call on an old lady?" he said to himself. "It is a little too suggestive of her weakness for lieutenant-colonels!"

But in spite of his bitter disapproval he added:

"Very well then, I shall love her—but not seriously."

While he was making this good resolution, he was not three steps away from her and trembling like a leaf, but with happiness.

At this moment, Lucien made a polite inquiry about her indisposition; Madame de Chasteller replied with the greatest courtesy, and in a charming tone of voice but, at the same time, with a composure that was all the more convincing since it was neither serious nor sad but, on the contrary, affable almost to the point of gaiety. Completely disconcerted, Lucien did not realize the full extent of the misfortune this tone seemed to presage until after he had left, and had had time to think it over. As for his own manner, it was as dull and stupid as possible. Perfectly aware of this, he made a great effort to give a little grace to his gestures and voice—with what success may well be imagined!

"Here I am displaying exactly the same degree of idiocy as during the first moments of our conversation at the ball . . ." he thought, passing judgment on himself. And he was right, he in no way exaggerated his lack of charm and wit. But what he did not know was that the only person in whose eyes he longed not to appear an idiot, had judged his embarrassment quite differently.

"M. Leuwen," thought Madame de Chasteller, "was expecting the natural sequel to my inconceivably frivolous behavior at the ball, or at least he had a right to hope for an agreeable, even an affectionate manner, recalling that friendly tone. He meets instead with an extremely courteous manner, but one which actually implies that he is even less to me than a simple acquaintance."

In order to say something, and not finding an idea in his head, Lucien suddenly decided to expatiate upon the talents of Madame Malibran who was then singing at Metz, and whom all Nancy society had announced its intention of going to hear. Madame de Chasteller, delighted not to have to struggle to find words both polite enough and, at the same time, cold enough, silently watched him as he talked. Soon he was floundering hopelessly, and so ridiculous in his confusion that even Madame de Commercy noticed it.

"The accomplishments of these fashionable young men are remarkably subject to change," she murmured to Madame de Chasteller. "He has not the slightest resemblance to the charming young second-lieutenant who often calls on me."

This remark was a joy to Madame de Chasteller: a sensible woman, famous in the city for her good sense and cool judgment, had just confirmed what she herself had been thinking, and with what pleasure!

"How different from that man I saw at the ball—so merry, so quick, so sparkling with wit, embarrassed only by the overabundance and vivacity of his ideas! And here he is trying to talk about a famous singer without being able to find one single intelligent word to say, although he reads reams about Madame Malibran's perfections in the papers every day."

Madame de Chasteller felt so extremely happy that all at once she thought:

"I am in danger of forgetting myself by some friendly word or smile that will spoil all the happiness of the evening. This is indeed very sweet to me, but if I don't want to be angry with myself, I must stop right here."

She rose and took her departure.

Soon after, Lucien also left; he needed to meditate calmly on the extent of his own imbecility and on Madame de Chasteller's cool indifference. After five or six hours of heartbreaking reflection, he arrived at this glorious conclusion:

He was not a lieutenant-colonel and as such worthy of Madame de Chasteller's attention. Her behavior toward him at the ball had been mere trifling on her part, a passing fancy, to which such naturally affectionate women are subject. For an instant the uniform had given her an illusion; for an instant, nothing better being at hand, she had mistaken him for a colonel. All this was cold comfort.

"I am a complete fool and this woman an actress and a coquette—and wonderfully beautiful! The devil if I ever so much as glance at her windows again!"

After this heroic resolution, Lucien's expression could not have been gayer if he had been about to be hanged. In spite of the lateness of the hour he started out for a ride. He had hardly left the city than he perceived that he was incapable of controlling his horse. He handed it over to his servant and continued on foot. Not long afterwards, as midnight was striking, in spite of all the insults he had heaped on Madame de Chasteller, he was once more installed on the stone opposite her window.

CHAPTER TWENTY-ONE

HIS ARRIVAL filled her with joy. Leaving Madame de Commercy's, she had said to herself:
"He must be so very displeased with himself and with me, that he will make up his mind to forget me; or, at least, if he comes here again, it will not be for several days."

Now and then, in the intense darkness, Madame de Chasteller could make out the lighted tip of Lucien's little cigar. She loved him madly at this moment. If only in the great universal silence of the night, Lucien had had sense enough to come up close to her window and say very softly something ingenious and original such as:
"Good evening, Madam. Won't you deign just to make a sign that I am heard?"

Whereupon Madame de Chasteller would probably have whispered: "Goodnight, M. Leuwen." And the intonation of those three words would have left nothing to be desired by the most exigent lover. To speak to Lucien, if it were only to pronounce his name, would have been the height of voluptuousness for Madame de Chasteller.

After having played the fool, as he said to himself, Lucien sought out a billiard parlor located at the rear of a filthy courtyard, where he was sure of finding some of the lieutenants of his regiment. He was in so piteous a state that it actually gave him pleasure to see them. His pleasure was apparent and pleased these young men who were being jolly good fellows that evening, but quite prepared to resume their fashionable haughtiness the following day.

Lucien had the pleasure of playing and of losing. It was decided that the few napoleons which had been won should not be spent at once. Champagne was brought, and Lucien had the wit to get drunk, so drunk that the attendant, together with one of the neighbors he called in, was obliged to take him home.

Thus it is that love raises one above the swinish herd!

The next day Lucien behaved exactly like a madman. His comrades, the lieutenants, having reverted to their normal hostility, remarked among themselves:

"This little fop from Paris is not used to champagne, he hasn't got over last night yet. We'll have to get him to drink often, and we'll make a fool of him before, after, and during; wonderful!"

The morning after the first meeting since the ball with the woman he had felt so sure of, he was altogether out of his mind. He understood absolutely nothing of all that was happening to him—neither the novel sensations stirring in his heart, nor other people's behavior toward him. He kept imagining that they were making allusions to his feeling for Madame de Chasteller, and it took all the reason he could muster not to give way to his anger.

"I shall just live from day to day," he finally decided, "doing whatever I please at the moment I please. Provided I confide in no one, and that I don't write to a soul about my folly, no one will be able to say to me later on: 'You were mad.' If this disease doesn't kill me, at least I won't ever have to blush. A folly well hidden loses half its ill effects. The main thing is to prevent people guessing my true feelings."

In the space of a few days a complete change took place in Lucien Leuwen. Society was amazed at his gaiety and his wit.

"He is unprincipled, he is immoral, but he is really eloquent," everyone at Madame de Puylaurens kept saying.

"My friend, you are deteriorating," said that witty woman to him one day.

Lucien talked for the sake of talking, was on both sides at once, he exaggerated and distorted everything he recounted, and he recounted a great deal and at great length. In short, he ran on like a provincial wag, and in consequence his success was enormous. The inhabitants of Nancy now recognized what they were in the habit of admiring; formerly they had found him queer, eccentric, affected, often incomprehensible.

The truth was that Lucien was in mortal terror of letting people see what was happening in his heart. He felt himself closely watched and spied on by Doctor Du Poirier whom he had begun to suspect of having some understanding with M. Thiers, Louis-Philippe's clever Minister of Police. But Lucien could not very well break with Doctor Du Poirier. He could not hope to get rid of him by ceasing to talk to him. Du Poirier was entrenched in this society into which he had introduced Lucien, and to break with him would have been extremely ridiculous, as well as embarrassing. And not to break with so active, insinuating, and also so susceptible an individual, meant treating him as an intimate friend, as a father.

"It is impossible to overplay a part with these people," Lucien thought, and he began talking like a veritable actor. He acted a role all the time and the silliest one he could think of, wilfully using the most absurd terms. He had to have someone with him every minute, solitude having become unbearable. The more preposterous the theories he upheld, the more completely his mind was diverted from the serious side of his life which was not satisfactory, and his mind was his soul's buffoon.

He was no Don Juan, far from it. We can't say what he might become some day, but at that time, when alone with a woman he had no aptitude for acting in any way except the way he felt. Until now, he had treated with the profoundest scorn this sort of talent, the lack of which he was beginning to regret. At least he had no illusions on this score.

The terrible remark of Ernest, his learned cousin, on his total lack of sense where women were concerned, echoed almost as insistently in his mind as the frightful remark of the post-master about the lieutenant-colonel and Madame de Chasteller.

Dozens of times his reason told him that he should try to see this Bouchard again, that with money and flattery he could probably learn many more details. It was beyond him. The mere sight of the post-master in the distance gave him goose flesh.

His mind thought it was justified in despising Madame de Chasteller, but every day his heart found new reasons for adoring her as the purest, the most celestial being, and the farthest removed from all considerations of vanity and money—which constitute a second religion in the provinces.

The struggle between his mind and heart literally almost drove Lucien crazy, and certainly made him one of the most miserable of men. It was just at the moment when, because of his horses, his tilbury and his liveried servants, he was the object of envy of all the lieutenants of the regiment, and of all the young gentlemen of Nancy and the surrounding countryside who, seeing him rich, handsome enough, and brave, looked upon him as, without a doubt, the luckiest man they had ever met. His dark melancholy mien, as he walked the streets alone, his absent-mindedness, his sudden bursts of temper that seemed like ill nature, were all considered as the highest and noblest form of fatuity. The more enlightened ones saw in all this an artful imitation of Lord Byron, who was being talked about a great deal at that time.

His first visit to the billiard parlor was not the last. Gossip was quick to pounce upon it; and just as all Nancy had added a dozen or more liveries to the four Madame Leuwen had sent to her son from Paris, now everybody repeated that Lucien was carried home dead drunk every night. The indifferent were astonished, the former Carlist officers delighted. One heart alone was pierced to the quick.

"Could I have been mistaken in him?"

Losing his senses in order to forget his misery was evidently not very pretty, but it was the only remedy he could think of, or rather, he had simply let himself drift; garrison life was there and he succumbed to it. What else could he do if he was to avoid unbearable nights?

This was the first unhappiness he had ever known. Until now his life had been made up entirely of work and pleasure. For a long time he had been received, and with distinction, by all the best families of Nancy. But the very thing that assured his success took away all his pleasure. Lucien was like an old coquette: since he was always acting, nothing gave him pleasure.

"If I were in Germany I should speak German," he said to himself. "In Nancy I speak 'Provincial.' "

It would have seemed to him a blasphemy if he had said of a morning: "It is a beautiful morning." Frowning with the important air of a big landowner he would cry: "What wonderful weather for hay!"

His excesses in Charpentier's billiard parlor somewhat tarnished his reputation. But a few days before the news of his misbehavior burst over the city, he had bought an enormous calash, very suitable for holding large families in which Nancy abounded; and indeed, it was with this end in view that he had purchased it. The six Demoiselles de Serpierre and their mother had *handseled* it, as they say in this region. Several other families, equally numerous, ventured to ask to borrow it and instantly obtained permission.

"This M. Leuwen is a good sort, really," was said on all

sides. "Of course it doesn't mean much to him: his father speculates with the Minister of the Interior, and it's our poor public funds that pay for all this."

It was in the same amiable fashion that Dr. Du Poirier looked upon the "little present" which Lucien had given him at the end of his attack of gout.

Everything was going as smoothly as possible for Lucien, even his father raised no objections to his extravagance. Lucien was sure that everyone spoke well of him to Madame de Chasteller. But the fact remained that the house of the Marquis de Pontlevé was the only one in Nancy in which he seemed to be losing ground. In vain, Lucien tried to call; but, rather than receive him, Madame de Chasteller closed her door to everyone on the pretext of illness. She had even deceived Doctor Du Poirier himself, who told Lucien that Madame de Chasteller would do well not to go out for some time to come. Using this excuse furnished by Du Poirier, Madame de Chasteller paid only a very few calls without being accused of being arrogant or unsociable by the ladies of Nancy.

The second time Lucien saw her after the ball, he was barely treated as a casual acquaintance; it even seemed to him that to the few remarks he addressed to her she replied even less than the simplest courtesy demanded. For this second interview Lucien had formed the most heroic resolutions. His scorn for himself was redoubled by the discovery of his lack of courage when the moment for action arrived.

"My God!" he thought. "Will the same thing happen to me when my regiment charges the enemy?"

Lucien reproached himself bitterly.

The next day he had hardly arrived at Madame de Marcilly's when Madame de Chasteller was announced.

Her indifference was so pronounced that toward the end of the call he suddenly revolted. For the first time he took advantage of the position he enjoyed in society to offer Madame de Chasteller his hand to escort her to her carriage, although it was evident that this hypocritical courtesy annoyed her exceedingly.

"Forgive me, Madam, if I seem a little indiscreet; I am very unhappy!"

"That, sir, is not what people say," replied Madame de Chasteller with an ease which was anything but natural, as she hurried toward her carriage.

"I have made myself the sycophant of all the inhabitants of Nancy in the hope that they will speak well of me to you; and at night I try to forget you by losing my senses."

"I do not think, sir, that I have given you the right . . ."

At that moment Madame de Chasteller's footman came forward to open the carriage door, and the horses bore her away more dead than alive.

CHAPTER TWENTY-TWO

IS THERE anything more degrading," cried Lucien to himself, standing stock still where he was, "than to persist in struggling against the demon of rank; never can I hope to be forgiven for not having epaulets with bullion fringe."

Nothing could have been more disheartening than this reflection, and yet, during the visit which had terminated with the little dialogue we have just reported, Lucien had been fairly intoxicated by Bathilde's divine pallor (Bathilde was one of the Christian names of Madame de Chasteller), and by the amazing beauty of her eyes.

"One certainly cannot accuse that icy reserve of having

betrayed the least spark of interest during the whole half-hour in which so many things were talked about. But, in spite of all the prudence she imposes on herself, I can see something dark and mysterious and eager stirring in the depths of those eyes, as though they were following a conversation far more intimate and exciting than the one our ears were listening to."

Neglecting nothing that would make him ridiculous, even in his own eyes, our poor Lucien, thus encouraged as we have seen, decided to write to her. He wrote a very fine letter which he went to post himself at Darney, a town on the road to Paris about six leagues from Nancy. A second letter had the same fate as the first: it remained unanswered. Fortunately in the third he let slip by chance and not by wit (of which, in all conscience, we cannot suspect him) the word *suspicion*. The word was a precious ally on the side of love which was waging a ceaseless battle in Madame de Chasteller's heart. The fact is, in spite of all her self-reproaches, she loved Lucien with her whole soul. Days counted, and were prized by her, only because of the hours spent at night behind the shutters of her drawing room listening for his footsteps. For Lucien, little dreaming of all the success of this strategy, would remain hours on end in the Rue de la Pompe.

Bathilde (the title of *Madame* is far too dignified for such childish behavior) spent her evenings behind the shutters, breathing through a little tube of licorice paper which she placed between her lips as Lucien did his little cigars. In the midst of the deep silence of the Rue de la Pompe (deserted even by day, but how much lonelier at eleven o'clock at night) she enjoyed the not too sinful pleasure of listening to the crackling of licorice paper in Lucien's hands as he tore off a sheet from the little book to make his *cigarito*. It was M. de Blancet who had had the honor and the happiness of procuring for Madame de Chasteller some of these little books of licorice paper which, as everyone knows, are imported from Barcelona.

During the first days following the ball, reproaching herself bitterly for having failed in all that a woman owes herself, and rather because of her esteem for Lucien, whose respect she craved more than anything in the world, than because of her own reputation, she had imposed on herself the boredom of pretending to be ill and of scarcely ever going out. It is true that by this judicious behavior she succeeded in making people forget entirely her misadventure at the ball. She had been seen to blush while talking to Lucien, but since in two months she had not once received him, although nothing in the world would have been simpler, people had ended by supposing that it was during her conversation with Lucien that she had begun to feel the first effects of that indisposition which a little later forced her to leave the ball. Since her fainting fit at the ball she had said to two or three ladies of her acquaintance:

"I have not yet recovered my customary health; I lost it in a glass of champagne."

Disturbed at seeing Lucien again, and by what he had dared say to her at their last encounter, she became more and more faithful to her vow of complete solitude.

Madame de Chasteller had satisfied the claims of discretion. Nobody suspected any moral cause for her indisposition at the ball, but her heart suffered cruelly. She had lost her self-respect. That inner peace, which, since the revolution of 1830, had been her only solace, was now completely unknown to her. This state of mind and her enforced retirement began really to affect her health. All these various circumstances, and also, no doubt, the resultant boredom, combined to give an added value to Lucien's letters.

For a month now, Madame de Chasteller had done much for the cause of virtue, or at least what is the clearest evidence of virtue: she had been ceaselessly tormented. What more could the stern voice of duty demand? Or, in other words: could Lucien now possibly think that she had been lacking in feminine reserve? Whatever that frightful word *suspicion* he had pronounced might imply, could Lucien find anything in her subsequent behavior to strengthen that suspicion? For several days she had the pleasure of answering *No* to this question she endlessly put to herself.

"But what in the world was that suspicion he had about me? It must have been something of a really serious nature. . . . Why! in a flash, it changed his whole expression. And, oh!" she added, blushing, "what a question that sudden change wrung from me!"

Then bitter remorse, inspired by the recollection of that question she had dared to ask, once more took complete possession of her.

"How little control I had over myself! . . . Oh, what it must have taken to produce such a change in his whole expression! Was it so serious then, that suspicion which suddenly made him pause in the midst of the liveliest outburst of sympathy?"

Just at that lucky moment Lucien's third letter arrived. The first two had given her keen pleasure, but she had not felt the least temptation to answer them. After reading this last one, Bathilde quickly hurried to get her *escritoire,* set it on a table, opened it, and began to write before giving herself time to think.

"It is *sending* a letter, not writing it that might be reprehensible," she observed vaguely to herself.

It need hardly be said that the reply was written in a style of studied haughtiness. It advised Lucien two or three times to give up all hope, even the word *hope* was avoided with an infinite skill on which Madame de Chasteller congratulated herself. Alas! Without knowing it, she was a victim of her

Jesuitical education; she was deceiving herself, all unconsciously making use in her own case of that art of deceiving
others which she had been taught at the Sacred Heart: she
answered him: that was the one important thing she failed
to realize.

Having finished her letter of a page and a half, Madame
de Chasteller almost danced for joy as she began pacing up
and down her room. After an hour's reflection, she ordered
her carriage. As they drew near the post office, she pulled the
bellrope:

"I forgot," she said to the footman, "I have this letter to
mail. Please be quick about it."

The post office was only a few steps away. She followed
the footman with her eyes and saw that he did not glance
at the address which she had written in a somewhat disguised
hand:

To M. Pierre Lafont
General Delivery
Darney.

This was the name (that of one of Lucien's servants) and
the address which Lucien had given her in his letter, with
all proper humility and without any improper show of hope.

Nothing could possibly convey Lucien's surprise, almost
his terror, when the next day, having gone in the most
perfunctory way and without the least hope, to wait on the
road to Darney for his servant Lafont to return from the post
office, he saw the man as he rode up take a letter out of his
pocket. Lucien fell rather than dismounted from his horse,
and without opening the letter and scarcely knowing what he
was doing, plunged into the nearby woods. When he found
himself in the middle of a thicket of chestnut trees, and felt
sure that he was hidden from view on all sides, he sat down and
settled himself comfortably like a man who, awaiting the

stroke of the axe that will dispatch him into the next world, wants to relish the sensation.

How different from the reaction of a man of the world to whom fortune has not accorded that uncomfortable gift, father of so many absurdities, that is called a soul! For sensible people, wooing a woman is an agreeable duel. Kant, the great philosopher, adds: "The sense of duality is powerfully revealed when the perfect happiness to be found in love, can only be found in *complete* sympathy, that is, in the total absence of the sense of being two."

"So Madame de Chasteller has replied!" any young man from Paris, somewhat less delicately reared than Lucien, would have said to himself. "Her lofty soul has compromised at last. That is the first step. The rest is merely a matter of form; it will take a month or two months, depending on how more or less adroit I may be, how more or less exaggerated are her ideas on the length of time a truly virtuous woman should hold out."

Lying on the ground reading those terrible lines, Lucien did not yet perceive the principal point of the letter which, for him, should have been: "Madame de Chasteller has replied!" He was horrified by the severity of the language and the tone of profound conviction with which she exhorted him never again to mention sentiments of such a nature, at the same time enjoining him, in the name of honor, in the name of that which all respectable people regard as most sacred in their intercourse with each other, to abandon those singular ideas with which, no doubt, he had merely wished to test her heart, before giving himself up to a folly which in their respective positions, and above all, considering her way of thinking, was an aberration (she dared employ the word) impossible to understand.

"That is a dismissal in proper form!" thought Lucien after reading the appalling missive five or six times at least. "I am in no state, at the moment, to compose any sort of an answer," he said to himself. "Yet, as the Paris mail comes through Darney tomorrow morning, if my letter is not mailed tonight, Madame de Chasteller will not receive it for at least four days."

This decided him. There, in the midst of the woods, with a pencil he happened to find in his pocket, and using the top of his shako to write on, he composed a reply with about the same amount of sagacity as had governed his thoughts for the past hour. It was, he thought, very bad. It dissatisfied him particularly because it left no chance for hope, or for opening a future attack. Thus we see how much of a coxcomb there is in the heart of every child of Paris! And yet his reply revealed, in spite of the corrections he made on reading it over, a heart really grieved by the insensibility and the disdain of Madame de Chasteller's letter.

He went back to the road and sent his servant to buy paper and writing materials in Darney. He copied his reply, but after his servant had started off for Darney again, he was on the point of galloping after him two or three times to recover it, so inept did it seem to him, and without the least chance of advancing his suit. The only thing that restrained him was the utter impossibility, in his present state, of composing anything better.

"Ah, how right Ernest was!" he thought. "Heaven never intended me to be a success with women! I shall never raise myself above the ladies of the Opera who think highly of me because of my horses and my father's fortune. I could, perhaps, add a provincial marquise or two to their number if intimate friendship with their husbands were not so irksome."

While indulging in these reflections on the meagerness of his talent in that direction, and waiting for his servant to return, he took advantage of the remaining paper to compose a second letter, and having finished it, he found it even more in the *languishing swain* style and insipid than the one now in the mail.

That night he did not go to the Charpentier billiard parlor. His author's pride being too humiliated by the style of the two letters he had written, he spent the night composing a third which, after he had made a fair copy in a legible hand, reached the formidable length of seven pages. He worked on it until three o'clock in the morning; at five, before going to drill, he had the courage to dispatch it to the post at Darney.

"If the Paris mail is a trifle late, Madame de Chasteller will receive it at the same time as the little scribble I wrote on the road yesterday, and perhaps will not think me such a complete idiot."

Fortunately for him, the Paris mail had already left when the second letter arrived at Darney, and Madame de Chasteller received only the first one next morning.

The distress, the almost childish simplicity of this letter, the perfect and ingenuous devotion, without effort and without hope, that it displayed, seemed to Madame de Chasteller in marked contrast to the assumed fatuity of the elegant young second-lieutenant. Were these really the words and the sentiments of that brilliant young man who, in his dashing calash, thundered through the streets of Nancy? All that, however, had never really worried Madame de Chasteller. But the clever ones of Nancy called Lucien a coxcomb and even believed it themselves, because with all the advantages he enjoyed on account of his wealth, they, in his place, would have been coxcombs.

Lucien was really more modest than conceited. He had the good grace not to know his worth in anything except mathematics, chemistry, and horsemanship. With what joy he would have exchanged these talents, generally accorded him, for the art of making himself loved by the ladies which, as he had observed, was enjoyed by several of his acquaintances in Paris.

Madame de Chasteller had repented many times for having written to Lucien; the reply she might receive from him filled her with a sort of terror. But now all her fears seemed to be belied in the most charming manner.

Madame de Chasteller was certainly much occupied that day. She had to read this letter five or six times, after first closing and locking three or four doors in her apartment, before she could decide what her idea of Lucien's character ought to be. There seemed to her to be a contradiction: his conduct in Nancy was that of a coxcomb, his letter that of a child.

No, really, this was not the letter of a presumptuous, even less of a vain man. Madame de Chasteller possessed enough knowledge of the world and enough intelligence to be sure that the letter revealed a charming simplicity and not the affectation and fatuous conceit, more or less disguised, of a man very much in vogue; for such was Lucien's role in Nancy, had he only had the wit to realize his good fortune and profit by it.

CHAPTER TWENTY-THREE

THE ONLY CLEVER THING about Lucien's letter was his request for a reply.

"Grant me your forgiveness, Madam, and I swear eternal silence."

"Ought I to write him that reply?" Madame de Chasteller asked herself. "Would that not be the beginning of a correspondence?"

A quarter of an hour later she said to herself:

"Forever to deny oneself every happiness that comes along, even the most innocent—what a miserable existence! What is the use of living on stilts? Haven't I been bored enough for the past two years, being kept away from Paris? What harm can it do to write this letter, the last one he will ever receive from me, provided it is written so that it may be read and commented upon without danger even by the ladies who forgather at Madame de Commercy's?"

Long mulled over and so absorbing to write, this letter was sent at last. It was full of wise counsels offered in a friendly tone. He was exhorted to guard against, or to cure himself of, a weakness which, to be sure, was no more than a passing fancy—unless of course it were just a little fabrication he had been naughty enough to indulge in as a relief from the idle boredom of garrison life. The tone of the letter was in no way tragic; Madame de Chasteller had even tried to adopt that of an ordinary correspondent, and to avoid the high-sounding phrases of outraged virtue. But unknown to herself there had crept into her letter phrases of a profound seriousness that were the echo of her real feelings, the pain and presentiments of a deeply troubled soul. Lucien felt rather than perceived these nuances; a letter written by a really frigid soul would have discouraged him altogether.

Her letter had hardly been mailed when Madame de Chasteller received the long one of seven pages which Lucien had been at such pains to write. She was outraged, and bitterly regretted the indulgent tone she had used in hers. Thinking he was acting for the best, Lucien, without realizing it, was following the doubtful lessons in conceit and crude cunning toward women which form the greater share of the elevated conversations of young men of twenty when they are not talking politics.

Forthwith Madame de Chasteller sat down and wrote four lines, begging M. Leuwen not to continue a pointless correspondence; otherwise she would be under the disagreeable necessity of returning his letters unopened. She hastened to have this letter mailed. Nothing could have been colder.

Strong in her fine resolution, irrevocable since she had written it, to return unopened any future letters Lucien might write, and believing that she had now broken with him completely, Madame de Chasteller found herself very poor company. She ordered her carriage and decided to repay some of the calls she owed. She began with the de Serpierres. It was as though a knife had pierced her heart when, on entering the drawing room, the first person her eyes fell on was Lucien, who was playing with the young ladies like so many children, in the presence of their father and mother.

"Is Madame de Chasteller's presence really so disconcerting?" asked Mademoiselle Théodelinde a few moments later, without the slightest desire to be disagreeable but simply because it was a fact she had observed. "You are no fun any longer. Does she frighten you?"

"Well, if you must know, she does!" replied Lucien.

Madame de Chasteller could not very well help adopting the general tone of the conversation, and, in spite of herself, spoke to Lucien without severity. Lucien discovered that he was able to reply readily, and for the second time in his life ideas flocked into his head and, in addressing Madame de Chasteller, he was able to find words to express them.

"It would be out of place to treat M. Leuwen with the proper coldness," thought Madame de Chasteller in order to justify herself in her own eyes. "M. Leuwen cannot have received my letters yet . . . Besides, I am seeing him perhaps for the last time. If my unworthy heart continues to be occupied with him, I shall find some means of leaving Nancy."

The vision called up by this thought softened Madame de Chasteller in spite of herself; it was almost as though she had said:

"I shall have to leave the only place where I can hope to find a little happiness."

By means of this reasoning, Madame de Chasteller was able to forgive herself for being unconcernedly agreeable and gay, in keeping with the general good humor she had found in the drawing room. The gaiety was so contagious, and everybody was so pleased with the company present, that the idea occurred to Mademoiselle Théodelinde of taking a drive in Lucien's calash, which they all used without ceremony. She consulted her mother in a whisper.

"Let's all go to the *Green Huntsman,*" she then proposed aloud.

Her suggestion was approved by acclamation. Madame de Chasteller was so miserable at home that she had not the courage to refuse this outing. She took two of the girls with her in her carriage, and together they started off for a charming café situated about a league and a half from the city, in the midst of the first tall trees of the Burelviller woods. Cafés of this kind in the woods, which are of German origin and where there is usually music played by a band of wind instruments, are happily gaining in popularity in several cities of France.

In the woods of the *Green Huntsman* their conversation took on a quiet gaiety and friendly ease that was ideal. It was the first time that Lucien had dared to talk so much in front of Madame de Chasteller and to address her directly. She answered him, and even once or twice could not help looking at him with a smile. Later she even took his arm. He was utterly happy. Madame de Chasteller observed that the eldest of the young ladies was on the point of falling in love with him.

That evening in the coffee-house there was a band of Bohemian horn players who performed ravishingly some simple, sweet and rather slow music. Nothing could have been more tender, more engaging, more in harmony with the late after-noon sun as it sank behind the tall trees. From time to time it sent its rays darting through those green depths, lighting for a moment that semi-darkness—the mysterious twilight of great forests which is always so troubling. It was one of those enchanting evenings that is an enemy of the heart's tranquillity. It may have been because of all this that Lucien, less shy than usual, but without being too bold, turned to Madame de Chasteller as though carried away by an involuntary impulse and said:

"How can you doubt the sincerity and the purity of the sentiment that inspires me? I may not be worth much, I count for nothing in the world, but can't you see that I love you with my whole soul? From the day of my arrival when my horse fell under your windows, I have thought of nothing but you, and that in spite of myself, for you cannot be said to have spoiled me with your favors. I can swear, although it may seem childish and perhaps terribly ridiculous to you, that the sweetest moments of my life are those I spend under your windows every night."

Madame de Chasteller, who had taken his arm, did not protest, seemed even to lean on him a little. She looked at him with eyes grown intent, if not a little tender, for which Lucien was almost ready to reproach her!

"As soon as we are back in Nancy, when you are caught up in life's vanities again, you will see in me nothing but a little second-lieutenant. You will be severe and even, I dare say, unkind. You won't have to do much to make me miserable; the mere fear of displeasing you is enough to take away all my peace of mind."

This was said with such touching sincerity and simplicity that Madame de Chasteller impulsively replied:

"You mustn't believe the letter you will receive from me!"

She spoke quickly and Lucien replied in the same way:

"My God! Could I have displeased you?"

"Yes; your long letter dated last Tuesday seems to have been written by another person; it reveals an unfeeling heart and one that harbors intentions inimical to me; it is almost the letter of a fatuous and vain little man."

"But you can see for yourself if I have any pretensions where you are concerned! You can see very well that you are the mistress of my fate! And you are, apparently, going to make me very unhappy."

"No, or else your happiness does not depend on me."

Involuntarily, Lucien stopped and looked at her: he saw the same tender and friendly eyes gazing into his as during their conversation at the ball; but this time they seemed to be veiled with a sort of sadness. If they had not been in a clearing of the woods within a hundred steps of the Demoiselles de Serpierre where they might be seen, Lucien would have embraced her, and she, in truth, would have allowed herself to be embraced. Such is the danger of sincerity, music, and great forests!

Madame de Chasteller saw all her imprudence written in Lucien's eyes, and was frightened.

"Remember where we are. . . ."

And ashamed of her exclamation and what it seemed to imply:

"Not another syllable," she said with resolute severity, "and let us continue walking."

Lucien obeyed, but with his eyes fastened on her, and she could see how hard it was for him to obey her and remain silent. Little by little he felt her leaning with a friendly pressure on his arm. Tears, which were evidently tears of happiness, rose to Lucien's eyes.

"Yes, my friend," she said after an endless silence, "I believe that you are sincere."

"How happy you make me! But the moment I leave you,

231

I shall begin trembling again. You inspire me with terror. Back in the drawing rooms of Nancy you will once more become for me the same severe and implacable goddess . . ."

"I was afraid of myself. I trembled for fear you had lost all respect for me after the silly question I asked you at the ball. . . ."

At that moment the little woodland path took a sudden turn, and they came upon two of the de Serpierre sisters strolling arm in arm, not twenty steps away. Lucien now feared that everything was over for him as it had been after the look she had given him at the ball; inspired by this danger he said precipitately:

"Allow me to call on you tomorrow."

"Oh! God!" she cried in terror.

"Have mercy!"

"Well then, I will receive you tomorrow."

After pronouncing these words, Madame de Chasteller was more dead than alive. The Demoiselles de Serpierre found her looking extremely pale, breathing with difficulty and with swooning eyes. Madame de Chasteller asked to lean on their arms.

"Imagine, my dears, the freshness of the evening air has made me feel quite faint. If you don't mind, let's go to the carriages right away."

In the life he had led, both as a student and a heedless and spoiled young man, Lucien had never felt a sensation comparable in the least to what he felt now. It is because of rare moments like these that life is worth living.

"You are really stupid," Mademoiselle Théodelinde said to him in the carriage.

"Shame on you, daughter. You are not very polite!" remonstrated Madame de Serpierre.

"But he is insufferable this evening," replied the little provincial miss.

And it is because of such artlessness that one sometimes loves the provinces where it is still possible. One may still find certain natural and sincere impulses among the young people that are perfectly harmless, and not invariably spoiled the next moment by little mincing hypocritical airs.

Hardly had Madame de Chasteller been restored to solitude and reason, than she was overcome with remorse at having given Lucien permission to call. She made up her mind to have recourse to a certain person the reader has already met; he may have a contemptuous recollection of one of those creatures, so common in the provinces where they are respected, but who hide themselves in Paris where ridicule is the rule, a certain Mademoiselle Bérard, a bourgeoise whom we found insinuating herself among the great ladies in the Chapel of the Penitents, the first time Lucien had had wit enough to visit it. She was a tiny, dried up little person of forty-five or fifty, with a pointed nose and shifty eyes, invariably dressed with the greatest care, a habit she had acquired in England, where for twenty years she had been companion to Lady Beatown, a wealthy Catholic peeress. Mademoiselle Bérard seemed to have been born for this odious role which the English, remarkable painters of everything disagreeable, designate by the name of *toadeater*. The endless mortifications that a poor lady's companion has to endure without a word as a vent for some rich woman's ill humor with the world she bores, have given rise to this lovely post. Malicious by nature, atrabilious, and a born gossip, not rich enough for her piety to win her any special deference, Mademoiselle Bérard needed an opulent house that could furnish her with facts to distort, gossip to spread, and win her consideration in the world of the sacristies. One thing there was that not all the treasures of the earth, nor even the order of our Holy Father the Pope, could have wrested from our worthy Mademoiselle Bérard, and that was a moment of discretion about anything she had happened to learn which would harm someone. This absolute lack of discretion was what decided Madame de Chasteller. She sent word to Mademoiselle Bérard that she desired to engage her as her companion.

"This horribly spiteful creature will answer to me for myself," thought Madame de Chasteller. And the severity of this punishment set her conscience at rest. Madame de Chasteller almost forgave herself for the interview she had so lightly granted.

The reputation of Mademoiselle Bérard was so well known that Doctor Du Poirier himself, who was the intermediary Madame de Chasteller had chosen, could not help exclaiming:

"But, Madam, consider what a viper you are bringing into your home!"

Mademoiselle Bérard arrived. Extreme curiosity, rather than pleasure at her preferment, gave her squinting eyes, ordinarily only deceitful and spiteful, a somewhat feverish look. She arrived with a list of pecuniary and other conditions. After agreeing to them all, Madame de Chasteller said:

"I shall ask you to remain in this drawing room where I receive my callers."

"I have the honor of pointing out to you, Madam, that at Lady Beatown's I was assigned a place in the second drawing room adjoining the one occupied by the ladies who accompanied my lady to the princesses, which is perhaps more in keeping with the rules of decorum. My birth . . ."

"Very well, Mademoiselle, in the second drawing room."

And Madame de Chasteller fled to her own room and locked herself in; Mademoiselle Bérard's eyes had made her actually ill.

"My indiscretion of yesterday is now partly repaired," she thought. Before she had had Mademoiselle Bérard in the house, she trembled at every sound, always imagining that a lackey was coming to announce M. Leuwen.

CHAPTER TWENTY-FOUR

OUR POOR SECOND-LIEUTENANT never dreamt of the strange company that was being arranged for him. Out of extreme delicacy he felt that he ought not to present himself at Madame de Chasteller's without first having asked permission of the Marquis de Pontlevé, and to be sure of not finding the old Marquis at home, he had to wait until he saw him leave his house at three o'clock, as the Marquis did every day to go to his *Henri V* Club.

No sooner had Lucien seen the Marquis crossing the Place d'Armes, than his heart started thumping. He arrived at the Hôtel de Pontlevé and knocked. He was so ruffled that he addressed the old paralytic porter with deference, and had hardly enough voice to make himself understood.

On his way up to the second floor, it was with a sort of terror that he looked at the great staircase of gray stone with its ornate iron balustrade, lacquered black and decorated, here and there, with gilded fruit. At last he arrived at the door of the apartment occupied by Madame de Chasteller. Stretching out his hand toward an English bell made of brass he almost hoped that he would be told that she was not at home. Never before in his life had Lucien been so overcome by fright.

He rang. The sound of the bell, echoing through the different stories of the house, almost made him ill. Finally the door opened. The servant went to announce his arrival, after requesting him to wait in the second drawing room where he found Mademoiselle Bérard. He could see that she was not merely paying a call but was there to stay. This sight completed his confusion. He made her a deep bow and went to the other end of the room, where he stood looking intently at an engraving.

In a few moments Madame de Chasteller appeared. Her face was flushed and she seemed agitated. She went over and seated herself on a couch very close to where Mademoiselle Bérard was sitting. She motioned Lucien to a chair. Never had a man found such difficulty in sitting down and running through the few ordinary formulas of politeness. While he was mumbling some perfectly prosaic words, Madame de Chasteller turned excessively pale; whereupon Mademoiselle Bérard put on her spectacles to examine them both.

Lucien's troubled eyes went from Madame de Chasteller's charming countenance to this shiny little yellow face whose pointed nose, with its gold spectacles, was turned toward him. Even in such a trying (thanks to Madame de Chasteller's prudence) moment as this first interview between two individuals who the day before had almost confessed their love for each other, Madame de Chasteller's expression radiated simple happiness, and seemed to reveal a readiness to be moved to a tender rapture. Lucien was touched by this noble expression, and it almost made him forget Mademoiselle Bérard.

He relished with delight the keen pleasure of discovering this new perfection in the woman he loved. This feeling brought a little life back to his heart, he breathed once more; he began to rise out of the abyss of disappointment into which he had been plunged by the unexpected presence of Mademoiselle Bérard.

There still remained one great difficulty to be overcome: what to talk about? And he must talk. The prolonged silence

236

was becoming dangerous in the presence of this spiteful bigot. To lie seemed horrible to Lucien, yet Mademoiselle Bérard must not be given a chance to gossip.

"What a lovely day, Madam," he said at last. After this terrible phrase he could hardly breathe. He plucked up his courage and was shortly able to add: "That is an exceptionally fine Morghen engraving you have there."

"My father is very fond of him. He brought it back after his last trip to Paris." And her troubled eyes tried not to meet Lucien's.

What made the interview so absurd, and so particularly humiliating for Lucien, was that he had spent a sleepless night preparing a dozen charming and touching speeches, admirably describing, and with art, the exact state of his heart. Above all, he had been careful to couch them in a simple, graceful style, studiously avoiding anything that could imply the slightest ray of hope.

After speaking of the engraving:

"The time is passing," he thought, "and here I am wasting it in these insignificant platitudes, as though what I most desired was to bring my visit to an end. How I shall reproach myself the minute I am outside the house!"

If only he had been in possession of his usual sang-froid, nothing would have been more natural to Lucien than to find charming things to say even in the presence of this old maid, who was malicious no doubt, but not very intelligent. But at the moment it happened that Lucien was incapable of improvising anything. He was afraid of himself, he was much more afraid of Madame de Chasteller, and he was afraid of Mademoiselle Bérard. And nothing is less favorable to the inventive faculty than fear. What increased the difficulty of finding anything passable to say, which afflicted Lucien at this moment, was that he realized only too well the blankness of his mind, and even exaggerated it to himself. At last a poor little idea came to him:

"All I hope for, Madam, is to become a good cavalry officer, since heaven, it would seem, has not destined me to become an eloquent orator in the Chamber of Deputies."

He saw Mademoiselle Bérard's little eyes open wide, that is, as wide as was possible for them. "Good," he thought, "she thinks I am talking politics, and is preparing her report."

"I should be utterly incapable *in the Chamber* of pleading the causes I felt most deeply, yet away from the tribune, I should be overwhelmed by the vehemence of the sentiments animating my heart. When I opened my mouth before that supreme judge, and, above all, severe, whom I am in terror of displeasing, all I could say would be: See what a state I am in, you have such complete possession of my heart that it has not even the strength to plead its own cause before you."

Madame de Chasteller had listened at first with pleasure, but toward the end of this little discourse she began to be afraid of Mademoiselle Bérard, Lucien's last sentence seeming to her much too transparent.

"And have you, indeed, some hope, sir, of being elected to the Chamber of Deputies?"

. "My father allows me complete liberty of choice. He is an excellent father, and as I desire this election with the most fervent passion, I have no doubt he will consent."

"But it seems to me, sir, that you are very young. I fear this may be an unanswerable objection! . . ."

Lucien was trying to couch his reply in terms that would prove the modesty of his expectations, when suddenly struck by this thought:

"So this is that interview which I had looked forward to as the crowning happiness!" he said to himself bitterly.

The thought froze him. He added a few platitudinous phrases that sounded pitiful to him, then rose abruptly, and hastily took his departure. He could hardly wait to leave that room, to enter which had seemed to him to promise the very height of happiness.

Hardly had he reached the street than he was overwhelmed by amazement and as though stunned.

"But I am cured," he cried after taking a few steps. "My heart is incapable of love. So that is the first interview, the first rendezvous with a woman one loves! What a mistake I made, despising my little ballet dancers! My poor little assignations with them only made me dream of the delight of a rendezvous with a woman I really loved! This thought has often made me sad at the gayest moments. How foolish I have been! But perhaps I was not in love . . . I was mistaken. . . . How ridiculous! How impossible! *I* in love with a woman belonging to the legitimists, with all their selfish, unjust ideas, jealous of their privileges, and vexed every other minute of the day because people make fun of them! To enjoy privileges that everybody makes fun of, what a satisfaction!"

As he said all this to himself, he was thinking of Mademoiselle Bérard. He saw her again sitting there before him with her little cap of yellow lace tied with a faded green ribbon. This decayed, and not very clean, magnificence made him think of a dirty hovel!

"That is what I should have thought of them all, if only I had studied them more critically."

His thoughts were miles away from Madame de Chasteller. He came back to her.

"I not only believed that I loved her, but was even sure that I saw in her a dawning affection for me."

At that moment it was a pleasure to think of anything except Madame de Chasteller! It was the first time in the last three months that he had known this strange sensation.

"To think," he cried with a sort of horror, "that ten min-

utes ago I was forced to lie when I was trying to find tender
things to say to Madame de Chasteller! And that, after what
happened to me yesterday in the woods of the *Green Huntsman,* after all the transports of joy I have known since that
instant and which this morning during drill caused me to fall
out of ranks two or three times. Great God! Can I never count
on myself? Who would have thought it yesterday! So I am
nothing but a fool or a child!"

These reproaches were sincere, but they made him realize
no less clearly that he was no longer in love with Madame
de Chasteller. It *bored* him to think of her. This last discovery
was the final blow; he despised himself.

"Tomorrow I may become an assassin, a thief, anything at
all! For I am sure of nothing about myself."

As he walked along the street, Lucien suddenly realized
that he was thinking about all the trifling things of Nancy
with an entirely new interest.

Not far from the Rue de la Pompe stood a small Gothic
chapel, built by René, Duc de Lorraine, which the inhabitants
of Nancy admired with artistic transports ever since they
had read in a Paris review that it was a thing of beauty. Before
that time, its walls had served an ironmonger as a convenient
support for his iron bars. Never before had Lucien stopped
to glance at this obscure chapel with its little gray nervures,
or if, by chance, his eyes rested on it for an instant, soon the
thought of Madame de Chasteller had come to distract his attention. Chance at this moment brought him face to face
with this Gothic monument, no bigger than one of the smallest
chapels in Saint-Germain-l'Auxerrois. He now stood and
looked at it for a long time, absorbed in studying all its
minutest details; in fact, he found in it a pleasant diversion.
Examining all the little heads of saints and animals, he was
astonished by what he felt, but even more by what he no
longer felt.

He remembered, all at once, with real pleasure, that there was to be a pool that evening at the Charpentier billiard parlor, and a tourney for the prize cue. In the emptiness of his heart he awaited with impatience the hour of the tourney, and was the first to arrive. He played with keen relish, was never absent-minded, and was, by chance, the winner. But he was careful not to get drunk; drinking to excess seemed to him that day a very silly pastime. But still, out of habit, he sought never to be alone.

CHAPTER TWENTY-FIVE

ALL DURING THE TIME Lucien was engaged in joking with his companions, his mind was filled with philosophic and somber thoughts:

"Poor women!" he mused to himself. "They risk their whole fate on our whims, they count on our love! And, after all, why shouldn't they? Are we not always sincere when we swear that we love them? Yesterday at the *Green Huntsman*, I may have been cautious, but I was certainly the sincerest of men. Great God! What is life anyway? From now on I shall be more indulgent."

Lucien watched everything that went on at the Charpentier billiard parlor like a child, he took an interest in everything.

"What in the world has happened to you?" asked one of his comrades. "You're the best-natured chap in the world tonight."

"No queer and superior airs!" exclaimed another.

"Until tonight," said a third, who was the poet of the regiment, "you have been like a jealous ghost come back to this earth to sneer at the pleasures of the living. Today jest and laughter seem to follow at your heels. . . ."

All these bantering remarks (the gentlemen were anything but subtle) neither offended Lucien, nor did he show the least sign of resentment.

At one o'clock in the morning, when he was once again alone, he said to himself:

"So now I think of everything in the world with pleasure except Madame de Chasteller! And how am I to get out of the sort of obligation I am under to her? I might ask the colonel to send me to N—— to wage a cabbage war on the workers. It would be uncivil, to say the least, to have nothing more to say to her. She would think I had been trifling. . . .

"And if I go to her and tell her truthfully that, at the sight of that horrible little bigot of hers, my heart froze, she will think I am an imbecile or a liar and despise me."

"But how is it possible," he thought, reverting to his own conduct, "how is it possible that such an extraordinary, such an overwhelming emotion, one that literally filled my whole life, all my nights and days, that drove sleep away, that might even have made me forget my duty to my country, could have been arrested, annihilated by such a miserable trifle! . . . Great God! Are all men like that? Or am I madder than the rest? Who will solve this riddle for me?"

The next day, when that sunrise bugle call, known in the army as reveille, woke Lucien at five o'clock, he began gravely pacing the floor. He could not get over his amazement. Not to think of Madame de Chasteller left an enormous void.

"Is it possible," he said to himself, "that Bathilde is nothing to me any longer?" And this charming name which used to have such a magical effect on him, now seemed no different from any other. His mind began to review all of Madame de Chasteller's good qualities, but seemed much less sure of those than of her divine beauty, and soon concentrated on the latter.

"What magnificent hair, with the sheen of finest silk, so long, so luxuriant! What a lovely color it was yesterday in the shade of the tall trees! What a charming blond! It is not the color of the golden hair praised by Ovid, nor that mahogany shade seen on some of the loveliest heads of Raphael and Carlo Dolci. The name I should give to hers—not very elegant perhaps—but really, under its silky sheen, it is the color of hazelnuts. And that admirable line of the forehead! What thoughts such a forehead hides, too many perhaps! . . . How it used to frighten me! As for her eyes, who has ever seen anything to equal them? Infinity is in her gaze, even when she looks at the most insignificant objects. How she looked at her carriage yesterday as we walked toward it at the *Green Huntsman!* And the exquisite modeling of the eyelids of those beautiful eyes! What a setting! They are most divine, those eyes, when they gaze at nothing. Then, it is the very music of her soul they seem to express. Her nose is indeed a bit aquiline. I don't care much for that in a woman. I never liked it even in her when I was in love with her. *When I was in love with her!* Great God! Where shall I hide? What am I to do? What can I say? And if she had given herself to me? . . . Well, I would have acted as a gallant gentleman then, as always. 'I am mad, dear friend,' I would have said. 'Name a place of exile anywhere, no matter how horrible, and there I shall fly!' "

This thought restored some life to his soul.

"Yes," he said, resuming his critical examination almost as an amusement, "yes, an aquiline nose, pointing, as the pompous Chactas puts it, toward the grave, gives too serious an expression to the face. But still worse, this feature, particularly a three-quarter view of it, always gives an air of pedantry to serious retorts, especially of refusal.

"But what a mouth! Is it possible to imagine a more delicate, a more finely drawn contour? It is as beautiful as the most beautiful antique cameo. And often this delicate, mobile mouth betrays Madame de Chasteller. Often, unknown to her, what a charming form it takes, and the contour of that upper lip, which protrudes a little, seems to change when something has been said that touches her. She is not given to mockery, she even disapproves anything of that sort, and yet, at the slightest pompousness, at the least suggestion of exaggeration in the discourses of these provincials, how the corners of her lovely mouth involuntarily curl! And this alone is what makes the ladies call her malicious, as M. de Sanréal said again the other day at Madame d'Hocquincourt's. She has really a charming, merry, and amusing mind, but she seems always to regret having revealed it."

But all this list of beauties, and more, did not help Lucien's love: it could not be revived. He talked of Madame de Chasteller to himself as a connoisseur might talk about a beautiful sculpture he wanted to sell.

"After all, she must be a bigot at heart," he said. "To have unearthed that execrable Mademoiselle Bérard as a companion only proves it. In which case I should soon have found her acrimonious, sanctimonious, and conscience-stricken. Ah, but what about the lieutenant-colonels? . . ."

This thought engaged Lucien for some time.

"I should prefer her to be a trifle too pleasing to lieutenant-colonels than a bigot; according to my mother there is nothing worse. Perhaps," he went on in the same vein, "it is just a question of class. Since 1830 people of her class have been convinced that if once they could make piety popular, they would find Frenchmen readier to concede them their privileges. Your true bigot is patient. . . ."

But it was evident that Lucien was not even thinking of what he was saying any longer.

At that moment his servant arrived from Darney, and handed him Madame de Chasteller's reply to his seven page letter. As we have said before, it consisted of four extremely curt lines. It stunned him.

"And here I am worrying and feeling ashamed for not loving her! A lot she cares! This is the true expression of her feelings."

He knew very well that almost the first words Madame de Chasteller had said to him at the *Green Huntsman* were a disavowal of this very letter. But it was so short, so curt! Lucien remained stunned, stunned to the point of forgetting all about drill. His orderly, Nicolas, came at a gallop to look for him.

"Ah, Lieutenant, you're going to catch it from the colonel!"

Without a word, Lucien jumped on his horse and started off at a gallop.

While drill was in progress, the colonel rode up behind the Seventh Company where Lucien was rear-file.

"I'm in for it now," he thought. But to his great astonishment no coarse or angry word was directed toward him. "My father must have had someone write to the brute."

However, the consciousness of having merited some blame made him very attentive that morning, and it was perhaps out of malice that the colonel had them repeat several operations when the Seventh was in the lead.

"But I'm a fool to think that I am the center of the universe," Lucien said to himself. "The colonel has his own troubles, and if he doesn't bother to take me down it's because he has forgotten all about me."

All during drill Lucien was too much afraid of some act of inattention to think of anything else. But returning to his rooms, when he dared delve into his heart again, he found his attitude toward Madame de Chasteller entirely altered.

Although he would not be able to present himself at the

de Serpierres' before four-thirty, Lucien was the first at the ordinary that day. He ordered his calash for four o'clock. He was so restless that he went himself to see his horses harnessed, and found a hundred things to find fault with in the stables. Finally, at fifteen minutes past four, he was happily ensconced in the de Serpierre drawing room, surrounded by the young ladies. Their conversation restored some life to his soul, as he told them with infinite grace. Mademoiselle Théodelinde, who had a very marked fondness for our second-lieutenant, was unusually gay and seemed to impart some of her gaiety to him.

Madame de Chasteller entered. They had not been expecting her that day. Never had he seen her looking prettier; she was pale and a little shy.

"And in spite of that shyness," he thought, "she *gives* herself to lieutenant-colonels!"

With these coarse words all his lost passion seemed to revive. But Lucien was young, not used to the world. Without realizing it, he was almost curt, and not in the least gracious to Madame de Chasteller. There was something of the tiger about his love. He was not the same man he had been yesterday.

The young ladies were all of a twitter at this moment: one of Lucien's servants had just entered carrying magnificent bouquets for each of them; these Lucien had had brought all the way from the greenhouses of Darney, famous for their flowers. As there was none for Madame de Chasteller, they divided the largest one in two.

"An unhappy omen," she thought to herself.

In the midst of all the young girls' merriment, she felt a little crestfallen. She could not understand Lucien's brusque and ungracious manner toward her. She wondered whether, to preserve his esteem, and to show a proper regard for her honor, without which no woman can expect to be loved by a man of any delicacy, she should not leave at once or, at least, appear to be offended.

"No," she said to herself, "because I am not really offended. In my present state of distress only by not allowing myself the least little hypocrisy can I be sure of not failing in the amenities."

In this observation I find that Madame de Chasteller displayed sublime wisdom, as well as in following the dictates of that wisdom. Never in her life had she been more amazed.

"Is M. Leuwen really only a coxcomb as people say? And was his object merely to obtain the indiscreet admission I made day before yesterday?"

Madame de Chasteller reviewed all those signs she had observed in Lucien of a heart that has been touched.

"Could I have been mistaken? Could vanity have blinded me to such a degree? There is no truth in the world for me if M. Leuwen is not really sincere and good."

Then again she fell into the most cruel uncertainty, and rejected with difficulty the word *coxcomb* that all Nancy attached to Lucien's name.

"No, it is not so! I have told myself a thousand times, and at moments when I was perfectly cool and collected, that it is M. Leuwen's tilbury, and especially his servants' liveries that have won him this appellation, and not his true character. To all these people, that is invisible. They know very well that in his place they themselves would certainly be coxcombs! But, as far as he is concerned, it is only innocent vanity, which is a sign of his youth. He enjoys feeling that these fine horses and handsome liveries belong to him. This word *coxcomb* simply betrays all the envy of our ex-officers."

However, despite the incisive character of her reasoning and its striking perspicuity, the word *coxcomb* in her present troubled state still held a terrible weight in influencing her judgment.

"I have spoken to him only five times in my life; I certainly have no great knowledge of the world. One would have to have extraordinary self-confidence to pretend to understand a man's heart after five conversations with him . . . And besides," she continued, growing more and more depressed, "whenever I talked to him I was always much too much concerned with hiding my own feelings to study his. . . . It is, I must admit, a trifle presumptuous for a woman of my age to think that she can judge a man better than an entire city."

After this observation, Madame de Chasteller became distinctly gloomy. Lucien began looking at her again with his old anxiety. He thought:

"So, the insignificance of my rank and my diminutive epaulets are having their effect. What consideration can any lady enjoy in the eyes of Nancy society with a modest second-lieutenant as an admirer, especially when she has been accustomed to leaning on the arm of a colonel, or if there's no presentable colonel at hand, a lieutenant-colonel, or, at least, a major. Nothing less than epaulets with bullion fringe can suffice."

It can be seen that our hero was quite absurd in his reasoning, and it must be admitted that he was no happier than he was clairvoyant. Hardly had he stopped reasoning thus than he wished himself a hundred feet under ground, for he had begun to be in love again.

Madame de Chasteller's heart was not in a much more enviable state. They were both paying, and dearly, for the happiness they had enjoyed two days before at the *Green Huntsman*. And if novelists, as in the old days, still had the happy privilege of drawing a moral to adorn a tale, we should here exclaim: "Just punishment for the temerity of loving somebody one hardly knows! The idea of entrusting one's happiness to a person one has seen only five times!" And if the novelist should translate his thoughts into a pompous style and even end up with some religious allusion, then the imbeciles would say to each other: "What a moral book, the author must be a most respectable man." But these imbeciles would certainly not say to themselves, not yet having read it in enough books recommended by the Academy: "Considering the present refinement of polite manners, what can a woman know of a *correct* young man even after *fifty* visits, except the extent of his wit or how far he has progressed in the art of saying nothing elegantly? But of his heart, of his particular fashion of going hunting after happiness, not one thing; otherwise he is not a correct young man."

During these moral speculations, the two lovers were looking utterly miserable. A little before the arrival of Madame de Chasteller, Lucien, in order to explain and excuse the impropriety of so early a call, had proposed taking the Serpierre ladies to the *Green Huntsman* for coffee. They had accepted. Now, after a few polite exchanges with Madame de Chasteller, and after the invitation had been repeated and accepted, the young ladies rushed into the house to get their hats. Madame de Serpierre followed at a more dignified pace, and Madame de Chasteller and Lucien were left alone in the long avenue of locust trees. They walked together in silence but separated by the entire width of the wide avenue.

"Is it consistent with what I owe myself," thought Madame de Chasteller, "to go with them to the *Green Huntsman?* Will it not seem to be allowing M. Leuwen somewhat too great an intimacy?"

CHAPTER TWENTY-SIX

SHE had only an instant to make up her mind; love quickly took advantage of this added embarrassment. All at once, instead of walking with eyes downcast to avoid meeting Lucien's gaze, Madame de Chasteller turned and looked at him:

"Has M. Leuwen had some cause for annoyance in his regiment, that he should seem so lost in the depths of melancholy?"

"It is true, Madam, that ever since yesterday I have been deeply troubled. I am at a loss to understand what has happened to me." He looked directly at Madame de Chasteller, and by their profound gravity, his eyes showed that he was telling the truth. Madame de Chasteller was startled, and stood still as though rooted to the ground; she was incapable of taking another step.

"I am ashamed of what I am going to say, Madam," Lucien continued, "but my duty, as a man of honor, forces me to speak."

This extraordinarily serious preamble made Madame de Chasteller blush.

"I am afraid that what I have to say, the very words I am forced to use, are as ridiculous as the subject is strange and even idiotic."

There was a little silence. Madame de Chasteller glanced at Lucien with anxiety. He looked really distressed. Finally, as though painfully mastering his mortification, he said hesitatingly and in a low, scarcely audible voice:

"Will you ever believe it, Madam? Will you be able to

listen without laughing at me, without thinking me the most pitiful of men? I cannot rid my mind of that person I met at your house yesterday. The sight of that dreadful face, that pointed nose with its spectacles, seems to have poisoned my soul."

Madame de Chasteller could hardly keep from smiling.

"Never, Madam, since my arrival here in Nancy, have I experienced anything resembling what I felt at the sight of that monster; my heart froze! Since then I have actually spent as much as an hour at a time without thinking of you, and what is even more amazing, it seemed to me that my love was dead."

Madame de Chasteller's face now grew very grave; Lucien could no longer detect the least trace of a smile nor any irony.

"Really, I thought I was mad," he added, reverting to all the simplicity of his usual tone which, in Madame de Chasteller's eyes, precluded the least possibility of deceit or fraud.

"Nancy appeared to me as a new city which I had never seen before, because I had never before seen anything in it but you. A lovely sky would make me say: 'Her soul is purer!' The sight of a gloomy house: 'If Bathilde lived there, how I should love that house!' Please forgive my daring to speak to you like this."

Madame de Chasteller made a little gesture of impatience, as much as to say: "Do go on! Don't bother me with such trifles."

"Well, Madam," continued Lucien who seemed to be scrutinizing her eyes to study the effect of his words, "this morning that gloomy house appeared to me a gloomy house, the beautiful sky seemed to me beautiful without recalling another beauty; in short, I had the misfortune of being in love no longer. Then, suddenly, four terribly severe lines in reply to a letter of mine (undoubtedly much too long) began to dispel the effect of the poison. I had the joy of seeing you, and my frightful nightmare vanished. I have resumed my chains, but I still feel the chill of the poison. . . . I am afraid I am being a little bombastic, but I don't know how else to express what happened to me ever since I set eyes on your companion. The fatal proof is that I have to make an effort to speak the language of love."

After this frank confession, it seemed to. Lucien that a hundred-pound weight had been lifted from his chest. He had so little experience of the world that he had not expected this joyous result.

Madame de Chasteller, on the contrary, was apparently stunned. "It is plain, he is nothing but a coxcomb. How can I possibly take this seriously?" she thought. "Am I to believe that it is the ingenuous confession of a loving heart?"

Lucien's way of speaking, when talking to her, had always been so natural that Madame de Chasteller inclined to the latter view. But she had often noticed that, addressing anyone but herself, he often said the most absurd things intentionally. This recollection of Lucien's posturing sickened her. On the other hand, Lucien's manner, the whole tone of his remarks, were now so different, the end of his discourse had seemed so sincere, how could she help believing him? Could he possibly be such an accomplished actor at his age? But if she were going to credit his strange confession, if she believed it to be sincere, first of all she must not appear to be offended, still less dejected. But what should she do to appear neither the one nor the other?

Madame de Chasteller could hear the young girls as they came running back to the garden. M. and Mme. de Serpierre were already installed in Lucien's big calash. She refused to listen to the voice of reason any longer.

"If I don't go to the *Green Huntsman,* two of these poor children will be deprived of their outing."

And so she got into her own carriage taking the two younger girls with her.

"At least, I shall have a little time for reflection."

Those reflections were very sweet.

"M. Leuwen is an honorable man, and, although it seems perfectly unbelievable and extravagant, I am sure what he says is true. Even before he spoke, his expression, his whole attitude, told me so."

When they left the carriages at the entrance to the Burelviller woods, Lucien was a different man. Madame de Chasteller saw this at a glance. His expression had resumed all its youthful serenity, his manners all their habitual ease.

"His is an upright heart," she thought with delight, "the world has not yet turned him into one of those false, calculating men of fashion; quite amazing at the age of twenty-three! And he has always moved in fashionable society!"

In this Madame de Chasteller was mistaken. From the age of eighteen, Lucien, far from living in the society of the court or of the Faubourg Saint-Germain, had passed his days amidst the retorts and alembics of a chemistry class.

Pretty soon, as they walked along with the two younger girls beside them and the rest of the family some ten paces distant, Madame de Chasteller was leaning once more on Lucien's arm. Not to arouse the curiosity of the two young girls, Lucien assumed a sprightly tone.

"Ever since I had the courage to tell the truth to the person I most esteem in the whole world, I am another man. Already I feel how ridiculous my words were in speaking of that old maid, the sight of whom had poisoned me. . . . How beautiful it is here today, as beautiful as the day before yesterday! But before I can give myself up entirely to the joy this lovely spot awakens, I must know, Madam, your opinion on the absurdity of that part of my harangue where there was question of chains, of poison, and a lot of other tragic words."

"I must admit, sir, that I am not sure. But in general," she added after a little pause, and with gravity, "I think it showed sincerity. If there was some self-deception, at least, there was no intention of deceiving. And the truth makes anything acceptable—even chains and poison."

Madame de Chasteller tried not to smile at these words.

"Why is it," she asked herself in real distress, "that I can never keep a proper tone in speaking to M. Leuwen! Is talking to him then such happiness for me? And who can say if he is not a coxcomb who looks upon me as just one more poor little provincial he can trifle with? Or perhaps, without being exactly dishonorable, he has only the most casual feeling for me, a love born of the boredom of garrison life?"

So spoke the attorney for the anti-love party in her heart, but decidedly with much less effect. She found an exquisite pleasure in day-dreaming, and spoke only just enough not to seem strange to the Serpierre family that now surrounded the two of them. But, happily for Lucien, the German band finally arrived and began to play Mozart waltzes followed by duets from *Don Giovanni* and *The Marriage of Figaro*. Madame de Chasteller grew even more serious, but little by little she began to feel much happier. As for Lucien, he was living to the full the romance of life—the hope of happiness now seemed a certainty. He had the temerity to say to her in one of those brief instants of semi-freedom that can be snatched even while walking in the midst of a whole family:

"One must never deceive the God one adores. I have been sincere, that is the greatest mark of respect I could offer; am I to be punished for it?"

"What a strange man you are!"

"It might be more polite to agree with you. But the truth is, I don't know what I am, and I'd give a lot if anyone would enlighten me. I only began to live, and to try to know myself, the day my horse fell with me underneath the window with the parrot-green shutters."

He said this as one whose words come spontaneously as he speaks. Madame de Chasteller could not help being touched: his whole demeanor was sincere and at the same time noble. He had felt a certain diffidence about speaking of his love thus openly; now he was rewarded by a tender smile.

"Do I dare ask to come to see you tomorrow?" he added. "But I have another and almost as great a favor to ask, and that is, not to be received in the presence of that old maid."

"You will gain nothing," replied Madame de Chasteller sadly. "I am much too reluctant to listen to you tête-à-tête treating of a certain subject, which seems to be the only one you can talk to me about. Come only if you are gentleman enough to promise me that you will talk on some entirely different subject."

Lucien promised. This was about all they had a chance to say to each other that afternoon. He was even glad for both of them that, being surrounded by people, they were practically prevented from talking to each other. Even had they been free to do so, they would not have had much more to say, and they were not yet intimate enough not to be embarrassed, Lucien especially, by silence. But, although they said nothing, their eyes seemed to agree that there was no cause for quarrel between them! They loved each other in a way quite different from two days before. They no longer felt those transports of youthful happiness free from suspicions, but rather passion now, and intimacy, and the keenest desire to be able, at last, to trust each other.

"Let me only believe you, and I am yours," Madame de Chasteller's eyes seemed to say. And she would have died of shame if she could have seen their expression. That is one of the misfortunes of extreme beauty, it cannot hide its feelings. But its language is only understood by an indifferent observer. For an instant Lucien thought he understood it, but a moment later was plunged in doubt again.

Their happiness in being together was secret and profound. Lucien almost had tears in his eyes. Several times in the course of their stroll, Madame de Chasteller avoided taking his arm, but without any appearance of affectation in the eyes of the Serpierres, or of coldness toward Lucien.

Finally, as it was now quite dark, they left the *café-hauss* and began walking toward the carriages which had been left at the entrance of the forest. Madame de Chasteller said to Lucien:

"Will you give me your arm, M. Leuwen?"

Lucien pressed the arm offered him and felt the pressure faintly returned. The Bohemian band could be heard in the distance. It was delightful. Then a profound silence fell.

By a lucky chance, when they arrived at the carriages, it appeared that one of the young ladies had dropped her handkerchief in the gardens of the *Green Huntsman*. At first it was suggested that a servant be sent to fetch it, then that they should all drive back. But Lucien, coming out of his reverie to join the discussion, pointed out to Madame de Serpierre that the night was superb, that because of the warm and almost imperceptible breeze, there was no dew, that the young ladies were less overheated than two days ago, that the carriages could follow them, etc., etc. Finally, after offering a quantity of excellent reasons, he concluded by saying that, if the ladies were not tired, it would be agreeable to go back to the garden on foot. Madame de Serpierre referred the decision to Madame de Chasteller:

"To be sure!" replied Madame de Chasteller. "But on condition that the carriages do not follow; that noise of wheels behind one, always stopping if one happens to stop, is too annoying."

Thinking that the musicians, having been paid, would be leaving the garden, Lucien sent a servant ahead to engage them to stay on, and to begin playing once more the selections from *Don Giovanni* and *Figaro*. Returning to the ladies, he casually took Madame de Chasteller's arm. The young ladies were overjoyed at this renewed promenade. Their conversation, as they all strolled along together, was very gay and agreeable. Not to call attention to himself, Lucien did his share of the talking, but he and Madame de Chasteller avoided saying anything directly to each other: they were too happy as it was.

Soon they heard the music beginning again. When they reached the garden, Lucien pretended that M. de Serpierre and he were dying for a glass of punch, and proposed that a very weak one should be made for the ladies. As it was most agreeable being together like this, the suggestion of a punch was greeted with general approval, in spite of the opposition of Madame de Serpierre who insisted that there was nothing more injurious to young girls' complexions. This opinion was seconded by Mademoiselle Théodelinde who was a little bit too fond of Lucien not to be just a little bit jealous.

"You must plead your cause with Mademoiselle Théodelinde," said Madame de Chasteller in the blithest and friendliest of tones.

And in the end, they did not get back to Nancy until half past nine in the evening.

CHAPTER TWENTY-SEVEN

LUCIEN had missed the evening muster, and it was his week on duty at the barracks. He made haste to look up his adjutant who advised him to go directly to the colonel and make a clean breast of it. The colonel was what was called in 1834 a *Juste-milieu,* and a rabid one. As such, he was extremely jealous of the reception Lucien was accorded in Nancy society. His own lack of success in that quarter, as the English say, might well retard the moment when this devoted colonel would be made a general, aide-de-camp to the King. He replied to the second-lieutenant's initiative with a few very curt words that ordered Lucien to keep quarters for twenty-four hours.

This was exactly what Lucien had dreaded. He went home to write to Madame de Chasteller. But what torture to write a formal letter, yet how imprudent to put into writing the things he had dared to talk to her about! The subject occupied his entire night.

After a thousand misgivings, Lucien sent his servant to the Hôtel de Pontlevé with a letter that could be read by anyone. As a matter of fact, he was afraid to write otherwise to Madame de Chasteller: all his love had returned and with it the extreme terror she inspired in him.

Two days later, at four o'clock in the morning, he was awakened by the order to horse. At the barracks he found everything in confusion. A second-lieutenant was very busy distributing cartridges to the lancers. It was said that mill-workers of a town eight or ten leagues away had just organized and formed a protective society.

Colonel Malher went from one end of the barracks to the other shouting to the officers so that all the lancers could hear:

"What we have to do is to give them such a lesson they'll never forget it. No mercy for the b——! There are crosses to be won."

Riding past Madame de Chasteller's windows Lucien looked up searchingly, but there was no sign of life behind the closely drawn curtains of embroidered muslin. Lucien could not blame Madame de Chasteller: the least sign might be noticed and talked about by the officers of the regiment.

"Madame d'Hocquincourt," he thought, "would certainly have been at her window. But then, would I ever love Madame d'Hocquincourt?"

If Madame de Chasteller had been at her window, Lucien would have found this mark of attention adorable. As a matter of fact, the ladies of Nancy were occupying all the windows along the Rue de la Pompe and the next street, through which the regiment had to pass on its way out of the city.

The Seventh Company, to which Lucien belonged, rode directly in front of the artillery consisting of half a battery with linstocks lighted. The wheels of the ordnance gun carriages and caissons shook the frame houses of Nancy and gave the ladies a pleasurable thrill of fear. Lucien bowed to Madame d'Hocquincourt, Madame de Puylaurens, Madame de Serpierre and Madame de Marcilly.

"I should like to know whom they hate most," thought Lucien, "Louis-Philippe or the mill-workers. . . . Why couldn't Madame de Chasteller have shared the curiosity of all these ladies and so given me that tiny proof of interest? Well, here I am, off to slaughter weavers, as M. de Vassigny so elegantly puts it. If the affair is hot enough, the colonel will be made a *commandeur* of the *Legion d'Honneur,* and as my reward, I shall have won remorse."

The Twenty-seventh Lancers took six hours to cover the eight leagues which separated Nancy from N——. The regiment was delayed by the artillery. Colonel Malher received three couriers, and each time he had the horses of the ordnance changed, dismounting the lancers who seemed to have the strongest horses for hauling the heavy gun carriages.

When they had proceeded about half way, M. Fléron, the prefect, caught up with the regiment, arriving at a fast trot. To speak to the colonel, he was obliged to pass along the whole length of the column from its tail to its head, and had the pleasure of being hooted by all the lancers. He wore a sword which, because of his tiny stature, seemed enormous. The muffled jeering swelled into a burst of laughter which he tried to escape by spurring his horse to a gallop. The laughter redoubled with the usual cries of: "He *will* fall! He *won't* fall! He *will* fall! He *won't* fall!"

But the prefect soon had his revenge. Hardly had they started through the dirty, narrow streets of N—— than the lancers were hooted by all the women and children crowding the windows of the poorer quarters and by some of the weavers themselves who, from time to time, appeared at the corners of the narrowest little alleys. They could hear the shops being hastily closed on all sides.

Finally the regiment came out onto the city's chief business thoroughfare; shops were all shut up, not a head in any of the windows, a death-like silence. They reached an irregular and very long square, ornamented with five or six stunted mulberry trees, and with a foul stream, full of all the filth of the town, running down its entire length. And, as it also served as a sewer for several tanneries, the water was blue.

The garments hanging in the windows to dry were so miserable, so tattered and filthy, they made one shudder. The windowpanes were tiny and dirty and in many of the windows the glass had been replaced by old paper covered with writing and oiled. Everywhere a flagrant picture of poverty that made the heart ache, but not hearts that hoped to win a cross by delivering saber blows in this miserable little town.

The colonel drew up his regiment in order of battle all along the little stream. There the unhappy lancers, dying of hunger and fatigue, spent seven hours exposed to the blazing August sun without anything to eat or drink. As we have said, at the arrival of the regiment, all the shops had been quickly closed, and the taverns even more quickly than the rest.

"We're in a nice mess," one of the lancers shouted.

"We're very popular around here," another voice replied.

"Silence, damn you!" bawled some *Juste-milieu* lieutenant.

Lucien noticed that all the self-respecting officers kept perfectly silent, and were looking grave.

"So, we are facing the enemy," thought Lucien.

He was watching himself, and was pleased to discover that he was as cool as though he were performing an experiment in chemistry at the École Polytechnique. This egotistical thought greatly diminished his distaste for this sort of service.

The tall thin lieutenant, whom Lieutenant-Colonel Filloteau had mentioned, came to speak to him, cursing the mill-workers. Lucien did not answer but looked at the officer with unutterable contempt. As the lieutenant walked away several voices, loud enough to be heard, cried out: "Spy! Spy!"

The soldiers were suffering horribly. Two or three were forced to dismount. Men on fatigue duty had been sent to the public fountain. In its basin, which was immense, they found three or four dead cats, recently killed, that had reddened the water with their blood. The thread of warmish water flowing from the ornamental spout was so scanty that it took several minutes to fill one bottle—and there were three hundred and eighty men under arms.

The prefect and the mayor were often to be seen together

going back and forth across the square, trying, it was said in the ranks, to buy wine.

"If I sell you any," each wine-merchant replied, "my house will be pillaged and destroyed."

The regiment was now being regularly assailed every half hour with redoubled jeers and cat-calls.

After the spying lieutenant had left him, Lucien conceived the idea of sending his servants to a village two leagues away which, having neither looms nor workers, was probably peaceable. These servants were told to buy, at any price, one hundred loaves of bread and three or four loads of fodder. The servants having been successful in their mission, at about four o'clock four horses loaded with bread, and two others with hay, appeared on the square. Suddenly there was a dead silence. The peasants came over to Lucien who, after paying them well, had the pleasure of distributing a little bread among the privates of his company.

"Look at our republican beginning his intrigues," exclaimed several of the officers who disliked Lucien.

With less hypocrisy, Filloteau came to ask him for two or three loaves for himself, and hay for his horses.

"It's my horses that worry me," cynically observed Colonel Malher, passing in front of his men.

A moment later Lucien heard M. Fléron saying to the colonel:

"Damn it all, aren't we going to get in a single blow at these blackguards?"

"He is much more rabid than the colonel," thought Lucien. "Colonel Malher can hardly expect to be made a general for killing a dozen or more weavers, but Fléron might well be made prefect and would be sure of the post for two or three years."

Lucien's timely distribution had given them the ingenious idea that there were actually villages in the neighborhood of the town. Toward five o'clock, a pound of black bread was distributed to each lancer and a small quantity of meat to the officers.

At nightfall one shot was fired, but nobody was hurt.

"I don't know why," thought Lucien, "but I'd be willing to wager that that shot was fired by order of M. Fléron."

About ten o'clock at night, they noticed that all the workers had disappeared. At eleven, some infantry soldiers arrived. The cannons and the howitzers were turned over to them, and at one o'clock in the morning the regiment of lancers, dying of hunger—both men and horses—departed for Nancy. They halted for six hours in a very peaceful village where they were sold bread at eight sous a pound and wine at five francs a bottle; the warlike prefect had forgotten to make arrangements for provisioning the regiment.

For all the military, strategic, political, etc., details of this notable affair, see the newspapers of that time. The regiment had covered itself with glory and the workers had given evidence of the most signal poltroonery.

Such was Lucien's first campaign.

"I wonder if I dare, when I get back to Nancy, present myself at the Hôtel de Pontlevé, provided it is by day?"

He dared. But he was dying of fright when he knocked at the porte-cochère, and as he rang the bell of Madame de Chasteller's apartment, his heart was pounding so that he said to himself:

"My God! Am I going to stop loving her again?"

She was alone, with no Mademoiselle Bérard. Lucien seized her hand passionately. Two minutes later he perceived that he loved her more than ever. Had he had a little more experience he would have succeeded in getting himself told that he too was loved. If he had only had the audacity to throw himself into her arms, he would not have been repulsed. It would at least have been possible to establish a treaty of peace extremely advantageous to the interests of his love. Instead he did not advance his affairs in the least, and was serenely happy.

It had been reported and believed that the pistol-shot fired by the workers of N—— had killed a young officer of the Lancers. Frightened at first, after learning the facts, relief put Madame de Chasteller in a melting mood.

"I must send you away now," she said with a tone of regret which she had intended to make severe.

Lucien was afraid of offending her, and yielded.

"May I hope, Madam, to see you later at Madame d'Hocquincourt's? It is her day at home."

"Very likely. And I am sure that you will not fail to be there. I know that you are not averse to the company of that very charming lady."

An hour later Lucien presented himself at Madame d'Hocquincourt's, but Madame de Chasteller did not arrive until very late.

After that, time flew for our hero. But lovers are so blissful in their scenes together that the reader, instead of sympathizing with the description of their happiness, becomes jealous of it, and out of revenge is apt to say: "My God! What an insipid book!"

CHAPTER TWENTY-EIGHT

WE SHALL NOW beg leave to take a standing leap over the two following months. This will be all the simpler for us in that Lucien, at the end of those two months, was no further advanced than on the first day. Convinced that he had no gift for making himself desirable to a woman, especially when he was seriously in love with her, he contented himself every moment of the day with trying to do what pleased him the most at that moment. Never in any given quarter of an hour did he impose on himself the least constraint, pain, or act of prudence that might during the next quarter-hour further his amorous interests with Madame de Chasteller. He told her the truth about everything. For example, one evening:

"But it seems to me," she said to him, "that you say things to M. de Serpierre which are absolutely the contrary of what you say to me. Could it be that you are just a little false? In that case the persons who take an interest in you will be most unhappy."

Mademoiselle Bérard having usurped the second drawing room, Madame de Chasteller received Lucien in a large study or library adjoining it, the door of which was always left open. In the evening when Mademoiselle Bérard retired, Madame de Chasteller's maid took her place; and on this particular evening they could, with perfect security, talk freely about everything and name things by their names: Mademoiselle Bérard had gone to pay calls and the maid was deaf.

"Madam," Lucien replied warmly and with a sort of virtuous indignation, "I have been thrown into the middle of the ocean. I swim so as not to drown and you say: 'He moves his arms too much!' Have you such an exaggerated opinion of the strength of my lungs that you think they alone suffice to re-educate all the inhabitants of Nancy? Do you want me never to see you except here in your house? And even so, they would soon make you ashamed of receiving me just as they have made you ashamed of your desire to return to Paris. It is quite true that on every subject, even on the time of day, I think and believe the exact opposite of the natives of these parts. Do you want me to be reduced to absolute silence? To you alone, Madam, I say what I think about everything, even politics—about which we are so much at variance. And it is for you alone, in order to be nearer to you, that I have perfected myself in that habit of lying which I adopted the day when, to rid myself of my republican reputation, I went to the Chapel of the Penitents with the worthy Dr. Du Poirier as my guide! Would you prefer, beginning tomorrow, to have me say exactly what I think and to measure swords with the whole world? I shall no longer go to the Penitents, at Madame de Marcilly's I shall no longer look at the portrait of Henri V, at Madame de Commercy's I shall no longer listen to Abbé Rey's absurd homilies; and in less than a week I shall be unable ever to see you again."

"No, that is not what I want," she replied sadly. "And yet I have been deeply distressed ever since yesterday evening. After I urged you to go and talk with Mademoiselle Théodelinde and Madame de Puylaurens, I overheard you telling M. de Serpierre exactly the opposite of what you had just said to me."

"M. de Serpierre buttonholed me as I passed. Blame the provinces where one cannot live without being a hypocrite, or blame the education I have received which has opened my eyes to a good three quarters of all human imbecility. You object sometimes that a Paris education prevents a person from *feeling;* perhaps, but as compensation, it teaches one to see clearly. I take no credit to myself for it, and you would be wrong to accuse me of pedantry, for the fault rests with the witty people who are brought together in my mother's salon. One has only to see clearly to be struck by the absurdity of MM. de Puylaurens, Sanréal, de Serpierre and d'Hocquincourt, and to understand the hypocrisy of Dr. Du Poirier, M. Fléron and Colonel Malher, the three latter blackguards and far more despicable than the former who, out of stupidity, rather than selfishness, naïvely prefer the happiness of some two hundred thousand privileged individuals to that of the thirty-two million people in France. But here I am, engaged in propaganda! A very stupid way of spending my time with you. Yesterday, which of us seemed to you to be in the right—M. de Serpierre whose arguments I failed to contest, or myself whose real thoughts you know?"

"Alas! both of you! You are changing me, perhaps for the worse! When I am alone, I surprise myself wondering if they did not at the Sacred Heart intentionally teach me some singular lies. One day during a quarrel with the General (that is, M. de Chasteller), he plainly told me so, and then seemed to regret having said it."

"Naturally! He was jeopardizing his best interests as a husband. It is preferable for a wife to bore her husband by her lack of intelligence, but to remain faithful to her duties. In this, as in everything else, religion is the strongest ally of despotic power. As for me, I am not afraid of endangering my interests as a lover," replied Lucien proudly. "And after this test, I am sure of myself in all possible eventualities."

Taking a lover, as Lucien explained, is one of the most decisive steps a young woman can permit herself. If she does not take a lover she dies of boredom, and around forty becomes an imbecile; she either loves a dog to whom she devotes all her attention, or a confessor who devotes all his attention to her; for a truly feminine heart needs a man's sympathy, as we men need a partner in conversation. If she takes a dishonorable man for lover, a woman, in all probability, throws herself headlong into the most horrible afflictions. . . . Nothing could have been more naïve than Madame de Chasteller's objections to all this, nor more tender than the tone in which they were said.

After conversations of this sort it always seemed utterly

impossible to Lucien that she had ever had an affair with the Lieutenant-Colonel of the Twenty-seventh Regiment of Hussars.

"My God! What wouldn't I give to have my father's flair and experience for one single day!"

Although ordinarily very well treated by Madame de Chasteller, and in his calmer moods believing himself loved by her, Lucien, nevertheless, always approached her with fear and trembling. He had never been able to get over a certain feeling of perturbation every time he rang her bell. He was never sure of the welcome he would receive. As soon as his eyes fell on the Hôtel de Pontlevé, even before arriving, he was no longer himself. For him the old porter was a fatal being, whom he could address only with bated breath.

Often when talking to Madame de Chasteller his words would become tangled on his tongue, a thing which never happened to him with anyone else. And this was the man Madame de Chasteller suspected of being a coxcomb and regarded with a bewilderment that equaled his. He was, for her, the absolute master of her happiness.

One evening Madame de Chasteller had an urgent letter to write.

"Here is a newspaper to while away your idle moments," she said, laughing and tossing him a copy of the *Débats*. She jumped up to fetch a closed escritoire which she then set on the table between Lucien and herself.

As she was opening the desk with a little key attached to her watch-chain, Lucien leaned over the table and kissed her hand.

Madame de Chasteller raised her head: she was no longer the same woman. "He might just as well have kissed my forehead," she thought. She bristled with offended modesty.

"I can never trust you, it would seem." And her eyes flashed with sudden anger. "I not only receive you when I should have closed my door to you as to everyone else, but I allow you an intimacy that endangers my reputation, whose rules you might at least have respected (here her voice and entire bearing became even more withering); I treat you as a brother and ask you to read for a moment while I am writing an urgent letter and, in a most ill-timed and graceless way, you take advantage of my total lack of misgiving to indulge in a gesture that is, as a matter of fact, just as humiliating for you as it is for me! I have made a mistake, I should never have received you. Please go!"

In her manner and in her voice was all the firmness and all the coldness her pride could demand. Lucien saw this and was stunned.

This cowardice on his part strengthened Madame de Chasteller's courage. What he should have done was to rise, bow coldly, and say:

"Really, Madam, you exaggerate. One little indiscretion of no consequence, and perhaps a little silly on my part, and you turn it into a monstrous crime. I loved a woman as remarkable for her intelligence as for her beauty. At the moment I only find her pretty."

And with these words he should have picked up his sword, tranquilly put it on, and departed.

But far from thinking of such a course of action which he would have found too painful and too perilous, Lucien confined himself to falling into a state of despair at his dismissal. He had, it is true, risen, but he did not take his leave. He was very obviously trying to find a pretext for staying.

"I shall relinquish my place to you, sir," Madame de Chasteller continued with finished politeness which, by its coldness, seemed to accentuate the scorn she felt at his not leaving.

She closed her escritoire, preparing to take it to another room. Lucien, in a sudden access of anger, said to her:

"I beg your pardon, Madam, I forgot myself."

With that he left, overcome by rage both against himself and against her.

There had been nothing satisfactory about his behavior except those last words, but they had been entirely the result of impulse and not of art.

Once outside the unfortunate house, and free from the curious glances of the servants who were not accustomed to seeing him depart at such an early hour:

"It must be admitted," he said to himself, "that I am a small boy indeed to permit myself to be treated like that! I have only got all I deserved. When I am with her, instead of seeking to improve my position, I just sit and stare at her like a child. On my return from N—— there was a moment when it only depended on me to secure the most substantial privileges for myself. I could have induced her to say plainly that she loved me, and won the right to embrace her every time I arrived or departed. As it is I can't even kiss her hand! What a fool I am!"

Thus spoke Lucien to himself as he fled down the main street of Nancy, and continued with many another bitter self-reproach.

Full of contempt for himself, he still retained sense enough to say:

"Something must be done about it."

He looked forward to the evening with repugnance. For this was Madame de Marcilly's evening at home, and in that virtuous house, in the presence of a bust of Henri V, all the right-thinking heads of the city forgathered to discuss the day's news in the *Quotidienne* and lose thirty sous at whist.

Lucien felt that he was in no state of mind to act a part. He had the happy idea of going to see Madame d'Hocquincourt instead. Of all provincial ladies that ever existed she was the most natural, and almost reconciled one to the provinces. Hers was a naturalness that would have been impossible in Paris, where her *stock would have gone down.*

CHAPTER TWENTY-NINE

A H!" she cried on seeing him enter. "You make up my mind: I shan't go to Madame de Marcilly's."

And she called back the servant who had been sent to order her carriage.

"But how does it happen that you are not at the feet of the sublime Chasteller? Has there been a lovers' quarrel?"

Madame d'Hocquincourt scrutinized Lucien with a gay and knowing look.

"Ah, it's plain enough!" she cried merrily. "That contrite air betrays you. My misfortune is written all over those afflicted features, in that forced smile: I am nothing but a make-shift. Out with it! Tell me, since I am only a humble confidante, tell me all your troubles! Have you been driven away for some more amiable young man, or have you been driven away because you deserve it? But, first of all, you must tell me the truth if I am to console you."

Lucien had a great deal of difficulty in evading Madame d'Hocquincourt's questions. She was by no means lacking in wit, and this wit, being constantly at the service of a strong will and a passionate nature, had acquired all the idiosyncrasies of common sense. Lucien was too immersed in his anger at first to find a way to throw her off the scent. But the next minute, still rankling from the treatment he had received from Madame de Chasteller, he was very much surprised to hear himself addressing the most gallant remarks, charming personal nothings to the young woman in an elegant negligee half-reclining on the couch with an air of keenest interest, not two feet away from him.

Such language on Lucien's lips had, for Madame d'Hocquincourt, all the advantage of novelty. He observed that, engaged in trying the effect of a charming pose in the long mirror of an adjacent wardrobe, she had stopped tormenting him on the subject of Madame de Chasteller. Lucien, whom misfortune had made Machiavellian, said to himself:

"The language of gallantry when one is tête-à-tête with a young woman who honors it by listening with an almost serious attention, must of necessity take on a bold, almost passionate tone."

We must admit that in reasoning thus Lucien felt the keenest pleasure in demonstrating to everyone that he was not a very small boy. During this time Madame d'Hocquincourt, for her own part, was making one discovery after another. She was beginning to find Lucien the most delightful man in the whole city of Nancy. This was all the more dangerous, considering the fact that M. d'Antin had already lasted more than eighteen months, an extremely long reign which had astonished everybody.

Happily for the tête-à-tête it was interrupted by the arrival of M. de Murcé. A tall thin young man, he carried his small head covered with very black hair proudly. Invariably taciturn at the beginning of a visit, his whole merit consisted in a gaiety that was perfectly natural and very comical because of its artlessness, but which began to display itself only after he had been an hour or two in gay company. He was essentially provincial but, nevertheless, very amiable. None of his quips would have passed muster in Paris but they were quite comical nonetheless, and became him very well.

Soon there appeared another habitué of the house, M. de Goëllo. He was a large man, pale and blond with a great deal of learning and very little wit, who listened to himself talk and said at least once a day that he was not yet forty, which was indeed true since he was something over thirty-nine. Moreover he was a cautious man; to answer yes to the simplest question, even to bring up a chair for anyone, were weighty matters taking a quarter of an hour for deliberation. When he finally made up his mind to action he affected the most childish kind of alacrity and impetuosity. He had been in love with Madame d'Hocquincourt for the past five or six years, kept hoping that his turn would come, and sometimes even tried to make newcomers believe that it had already come and gone.

One day at a tavern, Madame d'Hocquincourt, catching him assuming this role, said to him:

"You are a future, my poor darling, that pretends to be a past but that will never be a present." For she always "darlinged" her friends when on one of her witty flights, without, for all that, shocking anybody. It was plainly only the intimacy of a sprightly mood which is a thousand leagues removed from tender sentiments.

M. de Goëllo's arrival was followed at short intervals by four or five young men.

"Here we have all that is best and gayest in town," said Lucien to himself as he watched them enter one after the other.

"I have just come from Madame de Marcilly's," said one of them. "They are all gloomy there and pretend to be even gloomier than they are!"

"It's what happened at N—— that makes them so cheerful."

"As for me," said another, annoyed at the way Madame d'Hocquincourt sat gazing at Lucien, "I decided that if I failed to find Madame d'Hocquincourt, or Madame de Puylaurens, or Madame de Chasteller at home, there was nothing for it but to drown my evening in a bottle of champagne. And that is the course I would have pursued had I found Madame d'Hocquincourt's door closed to the common herd."

"But my poor Téran," retorted Madame d'Hocquincourt at this malicious thrust at Lucien, "one doesn't threaten to get drunk, one gets drunk. You should have sense enough to see the difference."

"Nothing, it is true, is more difficult than to know how to drink," insisted Goëllo, the pedant. (It was a critical moment.)

"What are we going to do? What are we going to do?" cried Murcé and one of the Roller brothers in the same breath.

This was the question everyone was asking without anyone finding the answer, when M. d'Antin appeared. At the sight of his jovial air all faces brightened immediately. He was a tall blond young man of twenty-eight or thirty. It was utterly impossible for him to assume a serious or solemn air, and were he ever to announce that the street was on fire it would most certainly not be with a lugubrious face. He was a very good-looking man, but at times one might have objected to a somewhat vacuous, stupid expression on his charming face, like that of a man beginning to get drunk. When you knew him this was only an added charm. As a matter of fact, he was quite devoid of sense but had the best heart in the world and an unbelievable fund of gaiety. He had just managed to run through a large fortune which his miserly father had left him three or four years before. He had deserted Paris, or rather he had been driven from that city for indulging in certain pleasantries on the subject of an august personage. He was absolutely unique as an organizer of all kinds of amusing parties, for wherever he appeared dullness fled. Unfortunately

Madame d'Hocquincourt was familiar with all his gifts by now, and the element of surprise, so essential to her happiness, was no longer operative. M. de Goëllo, who had heard Madame d'Hocquincourt remark as much, was teasing M. d'Antin with heavy wit about his no longer being able to contrive anything new, when Count de Vassigny entered.

"There is only one thing for you to do if you want to last, my dear d'Antin," said M. de Vassigny. "You must turn sensible!"

"I should bore myself! I haven't the courage! I shall have plenty of time to be serious when I am completely ruined. Then, to bore myself in a useful fashion, I shall plunge into politics and the secret societies in honor of Henri V who is my very own king. Will you promise me your support? Meanwhile, gentlemen, as you all seem so serious, still numbed apparently by the amiability of the Hôtel Marcilly, let's play faro—that Italian game I taught you the other day. M. de Vassigny, who does not know the game, will deal. Then Goëllo cannot accuse me of arranging the rules for my benefit! Who knows how to play faro?"

"I do," said Lucien.

"Good! So, will you be so kind as to coach M. de Vassigny and to see that he follows the rules of the game. You, Roller, will be croupier."

"I," replied **Roller** coldly, "will be nothing—for I am leaving."

The truth was that Count Roller could see that Lucien, whom he had never before met at Madame d'Hocquincourt's, was going to play a most agreeable role this evening, and as that was something he could not stomach, he took his departure.

A good part of Nancy society, especially the younger men, detested Lucien. He had the dubious advantage of having made two or three rejoinders which even to them seemed witty, and had thereby turned them into enemies for life.

"After our game," continued d'Antin, "at midnight when you are all ruined, we shall, like perfectly respectable people, go to supper at the *Grande Chaumière*." (This was the best tavern of Nancy, situated in the garden of a former Carthusian monastery.)

"I agree," said Madame d'Hocquincourt, "provided it's a *Dutch treat.*"

"Naturally," said d'Antin. "And as M. Lafiteau, who has excellent champagne, and M. Piebot, the only ice-dealer in Nancy, may be going to bed, I shall, in the name of the *Dutch treat,* see that there is wine and that it is properly chilled. I'll have it all sent over to the *Grande Chaumière*. In the meanwhile, M. Leuwen, here are a hundred francs. Please do me the honor of playing for me, and try not to seduce Madame d'Hocquincourt or I shall take my revenge and go straight to the Hôtel de Pontlevé to denounce you."

Everybody followed M. d'Antin's instructions obediently, even that inveterate politician, Vassigny. The game started and after half an hour everyone was very much excited. That is what d'Antin had counted on to chase away the inclination to yawn they had acquired at Madame de Marcilly's.

"I'll throw my cards out of the window," cried Madame d'Hocquincourt, "if anyone punts more than five francs. Do you want to make a queen of gamesters out of me?"

D'Antin returned, and at half-past twelve they left for the *Grande Chaumière*. A little flowering orange tree, the only one of its kind in Nancy, had been placed in the center of the table. The wine was chilled to perfection. The supper was very gay, no one got drunk, and at three o'clock in the morning they all parted the best friends in the world.

And it is in this way that a woman loses her reputation in

the provinces, a thing that worried Madame d'Hocquincourt not the least in the world. Getting up the next morning, she went to see her husband, who embraced her, saying:

"You are quite right to enjoy yourself, my poor child, if you have the courage. Do you know what happened at X——? That king we all hate so much is losing ground, and after him will arrive the Republic which will chop off his head and ours too."

"His head? Ah, no! He is far too clever. And as for you, I'll carry you off across the Rhine."

Lucien had prolonged his stay at the Hôtel d'Hocquincourt as long as possible, leaving with the last of his companions of the evening and attaching himself to the little group, which grew smaller at each street corner as each member took the direction of his house; finally he accompanied the last one, who lived the farthest away, all the way to his door. He talked a great deal and felt a mortal terror of being left alone. For, at the Hôtel d'Hocquincourt, while listening to the stories and jests of these gentlemen, and trying by well-timed remarks to maintain the position that Madame d'Hocquincourt seemed inclined to accord him and which was not that of a small boy, he had made a resolution for the next day.

He would *not* go to the Hôtel de Pontlevé. And right away he began to suffer.

"But it is important to maintain one's honor and if I give in now I shall soon see that preference, which it is evident at times she feels for me, change to contempt. And besides, God knows what new insult she has ready for me if I go to see her tomorrow."

These two thoughts, occurring in quick succession, became torture to him.

The next day arrived all too quickly and with it the cruel

sensation of the happiness he was to be deprived of by not going to the Hôtel de Pontlevé. Everything seemed insipid, colorless, odious by comparison with the delicious perturbation he would feel in that little library, beside that little mahogany table where she always sat working as she listened to him. The decision to present himself after all was enough to change his whole frame of mind.

"For," he added, "if I don't go this evening how am I to present myself tomorrow? (In his mortal perplexity he had recourse to cant.) Do I really want to have the house closed to me? And for such nonsense! Besides, perhaps I was really to blame. I might ask permission to go to Metz for a few days. . . . But I should be punishing myself. I should die of despair."

On the other hand, had not Madame de Chasteller, with her exaggerated idea of feminine delicacy, wanted to make him understand that he should simply make his calls less frequent, limit them, for example, to one visit a week? By presenting himself so soon at a house from which he had been so summarily dismissed, would he not expose himself to Madame de Chasteller's redoubled wrath and moreover give her just cause for complaint? He knew how susceptible she was on the subject of what she called the deference due to her sex. It is true that in her struggle against her feelings for Lucien, Madame de Chasteller, distressed at being so little able to count on her most sternly formed resolutions, was often irritated with herself and, in consequence, would pick quite unwarrantable quarrels with him.

With a little more experience of life, these unreasonable quarrels on the part of a woman as intelligent as Madame de Chasteller and one whose natural modesty and sense of justice usually kept her from exaggerating other people's faults, would have made Lucien realize how torn by conflict was that heart he was engaged in besieging. But Lucien's patriotic soul had always despised love and knew nothing of the very necessary art of making love. Until chance had placed Madame de Chasteller in his way, and an access of vanity had made the idea that the prettiest young woman of the city should have reason to laugh at him unendurable, he had always said to himself:

"What would be thought of a man who, during an eruption of Vesuvius, should be wholly taken up with playing cup-and-ball?"

This imposing illustration has the advantage of summing up Lucien's character and the character of the best of the young men of his generation. When love had come to take the place of that sterner sentiment, duty to the fatherland, in the heart of this young Roman, all that remained of his sense of duty was transformed into a sense of honor—badly understood.

In Lucien's present position, the most insignificant young man of eighteen, provided he had a soul barren enough and that contempt for women which is so fashionable today, would have said to himself: "What could be simpler than to go to see Madame de Chasteller without seeming to attach the slightest importance to what happened yesterday, without showing any sign that one even remembers her little outburst of temper, but prepared to make all due amends in the way of excuses and then to begin speaking of something else if Madame de Chasteller should still seem inclined to give importance to the heinous crime of kissing her hand."

But Lucien was very far from harboring any such ideas. From the point of view of common sense and in our present state of moral decrepitude, it takes quite an effort, I admit, for us to understand the frightful battles raging in our hero's soul and, after that, not to laugh.

Toward evening Lucien, no longer able to remain quiet, was pacing with restless step along a deserted part of the ramparts not a hundred paces from the Hôtel de Pontlevé. Like Tancred he was battling phantoms and needed all his courage. He was more undecided than ever when a certain clock close by which he always heard from Madame de Chasteller's little library, began striking half-past seven with all the quarters and half-quarters with which the hours are surrounded in the German clocks of the East of France.

The sound of this clock settled it! Without realizing why, there came to him the poignant recollection of his state of happiness on the evenings when he heard those quarters and half-quarters, and he was seized with a profound disgust for the sad, painful, egotistical feelings that had been afflicting him ever since the day before. Walking slowly along that melancholy stretch of rampart, all men had appeared to him in a mean and sordid light. Life had seemed arid and stripped of all joy, of everything that made life worth living. But at the sound of the clock, electrified by the thought of that community of sentiment uniting two great and generous souls with scarcely the need of words, he quickly turned his steps toward the Hôtel de Pontlevé.

He was hurrying past the porter's wife when she stopped him:

"Where are you going, sir?" she cried in a tremulous little voice, getting up from her spinning wheel as though to run after him. "Madam has gone out."

"What!" exclaimed Lucien. "Gone out! She has gone out?" And he stood there as though petrified.

The porter's wife mistook his attitude for one of incredulity.

"She left almost an hour ago," she explained with an air of candor, for she liked Lucien. "You can see for yourself, the carriage house is open and the coupé isn't there."

Lucien fled at these words, and two minutes later was once more on the rampart. He looked down at the muddy moat without seeing it, and beyond it at the desolate, arid plain.

"A pretty maneuver that was, to be sure! She despises me . . . and to show it she intentionally goes out an hour before the time she is in the habit of receiving me every day. Just punishment for my cowardliness! This should be a lesson to me for the future. If I haven't the courage to resist temptation while in the same city, then I must ask permission to go to Metz. Certainly I'll suffer, but no one will be able to see into my heart, and distance will save me from the possibility of committing more blunders like this one which is a stain on a man's honor. Forget this proud woman . . . After all, I am not a colonel. This is worse than folly on my part. To persist in struggling against my lack of rank is a proof of utter insensibility."

He flew home, saw to the harnessing of his calash himself, all the while cursing the slowness of the coachman, and had himself driven to Madame de Serpierre's. Madame was out, and her door was closed.

"Evidently all doors are closed to me today."

He climbed into the driver's seat and drove himself at a gallop to the *Green Huntsman*. The Serpierre ladies were not there. He rushed furiously through all the alleys of its beautiful garden. The German musicians were drinking at a nearby tavern. Catching sight of Lucien, they ran after him.

"Sir, O sir! Do you want us to play those Mozart duets?"

"Of course."

He paid them, jumped into his carriage, and drove back to Nancy.

He was received at Madame de Commercy's where he displayed an edifying gravity. He played two rubbers of whist with M. Rey, Grand Vicar of the Bishop of Nancy, without his cantankerous old partner's being able to reproach him for a moment's inattention.

CHAPTER THIRTY

AFTER TWO RUBBERS of whist, which seemed to him endless, Lucien was in addition called upon to take sides in a dispute over an incident which had occurred that morning: one of the priests of the city had refused to allow the funeral of a certain shoemaker to take place in his church.

Lucien was listening to this disgusting story without paying much attention when the Vicar exclaimed:

"Although he is in the service, I ask for no better judge than M. Leuwen."

"It is precisely because I am in the service and not *although*," Lucien retorted, "that I have the honor to beg the Grand Vicar to say nothing that might force me to give a disagreeable reply."

"But, my dear sir, there were four grounds against this man: as a purchaser of national property, holder of . . . , for being married by the state only, and refusing a proper marriage on his deathbed."

"You are forgetting a fifth, sir: paying his part of the tax that provides your salary and mine."

And with that Lucien departed.

A few more retorts of the sort would have ruined the good reputation he had acquired, but this one was really to the point.

Nevertheless, the remark would certainly in the end have

hastened his ruin or, at least, it would have lost him half of the consideration he enjoyed in Nancy had he been destined to stay much longer in that city.

As he was leaving, he ran into his friend Dr. Du Poirier who buttonholed him and, willy-nilly, carried him off for a walk on the Place d'Armes to finish explaining to him his system for the restoration of France. The civil code, with its equal partition of the estate on the decease of the head of the family, will result in the subdivision of the land to infinity. The population will increase but it will be a paupered population without bread. The great religious orders, of necessity, must be re-established in France. Holding enormous properties, they would make for the greater happiness of a limited number of peasants required for the cultivation of those vast domains.

"Believe me, sir, there is nothing more disastrous than an over-numerous and over-educated population. . . ."

Lucien behaved admirably.

"It sounds plausible," he replied. . . . "There is much to be said. . . . I am not sufficiently versed in these weighty matters. . . ."

He put forward several objections, but finally appeared to admit the doctor's general principles.

"But does this old rascal really believe what he is saying?" he wondered as he listened, at the same time examining attentively that large head with its deeply lined face. "I seem to recognize, underneath, the clever scheming of a pettifogging lawyer from Lower Normandy, not the goodnatured simplicity capable of believing in all this humbug. Besides one cannot deny that this man has a keen intelligence, the gift of persuasion, and the art of getting the best possible conclusions from the worst possible premises, the most gratuitous assumptions. His manners are coarse, but being a clever man and one who understands his century, far from trying to correct this coarseness he revels in it; it constitutes his originality, his mission and his force. He seems to exaggerate it intentionally. These provincial nobles need have no fear that it would ever be mistaken for their noble haughtiness. The stupidest of them are able to say: 'What a difference between this man and me!' and swallow more readily all the doctor's humbug. If he succeeds in triumphing over 1830, they will make him a minister, he will be their Corbière.

"But there's nine o'clock striking already," cried Lucien suddenly. "Good-by, my dear doctor, I must leave you and your sublime arguments which will lead you to the Chamber one of these days and which you will end up by making fashionable. You are really a man of superior eloquence and persuasion, but I must go now and pay my court to Madame d'Hocquincourt."

"That is to say, Madame de Chasteller. Don't think you can fool me, young man!"

And Dr. Du Poirier, before going to bed, visited five or six more noble families to find out, as usual, everybody's business, to direct them, to help them understand the simplest things with, of course, due regard to their vanity, mentioning at least once a week each one's ancestors, or, when there was nothing better to do or when carried away by enthusiasm, preaching his doctrine of the re-establishment of the great monastic orders.

At one house he would decide what day the washing should be done, at another . . . And he always decided for the best since he had good common sense, much sagacity, and a great deal of respect for money, besides being quite free from passion in regard to the washing. . . .

Whilst the doctor was engaged in talking washing, etc., Lucien, holding his head high, was walking with a firm step and the intrepid look of resignation and true courage.

He was satisfied with the way he was fulfilling his duty. He went directly to Madame d'Hocquincourt's, or "Madame d'Hocquin," as her Nancy friends familiarly called her.

He found M. de Serpierre and M. de Vassigny there, everlastingly talking politics. M. de Serpierre was explaining at length, and unfortunately with proofs, how much better things had been before the Revolution, at the Intendancy of Metz under M. de Calonne, later the famous Minister.

"That courageous magistrate," said M. de Serpierre, "who succeeded in prosecuting the wretched La Chalotais, the first of the Jacobins. That was in 1779. . . ."

Lucien leaned over towards Madame d'Hocquincourt and said gravely:

What language, Madame, both for you and for me!

She burst out laughing, much to the annoyance of M. de Serpierre.

"You must know, sir . . ." he continued, addressing Lucien. . . .

"My God," thought Lucien, "this is my cue! It was written that I should fall from the frying pan into the fire, from Du Poirier to Serpierre!"

"You must know, sir," continued M. de Serpierre in a thundering voice, "that these gentlemen of the petty nobility, or related to them, had the tallage and capitation tax of their protégés reduced, as well as their own land-tax. Do you know that whenever I went to Metz there was no other inn for me, as for all the first families of Lorraine, but the Hôtel de l'Intendance of M. Calonne? And there you would be sure to find a sumptuous table, charming women, the first officers of the garrison, gaming-tables and perfect manners! Instead of which you now have a dreary little prefect in a shabby suit who dines alone and badly, that is, if he dines at all!"

"God!" thought Lucien, "this man is an even worse bore than Du Poirier."

Hoping to bring the harangue to an end, he made only vaguely admiring gestures by way of reply, and the slight attention he paid to what he heard and what he said, once more left free scope to all his amorous thoughts.

"It is evident," he decided, "that without appearing the most abject of men, I can no longer present myself at Madame de Chasteller's. All is over between us. The most I can allow myself is a formal call from time to time. In other words, I have received my dismissal. My enemies, the Roller brothers, my rival, her tall cousin M. de Blancet who dines five nights a week at the Hôtel de Pontlevé and takes tea with father and daughter every evening, will all of them soon learn of my disgrace. Look out for their contempt then, my fine gentleman of the charming yellow liveries and mettlesome horses! All those whose windowpanes have trembled at the clatter of your carriage wheels, that shake the very pavements, will vie with each other in celebrating your ridiculous disgrace. You will sink low indeed, my poor friend! Perhaps you will be hooted out of the Nancy which you so despised. A nice way for a city to remain engraved on one's memory!"

All the while that he was immersed in these pleasant reflections, his eyes were fixed on the lovely shoulders of Madame d'Hocquincourt which a summer bodice, newly arrived from Paris the day before, left generously uncovered. Suddenly a brilliant idea occurred to him:

"Behold my buckler against ridicule! Now for the attack!"

He leaned over toward Madame d'Hocquincourt and said softly:

"What he thinks of M. de Calonne whom he mourns so bitterly, is just what I think about our lovely tête-à-tête of the other evening. It was really gauche of me not to take advantage of the serious attention I seemed to read in your eyes, to try to divine whether or not you would accept me for your adorer."

"Try to make me mad over you, I do not object," rejoined Madame d'Hocquincourt simply and coolly. She gazed at him in silence with great attention and a philosophic little pout that was altogether charming. Her beauty was heightened at this moment by a delicious air of grave impartiality, which she allowed to have its effect before adding:

"But, since what you ask is not a duty—quite the contrary, until I am mad about you, but raving mad, expect nothing of me."

The rest of their conversation in lowered tones was pursued in the same vein as this auspicious beginning.

M. de Serpierre still endeavored to engage Lucien in his discussion, having been accustomed to the greatest deference on the latter's part whenever they met at Madame de Chasteller's. At last he could not fail to understand, from Madame d'Hocquincourt's smiles, that Lucien's attention was nothing but painful politeness. The venerable old man decided to fall back entirely on M. de Vassigny, and the two gentlemen began pacing the drawing room from one end to the other.

Lucien was as cool and collected as possible. He made every effort to become intoxicated by that skin, so white and fresh, and those voluptuous curves almost directly under his eyes. But all the time he was admiring them, he could still hear Vassigny replying to his companion and trying to inculcate Du Poirier's ideas on the great religious orders and the inexpediency of the partition of estates and of too large a population.

The political promenade of the two gentlemen and Lucien's gallant conversation had lasted about a quarter of an hour when Lucien began to notice that Madame d'Hocquincourt was by no means indifferent to the tender remarks he was improvising with the laborious aid of his memory, and the lady's obvious interest at once inspired new ideas and words which were not without grace. They expressed what he felt.

"What a difference between this pleasant courteous air, full of sympathy, with which she listens to me and what I meet elsewhere! And those round arms gleaming through transparent gauze, those lovely shoulders that caress the eyes with their soft whiteness! Nothing like that with the other one! A haughty air, a severe expression, and a dress all the way up to the neck! And worse still, a taste for officers of high rank. Here I, a lowly second-lieutenant, am made to feel that I am the equal of everybody at the least."

Lucien's wounded vanity made him feel keenly the pleasure of success. In the heat of their colloquy M. de Serpierre and M. de Vassigny often paused at the other end of the drawing room, and Lucien, taking every advantage of these instants of complete freedom, was listened to with tender admiration.

The two gentlemen had been standing still at the far end of the room for some minutes, halted evidently by M. de Vassigny's striking arguments in favor of vast domains and large-scale cultivation so advantageous to the nobility, when, not two feet away from Madame d'Hocquincourt, suddenly Madame de Chasteller appeared. With her light and youthful step, she had entered immediately following the announcement of her name, which nobody had heard.

It was impossible for her not to read in Madame d'Hocquincourt's eyes, and even in Lucien's, the untimeliness of her arrival. She immediately began talking with great vivacity and volubility in a high-pitched tone of voice, about things she had observed on her round of visits that evening. The result was that Madame d'Hocquincourt was not put in an embarrassing position. Never had Lucien seen Madame de

Chasteller like this, bubbling over with gossip, even malicious gossip.

"I should never have forgiven her," he said to himself, "if she had assumed a virtuous air and tried to embarrass that poor little d'Hocquincourt. She saw very well that my talent for seduction was beginning to have an effect."

In saying this Lucien was almost half serious.

Madame de Chasteller spoke to him as freely and gracefully as usual. She said nothing very remarkable but, thanks to her, the conversation was lively, even brilliant, for nothing is more amusing than gossip if retailed with wit.

Monsieur de Serpierre and M. de Vassigny had abandoned their politics and come back to Lucien's group, attracted by the charms of slander. Lucien assumed his share in the conversation.

"She must not think that I am in despair because she has closed her door to me."

But as he talked and tried to be agreeable, he entirely forgot the very existence of Madame d'Hocquincourt. In spite of his gay and detached manner, his chief occupation was observing, out of the corner of his eye, whether his clever remarks met with any success with Madame de Chasteller.

"What miracles my father would have accomplished in my place," thought Lucien, "in a conversation like this directed toward one person but to be understood by another! He would even succeed in making it satiric or flattering for a third! With the same remark I should be able to affect Madame de Chasteller while continuing to pay court to Madame d'Hocquincourt."

This was the only time he thought of the latter and only, moreover, in relation to his admiration for his father's wit.

As for Madame de Chasteller, her sole concern was trying to discover if Lucien had noticed how painful it had been for her to find him talking to Madame d'Hocquincourt with such an air of intimacy.

"I wish I knew whether he went to my house before coming here," she thought.

Little by little many more people arrived: MM. de Murcé, de Sanréal, Roller, de Lanfort and a few others unknown to the reader and really, to tell the truth, not worth introducing. They talked too loudly and gesticulated like actors. Soon Madame de Puylaurens appeared, and finally M. d'Antin himself.

In spite of herself, Madame de Chasteller kept watching the eyes of her brilliant rival. She noticed that while Madame d'Hocquincourt was greeting all her callers and making a quick tour of the room, her eyes invariably returned to Lucien and seemed to contemplate him with lively interest.

"Or rather, they are asking him to amuse her," said Madame de Chasteller to herself. "It is simply that M. Leuwen arouses her curiosity more than M. d'Antin. Her feelings go no further than that *for today*. But with a woman of her temperament, indecision never lasts long."

Rarely had Madame de Chasteller displayed such quick discernment. A budding jealousy that evening made her older than her years.

When the conversation became very animated and Madame de Chasteller felt that she could safely remain silent, her face clouded. Suddenly it cleared again as she thought:

"M. Leuwen does not talk to Madame d'Hocquincourt in the tone one uses toward a person one loves."

In order to avoid the civilities of the new arrivals, Madame de Chasteller went over to a table covered with a profusion of cartoons, satirizing the existing order. Lucien stopped talking. She noticed it with delight.

"Am I right?" she asked herself. "And yet what a difference between my severity which borders on prudishness, the result of my serious character, and the vivacity and unconstraint and the natural and ever-changing attractions of that brilliant little d'Hocquincourt. She has, it is true, had too many lovers but, after all, is that any drawback in the eyes of a second-lieutenant twenty-three years of age? And one who has such singular opinions? Besides, I wonder if he knows it?"

Lucien kept moving about the drawing room from one group to another. He was emboldened in this restlessness seeing that everybody was occupied with the news that a camp of cavalry had been established at Lunéville. This fresh subject for gossip made everybody forget Lucien and the signal attention paid him that evening by Madame d'Hocquincourt. On his part, he was equally oblivious of the people present. If he thought of them at all it was only to dread their curious glances. He was dying to go up to the table of caricatures, but feared that this would show an unpardonable lack of dignity.

"Even perhaps a lack of proper respect for Madame de Chasteller," he added bitterly. "She wished to avoid me at her house, and I take advantage of the fact of her presence in the same drawing room to compel her to listen to me!"

While finding this argument unanswerable, Lucien in a few moments found himself so near the table over which Madame de Chasteller was bending, that to ignore her would have been noticeably rude.

"It would seem like pique," Lucien said to himself. "And that is just what I want to avoid."

He blushed outrageously. The poor boy at that moment had lost all notion of the rules of fashionable behavior, they had vanished; he had forgotten them.

Madame de Chasteller, laying down one of the caricatures to take up another, raised her eyes slightly and noticed Lucien's flushed face. It was not without its effect. Across the room, Madame d'Hocquincourt saw plainly all that was going on beside the green table, and M. d'Antin's efforts at that moment to entertain her with an amusing story seemed to her unbearably tiresome.

Lucien at last summoned courage enough to raise his eyes to Madame de Chasteller, but he trembled with the fear of meeting hers and of being forced to speak at once. She seemed to be studying an engraving but with a haughty and almost angry expression. The poor woman had just had the unheard-of idea of taking Lucien's hand which was resting on the table, while the other held a cartoon, and of lifting it to her lips. This impulse filled her with consternation and unspeakable anger against herself. . . .

"And in my arrogance I sometimes dare blame Madame d'Hocquincourt!" she thought. "Only a moment ago I dared to despise her. But I am perfectly sure that no such infamous temptation has ever occurred to her all evening. God! Wherever can such horrible ideas come from?"

"I must clear up all this," Lucien said to himself, rather shocked by her distant air, "and then not think of it any longer."

"Is it possible, Madam, that I am unfortunate enough to have inspired your anger once more? If that is so, I shall leave you instantly."

She raised her eyes and could not help smiling at him very tenderly.

"By no means, sir," she said as soon as she was able to speak. "I was merely annoyed at myself for a stupid idea that came to me."

"My God! What am I about? Am I going to confess to him . . . that would be the last straw!"

She grew suddenly so red that Madame d'Hocquincourt, who had never taken her eyes off the two of them, said to herself:

"So, now they are reconciled, and closer than ever. As a

matter of fact, if they dared, they would fall into each other's arms." Lucien was about to move away. Noticing it, Madame de Chasteller said to him:

"No, do stay where you are, beside me. But for the moment I really cannot speak."

And her eyes filled with tears. She leaned down over the table, looking fixedly at an engraving.

"Ah!" thought Madame d'Hocquincourt. "Now we have reached the stage of tears."

Lucien was utterly amazed and said to himself:

"Is it love? Is it hate? It can hardly be indifference, it seems to me. All the more reason to clear things up and have done with it."

"You inspire me with such fear that I dare not reply," he said with a look of sincere distress.

"And what could you have to say to me?" she rejoined with dignity.

"That you love me, my angel. Only say it, and I swear that I will never take advantage of it."

Madame de Chasteller was on the verge of saying: "Yes, it is true, but have pity on me!" Just then Madame d'Hocquincourt, who had come quickly across the room, brushed against the table with her stiffly starched skirt of English muslin, and it was thanks to this rustling sound alone that Madame de Chasteller became aware of her presence. A tenth of a second more and she would have made her confession to Lucien within hearing of Madame d'Hocquincourt.

"God! how frightful!" she thought. "What terrible disgrace is in store for me this evening? If I raise my eyes, Madame d'Hocquincourt, and he himself, and everybody else will see that I am in love with him. Ah! what imprudence my coming here this evening! There is but one thing for me to do, even if I die on the spot, and that is to stay where

I am without moving, without speaking. Perhaps then I shall succeed in doing nothing for which I should have to blush."

Madame de Chasteller's eyes indeed remained fastened on the engraving as she continued to bend low over the table.

Madame d'Hocquincourt waited an instant for Madame de Chasteller to notice her, but her malice went no further. It never even occurred to her to address some facetious remark to her rival that would force her to raise her eyes and make a spectacle of herself. She even forgot Madame de Chasteller completely, having eyes for no one but Lucien. She found him irresistible at that moment: his eyes wore a tender expression but at the same time there was a little air of obstinacy about him. This obstinate air in a man, unless she could make fun of it, was fatal to Madame d'Hocquincourt and invariably decided the victory.

CHAPTER THIRTY-ONE

MADAME DE CHASTELLER had forgotten her love to think of nothing but safeguarding her reputation. She now turned her whole attention to the general conversation.

The camp of Lunéville and its probable consequences (nothing less than the immediate fall of the usurping power which had had the imprudence to order its establishment) still occupied the attention of everyone. But they were reduced to repeating opinions and facts that had already been reiterated over and over again: the cavalry could be counted on with more certainty than the infantry, etc., etc.

"Such endless repetition," thought Madame de Chasteller, "will soon irritate Madame de Puylaurens, and in order not to die of boredom, she will soon take sides. If I sit near her, in the rays of her glory, I shall be able to listen without talking, and, above all, M. Leuwen will not be able to talk to me."

Madame de Chasteller crossed the room without meeting Lucien. This was a great point gained. If that handsome young man had been endowed with a little natural talent, he would have obtained an avowal of love and the promise of being received every day of his life.

Everyone knew of Madame de Chasteller's admiration for Madame de Puylaurens' wit. She took a seat near Madame de Puylaurens who was describing the unseemly neglect and the boring solitude which were going to be the fate of the prince deserted by good society in the vicinity.

Having taken refuge in this safe harbor, Madame de Chasteller, who felt herself on the verge of tears and in no state to meet Lucien's glance, laughed a great deal at Madame de Puylaurens' witty way of ridiculing everything connected with the camp at Lunéville.

Now that she had escaped from her awkward predicament and had recovered from the terror which had made her oblivious of everything else, Madame de Chasteller noticed that Madame d'Hocquincourt never left Lucien's side for a moment. She seemed to be trying to induce him to talk, but, even at that distance, Madame de Chasteller thought she could see that Lucien remained taciturn.

"Is he shocked by the ridicule being heaped on the prince he serves? But he has told me a hundred times that he is not in the service of any prince; that he serves his country; and that he finds absurd the pretension of the first magistrate in calling the profession of soldier *being in his service*. M. Leuwen even goes so far as to say: '*And that is what I intend to show him by helping to dethrone him if he continues to violate his promises, that is, if we can find a thousand citizens*

who think as we do!'" * These thoughts were accompanied
by a thrill of admiration for her lover, otherwise all these
political details would have been quickly forgotten. Lucien
had made her the sacrifice of his liberalism and she had sacrificed her ultraism for his sake. On that score they had long
been in perfect accord.

"This silence of his—" continued Madame de Chasteller
to herself, "does it not mean that he wants to show his indifference to the marked favor Madame d'Hocquincourt is
showing him? He must feel very ill-treated by me. I wonder
if he is unhappy. Could I be the cause?"

Madame de Chasteller hardly dared believe it, but her attention redoubled. It is true that Lucien barely spoke, his
words had to be dragged out of him. His vanity warned him:
"It is possible that Madame de Chasteller is making sport of
you. If that is true soon all Nancy will follow suit. And perhaps Madame d'Hocquincourt is in the conspiracy! If that
is so, I must not appear to have pretensions until the day
after the victory. And here are forty persons who (if they
give me a thought) may be watching me. In any case my
enemies will not fail to say that I am courting Madame d'Hocquincourt to mask my discomfiture over my failure with
Bathilde. I must show these malicious provincials that it is
she who is running after me, and therefore I won't utter
another word for the rest of the evening. I shall even go so
far as to be impolite."

This capriciousness on Lucien's part only tended to increase
that of Madame d'Hocquincourt. She had no longer either
eyes or ears for d'Antin and told him more than once in
a very curt tone and as though in a hurry to be rid of him:

"My dear d'Antin, how boring you are tonight!"

And she would return quickly to the consideration of this
absorbing problem:

* This is a Jacobin speaking.

"Something must have shocked Leuwen. This silence is not natural in him. But what could I have done to displease him?"

As Lucien did not go near Madame de Chasteller, Madame d'Hocquincourt readily concluded that everything was over between them. Besides, she owed to a naturally happy disposition this marked difference from provincials in general, that she paid very little attention to other people's affairs. However, by way of compensation she pursued with unbelievable diligence any mad plan that happened to pop into her giddy head. The one she harbored in regard to Lucien was facilitated by the solemn circumstance that the following day was Friday. For M. d'Hocquincourt, a pious young man of twenty-eight with lovely chestnut mustaches, in order not to participate in the profanation of this day of penitence, had gone to bed long before midnight. The moment he retired Madame d'Hocquincourt ordered punch and champagne served.

"They say that my handsome lieutenant likes to get tipsy. He must be a pretty spectacle in that state. We shall now find out!"

But Lucien never deviated from a fatuity worthy of his native land. During the entire evening he did not condescend to say three words in succession; that was the only spectacle he offered Madame d'Hocquincourt. She was amazed beyond all bounds and, in the end, entranced.

"What an astonishing creature, and at twenty-three!" she thought. "How different from all the others!"

At the very same moment the partner of this silent duet was thinking: "With these provincial nobles it is impossible to exaggerate. One must lay it on with a heavy hand."

The stupidity of the arguments he heard concerning the camp of Lunéville, which was going to result, it seemed,

in the fall of the King, did not offend him because of the
uniform he was wearing, but once or twice it wrung from
him a kind of ejaculatory prayer:

"Dear God! by what ill chance have I been thrown into
such dull company? And one which, if it were more intelligent,
would be only more malicious! What could be more stupid
and meanly bourgeois? What a ferocious passion for anything connected with money! And these are the progeny of
the conquerors of Charles the Bold!"

Such were his thoughts as he gravely drank glass after
glass of champagne which Madame d'Hocquincourt took
such keen delight in pouring out for him.

"Isn't there something I can do to ruffle that haughty manner?" she asked herself.

And Lucien's thoughts ran on:

"The servants of these people, after two years of war in
a regiment commanded by a conscientious, decent colonel,
would be a hundred times better men than their masters.
You will find in them a sincere devotion to something. The
most ridiculous thing about these aristocrats is that they are
always prating about *devotion,* yet it is the last thing they
are capable of."

Such egotistical, philosophical and political thoughts, quite
false perhaps, were Lucien's only resource at moments when
Madame de Chasteller made him miserable. What had turned
Lucien into a philosophical second-lieutenant, that is to say
sad and rather dull under the effect of the champagne, admirably chilled in accord with the fashion of the day, was
this fatal idea which began to dawn on him:

"After what I had the audacity to say to Madame de Chasteller, after that expression *my angel,* so crudely familiar (in
fact when I speak to her I have no sense, I should write down
what I want to say; what woman, no matter how indulgent,

would not take offense at being called *my angel,* especially
when she does not respond in the same way?) after that expression, so woefully imprudent, the very first word she says to
me now will decide my fate. She will dismiss me, I shall never
see her again. . . . I shall be forced to see Madame d'Hocquincourt. And how tired I'll get of her persistent attentions,
so unremitting and so immoderate, and I shall have to put up
with them every evening. If I approach Madame de Chasteller
now, my fate will be decided at once. And I should be unable to
reply. Besides, she may still be in the first transports of anger.
What if she says: 'I shall not be at home until the fifteenth of
the month'?"

The thought made Lucien shudder.

"Well, let us at least save our reputation. I must simply
redouble my fatuous attitude toward this petty nobility. They
can't hate me any more than they do already, and these
base souls will respect me in proportion to my insolence." *

At that moment one of the Rollers said to M. de Sanréal,
already fairly excited by the punch:

"Come along. I'm going over to that coxcomb and tell him
a thing or two about his King Louis-Philippe!"

But at that precise second the German clock which had
such power over Lucien's heart began to strike one o'clock
in the morning with all its chimes. In spite of her love of
late hours, Madame de Puylaurens rose to go, and all the
rest of the company followed her example. Thus, our hero
was not put to the necessity of demonstrating his courage
that night.

"If I offer Madame de Chasteller my arm she may pronounce that decisive word."

He stood motionless by the door and watched her as she

* A coxcomb speaking.

passed him, very pale and with downcast eyes, on the arm of her cousin M. de Blancet.

"And this," thought Lucien as he traversed the lonely, filthy streets of Nancy on his way to his lodgings, "is the foremost nation of the universe! My God! what must it be like to spend one's evenings in the little towns of Russia, Germany, or England! What meannesses! What coldly atrocious cruelties! In those countries the privileged class openly wields power, while here, I find it half-numbed and checkmated by being banished from the Budget. My father is right; one should live in Paris and see only people who know how to enjoy themselves. They are happy and for that reason less malevolent. Man's soul is a fetid bog, if one doesn't cross it quickly one is submerged."

One word from Madame de Chasteller would have transformed these philosophical thoughts into paroxysms of happiness. An unhappy man looks to philosophy to fortify his courage, but its first effect is to poison his mind by showing him that happiness is impossible.

Next morning, the regiment was very busy: every lancer's book had to be prepared for the inspection that was to be held before the departure for the Lunéville camp; their equipment had to be examined piece by piece.

"You'd think," said the old-timers, "that we were going to be reviewed by Napoleon!"

"It's more than it deserves, this war of chamber-pots and rotten apples we're expected to fight," said the young second-lieutenants. "It's sickening! But in case there's really a war we have to be on hand and know our *trade*."

After inspection in the barracks, the colonel allowed an hour for mess, then had the call to horse sounded and kept the regiment drilling for four hours. During all these divers occupations Lucien had a feeling of kindliness toward the soldiers; he was filled with tender pity for the weak, and after a few hours had once more become the passionate lover and nothing else. He had quite forgotten Madame d'Hocquincourt or, if she did find any place in his thoughts, it was only as a decoy that would save his honor, while boring him to death. The serious problem that he reverted to, whenever his thoughts were not forcibly focused upon his activities, was: "How will Madame de Chasteller receive me this evening?"

As soon as Lucien was alone, his uncertainty on this question turned to anxiety. As he left the ordinary, he looked at his watch before mounting his horse.

"It is five o'clock; I shall be back at seven-thirty, and at eight o'clock my fate will be decided. That expression, *my angel,* is probably in very bad taste at any time. A frivolous woman like Madame d'Hocquincourt might perhaps let it pass; some gay and gallant comment on her beauty would excuse it. But Madame de Chasteller! What possible excuse for the use of such a crude term had she ever given me, a woman so serious, so reasonable, so virtuous! Yes, *virtuous.* For, after all, I was not a witness of her intrigue with that lieutenant-colonel of Hussars, and people here are all such liars and slanderers! What trust can one put in anything they say? . . . Besides, for a long time now I haven't heard it mentioned . . . And finally, in plain words, I did not *see* it, and from now on I will believe only *what I see.* There were perhaps imbeciles there yesterday who, noticing the way I acted toward Madame d'Hocquincourt and her unbelievable assiduity in her attentions to me, will affirm that I am her lover . . . and some poor devil who happens to be in love with her will believe their gossip. . . . No, any sensible man believes only what he sees with his own eyes. What is there about Madame de Chasteller to mark her as a woman who cannot live without lovers? One might, on the contrary, accuse her of an excessive reserve, of prudishness. Poor thing! More than once yesterday she was even awkward out of sheer timidity. . . . She even blushes when she is alone with me, can't finish a sentence, forgetting apparently what she was going to say. . . . Compared to all the other women last evening, the poor woman is the Goddess of Chastity herself. Except for wit, there is no difference between the tone of her conversation and that of the Serpierre young ladies, whose virtue is proverbial. Half Madame de Chasteller's ideas are hidden from them, that is all, and those ideas can only be expressed in a somewhat philosophical language which, for that reason, seems less reserved. I can say many things to those young ladies the meaning of which only Madame de Chasteller grasps, and she is not shocked. In short, when it comes to a question of fact I should not readily believe the testimony of one of those people present yesterday evening. Against Madame de Chasteller, I have really only the testimony of the post-master, Bouchard. I made a mistake in not cultivating that man. What could have been simpler than to go to him for horses, to go to the stables myself to choose them? It was he who recommended my dealer in hay and my blacksmith, and, with them, I am in high favor. What a dolt I am!"

Lucien refused to admit to himself that the person of Bouchard was distasteful to him, because he was the only man who had openly spoken ill of Madame de Chasteller. The insinuations he had overheard one day at Madame de Serpierre's were all very vague. Madame de Chasteller's rather haughty air, which Nancy never thought of assigning to any cause other than the possession of an income of fifteen or twenty thousand francs which her husband had left her when he died, was really due to her irritation at all the rather too obvious compliments which she had to endure because of that fortune.

All the time these distressing thoughts were running through his mind, Lucien kept his horse at a fast trot. He heard the clock of the little village half way to Darney strike half past six.

"I must go back," he thought, "and in one hour and a half my fate will be decided."

Suddenly, instead of turning his horse's head toward home, he spurred it on to a gallop and did not stop galloping until he reached Darney, the little town where he had formerly gone in the hope of finding letters from Madame de Chasteller. He took out his watch. It was eight o'clock.

"Impossible to see Madame de Chasteller tonight," he said to himself, breathing more freely. He was like a man condemned to death who has obtained a reprieve.

The next evening, after the busiest day of his life during which he had changed his mind three or four times, Lucien was finally forced to present himself at Madame de Chasteller's. She received him with what seemed extreme coldness. This was due to her anger with herself and her embarrassment at seeing Lucien.

CHAPTER THIRTY-TWO

HAD HE PRESENTED himself the day before, Madame de Chasteller had made up her mind: she would have asked him, in the future, to come to see her only once a week. She was still dominated by her fright over those words Madame d'Hocquincourt had almost heard her say, the words she had almost spoken. Haunted by that dreadful evening at Madame d'Hocquincourt's, and by dint of repeating that it would be impossible much longer to hide from Lucien her feeling for him, it was not too difficult for

Madame de Chasteller to arrive at the decision not to see him so often. But hardly had this decision been reached when she felt the full force of its bitterness. Until Lucien's appearance in Nancy she had been a prey to boredom, but her boredom of that period would now have seemed a state of bliss compared to the misery of meeting, only at long intervals, this being who had become the sole object of her thoughts. The day before she had waited for him with impatience; she had thought she would find the courage to speak. But Lucien's failure to appear upset all her ideas. Her courage had been put to the severest test; a dozen times or more, during the two mortal hours of waiting, she had been on the point of abandoning her resolution. On the other hand the danger to her reputation was enormous.

"Never," she thought, "will my father, or any of my relatives, consent to my marrying M. Leuwen, a man of the opposite party, a *Blue,* and not of the nobility. It can't even be thought of; he himself does not dream of such a thing. Then, whatever am I doing? I can think of nothing but him. I have no mother to protect me, I am without a single friend to advise me, since my father so brutally cut me off from Madame de Constantin. Who in Nancy is there to whom I dare allow even a glimpse into my heart? It therefore behooves me to be adamant with myself. I must be all the more on my guard in this difficult position in which I find myself."

These arguments held their ground pretty well until ten o'clock struck, the hour after which, in Nancy, no one is supposed to call at a house which is not formally open that evening.

"That settles it!" said Madame de Chasteller, "he is at Madame d'Hocquincourt's. And," she sighed, "since he is not coming, and there is no chance of my seeing him tonight, what is the use of asking myself if I have the courage to speak to him about the frequency of his visits. It gives me a little respite. But maybe he won't come tomorrow, either! Perhaps without any effort on my part and quite naturally, he will stop coming every day of his own accord!"

When Lucien finally appeared the next day, she too had several times, since the day before, changed her mind about him. There were moments when she wanted to confide her perplexities to him as to her best friend, then to say: "Decide for me."

"If, as happens in Spain, I saw him at midnight through a lattice, he in the street and I in my room above, it wouldn't matter if I said those dangerous things. But, as it is, if suddenly he takes my hand and says, as he did yesterday, so simply and with such sincerity in his voice: 'My angel, you love me,' will I be able to count on myself?"

Once the usual polite greetings were over and they were seated opposite each other, both very pale, they looked at each other, and found nothing to say.

"Were you at Madame d'Hocquincourt's yesterday, sir?"

"No, Madam," replied Lucien, ashamed of his embarrassment and once more making the heroic resolution of bringing things to a head and having his fate decided once and for all. "I was on the road to Darney when I heard the hour strike at which I usually have the honor of presenting myself at your door. Instead of returning, I galloped on like a madman in order to make seeing you impossible. My courage failed me; I did not have the strength to expose myself to your customary severity. I seemed to hear my sentence on your lips."

He fell silent. Then, in a barely articulate voice which revealed all his timidity, he added:

"The last time I saw you standing beside the little green table, I confess it . . . I had the temerity of making use, in addressing you, of an expression which ever since has caused me untold remorse. I am afraid I shall be severely punished, for you are without indulgence toward me."

"Oh! since you are really repentant, sir, I forgive you the expression," said Madame de Chasteller, trying to assume a gay, careless air. "But I must speak to you about something which is of far greater consequence to me."

And her eyes, not able to keep up their pretense of gaiety, became profoundly serious.

Lucien trembled; for although he was annoyed with himself for his consternation, he was not vain enough to face with equanimity a life separated from Madame de Chasteller. What would become of him on the days he was not permitted to see her?

"Sir," continued Madame de Chasteller gravely, "I have no mother to provide me with wise counsels. A woman who lives alone, or practically alone, in a provincial city must be doubly careful of appearances. You come to see me often . . ."

"And so . . ." said Lucien, breathlessly.

Until that moment Madame de Chasteller's manner had been reasonable, decorous, cold, at least so it had seemed to Lucien. The tone of voice in which he pronounced the words: *and so . . .* might well have been beyond the powers of an accomplished Don Juan; with Lucien it was no trick of artifice but the impulse of his nature—it was natural. That simple exclamation changed everything. There was in it such wretchedness, such assurance of utter obedience, that Madame de Chasteller was, as it were, disarmed. She had gathered all her courage to resist someone strong and was confronted by extreme weakness. In an instant everything was changed. She no longer needed to fear her own lack of firmness, but rather to appear to be taking advantage of her victory. She was full of pity for the unhappiness she was causing Lucien.

In a dying voice, with lips pale and drawn in an effort to

appear inflexible, she explained to our hero her reasons for wishing to see him less frequently and for shorter periods at a time, for example every other day. People were beginning to show too great an interest in his visits. It was a question of not giving them an excuse for imagining things—entirely unjustified of course, and especially Mademoiselle Bérard who was a very dangerous witness.

Madame de Chasteller had scarcely the strength to complete these two or three sentences. The least word, the slightest objection from Lucien and her whole project would have crumbled. She felt the liveliest pity for his very evident unhappiness; she would never, she realized, have had the courage to persist. She was aware of nothing in the whole universe but him. Had Lucien been less in love and had he possessed more wit, he would have acted differently, but the fact was, and difficult to excuse in this day and age, that this twenty-three-year-old second-lieutenant was incapable of uttering one word of protest against this arrangement that would kill him. Imagine for yourself a coward who adores life and hears himself doomed to death.

Madame de Chasteller saw clearly what he was feeling; she herself was ready to burst into tears, she was overwhelmed with pity at the extreme distress she was causing.

"But," she suddenly said to herself, "if he sees a tear I shall be more deeply involved than ever. I must, at all costs, put an end to this visit so fraught with danger."

"After the wish I have expressed . . . sir . . . for some time already Mademoiselle Bérard, I fancy, has been counting the minutes you have spent with me . . . it would be prudent to cut your visit short."

Lucien rose; he could not speak, he could hardly find voice enough to murmur: "Madam, I shall be in despair. . . ."

He opened the door that led from the library onto a little inner stairway which he often used to avoid passing through the reception-room watchfully guarded by the terrible Mademoiselle Bérard.

Madame de Chasteller went to the door with him in order, by this courtesy, to mitigate a little the severity of the request she had just voiced. At the head of the little stairway Madame de Chasteller said to Lucien:

"Good-by, sir, until day after tomorrow."

Lucien turned. He was forced to rest one hand on the mahogany baluster to steady himself. Madame de Chasteller was touched and on a sudden impulse, as a sign of friendliness, after the English custom, held out her hand to him. Seeing Madame de Chasteller's hand drawing near his, Lucien seized it and slowly lifted it to his lips. As he did so his face came close to hers. He dropped her hand and took her in his arms, pressing his lips against her cheek. Madame de Chasteller did not find the strength to push him away, she remained motionless and unresisting in his arms. He pressed her to him in ecstasy, redoubling his kisses. Finally Madame de Chasteller gently disengaged herself, but her eyes, wet with tears, frankly betrayed the tenderest love. She succeeded, however, in saying:

"Good-by, sir . . ."

And as he gazed at her wildly, she quickly added:

"Good-by, *my friend*. Until tomorrow . . . but leave me now."

He left her and started down the stairs, but not without turning back to look at her again.

Lucien continued down the stairs in a state of unspeakable agitation. He was soon completely drunk with joy, which kept him from realizing that he was very young and very absurd.

Two weeks, three weeks passed. These were the happiest moments of Lucien's entire life, but he never again benefited by another such moment of weakness and surrender. And, as you know, he was incapable of bringing such a moment about himself, for the very reason that it meant too much to him.

He saw Madame de Chasteller every day. His visits often lasted two or three hours, to the scandalized disapproval of Mademoiselle Bérard. Whenever Madame de Chasteller felt that she could no longer keep the conversation within proper limits, she would propose a game of chess. Sometimes Lucien would timidly take her hand. One day he even tried to embrace her, and she burst into tears. She appealed to his pity and put him on his honor. As her appeal was in good faith, it was received in the same spirit. Madame de Chasteller made him promise not to talk to her openly of his love, but often, to make amends, she would put her hand on his epaulet and play with the silver fringe. When she was convinced that she need have no fear of any encroachments on his part, she displayed a gentle natural gaiety with him, which, for the poor woman, was ideal happiness.

They talked about everything with such utter sincerity that an indifferent onlooker might well have found this tone quite cavalier and always too ingenuous. It took the boon of this boundless frankness to compensate for the sacrifice they made in not speaking of their love. Often some indirect little word coming up in the course of the conversation would make them both blush; then a little silence would ensue, and it was when it became too painfully prolonged that Madame de Chasteller would have recourse to chess.

Most of all, Madame de Chasteller liked to have Lucien confide all the thoughts he had had about her at different times— in the first month of their acquaintance, at the present moment. . . . These confidences tended to stifle the whisperings of that great enemy of our happiness which is called prudence. Prudence said:

"This is an infinitely cunning and clever young man who is playing a part for your benefit."

Never had Lucien dared confide to her Bouchard's gossip about the lieutenant-colonel of Hussars. And dissimulation was so completely absent from their intercourse that twice this subject, mentioned by chance, came very near to starting another quarrel; for Madame de Chasteller saw in Lucien's eyes that he was concealing something.

"And that is a thing I will not forgive," she said to him with great firmness.

From Lucien, nevertheless, she hid the fact that almost every day her father made scenes on his account.

"What! my daughter, you spend two hours every day with a man of *that* party, and, what's more, a man whose birth makes it impossible for him to aspire to your hand."

Then followed touching words about an old father, almost an octogenarian, abandoned by his daughter, by his sole support.

The fact is that M. de Pontlevé lived in mortal fear of Lucien's father. Dr. Du Poirier had told him that M. Leuwen was a man of pleasure and wit, animated by a devilish propensity to what is the greatest of all enemies to the throne and the altar: irony. This banker might be disagreeable enough to divine the motive for M. de Pontlevé's passionate attachment to his daughter's ready money, and, what was worse, might say so.

CHAPTER THIRTY-THREE

WHILE MADAME DE CHASTELLER had forgotten the world and thought that the world had forgotten her, all Nancy was occupied with little else. Thanks to her father's complaints, she had become, for the good people of that city, the remedy that was *curing them of boredom.* For anyone who understands the profound boredom of a small provincial town, no more need be said.

Madame de Chasteller was about as artful as Lucien. He was unable to win the proof that she loved him completely; and she, the society of Nancy being less and less amusing for a woman passionately preoccupied with one sole idea, rarely appeared at Mesdames de Commercy's, de Marcilly's, de Serpierre's, de Puylaurens', etc., etc. Her absence was interpreted as contempt, and gave wings to slander.

In the Serpierre household, they had flattered themselves, I don't know why, that Lucien would marry Mademoiselle Théodelinde. For in the provinces, a mother never meets a rich or noble young man without looking upon him as a prospective husband for one of her daughters.

While all society was ringing with M. de Pontlevé's complaints about M. Leuwen's attentions to his daughter, addressed to anybody who happened along, Madame de Serpierre was infinitely shocked, even beyond the bounds of her naturally exacting virtue. Lucien was received in the house with all the acrimony of *marriage hopes betrayed,* which can appear under such a variety of amiable forms in a family composed of six young ladies by no means remarkable for their beauty.

Madame de Commercy, on the other hand, true to the manners of the court of Louis XVI, treated Lucien with the same unvarying courtesy. But that was not the case in Madame de Marcilly's drawing room. Since Lucien's indiscreet reply to the grand vicar, M. Rey, on the subject of the shoemaker's funeral, that worthy and prudent ecclesiastic had taken it upon himself to ruin our second-lieutenant's position in Nancy. In less than two weeks M. Rey succeeded in skillfully insinuating everywhere, and establishing as a matter of fact in Madame de Marcilly's drawing room, that the Minister of War had a decided fear of public opinion in Nancy, a city so close to the frontier, a city of considerable importance,

center of the Lorraine nobility, and perhaps, above all, a fear
of public opinion as it was manifested in the *salon* of Madame de Marcilly. This being the case, the Minister had sent
to Nancy a young man who was obviously of a different
stamp from his comrades, to observe the ways of this society
and probe into its secrets. "Is this," he asked, "merely a sign
of disapprobation or is there a question of taking action?
The proof of all this is that Leuwen listens, without batting
an eyelash, to things about the Duc d'Orleans (Louis-Philippe)
which would compromise anyone but a spy." Before he joined
the regiment he had been preceded by a reputation for republicanism which nothing justified, and which certainly never
seemed to bother him in front of the portrait of Henri V.

This discovery flattered the vanity of this salon where the
most exciting event hitherto had been the loss of nine or
ten francs at whist by Mr. So-and-So on a particularly unlucky
day. The Minister of War (perhaps, who knows, Louis-Philippe
himself?) trembled before their opinion!

So Lucien was a spy of the *Juste-milieu!* M. Rey was too
intelligent to credit any such nonsense, and as he might require a rather more plausible story for the salons of Madame
de Puylaurens and Madame d'Hocquincourt, he had written
to M——, Canon of ——, at Paris for further information on
Lucien. This letter had been sent to a vicar of the parish in
which Lucien's family lived, and M. Rey expected any day
now to receive a detailed report.

Thanks to M. Rey, Lucien found his credit waning in most
of the drawing rooms he frequented. It failed to worry him,
in fact he hardly gave it a thought, for the d'Hocquincourt
drawing room was an exception, and a brilliant exception. Ever
since the departure of M. d'Antin, Madame d'Hocquincourt
had managed things so well that her placid husband had
begun to show a special liking for Lucien. In his youth M.
d'Hocquincourt had had some slight knowledge of mathe-

matics and history. But far from diverting his thoughts from his melancholy ideas on the future, the study of history plunged him into even deeper gloom.

"Glance at the margins of Hume's *History of England.* You keep finding little marginal notes such as: *N. distinguishes himself, His deeds, His great qualities, His sentence, His execution.* And yet we imitate England; we began with the murder of a king, we have driven his brother out of the country, as they did the son of their king."

To avoid the fatal conclusion: *the guillotine awaits us,* he had decided to take up geometry again, useful, moreover, to a soldier. He bought books on the subject and two weeks later discovered that Lucien was just the man to guide his studies. He had indeed thought of M. Gauthier, but Gauthier was a republican; better a hundredfold to give up integral calculus altogether! But here right at hand was M. Leuwen, a charming man who, moreover, was in the habit of coming to the Hôtel d'Hocquincourt every evening. For this is how matters had been arranged:

At ten, or ten-thirty at the latest, the proprieties and the fear of Mademoiselle Bérard compelled Lucien to leave Madame de Chasteller's. Not being accustomed to retiring at such an early hour, he would then go to spend the rest of the evening at Madame d'Hocquincourt's. Whereupon two things had happened: M. d'Antin, a clever man who was not unduly attached to one woman more than another, seeing the part Madame d'Hocquincourt was preparing for him, received a letter from Paris that made a little trip imperative. The day of his departure, Madame d'Hocquincourt found him extremely amiable; but from that moment Lucien became infinitely less so. In vain the memory of Ernest Dévelroy's counsels urged him: "Since Madame de Chasteller is so virtuous, why not have a mistress in two volumes? Madame de Chasteller for the joys of the heart, and Madame d'Hocquincourt for somewhat less metaphysical moments?" But it seemed to Lucien that if he deceived Madame de Chasteller he would deserve to be deceived by her. The real reason for our hero's heroic virtue was that Madame de Chasteller was, alone in the whole world, a woman in his eyes. Madame d'Hocquincourt was merely a nuisance to him, and he mortally dreaded finding himself tête-à-tête with that young woman, reputed to be the prettiest in the province.

The sudden coldness of Lucien's conversation following the departure of d'Antin turned Madame d'Hocquincourt's caprice into a veritable passion; she would say the tenderest things to him in front of everybody. Lucien appeared to receive these advances with an icy gravity that nothing could move.

This madness on the part of Madame d'Hocquincourt more than anything else turned the so-called sensible men of Nancy against Lucien too. Even M. de Vassigny, a man of merit, and M. de Puylaurens who possessed quite a different order of intelligence from that of M. de Pontlevé, de Sanréal or Roller, and totally inaccessible to the insinuations so slyly disseminated by M. Rey, both began to find this little upstart very much in the way, for thanks to him, Madame d'Hocquincourt no longer paid the slightest attention to anything they said to her. These gentlemen found the greatest pleasure in chatting every evening for a quarter of an hour or so with this pretty woman—so young, so fresh and so smartly dressed! Neither M. d'Antin nor any of his predecessors had ever caused that cold and distant air with which Madame d'Hocquincourt now listened to their gallantries.

"He has appropriated this pretty woman who was our only refuge," said the grave M. de Puylaurens. "Impossible to organize a tolerable outing in the country with anyone else. And now when a drive is proposed, instead of seizing any and every excuse to start the horses trotting, Madame d'Hocquincourt categorically refuses."

Madame d'Hocquincourt knew very well that before ten-thirty Lucien was never free. Besides, whereas M. d'Antin could always be relied on to make things go, and merriment increased whenever and wherever he appeared, Lucien, through arrogance undoubtedly, spoke very little and made nothing go. He acted as a wet blanket.

Such began to be Lucien's position even in Madame d'Hocquincourt's drawing room, and all that remained to him was the friendship of M. de Lanfort, and the high esteem entertained for his wit by Madame de Puylaurens, a lady inexorable where wit was concerned.

When it was learned that Madame Malibran, on her way to Germany to pick up a few *thalers,* would be passing within two leagues of Nancy, M. de Sanréal had the brilliant idea of organizing a concert. It was a very grand affair and cost him a pretty penny. When the concert took place Madame de Chasteller failed to attend, but Madame d'Hocquincourt appeared surrounded by all her friends. Someone brought up the subject of a woman's favored suitor, her *ami-de-coeur* and this subject established the philosophic tone of the concert.

"To live without an *ami-de-coeur,*" pronounced M. de Sanréal, half drunk with glory and punch, "would be the greatest stupidity if it weren't an impossibility."

"One must hasten to make one's choice," said M. de Vassigny.

Madame d'Hocquincourt leaned forward toward Lucien who was sitting directly in front of her.

"And if the person one has chosen," she murmured, "has a heart of stone, what is a lady to do?"

Lucien turned his head laughingly, and was very much surprised to find tears in the eyes which were gazing into his. This miracle arrested his customary wit. He thought of the miracle instead of thinking of a reply. As for her, she said nothing but sat there with a conventional smile on her lips.

Leaving the concert, they returned on foot, and Madame d'Hocquincourt took Lucien's arm. She spoke hardly a word. When everyone was bidding her good-night in the courtyard of her hôtel, she squeezed Lucien's arm. Lucien left with the others.

She went up to her room and burst into tears. But she felt no animosity, and the next morning, paying a call on Madame de Serpierre, when the latter criticized Madame de Chasteller's conduct with the greatest acrimony, Madame d'Hocquincourt remained silent and uttered not a word against her rival. That evening, for something to say, Lucien complimented her on her costume:

"What a ravishing bouquet! What lovely colors! What freshness! It is the very image of the lady who wears it."

"You think so, really? Very well, it represents my heart, and I give it to you."

The look that accompanied the last word was without any of the gaiety which had, until then, reigned over the conversation. It lacked neither depth nor passion, and a sensible man would have had no doubt as to the significance of that gift. Lucien took the bouquet, said things more or less worthy of a Dorat, but his eyes remained gay and careless. He understood very well but did not want to understand.

He was desperately tempted but resisted the temptation. The following evening he felt like relating his adventure to Madame de Chasteller, as much as to say: "Repay me for what you have cost me." But he did not dare.

It was one of his mistakes: in love one must always dare, or expose oneself to strange reverses. Madame de Chasteller had already heard with distress of M. d'Antin's departure. The day after the concert, Madame de Chasteller learned from the all-too-frank pleasantries of her cousin Blancet that on the preceding evening Madame d'Hocquincourt had made a *spectacle of herself*. Her predilection for Lucien was turning into a *perfect frenzy,* said her cousin. That evening Lucien found Madame de Chasteller very gloomy. She treated him badly. This somber humor only increased with the days that followed, and between them would fall silences of fifteen or twenty minutes at a time. But these were no longer those delicious silences of the past which had forced Madame de Chasteller to take refuge in chess.

Could these be the same two people for whom a week ago all the minutes of two long hours were not enough to tell each other all they had to say?

CHAPTER THIRTY-FOUR

TWO DAYS LATER Madame de Chasteller was seized with a high fever. Believing her reputation ruined, she suffered unspeakable remorse. But all that was as nothing: she doubted Lucien's love.

Her womanly dignity was appalled by the strangeness of the feelings that took possession of her, and most of all by the vehemence of her emotions. This sentiment had grown all the stronger since she no longer feared for her virtue: in case of extreme danger a trip to Paris, where Lucien could not follow her, would keep her safe from all peril, although tearing her violently away from the only place on earth where she believed happiness was possible for her.

For several days the prospect of this remedy had reassured her, made her life more or less peaceful. A letter, dispatched by messenger and without the knowledge of M. de Pontlevé, to her closest friend, Madame de Constantin, asking her advice, had brought a favorable reply, approving the trip to Paris in case of emergency. Her conscience thus pacified, Madame de Chasteller had been happy.

Then, all at once, after M. de Blancet's account of what had taken place at Madame de Malibran's concert and all the coarse pleasantries of which he was prodigal (expressed, to be sure, in perfectly proper terms), she again became a prey to the most atrocious suffering, of which she was ashamed.

"Blancet has no tact," she said to herself. "He is one of those who suffer from the superiority of M. Leuwen. Perhaps he is exaggerating. Would M. Leuwen who is so sincere with me—one day even confessing that he had ceased to love me for a while—would he deceive me today? . . ."

"Nothing could be simpler to explain," replied the party on the side of prudence. "It is agreeable, and in perfect taste, for a young man to have two mistresses at the same time, especially if one of them is dismal, severe, always taking refuge behind the qualms of her tiresome virtue, while the other is gay, amiable, pretty, and does not have the reputation of driving her lovers to despair by her severity. M. Leuwen would have the right to say to me: 'Either stop being so loftily virtuous, and making scenes merely because I try to take your hand' . . . (it's true, I did treat him badly for such a trivial offense)" she paused a moment and sighed . . . " 'stop being so excessively virtuous or else allow me to take advantage of a momentary admiration Madame d'Hocquincourt entertains for my humble merits.' "

"Still, no matter how indelicate such reasoning may be," love's advocate retorted angrily, "he should have made some such declaration to me. That is what any honest man would have done. But perhaps M. de Blancet exaggerates . . . I must find out."

She ordered her carriage and was driven in haste to Madame de Serpierre's and then to Madame de Marcilly's. Everything was confirmed. Madame de Serpierre went even further than M. de Blancet.

By the time she got home again Madame de Chasteller was scarcely thinking of Lucien at all. Despair fired her imagination and it was entirely occupied in picturing the charms and seductive amiability of Madame d'Hocquincourt. She compared these with her own habitual reserve, so sad and so severe. This comparison tormented her all night. She experienced all those sensations which are the tortures of the blackest jealousy.

Everything about this passion, of which she found herself a victim, amazed and horrified her feminine modesty. For General de Chasteller, she had felt nothing but friendship and gratitude for his irreproachable conduct. She was even without the knowledge acquired from books. All novels had been represented to her at the Sacred Heart as obscene. Nor, since her marriage, had she read any novels, for a lady admitted to the conversation of royal princesses should know nothing of such literature. Besides, novels seemed crude to her.

"But am I even able to say that I am true to what a woman owes herself?" she questioned at dawn after that cruel night. "If M. Leuwen were sitting there opposite me now, looking at me as he does when he is afraid to tell me all he is thinking, made miserable by the mad restraints prescribed by virtue, that is, by my own selfish interests, would I be able to bear his silent reproaches? No, I would succumb . . . I am without virtue, and I cause the unhappiness of the one I love . . ."

Such a complexity of anxieties was too much for Madame de Chasteller's health, and a high fever broke out anew.

Excited by the fever, which from the first day made her

delirious, she kept seeing Madame d'Hocquincourt as she was at the Malibran concert—gay, amiable, happy, adorned with charming flowers (she had been told about the famous bouquet), embellished by a thousand seductive charms, and with Lucien at her feet. Then always the same argument would return:

"Wretched woman that I am, what have I ever accorded to M. Leuwen that he should feel himself bound to me? What right have I to keep him from responding to the advances of a charming woman, prettier than I, and above all, certainly more agreeable, and agreeable in just the way to please a young man accustomed to Parisian society: a gaiety that is ever fresh and never malicious?"

As she followed this sad reasoning she could not help asking for a little oval mirror. She looked at herself. With each new experience of this kind, she found herself less attractive. Finally she came to the conclusion that she was really ugly, and she loved Lucien all the more for his good taste in preferring Madame d'Hocquincourt.

The second day the fever grew worse; and even gloomier the phantoms that tortured her heart. The mere sight of Mademoiselle Bérard threw her into convulsions. She refused to see M. de Blancet. She loathed him. She kept remembering him as he had told her about the fatal concert. M. de Pontlevé paid her two formal calls every day. Dr. Du Poirier attended her with the same diligence and concentration he displayed in everything he undertook. He visited the Hôtel de Pontlevé two or three times a day. In the doctor's treatment the greatest blow to Madame de Chasteller was his strict order that she should not leave her bed; henceforth she could no longer hope to see Lucien. She was afraid even to pronounce his name, to ask her maid if he came to inquire for her. Due to the incessant and impatient attention with which she kept trying to distinguish the sound of his tilbury wheels she knew so well, her fever rose.

Lucien took the liberty of calling every morning. The third day he left the Hôtel de Pontlevé very much disturbed by Dr. Du Poirier's ambiguous replies. Climbing into his tilbury he drove off at a reckless pace, and on the square known as the promenade, which was planted with linden trees clipped to resemble parasols, he all but grazed M. de Sanréal. The latter had just finished breakfast, and while waiting for dinner was strolling idly through the streets of Nancy arm in arm with Comte Ludwig Roller.

This pair presented a ludicrous contrast. Although very young, Sanréal was extremely stout and not five feet tall, with a ruddy complexion and immense side whiskers that were startlingly blond. Ludwig Roller, tall, pale-faced and dismal, looked like a mendicant monk out of favor with his Superior. Topping a body at least six feet tall, his little head was ringed with a fringe of black hair, reminiscent of a monk's tonsure; fleshless and expressionless features set off his dull and insignificant eyes. A black suit, threadbare and too tight for him, completed the contrast between this ex-lieutenant of cuirassiers whose pay was his fortune, and the fortunate Sanréal whose coat had not buttoned across his middle for many long years, but who enjoyed an income of, at least, forty thousand francs. With the help of this fortune, he was credited with great valor, for he wore iron spurs three inches long, could not say two words without cursing, and never spoke for any length of time without embarking on some hair-raising account of duels. So it naturally followed, although he had never fought a duel himself, that he was brave, apparently because of the fear he inspired. Besides he had the gift of instigating the Rollers against anyone who displeased him.

Ever since the July Days, followed by their resignation, the three Roller brothers were far more bored than before. They owned one horse between them, and their apathy never gave way to the least sign of enjoyment except when there was a duel to fight, which they accomplished admirably and because of this talent were looked upon with considerable respect.

As it was only noon when Lucien's tilbury made the pavement tremble under the feet of the enormous Sanréal, the latter had not yet visited any café and was not yet entirely tipsy. Encouraged by Ludwig Roller, Sanréal was amusing himself chucking the chins of all the peasant girls who happened to pass. With his riding whip he kept slashing at the awnings of the cafés and at the chairs under them, as well as at the lower branches of the linden trees on the square.

Lucien's tilbury dashing by interrupted these pleasant pursuits.

"Do you think he intended that as a provocation?" Sanréal cried, turning to Roller with all the blustering fury of the bully.

"Listen," said Comte Ludwig, turning pale, "that young coxcomb is always polite, and I don't think he intended any offense with his tilbury. But I detest him even more because he's so damned polite. He has just left the Hôtel de Pontlevé. He means to carry off the prettiest woman in Nancy and our richest heiress, at least in the class from which you and I can choose a wife. . . . And that," added Roller firmly, "is something I'll not stand for."

"You are right," replied Sanréal, enchanted.

"In such matters, my friend," replied Roller acidly, "you ought to know that I never speak lightly."

"Are you putting on airs with *me?*" replied Sanréal in his best swashbuckling manner. "We understand each other. The essential thing is that he should not escape us. He's a crafty beggar and he's come off on top in the two duels he fought in his regiment."

"Sword duels! That's a joke! The wound he gave Captain Bobé was cured by the application of two leeches. But with me, egad! it will be a regular duel with pistols at ten paces, and if he doesn't kill me, I promise you he'll need more than two leeches."

"Let's go to my house. We shouldn't talk about these things with the spies of the *Juste-milieu* all around the promenade. I have just received a little cask of *kirschwasser* from Freiburg-im-Breisgau. Send word to your brothers and Lanfort."

"Why so many people? A half sheet of paper is all I need." And Comte Ludwig strode briskly toward a café.

"If you're going to play the fire-eater with me, I'm leaving you flat. . . . The important thing is to prevent this cursed Parisian from putting us in the wrong by one of his tricks and making a laughingstock of us. What can prevent his spreading the report in his regiment that we, the young nobility of Lorraine, have formed a protective society to prevent anyone from running off with young widows with sizable dowries?"

The three Rollers, along with Murcé and Goëllo, whom the café waiter had found playing pool not ten steps away, were soon assembled in M. de Sanréal's fine mansion, enchanted to find something to talk about, and all of them talking at once. The council was held around a massive mahogany table. Aping the English fashion, it was without a tablecloth, but over its mirroring mahogany surface circulated magnificent crystal decanters from the neighboring factories of Baccarat. A *kirschwasser* limpid as spring water, an eau-de-vie of a rich madeira yellow, gleamed in the bottles. Soon it became evident that all three Roller brothers wanted to fight Lucien. M. de Goëllo, a fop thirty-six years old, spare and wrinkled, who, during his lifetime, had aspired to everything, even to the hand of Madame de Chasteller, pleaded his cause with all due weight and circumspection, and insisted upon being the first to fight Lucien because he felt himself more injured than anyone else.

"Before he ever came here, wasn't I lending the lady Baudry's English novels?"

"Baudry be damned!" cried Lanfort who had just come in. "This fine fellow has offended all of us, and no one more than my poor friend d'Antin who has had to go away to get over it."

"To get used to his horns, you mean," interrupted Sanréal, laughing boisterously.

"D'Antin is my best friend," replied Lanfort, shocked at Sanréal's vulgarity. "If he were here he would fight every one of you rather than give up his right to have first chance at this amiable lady-killer. And for all these reasons, I too wish to fight."

For the last twenty minutes Sanréal's valor had been in a sorry plight. He saw plainly that everyone wanted to fight and he was the only one who had not put in his claim. After that of the gentle, amiable, preëminently elegant M. de Lanfort, there was no escape.

"In any case, gentlemen," he said finally, in a shrill and unnatural voice, "I am certainly second on the list; after all Roller and I were the ones who, under the lindens of the promenade, first conceived the plan."

"He is right," said M. de Goëllo. "Let's draw lots to see which of us is to rid the town of this public pest." (And he preened himself, very proud of this neat phrase.)

"By all means," said M. de Lanfort. "But, gentlemen, we cannot have more than one duel. If M. Leuwen is forced to meet four or five of us, I warn you that the *Aurore* will seize upon the story and you will all find yourselves written up in the Paris newspapers."

"And if he should kill one of our friends?" thundered Sanréal. "Are we to leave his death unavenged?"

The discussion lasted until dinner, which was both abundant and excellent. They all pledged their word of honor that they would not speak of the affair to a soul, and before eight hours had elapsed Dr. Du Poirier knew all about it.

Now there was a special order from Prague that quarrels were to be avoided between the nobility and the regiments of the camp of Lunéville and of the neighboring cities. That evening, with all the graciousness of an angry bulldog, Du Poirier approached Sanréal. His little eyes glittered like those of an infuriated cat.

"You will invite me to breakfast tomorrow morning at ten o'clock. You will also invite MM. Roller, de Lanfort, de Goëllo, and anyone else who is included in the plan. You will all listen to what I have to say."

Sanréal was dying to take offense, but he was afraid of one of Du Poirier's stinging remarks that would be repeated throughout the length and breadth of Nancy. He agreed with a nod of his head which was almost as gracious as Du Poirier's own manner.

The next day when his guests discovered with whom they had to deal, they made wry faces. The doctor arrived in a great hurry.

"Gentlemen," he said at once, without greeting anyone, "the Church and the Nobility have a great many enemies. Among others the newspapers which keep France informed, and make everything we do appear odious. If this were simply a question of chivalric valor, I should be satisfied merely to admire, and should take good care not to open my mouth, a poor plebeian like me, son of a small merchant who has the honor of addressing representatives of all that is noblest in Lorraine. But, gentlemen, I can see that you are all a trifle angry. Anger alone, no doubt, has kept you from stopping to reflect. That is my domain. You do not want a little second-lieutenant to carry off Madame de Chasteller? Very well! But what power on earth can prevent Madame de Chasteller from leaving Nancy and going to Paris to live? There, surrounded by friends who will give her the necessary courage, she will write the most touching imaginable letters to M. de Pontlevé: 'I can only be happy with M. Leuwen,' she will say, and she will say it well because that is what she feels. Will M. de Pontlevé refuse? It is doubtful, since his daughter is really serious, and he will not wish to break with someone who has 400,000 francs in the public funds. And Madame de Chasteller, her courage fortified by the advice of her Paris friends, among whom may be counted ladies of the highest distinction, can very well overlook the consent of a father in the provinces.

"Are you certain of killing Leuwen on the spot? In that case I have nothing more to say; Madame de Chasteller will not marry him. But, believe me, she will not, for that reason, marry one of you. According to my observation, she is a woman of a serious, tender, and obstinate disposition. One hour after the death of M. Leuwen, she has her horses harnessed to her carriage, takes fresh ones at the next post, and God only knows where she will stop! Brussels, Vienna, perhaps, since her father has invincible objections to Paris. No matter what happens, you may be sure of one thing: if Leuwen dies you will lose her forever. If he is wounded, the whole department will know the cause of the duel, and with her modesty she will think herself dishonored and, the day Leuwen is out of danger, will fly to Paris where Leuwen will join her a month later. In one word, it is only Madame de Chasteller's timidity keeps her here in Nancy; give her the slightest excuse and she will leave. In killing Leuwen you satisfy, I admit, an access of righteous anger, and between the seven of you, no doubt, you will succeed in killing him, but the lovely eyes and the beautiful dowry of Madame de Chasteller will be lost to you forever."

At this point everyone began to mutter protests and these only redoubled Du Poirier's impudence.

"If two or three of you," he went on, raising his voice, "fight Leuwen in succession, you will be looked upon as assassins, and the whole regiment will be up in arms against you."

"That is just what we want," cried Ludwig Roller with all the fury of his long pent-up rage.

"He's right!" cried his brothers. "We'll attend to those *Blues.*"

"And that is exactly what I forbid you to do, gentlemen— in the name of the King's commissioner for Alsace, Franche-Comté, and Lorraine."

All sprang to their feet at once. They rebelled against the insolence of this little bourgeois who dared to take such a tone with the flower of Lorraine's aristocracy. Such moments as these, indeed, were the delight of Du Poirier's vanity. His fiery temper rejoiced in battles of this kind. Not unmindful of their marks of contempt, on occasion he felt a need of humbling the overweening pride of these aristocrats.

After a torrent of wild words dictated by childish vanity, called pride of birth, the tide of battle turned in the favor of Du Poirier, the strategist.

"Do you wish to disobey, not me who am but an earthworm, but our legitimate King, Charles X?" he asked, after allowing each of them the pleasure of talking of his ancestors, his valor, and the place he had occupied in the Army before the fatal days of 1830. . . . "The King does not wish to quarrel with his regiments. Nothing more impolitic than a quarrel between his corps of nobles and a regiment."

Du Poirier repeated this truism so often and in such a

variety of terms that it ended at last by penetrating their heads, unaccustomed to the comprehension of anything new. Thanks to a flow of eloquence which Du Poirier calculated lasted from three quarters to one full hour, pride capitulated at last.

Hoping to lose less time, Du Poirier, whose ferocious vanity had begun to be tempered by boredom, undertook to say something flattering to each of them. He made the conquest of Sanréal, who had furnished Roller with arguments, by asking him for some of his spiced wine. Sanréal had invented a new way of concocting this adorable beverage, and hastened to the pantry to mix it himself.

When everyone had accepted the dictatorship of Du Poirier, he said:

"You really want to get rid of Leuwen, gentlemen, and at the same time not lose Madame de Chasteller?"

"Naturally!" they replied impatiently.

"Very well, then, I know one sure means. . . . You can doubtlessly guess what it is yourselves, if you stop to think."

And his malicious little eyes gleamed with satisfaction at their expectant air.

"Tomorrow, at the same hour, I shall tell you what that means is; nothing could be simpler. But it has one drawback, it demands the utmost secrecy for an entire month. You must allow me to divulge it only to two delegates, whom you, gentlemen, shall designate."

With these words he left abruptly, and hardly had he disappeared before Ludwig Roller began heaping him with terrible insults. Everyone followed his example with the exception of M. de Lanfort who said:

"His appearance is deplorable, he is ugly, dirty, his hat must be at least eighteen months old, he is familiar to the point of insolence. Most of his faults are due to his origin: his father, he admits, was a hemp merchant. But the greatest kings have made use of baseborn counselors. Du Poirier is far cleverer than I am, for the devil take me if I can guess his infallible means. And you, Ludwig, who have so much to say, can you?"

Everyone laughed except Ludwig, and Sanréal, enchanted by the turn things were taking, invited them to breakfast again the next day. But nevertheless before separating, stung though they were by Du Poirier's attitude, they named two delegates and naturally their choice fell on the two persons who would have objected the loudest had they not been chosen—M. de Sanréal and M. Ludwig Roller.

On leaving these fiery gentlemen, Du Poirier hastened to find, at the end of a little street, an obscure priest whom the prefect believed to be a spy in society and who as such drew a goodly share of the *secret funds*.

"You will go to M. Fléron, my dear Olive, and inform him that we have received a despatch from Prague, over which we have been deliberating for five hours at a meeting at M. de Sanréal's. But this despatch is of such importance that tomorrow at ten-thirty, we are to meet again in the same place."

Abbé Olive had obtained permission from Monsignor the Bishop to wear an extremely shabby blue coat and iron-gray stockings. It was in this costume that he went to betray Du Poirier and reveal his message to the Grand Vicar, M. Rey. After that he slipped off to the prefect who at the great news was unable to sleep all night.

Early the next morning he sent word to Olive that he would pay fifty *écus* for an exact copy of the despatch from Prague; and he had the audacity to write directly to the Minister of the Interior at the risk of displeasing his superior, M. Dumoral, a liberal renegade and a man who was in a perpetual state of anxiety. M. Fléron wrote to the latter as well, but the letter was mailed an hour too late, thus giving the important information sent to the Minister of the Interior by the humble prefect a whole hour's start.

CHAPTER THIRTY-FIVE

"BLOCKHEADS!" cried Du Poirier to himself when he learned the choice of the two delegates. "They don't even know how to select delegates. The devil if I tell them my plan."

At the meeting next day, Du Poirier, more serious and arrogant than ever, took Roller and Sanréal by the arm, led them into the latter's study, and locked the door.

Du Poirier was particularly punctilious in the observation of formalities, knowing that that was about all Sanréal would understand of the entire affair.

When they were all seated in armchairs, Du Poirier after a little silence began:

"Gentlemen, we are gathered here today in the service of His Majesty, Charles X, our legitimate King. Will you swear absolute secrecy even on the little I am permitted to reveal to you today?"

"My word of honor!" said Sanréal, overcome by respect and curiosity.

"Oh, f——!" exclaimed Roller impatiently.

"Gentlemen, your servants are being bribed by the republicans—that menial tribe can slip in everywhere; and unless we maintain absolute secrecy, even in regard to our closest friends, the good cause will not succeed and we shall find ourselves vilified in the *Aurore*."

For the sake of the reader I shall drastically curtail the discourse Dr. Du Poirier thought fit to address to these two gentlemen, the rich one and the brave one.

"The secret I had hoped to submit to you," he said finally, "is no longer mine. For the moment I am charged only to ask you to restrain your valor . . ." and here the doctor turned pointedly to Sanréal. "This will, I know, cost you a great deal."

"Certainly," said Sanréal.

"But, gentlemen, when one is a member of a great party, one must be ready to make sacrifices to the general will, even if it is wrong. Otherwise one is nothing, succeeds in accomplishing nothing. One deserves to be called a lost sheep. You must promise me that none of you will challenge M. Leuwen for the next two weeks."

"Must . . . Must . . ." Ludwig Roller repeated the word bitterly.

"By that time, M. Leuwen will either have left Nancy or he will no longer be paying calls on Madame de Chasteller—results which, as I have shown you, could not be obtained by a duel."

This had to be repeated in a variety of forms for an hour. The two deputies contended that it was not only their right but their duty to insist upon knowing the secret.

"A pretty figure we'll cut with the gentlemen waiting in the drawing room when they learn that we have been shut up here for a whole hour without learning a thing!"

"Then let them suppose that you do know," said the doctor coolly.

It took another hour, at least, to get this *mezzo termine* accepted by the vanity of the two gentlemen.

Dr. Du Poirier got through this trial of patience admirably and with great satisfaction to his pride. He liked, above all things, to talk, and to have to convince hostile listeners. A man of a repulsive exterior, he was endowed with a firm, lively and enterprising mind. Since he had got mixed up in political intrigue, the art of healing, in which he had acquired one of the foremost places, began to bore him. The service of Charles X, which he called *politics,* fed his desire for action, for work, for recognition. Flatterers assured him: "If Prussian or Russian battalions bring Charles X back, you are bound to be a deputy, a minister, etc. You will be our new Villèle."

"All in good time," Du Poirier would reply.

Meanwhile he was enjoying all the gratification of satisfied ambition. And it had come about in this way: M. de Puylaurens and M. de Pontlevé had received authority, from the proper source, to direct the Royalists' ventures in the province of which Nancy was the chief city. By rights, Du Poirier should have been simply the humble secretary of this commission, or rather of this occult power, which had only one rational thing about it; it was not divided against itself. Authority had been granted to M. de Puylaurens and in his absence, to M. de Pontlevé; but it was Du Poirier as a matter of fact who did everything. He gave the meagerest reports of his activities to the two titular heads, who did not object too much. For Du Poirier craftily saw to it that they should always glimpse the guillotine, or, at least, the Chateau de Ham, at the end of their plots, and these gentlemen, who were quite devoid of zeal, fanaticism, or devotion, were entirely happy to let this coarse and fearless bourgeois compromise himself—reserving for themselves the right to quarrel with him and put him in his place later on should they have any sort of success or in the event of a third Restoration.

Du Poirier had not the least feeling of animosity toward Lucien. With his passion for accomplishing whatever he set out to do, and now charged with the mission of getting rid of Lucien, he was determined to succeed.

Neither at the first meeting at Sanréal's when he asked for two delegates, nor at the second when he overcame their unsatisfied curiosity, had he as yet any very clear plan. It came to him by successive stages as he gradually realized that to allow the duel, which he had forbidden in the name of the King, to take place would be a marked defeat, a *fiasco,* not only for his reputation but for his influence in Lorraine among the younger members of the party.

He began by confiding to Mesdames de Serpierre, de Puylaurens, and de Marcilly, under the seal of secrecy, that Madame de Chasteller was much more seriously ill than had been supposed, and that her illness would certainly be a prolonged one. He persuaded Madame de Chasteller to submit to a blistering of her legs, thus preventing her from walking for a month. A few days later he arrived looking very grave, becoming even gloomier as he took her pulse, and he advised her to have the religious rites performed. All Nancy echoed with this news; and one can well imagine the effect on Lucien. Was Madame de Chasteller at death's door?

"And is death nothing more than this?" Madame de Chasteller said to herself, never dreaming that she was suffering from nothing more serious than a benign fever. "Death would be absolutely nothing if only M. Leuwen were with me. He would give me courage if mine should fail me. Indeed, life without him would have had little charm for me. I am forced to vegetate in this provincial town where, before he came, my life was so dismal. . . . But he is not an aristocrat and he is a soldier of the *Juste-milieu* or, much worse, of the Republic. . . ."

Madame de Chasteller now actually began to long for death. She was on the point of hating Madame d'Hocquincourt, and when she discovered this budding hatred in her heart, she despised herself. Since for two endless weeks she had not seen Lucien, her love for him gave her nothing but wretchedness.

In his despair, Lucien had gone to Darney to post three

letters, extremely discreet ones luckily, for they were intercepted by Mademoiselle Bérard, who was now in perfect accord with Dr. Du Poirier.

At this time, Lucien practically never left the doctor. It was a foolish move. He was far from being sufficiently wise in the ways of hypocrisy to permit himself the intimacy of such an unprincipled intriguer. Without knowing it, he had mortally offended Du Poirier. Piqued by Lucien's naïve contempt for rogues, renegades and hypocrites, the doctor began to hate him. Whenever they discussed the possibility of the return of the Bourbons he was amazed at the warmth and sound judgment of Lucien's arguments.

"But if that is the case," he cried one day at the end of his patience, "then I am nothing but an imbecile, I suppose?"

To himself he continued:

"We'll see, young fool, what is going to happen to your most precious interest! Go on reasoning about the future, repeat all the arguments you find ready made in your Carrel, *I* am the master of your present, as you will soon find out. Yes, old and wrinkled and shabby and uncouth as I am in your eyes, *I* am going to inflict the cruelest suffering on you, who are so handsome, young, rich and endowed by nature with noble manners, and in every way so different from me, Doctor Du Poirier. I spent the first thirty years of my life freezing on a fifth floor with a skeleton. You only took the trouble of getting born, and you secretly believe that when your *reasonable government* has been established you can punish strong men like me simply with contempt! That will be stupid of your party. Meanwhile it is stupid of you not to guess that I am going to hurt you—and hurt you badly. Suffer, little boy, suffer!"

And so the doctor began talking to Lucien about Madame de Chasteller's illness in the most alarming terms. If perchance he caught but the ghost of a smile on Lucien's lips he hastened to say:

"You see that church? The Pontlevé family vault is in there," adding with a sigh, "I'm very much afraid that it will soon have to be opened once more."

He had been waiting for several days for Lucien, who like all lovers was mad, to attempt to see Madame de Chasteller secretly.

Ever since his conference with the young men of the Party at Sanréal's, Du Poirier, who despised Mademoiselle Bérard's stupid aimless malice, had become reconciled to her. It was to her, rather than to M. de Pontlevé or M. de Blancet, or any other relative, that he confided Madame de Chasteller's supposed critical condition.

One great obstacle lay in the way of the project which was gradually taking shape in his mind: that was the constant presence of Madame de Chasteller's maid, Mademoiselle Beaulieu, who adored her mistress.

The doctor won her over, however, by showing how much he relied on her. He got Mademoiselle Bérard to consent to his often consulting with Mademoiselle Beaulieu instead of with her, as to what should be done for his patient until his next visit.

This good woman, like the none too good Mademoiselle Bérard, believed that Madame de Chasteller was dangerously ill.

The doctor confided to the maid that he thought some sentimental sorrow was aggravating her mistress's malady. He insinuated that it would seem to him only *natural* if M. Leuwen tried to see Madame de Chasteller.

"Alas, Doctor, for the last two weeks M. Leuwen has been pestering me to let him see Madame de Chasteller for five minutes. But what would people say? I refused absolutely."

The doctor replied with a quantity of phrases far beyond the intelligence of the maid to be able to repeat, but which in fact indirectly but clearly urged the good girl to permit the desired interview.

At last one evening it so happened that M. de Pontlevé, on the doctor's order, went to play a game of whist at Madame de Marcilly's, a game that was interrupted two or three times by his fits of weeping. And precisely the same day M. de Blancet, since it happened to be the season when woodcocks migrate, could not resist joining a hunting party. That very evening Lucien saw in Mademoiselle Beaulieu's window the signal which revived all his hopes and restored his interest in life. Lucien flew home, returned in civilian clothes, and at last, his presence being announced with infinite precaution by the faithful maid, who never went far from her mistress's sick-bed, he was able to spend ten minutes with Madame de Chasteller.

CHAPTER THIRTY-SIX

THE NEXT DAY when he arrived the doctor found Madame de Chasteller without fever and feeling so well that he was alarmed lest all the pains he had taken in the last three weeks should prove fruitless. In the presence of Mademoiselle Beaulieu he affected a very worried air and left like a man in a great hurry, returning some time later at an unprecedented hour.

"Beaulieu," he said, "your mistress is falling into a decline."

"Oh, my God, Doctor!"

Here the doctor expatiated upon the nature of a decline.

"What your mistress needs is mother's milk. If anything

can save her life, it is the milk of a fresh young peasant girl. I have scoured all Nancy, I find only workmen's wives whose milk would do Madame de Chasteller more harm than good. What we need is a young peasant girl. . . ."

While he was talking, the doctor noticed that Beaulieu kept looking at the clock.

"My village, Chefmont, is only five leagues from here. I'd get there at night, but that doesn't matter. . . ."

"Splendid, splendid! my good, my excellent Beaulieu! But, if you find a young nurse, be sure not to let her make the trip without a break. Do not return until day after tomorrow morning. The overheated milk would be a poison to your poor mistress."

"Do you think, Doctor, that it would hurt Madame to see M. Leuwen again? She has practically ordered me to let him in if he comes this evening. She is so fond of him! . . ."

The doctor could hardly believe his luck.

"Nothing could be more *natural,* Beaulieu." (He always insisted on the word, *natural.*) "But who will take your place?"

"Anne-Marie, a good girl and a pious girl."

"Very well, leave your instructions with Anne-Marie. Where does M. Leuwen wait until you announce him?"

"In the balcony of Madame's ante-chamber where Joseph used to sleep."

"In your poor mistress's present condition, she should not have too much excitement at one time. Therefore I advise you to allow no one else to see her, absolutely no one—not even M. de Blancet."

This, and many other details, were agreed upon between the doctor and Mademoiselle Beaulieu. This admirable girl left Nancy at five o'clock, after installing Anne-Marie in her place.

Now for a long time Anne-Marie, whom Madame de Chas-

teller had more than once been on the point of discharging
and had only retained out of pure kindness, had been entirely
devoted to Mademoiselle Bérard, even spying on Beaulieu
for her.

This is what occurred: at eight-thirty, while Mademoiselle
Bérard was engaged in talking to the porter, Anne-Marie had
signaled Lucien to cross the courtyard, and two minutes later
he was installed in the balcony of painted wood that occupied
a half of Madame de Chasteller's ante-chamber. From there
Lucien could see very well what was going on in the room
and hear almost everything that was said in the entire apartment.

All at once he heard what sounded like the wail of a new-
born infant. Then he saw the doctor come into the ante-
chamber out of breath and carrying a baby wrapped in a
cloth that seemed to be stained with blood.

"Your poor mistress," the doctor said quickly to Anne-Marie,
"is out of danger at last! The delivery was without complica-
tions. Is M. de Pontlevé out of the house?"

"Yes, Doctor."

"And that confounded Beaulieu is not here either?"

"She is on her way to her own village."

"I fixed up a pretext for her to go there for a wet nurse. The
one I engaged in the suburbs refuses to take a clandestine
baby."

"And M. de Blancet?"

"What is most singular is that your mistress refuses to see
him."

"And no wonder!" said Anne-Marie, "after a present like
that!"

"And, after all, the baby may not be his."

"Faith, these great ladies don't go to church very often, but
they make up for it by having as many lovers as they please."

"I think I heard Madame de Chasteller groaning," said the doctor, "I must go back to her. I'll send Mademoiselle Bérard to you."

Mademoiselle Bérard arrived. She detested Lucien, and in a conversation of a quarter of an hour said exactly the same things the doctor had said but managed to make them much more malicious. Mademoiselle Bérard was of the opinion that this little bratling, as she called it, belonged to M. de Blancet or to the Lieutenant-Colonel of Hussars.

"Or to M. de Goëllo," suggested Anne-Marie as naturally as possible.

"No, not M. de Goëllo," retorted Mademoiselle Bérard, "Madame can no longer endure him. He was responsible for the abortion which almost caused an open break with that poor Monsieur de Chasteller."

It can well be imagined in what a state Lucien found himself by this time. He was on the point of leaving his hiding place and fleeing despite the presence of Mademoiselle Bérard.

"No," he said to himself, "even if she has made a fool of me and treated me like the poor innocent I am, it would still be contemptible to compromise her."

At that moment, the doctor, fearing some really too improbable bit of malevolence from Mademoiselle Bérard, came to the door of the ante-chamber.

"Mademoiselle Bérard! Mademoiselle Bérard!" he cried with an air of alarm. "A hemorrhage. . . . Quick, quick! that bucket of ice I brought under my cloak."

As soon as Anne-Marie was alone, Lucien came out of his hiding place and handed her his purse. As he did so he could not help seeing the infant she was so ostentatiously holding and who, instead of being a few minutes old, was at least a month or two. But that was what Lucien failed to notice. With every sign of calm indifference he remarked:

"I am not feeling very well. I shall not see Madame de Chasteller until tomorrow. Will you kindly come and engage the porter in conversation while I am leaving?"

Anne-Marie looked at him in wide-eyed astonishment.

"Is he in on it too?" she wondered.

Happily for the doctor's scheme, as Lucien made a movement of impatience, she had no time to commit an indiscretion. She said nothing, put the baby on a bed in the next room, and went down to the porter's lodge.

"This purse is so heavy, I wonder if it's silver or yellow boys?"

She managed to get the porter away from the door and Lucien was able to cross the courtyard unnoticed.

He rushed home and locked himself in his room. It was only then that he allowed himself to realize the full extent of his misfortune. He was too deeply in love to be angry with Madame de Chasteller in this first moment.

"Has she ever said that she never loved anyone else before me? And, besides, living with me as with a brother because of my own imbecility, my unutterable imbecility, did she owe me any such confidence? Oh, Bathilde, can't I love you any longer?" he cried suddenly. "Must I really stop loving you?" And he burst into tears.

"A real man," he thought at the end of an hour, "would go to Madame d'Hocquincourt, whom I have neglected so stupidly, and seek his revenge."

He had to make a violent effort to get himself dressed, and, as he was leaving, he fell in a dead faint on the drawing room floor.

He came to himself a few hours later; a servant at three in the morning, going to see if he had returned, had stumbled over him.

"So, he's dead drunk again!" the man said. "It's disgusting in one's master."

Lucien heard these words plainly; and at first he thought he was in the state his servant mentioned; but suddenly the frightful truth came back to him, and he was far more unhappy than he had been the evening before.

He passed the rest of the night in a kind of delirium. For one second he had the ignoble idea of going back to Madame de Chasteller and loading her with reproaches. He was horrified at this temptation. To Lieutenant-Colonel Filloteau, who fortunately was then in command of the regiment, he wrote that he was ill, and left Nancy early in the morning, hoping that no one would see him.

It was during this lonely ride that he felt the full weight of his misfortune.

"I can no longer love Bathilde!" he would say to himself aloud, from time to time.

"I must go top speed to Paris. I must see my mother."

Military duties no longer counted for him. He felt like a man whose last hour is approaching. Everything in the world had lost all meaning; two things alone survived: his mother and Madame de Chasteller.

For his soul, worn out by sorrow, the mad idea of this trip to Paris was almost a consolation, the only consolation he could find. It was a distraction.

He sent his horse back to Nancy, and wrote to Filloteau requesting him not to let his absence become known.

"I have been sent for secretly by the Minister of War."

This lie fell involuntarily from his pen, for he had an insane fear of being pursued.

He ordered a post horse, and because of his wild appearance, some objections were raised. But he told them that he had been sent by Colonel Filloteau of the Twenty-seventh Lancers, to a company of the regiment which had gone to Rheims to wage war on the mill-workers.

The difficulties he had had in obtaining the first horse were not repeated and thirty hours later he arrived in Paris.

He was on the point of going to his mother's when it occurred to him that he would startle her if he arrived at such an hour. He went first to a furnished hotel in the vicinity, and only returned home several hours later.

END OF BOOK ONE

[*The story of Lucien Leuwen is continued in a sequel*—The Telegraph.]

APPENDIX

TRANSLATOR'S NOTE

In the introduction to the forthcoming second volume of *Lucien Leuwen,* entitled *The Telegraph,* will be found all the circumstances relative to the composition of Stendhal's "third chef d'oeuvre" as Henri Martineau calls it when he compares it with *The Red and the Black* and *The Charter House of Parma.* Here, only certain relevant facts need be mentioned to explain minor rectifications that have been made in the translation.

In a series of wills, Stendhal provided for the manuscript of *Lucien Leuwen* in case he should die before preparing it himself for publication. He was very much afraid some editor "addicted to the style in vogue" would remove the Beyle flavor. He gives this prospective editor permission to "correct the style and suppress repetitions" but cautions him "to leave the extravagances." His French editors, with the exception of Jean de Mitty who published a mutilated version in 1849, have been even more scrupulous than Stendhal demanded. The text has been published almost exactly as Stendhal left it even where the style is careless or rough or tentative, and with some inconsistencies. Errors are inevitable in so long a work in which, as Stendhal said of Laurence Sterne, "the pen draws him on." And although he kept altering his manuscript as he went along, Stendhal never corrected *Lucien Leuwen* as a whole. He had a very bad memory. When new ideas for scenes or characters or comments occurred to him, he would hastily dash them off as though afraid of losing them before they could be committed to paper, often forgetting what had gone before. As he himself remarks in one of his innumerable marginal notes: "I put down everything, note everything, sometimes crudely—for fear of forgetting. I'll polish later." This, for reasons already mentioned in the introduction, he never did.

The present edition for American readers does not pretend to be a work for Stendhal specialists such as those edited by eminent French scholars for the Beylist cult in France. It is addressed to the general public which, having taken pleasure in Stendhal's other novels in English will be sure to enjoy reading this one. The French text has been faithfully followed, and is not altered by the few minor omissions made for the sake of consistency. For instance, in the present volume the mention of Madame Grandet has been omitted whenever she is represented as being a friend of Lucien's. Stendhal had first intended to give her a role in Nancy society. Later, having changed his original plan, he has Monsieur Leuwen introduce his son to her for the first time after Lucien's return to Paris. Again, a part of a sentence about Madame de Commercy has been suppressed in the third chapter because, although throughout the book she is depicted as a very old lady, here she is described as "perhaps even prettier than Madame d'Hocquincourt." It was impossible, however, without important omissions and changes in the text, to correct the inconsistency which makes Monsieur Fléron a prefect at the beginning of the story, and later only a sub-prefect.

In the case of the appellation of the hero, the given name has been used consistently, thus differing from Stendhal's French editors who have wished to respect his preference for the use of family names expressed in a letter to his friend Madame Jules Gauthier who had submitted a manuscript to him for criticism: "Don't designate your characters by their given names. In speaking of Crozet, do you say Louis? You say Crozet, or at least you should." However, the possibility of confusion in *Lucien Leuwen* because of the two Leuwens, father and son, occurred to Stendhal. In a marginal note he suggested: "Call the protagonist Lucien and not Leuwen. There might be some confusion in the second volume in Paris." Despite this suggestion of Stendhal's to himself, and his tacit permission to his editors, both Debraye and Martineau call the hero Leuwen and Lucien by turn. As there seems no valid reason for not using the given name of the hero, Stendhal's suggestion to call the protagonist Lucien has been adopted.

AUTHOR'S FIRST PREFACE

THIS WORK is written simply and straightforwardly, without any surreptitious allusions. It even goes out of its way to avoid a few. But, except in the case of the hero's passion, the author thinks a novel should be a mirror.

If the police render its publication impolitic, it will be postponed for ten years.

August 2, 1836

AUTHOR'S SECOND PREFACE

RACINE was a sly and cowardly hypocrite because he described Nero; just as Richardson, that puritanical and envious printer, was undoubtedly an admirable seducer of women because he invented *Lovelace*. The author of the novel you are about to read, O Indulgent Reader, if you have a great deal of patience, is an enthusiastic republican and a disciple of Robespierre and Couthon. But, at the same time, he longs passionately for the return of the elder branch and the reign of Louis XIX. My publisher assures me that I will be accused of all these fine things, not through any malice, but because of the scant attention Frenchmen give to what they read. It is the fault of the newspapers.

The moment a novel sets out to depict the ways of contemporary society, the reader, even before he becomes familiar with the characters, asks: "What party does this man belong to?" Here is my answer: "The author is simply a moderate partisan of the Charter of 1830. That is why he has dared give detailed examples of both republican and legitimist conversations without lending to those opposing parties any more ab-

345

surdities than they themselves display, that is, without carica-
turing them—a dangerous proceeding which might lead each
party to suspect the author of being a rabid partisan of the
other."

The author would not live in a democracy like that of
America for anything in the world, because he prefers to pay
court to the Minister of the Interior rather than to the corner
grocer.

In the case of extremist parties, the last to be observed always
seem the most ridiculous. What sorry times when a publisher
of a trifling novel must ask the author to write a preface of
this kind! Ah, how much better to have been born two and
a half centuries ago under Henri IV, in 1600! Old age is the
friend of order and afraid of everything. In his old age our
man born in 1600 readily put up with the eminently noble
despotism of Louis XIV, and that government so admirably
depicted for us by the inexorable genius of the Duc de Saint-
Simon. Saint-Simon was honest and, in consequence, he was
called malicious.

If, by chance, the author of this futile romance has succeeded in being truthful, will he meet with the same reproach?
He has done everything in his power not to deserve it in
any way. In delineating these characters he has let himself be
carried away by the sweet illusions of his art, and his heart has
been far indeed from any corroding thought of hate. Between
two clever men, the one extremely republican, the other extremely legitimist, the author's secret predilection would be
for the one who was most agreeable. Generally speaking, the
legitimist would have more elegant manners and a greater
store of amusing anecdotes to relate; the republican would
have a more passionate soul, his behavior would be more
natural and more youthful. After weighing these two opposite
sets of qualities, the author, as he has just stated, would prefer

the more amiable of the two; and his preference would in no way be influenced by their political views.

AUTHOR'S THIRD PREFACE

ONCE upon a time there was a man who had a fever and who had just taken some quinine. Still holding the glass in his hand and making a wry face because of the bitter taste, he happened to look at himself in the mirror and saw that he was very pale and even a little green. He quickly dropped his glass and hurled himself at the mirror.

Such will perhaps be the fate of the following volumes. Unfortunately for them, they do not recount events that happened a hundred years ago; the characters are contemporary; they were, I suppose, still living two or three years ago. Is it the author's fault if some of them are pronounced legitimists, and if others talk like republicans? Will the author stand convicted of being both a legitimist and a republican?

To tell the truth, since we are forced to make a frank confession for fear of worse, the author would be in despair if he had to live under the government of New York. He prefers to pay court to M. Guizot rather than pay court to his bootmaker. In the Nineteenth Century, democracy, of necessity, introduces the reign of mediocre, rational, narrow-minded and *dull* people—that is, from a literary point of view.

October 21, 1836

ADDITIONAL CHARACTER STUDIES

MADAME D'HOCQUINCOURT

SHE LACKED entirely that starchy manner so much admired in the provinces, and her gay, free, familiar and unassuming ways won her the furious hatred of all the women. The prudish bigots in particular never spoke of her without horror. They would insinuate, hoping to infuriate her, that they thought her really almost plain. This only made her laugh, was, in fact, one of her favorite subjects of amusement. Seeing how Madame de Serpierre addressed her, Lucien realized all the animosity she had inspired. He found both the hatred of the prudes and the what-do-I-care attitude of the young woman herself a little exaggerated. Mad and merry and a born coquette, this young marquise had nothing of the stiffness of her rank. Moreover, her reputation was much worse than she deserved. By some chance, extraordinary in the provinces and a thing which particularly struck Lucien, Madame d'Hocquincourt was incapable of the slightest hypocrisy. She used her superb eyes with a coquetry so full of naturalness that it was no longer coquetry. She would go driving in her calash with her lover and her husband on the road to Paris, which was the fashionable promenade; a young man of the elite passing on horseback would put his horse through some singular and graceful paces or would say something that delighted her, and instantly she had eyes for no one else. And if, by chance, M. d'Antin took it into his head to speak to her before the impression of the graceful young horseman had been forgotten, he was pretty certain to see a look of impatience and disgust take the place of the heavenly light that had shone in her eyes a moment before. Lucien discovered another rare and precious quality in Madame d'Hocquincourt. She never had the least recollection today of what she had said or done the day before. She should have been the mistress of a great king bored by all the ambitions and intrigues of his courtiers and mistresses. Lucien thought seriously of attaching himself to this agreeable young woman. "Perhaps then this town would seem a little less loathsome." But to take a mistress was no small enterprise. It is even truer in the provinces than in Paris that one must begin by becoming the husband's friend, and the woebegone M. d'Hocquincourt, always sad, always harking back to the events of '93, always distorting them completely, was for Lucien, of all the inhabitants of Nancy, the most tiresome.

"The great motive force of these people," thought Lucien, "is the fear of a new Robespierre whom they see looming in the future, and they envy the people who have taken their places on the Budget. The marked hostility of all these young men comes, above all, from the ninety-three francs I steal from them." Every day Lucien noticed new feelings of envy for the middle classes who, killing themselves with hard work, had made a fortune in business.

MADAME DE CHASTELLER

MADAME DE CHASTELLER had been blessed by heaven with a quick, profound, discerning mind, but she was far from realizing her own intelligence. The Bourbons were in distress and she thought only of how to serve them. She imagined that she owed everything to them. Even to discuss this debt would have seemed base and craven in her eyes.

She did not believe in her own abilities, she reproached herself for the many times she had been mistaken in questions of politics, as well as in other minor matters. She did not perceive that it was in following the opinions of other people that she had been misled. If she had always trusted in all things, great and small, to her own first impressions, she would rarely have had to repent it. An impartial philosopher desiring to estimate the soul hidden behind that pretty face, would have observed a singular propensity to unselfish devotion and a horror, equally unreasoning, of anything that was spurious or hypocritical. From the fall of the Bourbons to the July Revolution one sentiment had been uppermost: admiration for those divine beings. She thought continually of the objects of her devotion. As she possessed a naturally noble soul, petty things seemed to her just what they are, that is, unworthy of engaging the attention of anybody born for great ones. This disposition made her entirely indifferent to and negligent of little things; and as nothing of secondary importance could touch her, she had a fund of practically unalterable gaiety. Her father called it childishness. This father of hers, M. de Pontlevé, spent his whole life dreading a second '93, and thinking of his daughter's fortune, which was his lightning-rod against that too inevitable thunderbolt. One might say of M. de Pontlevé that he was motivated not so much by his love of the Bourbons as by his fear of '93.

Madame de Chasteller spoke naturally and with a charming ease. She had definite and brilliant ideas, but was, above all, always gracious to her listener. She had only to meet the worst egoist or the most rabid republican *ideologist* two or three times in a drawing room to convert him to a love for the Bourbons, or, at least, mitigate whatever antipathy he might have for them. Both because of her love for the Bourbons as well as her natural generosity she maintained a very large establishment. In spite of all M. de Pontlevé's entreaties, she could not bring herself to discharge any of M. de Chasteller's servants. Her Tuesdays displayed all the amenity and good taste of the first houses of Paris, which was hardly short of miraculous in the provinces. Saturdays (her *petit-jour*) her drawing room was crowded with all that was most aristocratic and wealthy in Nancy and its surrounding countryside. All this might have been expected to arouse the envy of the other noble ladies, if it had not been for the fact that Madame de Chasteller was so unassuming and the rival ladies saw so plainly that had she followed her own inclination she would have lived alone in the country with her friend Madame de Constantin. Since all this luxury did not seem to give her any great satisfaction, it failed to excite their resentment—a remarkable anomaly in the provinces.

Madame de Chasteller was really only hated by the young republicans who knew that they would never have a chance of addressing a word to her.

Madame de Chasteller was well-versed in the proper manner of conducting herself, and even with grace, in the grand drawing room of the Palace of the Tuileries, how to address the King and the royal princesses, how to ingratiate herself with the great ladies; but beyond such essential matters, she had not the slightest experience of life. As soon as she felt herself moved she lost her head, and on such occasions her only measure of caution was to say nothing and to do nothing.

"I wish to God I had not spoken a word to M. Leuwen," she now said to herself. At the Sacred Heart, a nun who had acquired an influence over her by indulging all her childish caprices, could get her to perform all her tasks with a sort of devotion, simply by saying to her: "Do it for my sake." For it is an act of impiety, almost a temerity leading to *protestantism,* to say to a little girl, "Do such and such a thing because it is reasonable." *"Do it for my sake"* answers any purpose and does not lead one to question what is reasonable and what is not. And as a result, even with the best intentions in the world, Madame de Chasteller could find no rule of conduct to guide her in moments of emotional stress.

Leaning back in her chair beside the marble table, Madame de Chasteller was in despair. She knew not where to seek refuge from the terrible shame she felt at having appeared to Lucien to be lacking in reserve. Her first impulse was to retire to a convent for the rest of her life.

"My vows of eternal renunciation will prove to him that I have no designs on his freedom."

The only objection to this project was that it would start everybody talking about her, discussing her reason, lending her secret motives, etc.

"But what difference does all that make? I shall never see them again. . . . Yes, but I should know all the time that they were talking about me and so maliciously. It would drive me mad! Such a scandal would be unbearable. . . . Ah!" she cried with a new access of torment, "would it not only serve to confirm M. Leuwen in his idea that I am a brazen woman incapable of restraining myself within the sacred limits of feminine reserve?"

Madame de Chasteller was so upset and so little accustomed to calculating her own actions that she forgot for the moment those details of her behavior which constituted the foundation of her despair and of her shame. Never had she sat down at her embroidery frame behind the shutters without first dismissing her maid and locking the door.

"I have compromised myself in the eyes of M. Leuwen," she kept repeating to herself almost hysterically, leaning her elbows on the marble table. "There was a fatal moment when I forgot in the presence of this young man that sacred reserve without which my sex can never hope to gain the world's esteem, nor even one's

own self-respect. If M. Leuwen has any of that idealism so natural to his age, and which I imagined I could detect in his manner when he rode past my window, I have forfeited it forever, I have destroyed in one heedless moment the idea of purity he may have had of me. Alas! my only excuse is that for the first time in my life I have felt the stirrings of disordered passion. But can such an excuse be spoken? Can it be so much as thought? Yes, I have forgotten all the laws of modesty!"

She had the courage to pronounce this terrible word. Almost at once the tears that rose to her eyes disappeared.

"My dear cousin," she said to the Vicomte de Blancet with a somewhat factitious assurance (but he was incapable of appreciating this nuance, being entirely absorbed by the problem of the degree of intimacy that had been accorded him), "this is just a fit of nerves with everything that goes with it. But for the love of God don't let anyone at the ball hear of it, and do please bring me a glass of water. Water with ice if possible," she called out after him.

The attention it took to play this little scene provided a slight diversion from her terrible suffering, and with haggard eye she followed the Vicomte as he disappeared. When she was sure that he was out of hearing, she gave herself up to the bitterest despair. She was almost strangled by her sobs. Hers were the tears of utter distress and, above all, of shame.

"I have compromised myself forever in M. Leuwen's regard. My eyes said to him: 'I love you madly,' and I talked to him like this the very first time he addressed a word to me. In my madness I had the temerity to ask him questions that would hardly be permissible after six months of acquaintance and friendly intercourse. God! What could I have been thinking of!

"When you found nothing to say to me at the beginning of the evening, that is, in the century of waiting during which I passionately longed for a word from you—*was it timidity?* Timidity, my God! (She was choked with sobs.) *Was it timidity?"* she repeated, shaking her head, her eyes haggard, *"was it timidity, or was it that suspicion?* They say that every woman is mad once in her lifetime; apparently my hour had come."

And all at once the significance of the word *suspicion* came to her.

"And even before I threw myself at his head with such horrible indecency, he already had a *suspicion*. And to think that I should have *ignominiously* stooped to justify myself against that *suspicion!* And to an utter *stranger!* Great God! if anything could be calculated to make him think the very worst of me, is it not my atrocious conduct?"

Hers was a simple nature, and she had but little knowledge of life or of herself. She had spent ten years in a convent and sixteen months in the great world. Married at seventeen, a widow at twenty, she had found nothing in Nancy that seemed agreeable to her.

For a long time Lucien had known nothing of Madame de Chasteller. What we have just recounted in two words, and the malicious gossip of M. Bouchard, the post-master, constituted his whole stock of knowledge on this delicate subject.

MADAME DE CHASTELLER AND LUCIEN LEUWEN

"And even if she weren't so full of indulgence for lieutenant-colonels, or even plain lieutenants, have I the necessary talent to succeed with a woman of real delicacy? Would I be able to make her lose her head to the point of forgetting what she owes to herself?"

But if this reiteration of the same arguments did much to bear witness to our hero's modesty, it did nothing to further his happiness. His heart's need was to find Madame de Chasteller's merit without a stain. That was the way he loved her, he had to think of her as sublime; yet his reason showed him that she was very different. Furious with himself, he cried:

"Have I the gift of succeeding with a woman of society? It has never yet happened to me."

He was in love for the first time. Madame de Chasteller had that simplicity of character which harmonizes so well with true nobility. She would have condemned as a degrading crime the least falseness in herself, the least affectation toward the people she loved. With the exception of her passionate predilection for him, she told Lucien the truth about everything, with a naturalness and ardor that is seldom met with in a young woman of twenty-one.

"Even if I didn't love her, the evenings I spend with her would be the most amusing of my whole life."

She had never actually told him that she loved him, but when he reasoned coolly (which was, it must be admitted, rarely), he was sure of it. Madame de Chasteller enjoyed the recompense of a pure heart: unless frightened by the presence of ill-disposed individuals, she still possessed all the mad gaiety of youth. Toward the end of Lucien's visits, when, for three-quarters of an hour or an hour, he had not actually spoken of love, she was as merry as a child. Sometimes she even played ridiculous schoolgirl pranks on him such as hiding his shako, which Paris would have deemed indecorous. But if, in hunting for the shako together, Lucien was rash enough to take her hand, Madame de Chasteller would instantly draw herself up haughtily. No longer was she the happy heedless girl of a moment before. One would have thought her a censorious woman of thirty, self-reproach altered her features to such a degree.

Lucien was much given to this sort of imprudence; and to his shame be it said that sometimes, though not often, his Parisian education got the better of him. Not for the mere happiness of holding the hand of the woman he loved would he take Madame de Chasteller's, but because something in him whispered that it was ridiculous to spend two hours alone with a woman whose eyes sometimes showed such good will toward him, without once, at least, holding her hand.

It is not with impunity that one lives in Paris from the age of ten. No matter what salon one frequents, nor in what honor simplicity and naturalness are held, nor how much contempt is shown for all flagrant hypocrisies, nevertheless the affectation and vanity of the place, and all its petty scheming, penetrate even the heart that believes itself the most unsullied.

The result of Lucien's indiscretions, especially considering the habitual frankness of his manner toward this woman for whom his heart held no secret, and who seemed to him so infinitely intelligent, was to make these bold tentatives stand out like a blot on his habitual conduct.

Madame de Chasteller recognized in these affected transports of love the execution of a preconceived plan. At such moments she noticed with terror a certain change in Lucien's expression that seemed to her a sinister portent. This strange expression, recalling her worst suspicions, was, for a woman of her character, the surest hindrance to Lucien's hopes.

When Lucien began disturbing their peaceful and intimate happiness with his ridiculous tactics, the most unpleasant ideas would come flocking back into Madame de Chasteller's troubled mind. The happiness of her whole life depended on Lucien's probity. She found his manners charming, recognized his intelligence; but did he feel all that he said, or to his other talents did he add that of a clever actor?

"He is young, he is rich, he wears a handsome uniform, he comes from Paris: is he really a coxcomb after all? Everybody in Nancy says so. If he chooses to exaggerate his timidity with me, instead of the self-assurance natural to these gentlemen, is it not merely because he thinks I have a serious character? Yet I am simple enough to have boundless confidence in him! What will become of me if ever I am driven to despise him?"

The possibility of perfidy in a man she loved was enough to fill her with a rage against herself such as she had never known. At the moments when she was assailed by these doubts anyone might have thought she was ill, so prompt, so sudden, so profound was the change that came over her face. The mien she then assumed was enough to take away all the courage of the most confident lover, and Lucien was very far from being such a lover. He did not even have wit enough to see how profoundly his indiscretions irritated Madame de Chasteller.

End of Chapter VII and most of Chapter VIII, of the Edition du Rocher 1945

LUCIEN sat down on a stone. When he wanted to rise he was unable to and soon lost consciousness. He was roused to his senses by a little noise. Opening his eyes, he saw a lancer standing over him and staring down at him, laughing.

"Look at that! Our *Milord,* dead drunk!" he said. "It may be true that I drink all the money I make, but no one's ever caught me like that. But then, by gad, he's got more pennies than I have, and if he sets out to drink them all, he can certainly outdo yours truly, Ménuel." Lucien looked up at the lancer but was unable to speak.

"How about it, Lieutenant, you don't seem able to walk. Do you want me to set you on your legs?"

Ménuel would never have dared use such a tone if he had not been sure the officer was drunk. But he laughed heartily to see the *Milord,* as the soldiers called him, unable to stand up, and like all true Frenchmen was overjoyed to have a chance of being impudent to a superior. Lucien continued to look at him in silence, but at last found strength enough to say:

"Will you help me, please."

Ménuel put his hands under the second-lieutenant's arms and assisted him to his feet. Ménuel's left hand felt wet. He looked at it. It was covered with blood.

"Well! If that's how it is," he said, "you'd better sit down."

His voice was now full of sympathy. "The devil!" he thought to himself. "It's not drink, it's a blasted sword wound."

"Lieutenant, do you want me to carry you home? I'm strong. But first, better let me take off your coat, and bind up your wound."

Lucien did not reply. In an instant, Ménuel had taken off Lucien's coat, ripped up his shirt and made a bandage with one of the sleeves, tying his handkerchief tightly around it. Then he ran to a nearby tavern and came back with a glass of brandy in which he soaked the bandage. There was a little brandy left which he made Lucien drink.

"Stay with me," Lucien said. And an instant afterwards was able to add:

"This must remain a secret. Go to my place, have the calash harnessed and come and fetch me in it. You will be doing me a great service if no one finds out about this little accident, above all, the colonel."

"Milord is no fool, after all," thought Ménuel as he went to get the carriage. The lancer felt very proud. "I'm about to give orders to those cocky lackeys in their fine liveries." Ménuel had despised Lucien. Now that he found he was wounded and taking his accident so courageously, he admired him just as vigorously and with as much reason as he had despised him a quarter of an hour before.

Once in the calash, Ménuel dropped his compassionate tone, and became most entertaining, not because he was witty but because of the comical way he had of saying things.

"Will you give me your word of honor, comrade," Lucien insisted, "never to mention what you have seen?"

"All the words in the world, but what's much more to the point, would I be likely, Lieutenant, to do anything to displease the Lieutenant-Colonel Filloteau's special pet?" Ménuel went off to look for the surgeon of the regiment. He failed to find him, and stayed on with the wounded man who was not suffering in the least. Lucien was struck by the natural wit of this Ménuel, a poor sort of devil who took everything cheerfully, and who now installed himself in our hero's quarters. Bored to death, surrounded by convention-ridden people, and still not overly enthusiastic about the character of the ordinary soldier, Lucien, instead of indulging in his somber thoughts, listened with interest to Ménuel's endless yarns.

To our wounded hero Ménuel related parts of his life, but was very careful to keep certain others to himself. By way of episode, we shall relate in passing this story of a simple soldier. Although usually the muster rolls of a regiment contain only the names of men whose stories are pretty humdrum and always the same, it happens now and then that the simple soldier's uniform covers a heart that has known curious emotions.

Ménuel had been assistant to a bookbinder at Saint-Malô, his native city. Falling in love with the soubrette of a troupe of strolling players who had come to Saint-Malô, Ménuel had deserted his master's shop and become an actor. Sometime later at Bayonne, where he had been living for several months, and where he had made himself very popular and accumulated a little store of money by giving fencing lessons, he was importuned by a young man of that city for the return of fifty francs he had loaned Ménuel out of friendship. Ménuel's savings amounted to a little more than this debt, but he felt such distaste at the thought of tapping it, or rather of practically wiping it out by paying his debt, that he had the idea of committing a forgery, in other words a receipt conceived in these terms: *Received from bearer one hundred and fifty francs. Perret, jr.* When a friend of M. Perret, the latter having gone to Pau, came to collect the money in his name, Ménuel had the audacity to tell him that he had already sent the money to Perret before his departure. Perret returned from his trip and came to demand what was still owing him. Ménuel's reply did not please him, and Perret, in spite of the fact that Ménuel was a fencing master, forthwith challenged him to a duel.

Ménuel, already goaded by remorse, was horrified at what he was about to do; to kill a man for a hundred and fifty francs! He offered to pay the debt. Perret retorted that he was a coward. This word restored all Ménuel's defiance, and made him feel better. He would fight, but he would try to spare Perret's life. Going to the grounds where they were to fight, Ménuel said to him:

"Always disengage, never lunge, and it will be impossible for me to kill you."

This was said in all good faith and spoken as a fencing master. Unhappily Perret gave his adversary credit for a depth of villainy of which poor Ménuel was quite incapable.

After two or three reprises, Perret felt that he should do the reverse of what his adversary had advised him. He lunged and impaled himself on Ménuel's sword. His wound was critical. Ménuel was in despair, but his grief was taken for hypocrisy and fear.

Disgraced and despised throughout the city, he was prosecuted for forgery by Perret's father. All Bayonne was up in arms against him, and as everything is a question of the fashion of the moment, even the decisions of juries, Ménuel was condemned to hard labor.

In prison Ménuel had wine brought to him and did his best to be gay. Feeling remorse, and looking upon himself as irrevocably doomed, he wanted to spend the short time he had left as merrily as possible.

He was liked by all the jailors and turnkeys of the prison. One day, in the porter's lodge, he noticed eight or ten great coils of rope, brought there to replace the worn ones of all the prison blinds. An idea occurred to him. He promptly stole one of the coils. Luck being with him, he was not caught, and that very night, by scaling two very respectably high walls, he succeeded in making his escape. He went straight to a friend of Perret and gave him the one hundred and fifty francs he still owed. This friend had been one of those most active in helping Perret's father to have Ménuel condemned. But in Bayonne public opinion changes quickly, and people were beginning to think that Ménuel's punishment had been too severe. Perret's friend took pity on Ménuel and lost no time in putting him aboard a vessel that was to sail before daylight.

The wind rose in the night and the ship from Bayonne ran aground not far from Saint-Sebastien. Ménuel hailed a Spanish ship, and that same evening was wandering along the wharves of Saint-Sebastien. He was accosted by a recruiting officer and invited to join the *legitimist* army of Don Carlos. Ménuel accepted, and a few days later arrived at the army of the Spanish Pretender. He demonstrated that he could ride a horse; they discovered that he had the gift of gab; they put him in the cavalry.

One month later Ménuel made a sortie with his company to cover a convoy. The *Christinos* attacked; Ménuel was scared out of his wits. After a few rounds of musket-shot, Ménuel made off for the mountains at a gallop. When his horse could no longer make his way up the precipitous rocky slopes, Ménuel tied his forelegs together, left him in the dry bed of a stream, and proceeded to flee on foot. At last his ears ceased to be offended by the noise of musket-fire. He then stopped to deliberate.

"After such gallant behavior, how can I return to the army where, because of three little duels, I enjoy the reputation of being as brave as a lion?

"What a miserable wretch I am," thought Ménuel. "Forger, convict and now a coward for good measure!" The thought of killing himself occurred to him, but when he reviewed all the methods of suicide the idea horrified him. After it grew dark, our Ménuel, dying of hunger, began to think that perhaps the mule of some sutler might have been wounded or killed, in which case its panniers would still be lying on the battlefield. Stealthily, and not without a good deal of trepidation, he retraced his steps. Every two minutes he would halt, lie down and put his ear to the ground; he heard nothing but the gentle night wind rustling the brush and the little cork trees.

He arrived at last and, to his great surprise, he saw that after six hours of musket-fire the terrible carnage had left only two corpses on the battlefield. "What a miserable wretch I am," he said to himself, "to have had such a great fright for such a small danger!" He was in despair when suddenly he came upon a half-full wine-skin, and farther along a whole loaf of bread. He took the precaution of going several hundred paces away from the battlefield to eat his supper. He then returned, always on the alert.

One of the corpses was that of a young Frenchman named Ménuel who had a wallet full of letters as well as his passport. Our hero had the luminous idea of changing his name. He took the passport, the letters, the wallet, the shirts, far superior to his own, and finally the name of Ménuel. Until that moment his name had been quite different.

Once he had this name he said to himself: "Why shouldn't I go back to France? I am no longer a convict posted in all the police stations. As long as I avoid Bayonne where I shone with a false luster, and Montpellier where this poor Ménuel was born, I am free to go anywhere in France." Day was beginning to dawn. He had found a hundred francs in the pockets of the two corpses and was continuing his search when he saw two peasants approaching. He decided to tell them that he was wounded. Then he went to get his horse, but when he returned to the peasants he quickly noticed that, thinking him weakened by his wound, they were about to treat him as he had treated the corpses. His wound was cured on the instant, and the peasants, reverting to a more humane turn of mind, promised, in return for a *piastre* paid every morning and another paid every night, to take him to the Bidassoa, the stream which, as you know, forms the boundary of France.

Ménuel was very happy. But he had hardly set foot in France before he began imagining (he had a vivid imagination) that all the gendarmes he met looked at him suspiciously. He rode as far as Bézier where he sold his horse and took the diligence to Lyons. But his funds were running low. Partly by steam-boat, partly on foot, he finally reached Dijon, and a few days later Colmar. When he arrived at that fair city he had only five francs left. "I know how to handle a sword," he thought. "If I'm angry enough I'm a good fighter; I know how to ride a horse; the papers all say that there won't be a war for a long time and, anyway, I can always desert, so why shouldn't I join the regiment of lancers whose recruiting center is Colmar? I'll give the commander my passport and later I'll manage to steal it back again. If I destroy this indiscreet document, I shall say I was born at Lyons which I have just thoroughly explored. I shall call myself Ménuel and the devil if anyone will take me for a convict!"

All of which had been duly accomplished six months after he had entered the recruiting station. Ménuel, the very paragon of a soldier, had burned his passport after having most adroitly stolen it from the desk of the recruiting captain. He was now very popular, famous as a fencing master, and had the reputation of being a merry fellow. To forget his misfortunes, he spent in the taverns all the money he earned with his foil. Two things he had promised himself: to make friends in the regiment by never drinking alone, and never to get completely drunk for fear of letting some indiscreet word escape him.

Since he had joined the regiment six years ago, his life was apparently a happy one. If he had not been careful to conceal the fact that he could write, the officers of his company, who liked his neat appearance and whom he endeavored to please, would certainly have had him made a corporal. Ménuel was considered the *wag* of the regiment. He had a most fortunate duel with a fencing master. His valor no less than his skill had given him an enviable reputation throughout the garrison. But whenever he caught sight of a gendarme he would tremble in spite of himself; their presence was the bane of his existence. He had only one resource against this evil: the nearest tavern.

When he had the good fortune to attach himself to Lucien he felt that his fate had changed. "A man as rich as that," he thought, "could get me pardoned even if I was recognized. He only has to be willing to do it. He is a fool with his money, and what would it be for him, at the right moment, to give some head-clerk a thousand crowns for my pardon!"

LORD LINK

Chapter XXXI, of the Edition du Rocher 1945

OFTEN on his rides through the countryside around Nancy, Lucien had passed a magnificent English horse.

"That horse is worth ten, twelve, fifteen thousand francs. I don't know how much! Unless perhaps it has some hidden defect. . . . It seems possibly a little narrow in the shoulders."

Its rider was an excellent horseman, but his general appearance was that of a groom who had won first prize in a Viennese lottery.

"I wonder if the horse is for sale?" Lucien asked himself. "Although it would certainly cost more than I'd ever dare to pay."

The second or third time Lucien came upon horse and rider, he was close enough to see the man's face. He was dressed with extraordinary care, and appeared affected, by very dint of trying to look as natural as a man alone in his room shaving.

"My mother is right," thought Lucien. "These Englishmen are the kings of affectation." And he thought no more of the horse, but every time he saw it his admiration grew.

One day Madame d'Hocquincourt complimented him on his own horse.

"Not a bad animal," he replied, "and I'm very fond of it. But I sometimes meet one which, unless it has some hidden defect, in the amazing lightness of its movements, is far superior. Why, that horse seems hardly to touch the ground, or rather it makes you think that the ground is elastic, and in its rapid gait, when it trots, for instance, it fairly bounces in the air!"

"Your own feet, my dear Lieutenant, are walking on air! What fire! How beautiful your eyes are when you speak of something you love. Out of pure coquetry you really ought to fall in love, and always be indiscreet and talk about the object of your love."

"The person I am in love with at this moment does not take advantage of the power she has over me. I should be afraid of all my follies if I were to be seriously in love. They would soon extinguish whatever love a woman might feel for me and disaster would swiftly follow. You women are not noted for setting any great store by what is offered you constantly and too wholeheartedly."

Madame d'Hocquincourt threw him an appreciative little glance.

"And this beloved horse is ridden by a tall, blond, middle-aged man with a prominent chin and the face of a child?"

"Who rides extremely well, but flaps his arms too much."

"And he, for his part, claims that Frenchmen look stiff on horseback. I know him quite well. He is an English lord whose name is spelt in some outlandish way but is pronounced Link."

"And what does he do here?"

"He rides! They say he is banished from England. For three or four years now he has honored us by living among us. But how is it you haven't been taken to one of his Saturday balls?"

"I have enjoyed the honor of being admitted to Nancy society for such a short time!"

"Then it is I who shall have the honor of taking you to his next ball. He gives one regularly the first Saturday of every month, summer and winter. There has been none for the last two weeks because of Advent and M. Rey objected."

"He's a strange man, your M. Rey, and what power he exercises over you!"

"Lord! You should say that to Madame de Serpierre, who loves you so! What a sermon you would hear!"

"He is the master of all of you—this M. Rey!"

"What do you expect? He keeps telling us that unless the Jesuits return our poor privileges will never be what they used to be in the good old days. It is a sad thought, but necessity comes first. The Republic must never return to send us all to the scaffold as in '93. Besides, personally M. Rey is not too boring; he always amuses me for at least twenty minutes. It is his lieutenants who are tiresome. He is a man of real worth, at least one never yawns when he is talking. He has traveled. They sent him to Russia for four years and to America for two or three. They always assign him to the difficult posts. He came to us after the *Glorious Days.*"

"I find him rather American-looking."

"An American from Toulouse."

"Would you also introduce me to M. Rey?"

"No indeed! He would find such an introduction entirely *improper.* He is a man to be handled warily; he has a great influence with husbands. But I shall introduce you to Lord Link whose dinners are famous."

"I understood you to say that he did not give dinners."

"They are dinners he gives to himself. They say that he has three or four prepared for him every day in Nancy and the surrounding villages, and that he eats the one which happens to be nearest when he is hungry."

"Not a bad idea!"

"M. de Vassigny, who is such a savant, says that Lord Link is a strong partisan of the *utilitarian* theory in all things, which is especially preached by a famous Englishman . . . his name has something to do with a prophet . . ."

"Jeremy Bentham,* perhaps?"

"Exactly!"

---

* Jeremy Bentham (1748-1833), English philosopher and jurist. From Priestley's phrase, "the greatest happiness of the greatest number," he evolved a philosophic-ethic theory of pain-combating and pleasure-seeking calling for political and legal reforms. He was the first to use the terms "utilitarian" and "utilitarianism" in a philosophic sense.

"He is a friend of my father."

"Well, you shouldn't boast of it to English lords. M. de Vassigny says he is their *bête noire,* and M. Rey assured us the other day that Bentham would be worse than Robespierre if he had the same power. Lord Link is detested by his peers for being a disciple of that English terrorist; and, as the ultimate absurdity, he is ruined and can't live in the West End, the fashionable district of London, for he has barely four thousand pounds a year—that is a hundred thousand francs."

"And so he squanders them here?"

"No, in spite of his four dinners, he economizes here and goes to Paris every now and then to squander them in very bad company. He himself maintains that he only likes good society in the provinces. And in Paris, it is said, he actually *talks!* Here he does us the honor of spending a whole evening without opening his mouth. But invariably he loses at cards. I'll tell you what I suspect, but you must keep it a secret, I think I have noticed that he loses on purpose. It would be just like him to say: *I know I am not very agreeable, especially to fools, so I'd better lose!* The old ladies at Madame de Marcilly's adore him."

"Not bad, really! But it's you who lend him wit. Now that you describe the man, I seem to remember having seen him at Madame de Serpierre's. One day I happened to remark that no matter how amusing an Englishman might be, if you met him in the morning he always looked as though he had just learned that he was bankrupt. Come to think of it, Mademoiselle Théodelinde gave me a terribly reproachful look at the time and I always forgot to ask her why."

"She was wrong. Lord Link would not have minded. He has said that he despises men so much that unless a man actually buttonholes him and insults him to his face, he never asks for satisfaction. 'Does the heavenly Father pay me to correct all the stupidities of the human race?' he once remarked to M. de Sanréal who wasn't at all sure whether he shouldn't take offense, for Sanréal himself had just uttered three or four of the rankest stupidities. Ludwig Roller claims that Lord Link is not naturally inclined to anger. I don't know why, for Roller, poor dear, has never once, since the *July Days,* got himself *unangered.* His lieutenant's pay of two thousand francs really counts for him. Now he doesn't know what to talk about. He studied his profession seriously and always insisted that he would be a Marshal of France. They've had a *cordon-rouge* in the family."

"I don't know whether he ever will be a Marshal of France, but I do know that he is insupportable, with all his theories stolen from M. Rey, whose mouthpiece he has become. He maintains that the Civil Code is horribly immoral because it provides for the partition of inheritance among all the children. The monastic orders must absolutely be re-established and all French lands turned over to grazing. I have no objection to all France becoming a pasture, but I do object to anyone's talking about anything for more than twenty minutes at a time."

"Yes, but all that isn't at all boring when M. Rey is talking."

"M. Roller fully makes up for that, and two or three times has forced me to leave Madame de Serpierre's drawing room when he was holding forth; and what is worse he is not even capable of answering objections."

They came back to Lord Link.

"Lord Link is not sparing of his criticism of France either," said Madame d'Hocquincourt.

"Bah! I can hear him: land of democracy, of irony, of vicious political practices. We lack rotten boroughs, and with us there are always estates for sale. Therefore we are not worth a straw. Oh! there is nothing so boring as an Englishman who gets into a rage because all Europe is not a servile copy of England. The only good things about them are their horses and their patience in handling ships."

"Now it's you who are blaming *ab hoc* and *ab hac.* In the first place this poor lord always says what he has to say in two words and, moreover, says such true things that one never forgets them. Finally he is not at all English in one thing: if he finds that you ride well, he will let you ride his horses, even the famous *Soliman* which is apparently the one you admire so much."

"The devil he does!" cried Lucien. "That changes everything. I shall certainly pay court to him."

"Come to dinner tomorrow night. I shall invite him. He never refuses me and almost always refuses Madame de Puylaurens."

"Faith, the reason is not difficult to guess!"

"Ah, but one day, some insipid flatterer, I don't remember who, repeated this in front of us both together. I was trying to find some sort of rejoinder to such a crass compliment when Lord Link rescued me from my embarrassment by simply saying: 'Madame de Puylaurens has too much wit.' You should have seen d'Antin's face. He was sitting between Lord Link and me. In spite of all his wit he got as red as a beet.

"Madame de Puylaurens and d'Antin make a point of telling each other everything. I should like to know if he told her about this charming dialogue. What would you have done in his place? Etc. Etc. Etc.

"It does not, I admit, smooth the way for the declaration of a tender passion. But I should be very careful not to talk to you in such a tone: I am too fearful of falling in love with you. When you had succeeded in driving me completely mad, you would make fun of me."

THEY WERE DISPARAGING Louis-Philippe. Lord Link, who had been present for an hour without opening his mouth, observed in his phlegmatic way: "A man had a fine coat; his cousin stole it. While fighting the cousin for it, his friends slashed and ruined the fine coat. 'What will be left of my coat even if you win?' cried the man whose coat had been stolen. What will be left of the monarchy? Henri V might very well ask you: 'Where is the illusion necessary for that sort of farce to be found?' What Frenchman is in seventh heaven because the *King* speaks to him?" Having said this, Lord Link thought he had paid the price of admission and did not open his mouth again.

*   *   *

At the head of the above pages, Stendhal had written:
"Lord Link, a sardonic character. *Milord* Link is a Bishop of Clogher but must not be said.

"Milord Link has been expelled from England, he has four or five apartments in Montvallier [Stendhal later changed it to Nancy], a city he has chosen because of his deplorable reputation everywhere else. But this reason must not be explicitly stated.

"A cynical person, but too lazy to be malignant, easily gaining an influence over women because they produce no more effect on him than if they were seven-year-old children.

"Lucien takes long rides with Lord Link because he enjoys watching the movements of Lord Link's horse. Link's silence suits him admirably. Link's feminine vanity convinces him that Lucien is in reality courting him with his silence; and since he has always seen Lucien very talkative at Madame d'Hocquincourt's and elsewhere, he is delighted by the effect he has produced on this young Frenchman (whose good-looking legs he eyes with the same pleasure that I take in looking at Lady Clementine's lovely arms).

"By the end of six weeks, Lord Link has acquired great respect for Lucien, and in society—but not on their rides during which he respects Lucien's silence (humorous possibilities)—he shares with him all his Machiavellian sallies which now give Link, thanks to this echo, even greater pleasure."

Should it be disclosed to the reader that for Beyle, to be a Bishop of Clogher means to be addicted to certain peculiar practices?

ON THE BACK of the last manuscript page of this volume, Stendhal has a note which indicates that he may have intended adding the scene between Lucien and his mother after Lucien's return home.

"Mother, I am mad. Except that my honor is intact, I am the unhappiest of men."

"I forgive you anything," she cried, throwing her arms around his neck. "Is it a question of money? I have money."

"Much worse than that. I have loved, and I have been deceived."

APPENDIX

ADDITIONAL CHARACTERS

Character studies left among Stendhal's manuscripts of Lucien Leuwen *and incorporated in the text by Henri Martineau.*

Count Genevray is mentioned by Lucien in the list of aristocrats he has just met, but never appears in the story.

Count Genevray, a little fellow nineteen years old, plump and stuffed into clothes too tight for him; black mustaches; repeats twice every evening that there can be no happiness for France without *legitimacy;* a good little devil at that; beautiful hair.

NOTES

PAGE 3. *Lord Byron:* Stendhal quotes Lord Byron in French as follows:

Il y avait une fois une famille à Paris qui avait été préservé des idées vulgaires par son chef, lequel avait beaucoup, d'ésprit et de plus savait vouloir.

If these lines exist in Byron's works or correspondence they have not yet been ferreted out. Until such time as they have been discovered, this translation is offered with due apologies to Lord Byron and in the hope that he will not rise from his grave to haunt the translator.

PAGE 3. *Bibliothèque Bleue:* Collections of stories—especially popularizations of the medieval tales of chivalry always published in blue covers. Dating from the XVth Century, these collections were reprinted continually for several centuries. They included such well-known romances as *Lancelot du Lac, Les Quatre Fils Aymon, La Chanson de Roland, Tristan de Léonois, Flores et Blanchefleur*, etc., as well as, in some collections, old and naïve versions of *Tom Thumb* and *Cinderella*. Thus, Stendhal facetiously classes his great political and social satire with the romances of chivalry and fairy tales.

PAGE 3. *Cityold . . . 1837:* Stendhal had a mania for using his own peculiar English. This is simply the translation of Civita-Vecchia in Italy, where he served as consul. It was written, not in 1837, but in March 1835, according to Henri Martineau.

PAGE 5. *One of the famous days of June 1832:* Stendhal's manuscript reads: "One of the famous days of June, April or February 1832 or 34." But in a note he adds, "to be verified." I have therefore verified, and left only the correct date. In this I have followed

Henry Debraye and not Henri Martineau who leaves Stendhal's tentative sentence. This reference is to the two days of rioting (June 5th and 6th) which followed the funeral of General Maximilien Lamarque, one of the leaders of the opposition. The Republicans organized the funeral with the hope of turning it into a popular demonstration against the government and starting another revolution. The government, however, was fully prepared for hostilities and easily overcame the badly organized band of insurgents, who failed to gain the support of the populace. In spite of strict orders to the contrary, sixty or more Polytechnicians in uniform accompanied the funeral procession, and many of them took part in the street fighting. They were all expelled and henceforth bore the stigma of republicanism. Some of them, like Lucien at Nancy, tried hard to rid themselves of this stigma.

PAGE 5. *École Polytechnique:* first founded in 1794 by the National Convention to train young men for the army, engineering, and public works. It is now under the Ministry of War and supplies officers of artillery and engineers, while the *École Spéciale Militaire* provides graduates for cavalry and infantry.

PAGE 6. "Age of Lucien: 23; his mother 18 years older: 41; M. Leuwen, plus twenty-five, equals 66 years old." (Stendhal note in Ms.)

PAGE 7. *Gymnase: Théâtre du Gymnase-Dramatique,* theater in Paris, where for years the comedies and *vaudevilles* of Eugène Scribe (1791-1861) were given. *Vaudevilles* of that period were comedies interspersed with songs of topical interest set to light, popular airs. Thackeray, a younger contemporary of Stendhal's, also mentions the dashing colonels of the Gymnase in his *Paris Sketches* of about the same period: "Then there is the comedy of the day, of which Monsieur Scribe is the father. Good heavens! with what a number of gay colonels, smart widows, and silly husbands has that gentleman peopled the play-books."

PAGE 11. *Hampden:* John Hampden (1594-1643), English patriot, a cousin of Oliver Cromwell, opposed to the government of Charles

I. His name in Stendhal's day became a symbol of intransigent republicanism.

PAGE II. *nor a man to object to taxes even without the budget:* this probably has reference to those associations Guizot has described which, at the end of Charles X's reign, "were publicly formed to refuse taxes if the Government should attempt to collect them without a legal vote."

PAGE II. ... *a cigar he had just rolled in licorice paper.* Lucien smokes what we would call cigarettes. They were apparently a novelty at that time and still called cigars. Several English travelers who visited Spain in the late eighteenth century recorded that Spaniards smoked what were in effect cigarettes—finely shredded tobacco wrapped up in a small piece of paper. But the year 1845 is generally accepted as the earliest English reference to the cigarette.

PAGE II. *Halt in the mud:* an expression attributed to General Lamarque to characterize the period.

PAGE 12. *The Three Days:* or the *July Days* or *The Glorious Days (les Glorieuses)*, the July Revolution of 1830, which followed the violation of the Charter by Charles X, and brought Louis-Philippe to the throne. "Insurrectionary movements are emphatically called 'days' in France," comments Lewis Cass in *France, its King, Court and Government,* written anonymously when he was United States minister at Paris in 1840.

PAGE 13. ... *will not let himself be made a laughingstock by Nicholas:* After the uprising of Poland and its bloody suppression, the Russian Czar Nicholas I assumed a menacing attitude toward any nation that showed sympathy for Poland. Toward the government of Louis-Philippe the Czar became particularly insolent. The French envoy, who presented his king's obsequious letter announcing his accession to the throne, "was received," writes Louis Blanc, "by the chief of a yet semi-barbarous people with an insulting haughtiness to which the government of the Restoration itself would not have submitted." Stendhal comments in a marginal note: "Dangerous episode! But remember, Gentlemen of the Police, this is a Republican speaking." In *Henri Brulard* Stendhal calls Nicholas "the hypocritical Tartar."

PAGE 14. *Austerlitz and Marengo:* two of Napoleon's great victories. The battle of Austerlitz (December 2, 1805) was followed by the Peace of Pressburg between France and Austria. Marengo (June 14, 1800) completed Napoleon's conquest of northern Italy.

PAGE 14. . . . *took the trouble to get born:* reference to Figaro's famous soliloquy in Beaumarchais' *Mariage de Figaro.* "What has your lordship done to earn all this? . . . You have taken the trouble to get born."

PAGE 16. *Saint-Simonist:* a follower of Saint-Simonism, the socialistic system founded by Claude-Henri, Comte de Saint-Simon (1760-1825; a descendant of the author of the *Memoires*) and developed by his disciples. A school was founded after his death which included distinguished men of letters, artists, savants, and many students of the École Polytechnique. Saint-Simon's socialistic theory was tied up with novel religious ideas which he called the *New Christianity.* Both his social and religious doctrines were based on the principle of universal love. Probably because this is the ingredient most glaringly lacking in organized practical human relations, political, financial, social or religious, any movement or cult which founds its plans for reforming society on universal love is doomed to ridicule. Besides, the idealistic jargon of the Saint-Simonists under Père Enfantin, the "Father" of the Saint-Simonist "Family," even more than their ideal social doctrines, made them the natural butt for such cynical wits as Lucien's father. Stendhal himself was vehemently opposed to Saint-Simonism and denounced it in a pamphlet called *A Plot Against the Industrialists.*

PAGE 21. *Desaix and Saint-Cyr:* Louis Charles Antoine Desaix de Veygoux (1768-1800), one of Napoleon's victorious generals, killed at the battle of Marengo. Laurent de Gouvion, Marquis Saint-

Cyr (1764-1830), General under Napoleon and ambassador to Spain. After his great victory at Polotsk was made a Marshal. During the Restoration in 1815, he became Minister of War and again in 1817, serving until 1819. One of Stendhal's favorite books was Saint-Cyr's *Memoires,* which in *The Green Huntsman* he has the mathematician Gauthier recommend to Lucien.

PAGE 24. . . . *one of our cabbage-cutter brothers:* a foot soldier. In the monasteries the brothers who performed the humble office of the kitchen were called cabbage-cutter brothers. Under the Restoration the bayonet of the infantry was derisively called a cabbage-cutter, the foot soldier a cabbage-cutter brother.

PAGE 24. *Soult:* Stendhal in his manuscript first wrote Soult, later ruling out this "compromising" name, and replacing it by N——. In the second volume of *Lucien Leuwen,* the minister of war figures prominently, and at that time the minister of war was Marshal Soult. This was only one of the many reasons that made the publication of *Lucien Leuwen* impossible as long as Beyle held the post of consul at Civita-Vecchia. Nicholas Jean de Dieu Soult (1769-1851) entered the army as a private, was made Marshal of France in 1804, and later created Duke of Dalmatia by Napoleon. Banished after Waterloo, he was recalled in 1819 and became active in politics. Was minister of war and minister of foreign affairs under Louis-Philippe.

PAGE 25. *Court of Peers:* It was simply by a royal ordinance that the Chamber of Peers had been constituted a Court of Justice. Before this court in Paris were brought to trial all the insurgents arrested in the uprisings of April 1834, which occurred in Lyons, Paris, Marseilles, Saint Étienne, Besançon, Arbois, Chalons, Épinal, Lunéville and Isere. This was a violation of the Charter which provided that: "None should be withdrawn from his natural judges." *Lucien Leuwen* was being written at the time of this trial by the Court of Peers which began May 5, 1835.

PAGE 28. *Pear:* On this subject in *Caricatures and Lithography,* Thackeray wrote: "Everyone who was in Paris a few years since, must recollect the famous *poire* which was chalked upon all the walls of the city and which bore so ludicrous a resemblance to Louis-Philippe. The *poire* became an object of prosecution and M. Philipon (the caricaturist) appeared before a jury to answer to the crime of inciting to contempt against the king's person . . . the artist was acquitted and *La Poire* is immortal." But at the time Thackeray wrote, Louis-Philippe had already forsworn many of his liberal promises, and Thackeray continued: "No more political satires appear now . . . no more *poires* ripen on the walls of the metropolis." When Lucien came to Nancy the pear was considered a seditious emblem.

Charles Philipon (1800-1862), a caricaturist who was the avowed enemy of Louis-Philippe. He founded two satirical reviews, *La Caricature* in 1830, and the *Charivari* in 1832, which were frequently fined for violations of the censorship. Daumier was one of his most notable contributors.

P A G E 29. *Cannon of Saint-Roche:* From the steps of the Church of Saint-Roche in Paris during the uprising of the 13th Vende-miaire, the soldiers, on Bonaparte's order, fired on the opponents of the Convention.

P A G E 31. *Long live the Line:* that is, the troops of the line or the fighting troops of the regular army. The republicans are friendly toward the troops of the line and non-commissioned officers, but avowed enemies of the *Juste-milieu* officers attached to the government.

P A G E 31. *The Glorious Days (les Glorieuses):* name given to the first three days of the July Revolution, 1830.

P A G E 32. *Mme. de Chasteller preaches the gospel in her drawing room:* Henri Martineau explains this strange practice as follows: "To the reader who is surprised at the idea of Madame de Chastel-ler's preaching in her home, I refer to the volume of the *English Courier* in which Stendhal makes numerous allusions to the salons of the Paris aristocracy and the new customs encountered there. It was the fashion during the Restoration to begin evening receptions with a veritable sermon in favor of the Congregation and the *ultra* doctrines."

PAGE 32. *Duchesse d'Angoulême:* The Dauphine, daughter of Louis XVI, wife of the Dauphin, eldest son of Charles X.

PAGE 34. According to a note of Romain Colomb in his edition of the *Chasseur Vert* (*The Green Huntsman*) Stendhal never set foot in Nancy. "The new Rue de Paris," says Colomb, "is superb. . . . Everything the author writes about the fortifications and the physical appearance of Nancy is a series of absurdities." Stendhal himself says that he was in Nancy only once, and then only for two hours.

PAGE 38. *Montmirail:* Victory of Napoleon over the Prussians and Russians, February 1814.

PAGE 44. *"our province will end up by being a second Vendée":* reference to the Wars of the Vendée, a series of royalist insurrections that broke out in the Vendée during the French Revolution, fomented by the priests and the nobles.

PAGE 44. *Ultra:* name given to the court party headed by the Duc de Richelieu in the predominantly royalist Chamber, called the *Chambre introuvable,* after the second return of Louis XVIII, 1815. The *ultras* were fanatically Catholic and "more royalist than the King."

PAGE 45. *A cordon rouge:* a man who has received the Cross of Saint Louis. Literally the broad red ribbon to which the order is attached.

PAGE 45. *Jacobin:* originally a member of the Jacobin Club, the most extreme of the political clubs of the French Revolution, to which Robespierre belonged; by extension an ardent partisan of democracy. The word Jacobinism came to mean the most extreme democratic doctrines, as opposed to liberalism.

PAGE 46. *Mont-Saint-Michel:* the ancient Abbey perched on a granite cone in the Bay of Cancale off the Norman coast, which was converted into a political prison during the French Revolution.

PAGE 46. *the oath:* anyone who held a government office, as well as all electors, were compelled to take an oath of allegiance to Louis-Philippe. This was heresy to strict legitimists like M. de Pontlevé, whose king was Henri V.

PAGE 46. *Juste-milieu:* a partisan of Louis-Philippe. Literally *the just mean.* This expression was first brought into common political use by Louis-Philippe, in characterizing his own system of government—a middle-of-the-road government, as we would say.

PAGE 47. *Henri V:* Henri Charles Ferdinand Marie Dieudonné d'Artois, Duc de Bordeaux and Comte de Chambord. Born at Paris, 1820, died at Frohsdorf, near Vienna, 1883. The posthumous son of the Duc de Berry (younger son of Charles X), who was assassinated in 1820, Henri was the last of the elder branch of the Bourbons.

PAGE 55. *The Chateau:* the Chateau, or Palace of the Tuileries in Paris. It was the ancient residence of the French kings. Begun in 1563 by Catherine de Medici, it was abandoned for Versailles when that palace was built by Louis XIV. After the creation of the Empire, the Tuileries became once more the residence of the reigning sovereigns, including Louis-Philippe. It was burned during the Commune of 1871.

PAGE 55.

> *The ant is not a lender,*
> *That's the least of all his faults.*

> La fourmi n'est pas prêteuse,
> C'est la son moindre défaut.

PAGE 56. *the Gisquet musket contracts:* Allusion to a scandal at the beginning of the July Government. A partner in the banking house of Périer, Gisquet had been given an order by the government

NOTES

for 300,000 muskets. The opposition accused him—at the same time involving Marshal Soult and Casimir-Périer in the scandal—of having illicitly profited by the transaction. His accuser was fined and condemned to six months in prison and Gisquet was decorated. This, however, did not absolve him, nor the government, in the eyes of the public; and the "*affaire Gisquet*" remained a weapon in the hands of the opposition.

PAGE 57. *M. de Villèle's Three Hundred:* allusion to the subservient royalist majority returned to the Chamber at the elections of 1824, manipulated by Villèle, when only nineteen liberals were returned. The Comte de Villèle, French diplomat and a leader of the ultra-royalists under the Restoration, was premier from 1821 to 1828.

PAGE 66. *Aboukir:* A small village in northern Egypt, where Napoleon won a victory over the Turks, July 25, 1799.

PAGE 66. *Murat:* Joachim Murat (1767-1815). Napoleon's brother-in-law, married to Caroline Bonaparte, and one of his generals. He was King of Naples from 1808 to 1814.

PAGE 71. *the eloquence of M. de Lamennais:* Hughes Félicité Robert de Lamennais (1782-1854), French philosopher and theologian, was ordained priest, although with misgivings. After the July Revolution he became one of the founders of the journal *Avenir,* which advocated ideas alien to *Ultramontism* and was suppressed by spiritual authority. A member of the Assembly during the Revolution of 1848. At his death Lamennais refused to be reconciled to the Church.

PAGE 71. *Malibran:* Madame María Felicia García Malibran (1808-1836), internationally famous singer born in Paris, daughter and pupil of the Spanish singer Manuel García. One of the great prima-donnas who sang at Stendhal's beloved *Bouffes,* the Italian Opera, in Paris.

PAGE 71. *Pasta:* Madame Guiditta Negri Pasta (1798-1865), Italian singer, famous as well for her gift for tragic acting. Reigned

379

over Italian opera in Paris for ten years. Stendhal was supposed to have been her lover, but according to his own statement his relation with her was only a "liaison of friendship." For many years he finished all his evenings in her drawing room, going there "toward ten-thirty for faro." He finally moved into a room in the house where she lived because, he says, he was "tired of his porter's anger at having to open the door for him every day at three o'clock in the morning."

PAGE 71. *M. de Talleyrand:* Charles Maurice de Talleyrand-Périgord, Prince de Bénévent (1754-1838). French diplomat who served under the Directory, the Consulate, the Empire, the Restoration, and finally became Louis-Philippe's chief advisor. He was brilliant, witty, and unscrupulous.

PAGE 73. *Chateaubriand:* François René Vicomte de Chateaubriand (1768-1848), the celebrated French writer, was one of the most ardent adherents of the Bourbon cause. Under the Restoration, he was made a peer and a minister of state, and from 1822 to 1824 served as ambassador at the British Court.

PAGE 75. *The Bouffes: Théâtre-Italien* where Italian opera was given in Paris. When the first troop of Italian singers came to Paris they were called *Bouffons,* hence the name that clung to the Théâtre-Italien. In the 1830's, Italian opera was very fashionable in Paris, and every woman with any social pretensions had to have her box at the *Bouffes.* It will be remembered that Stendhal preferred Italian music to all other. Even in an early report of the French secret police of 1814 on Henri Beyle, will be found the observation that ". . . he never misses a performance of the *Opéra Bouffes.*"

PAGE 80. *Fourier's theories on the heat of the earth, or the soundness of the discoveries of Ampère:* Jean Baptiste Joseph, Baron de Fourier (1768-1830), French mathematician who wrote a famous work on heat, *Theorie Analytique de la Chaleur.* André Marie Ampère (1775-1836), French physicist, mathematician, and naturalist, discovered the principles of electric telegraphy and the fundamental law of electrodynamics. The ampere, or unit of electrical heat, is named after him. These scientific references are an echo of Stendhal's early predilection for mathematics.

PAGE 85. *. . . and the husbands subscribe in common to the newspapers they read:* This is not, as might be supposed today, because the citizens of Nancy were especially niggardly, but because of the high cost of subscriptions to newspapers in France at that time. To quote once more from Lewis Cass, commenting on the customs of Louis-Philippe's France: "Our system of newspaper subscription is very little known in this country. With us subscribers and advertisements support the journals, and he must be poor indeed who is not upon the subscription list of some newspaper printer. But here . . . the general subscription price is sixteen dollars . . ."

PAGE 87. *. . . he noticed a reading room . . .* The above authority goes on to explain: "It is in cafés and reading rooms and similar places of public resort, that all the journals of the day are to be found. These places are frequented by regular subscribers, as well as by other persons. They pay two *sous*—a little less than two cents—each; and for this sum the readers can remain in the reading rooms as long as they please, and peruse at their leisure all the papers of the day"—which can still be done in the cafés of France for the price of a *café-au-lait*.

PAGE 87. *National:* a republican newspaper; the *Journal de Paris* and the *Debats,* government papers.

PAGE 95. *Rue Transnonain:* Reference to the butchery of harmless citizens in a house on the Rue Transnonain in Paris by the soldiers during the April Riots of 1834.

PAGE 96. *. . . the meaningless cannon of Antwerp:* Reference to France's interference in the dispute between Belgium and Holland in regard to the settlement of the Treaty of Separation. France compelled the Citadel of Antwerp to capitulate December 29, 1832, thus transferring the fortress to the Belgians without further delay. This expedition in no way served French interests and was undertaken for purely political reasons. It succeeded in gaining a certain popularity for the government, as victories generally do. But Du Poirier is only interested in the cannon that will restore the elder line of Bourbons to the throne.

P A G E 96. . . . *as at Lyons:* General sympathy went to the striking silk weavers (the Mutualists) in their strike, and to the insurgents in the ensuing uprising of April 1834, which was so mercilessly quelled by the government.

P A G E 96. *Barême:* a ready-reckoner invented by the arithmetician, Bertrand-Joseph Barême (1640-1703).

P A G E 102. *"Grenadier, oh, how you grieve me!":* "*Grenadier que tu m'affliges!*", from *Les Cuisinières,* a vaudeville which was presented at the *Théâtre des Varietés* in 1822. (Note by Romain Colomb.)

P A G E 113. *Berryer:* Antoine Berryer (1790-1868) (son of Nicolas Berryer, the lawyer who defended Marshal Ney). A lawyer like his father, he was one of the leaders of the legitimist party, and a famous orator. Stendhal in his manuscript, to conceal his identity, gives him the name of Cochin.

P A G E 113. *Je fais mes farces:* Stendhal remarks: "Who knows this comedy? This is illustrating an obscurity by means of a greater obscurity." Henri Martineau notes that there was a *"Folie in One Act,"* given in Paris in 1815, written by Désaugier, Gentil and Brazier, but there was no mention of any M. Jabalot.

P A G E 121. *Béranger:* Pierre-Jean de Béranger (1780-1857), French song writer who introduced a new kind of political song that became very popular. Twice, on the publication of collections of his songs, the Restoration government found him dangerous enough to prosecute. He was tried, and both times fined and sentenced to imprisonment, in 1821 to three months at St. Pélagie (a prison mentioned several times in *Lucien Leuwen*) and to nine months, in 1825, at the prison of La Force.

PAGE 125. *the Colonel Caron affair:* Reference to an episode of the insurrectional movement of 1821, so severely suppressed by the government of Louis XVIII, when Lieutenant-Colonel Caron fell a victim to a despicable trap. At the instigation of agents provocateurs, he urged the troops to attempt the deliverance of the prisoners at Belfort. He was turned over to the agents of the government by his own troops, tried and executed.

PAGE 131. *the Almack Balls:* Almack's was a suite of assembly rooms in King Street, St. James, London. "The Almack ball was a reception that took place every Wednesday under the patronage of a committee of ladies of high rank. For fashionable society, it was the seventh heaven to obtain an invitation to Almack's. Stendhal was able to attend one of these balls during his trip to England in 1826." (Note by Henri Martineau.) "The first time I went to Almack's," writes Stendhal in his *Souvenirs d'Égotisme,* "my banker, when he saw my ticket, said with a sigh: 'I have been working twenty-two years, sir, to go to that ball, and you'll be there in an hour.'" Later these rooms were known as *Willis.*

PAGE 134. *Louis XVIII:* (1755-1824) grandson of Louis XV, brother of Louis XVI and of Charles X; one of the active leaders of the emigration; re-entered Paris in the wake of the Allies after the fall of the Empire; was made king; retired to Ghent during the Hundred Days; resumed the throne after Waterloo.

PAGE 138. *General Riego:* Rafael del Riego y Núñez, Spanish general and patriot, was betrayed when he fomented a revolt of the troops under his command, and was executed by Ferdinand VII in 1823.

PAGE 138. *Samuel Bernard:* (1651-1739) famous banker of Louis XIV, who enjoyed great favor with the King, and was received at the royal residences of Marly and Versailles.

PAGE 157. *Lavater's theories:* Johann Kaspar Lavater (1741-1801) was a Swiss philosopher, poet, and theologian who invented the pseudo-science of physiognomy, the art of judging character from the exterior appearance, especially from the features of the face. Goethe contributed a chapter to his book on physiognomy, which was published 1775-1778.

PAGE 160. *In which even* I hate you *is said with tenderness: Et jusqu'a* je vous hais *tout s'y dit tendrement.*

PAGE 161. *Millevoye* and *M. de Fontanes:* Louis de Fontanes (1757-1821) was a mediocre writer, but Napoleon's appointed intermediary with the men of letters of the Empire, exercising a good deal of useful patronage. Charles Hubert Millevoye (1782-1816) was a minor poet, author of a piece of sentimental verse, *La Chute des Feuilles (Falling Leaves)*, and of whom Sainte-Beuve wrote that "the poet died young though the man survived."

PAGE 161. *Foullon and Berthier:* Joseph François Foullon (1717-1789), Controller-General of the Treasury and Minister to the King's Household, he was anathema to the populace. Attempting to elude the mob's violence by having his death reported and arranging an elaborate funeral to cover his escape, his trick was unsuccessful, and he was caught, brought back to Paris, and hanged from a lamp-post. Mirabeau's correspondence, however, seems to prove that his death was not due to mob fury alone, but that assassins had been hired to murder him, as later in the case of Berthier. *Louis Alexandre Berthier* (1753-1815) fought under Lafayette in the American Revolution. In high favor with Napoleon who made him Prince of Neuchâtel and Wagram, and Marshal of the French Empire. After his surrender at Neuchâtel, he made his peace with Louis XVIII for which he was well rewarded. At his death it was said that he had committed suicide, but it was more generally believed that he had been assassinated by members of a secret society.

PAGE 161. *Alceste:* The atrabilious hero of Molière's comedy *The Misanthrope.*

NOTES

PAGE 163. Who does not have the spirit of his age
Of his age knows all the sorrows.

*Qui n'a pas l'esprit de son age
De son age a tout le malheur.*

PAGE 172. *Young Scotsman:* Comte de Chambord (or Henri V
for the legitimists) had been painted in Scottish costume while living with the royal family in exile at Holyrood Palace, near Edin-
burgh, Scotland. Later, the royal exiles were offered asylum in the
imperial castle of Hradschin, near Prague, by the Emperor of
Austria.

PAGE 203. *Capua:* According to legend, the ancient city of Capua
in southern Italy was a city of endless delights, and historians ascribe
Hannibal's lack of success, after he had wintered there with his
army, to the enervating and demoralizing effects of all the sensual
pleasures of that city.

PAGE 203. *Mutualist workers:* In 1828, a society for mutual assistance had been organized at Lyons by the master silk-weavers.
"Founded, in the first instance, with a view to mutual assistance between the working men," writes Louis Blanc, "the association
wished to extend its action; it wished to employ the strength it derived from the union of its members toward hindering the decrease
of wages." So when, in 1834, the wages of the plush workers were
reduced, joined by other classes of weavers, the Mutualist Society
called for a general stoppage of all the looms in Lyons. Such were
the timid beginnings of labor unions in France.

PAGE 207.

And if you must be damned, at least
Be damned for pleasant sins!

*Si vous vous damnez,
Damnez vous [donc] au moins pour des pechés aimables!*

Stendhal in a marginal note writes: "Look up these verses in Voltaire." He evidently never found them, nor, it seems, has anyone
else.

385

PAGE 229. *Coffee-house: café-hauss* in the French text.

PAGE 233. *Toadeater:* English in the French text, followed by *avaleur de crapaud.*

PAGE 237. *Morghen:* Stendhal was very fond of the engravings of Raphaël Morghen (1758-1833) who engraved Raphael's entire work. In the days of the Empire in Paris, Stendhal had bought several of Morghen's engravings to hang in his room.

PAGE 282. *. . . four grounds against this man:* the first two grounds refer to the property belonging to the nobles and to the Church that was confiscated by the revolutionary government and sold as national property. Realizing his dependence on the bourgeoisie, Louis XVIII was careful not to antagonize purchasers of national property and, in his declaration at Saint-Omer, affirmed that the purchasers of national property should never be molested. The *milliard* ($200,000,000) later voted as indemnity to the legitimists was far from satisfying them.

PAGE 284. *Corbière:* Pierre de Corbière, "antipope" in 1328, under the name of Nicolas V.

PAGE 285. *Calonne:* Charles-Alexandre de Calonne (1734-1802), French politician, Controller-General of the Treasury in 1785.

PAGE 285. *La Chalotais:* Louis René de La Chalotais (1701-1785), Attorney-General of the high Tribunal of Brittany. He instigated the suppression of the Jesuits.

PAGE 285. *What language, Madame, both for you and for me: Quel langage, Madame, et pour vous et pour moi!*—meaning how absurd all this talk for clever people like us! But since those indefatigable sleuths Henry Debraye and Henri Martineau, have not been able to track down this quotation, it is pretty safe to say that it is unknown. One can only surmise that it is probably a line from some currently popular play, opera, or song, used aptly enough to make Madame d'Hocquincourt laugh.

PAGE 304. *A Blue:* In the royalist wars of the Vendée during the Revolution, the *Whites* and the *Blues* were the nicknames given respectively to the insurgents under the white standard of the Bourbons, and to the soldiers of the Republic who wore a blue uniform. By extension afterwards applied in general to royalists or republicans.

PAGE 312. *Duc d'Orleans:* that is, Louis-Philippe, for he was still nothing more than the Duc d'Orleans to the legitimists.

PAGE 316. *Dorat:* Claude-Joseph Dorat (1734-1780), French poet who was the prototype of the elegant frivolity of the Eighteenth Century.

PAGE 345. *Robespierre and Couthon:* Maximilien de Robespierre (1758-94), Georges Couthon (1755-94), leaders of the French Revolution who, with Saint-Just, formed a sort of triumvirate during the "Reign of Terror." They were overthrown July 27, 1794, and guillotined the following day.

PAGE 345. *Louis XIX:* Louis-Antoine, Duc d'Angoulême, the Dauphin, son of Charles X. At Rambouillet, August 2, 1830, Charles X and the Dauphin abdicated in favor of Charles' grandson Henri, Duc de Bordeaux and Comte de Chambord, then ten years old. His claims were set aside and the younger, or Orleans, branch of the Bourbons was raised to the throne in the person of Louis-Philippe. The royalists, known as legitimists or *ultras,* refused to recognize Louis-Philippe. The majority, though not all, regarded Henri V as their king. Some like Sanréal and the Roller brothers in *Lucien Leuwen* "refused to concede the abdications of Rambouillet and looked forward to the reign of Louis XIX after that of Charles X." Others admitted the abdication of Charles X but not the enforced abdication of the Dauphin. Their king was therefore Louis XIX. Thus the legitimist party came to be divided into three classes—the Carlists, the Dauphinists, and the *Henri Quinquists.*

PAGE 345. *Charter of 1830:* Following the July Revolution, the Charter of 1814 was altered with the intention of making it more liberal. Among other changes, it provided for the abolition of Article 14 which authorized the sovereign to issue ordinances. On this article Charles X had based his claim that he was not repudiating the Charter in issuing his famous Ordinances by which he fully intended to override it and rule by royal decree. The publication of these ordinances was the spark that set off the Revolution. Louis-Philippe, with the parliamentary title of *King of the French,* was chosen because of his supposedly liberal views, democratic sympathies, and bourgeois tastes. He was affectionately called the "citizen king" and it was popularly believed that he would faithfully uphold the Charter and protect the liberties it provided. But very early in his troubled reign he, too, found it expedient to suppress certain liberties when they irked him and his ministers. Stendhal, who had welcomed the July Revolution and was a partisan of the new charter, soon came to despise Louis-Philippe and "his tricks and overreachings," as Queen Victoria later expressed it. Throughout this book Stendhal makes frequent allusions to the king's perfidy and, in the sequel to *The Green Huntsman,* to his inordinate love of money and his speculations on the stock-market.

P A G E 3 4 6. *Duc de Saint-Simon:* Louis de Rouvroy, Duc de Saint-Simon (1675-1755), soldier and diplomat under Louis XIV and Louis XV, famous for his *Memoires,* an intimate history of the court and courtiers.

P A G E 3 4 7. *M. Guizot:* François Guizot (1787-1874), French statesman and historian. Rival of Thiers and one of the most conservative ministers of Louis-Philippe's reign.

DATE DUE

GAYLORD			PRINTED IN U.S.A.